THE PRICE OF PASSION

THE BAD BOYS OF WALL STREET

EMBER LEIGH

Published by Ember Leigh, 2022

EmberLeighAuthor@gmail.com

Cover Model: Lucas Loyola

Photographer: Wander Aguiar

Cover art: Covers by Combs

Editing: Elisabeth R. Nelson

CONTENTS

This book is dedicated to all the women who chose to rise above, despite what their so-called friends/exes/toxic family/hometown community/society in general told them they could do.

You can fucking do it. Let's get to work.

CHAPTER ONE

JESSA

"Listen, you'll find someone else."

My roommate—no, *former* roommate now—shoved sparkly dresses from her closet into the open suitcase on her bed. She offered me a consoling smile, as though moving out four days before our *New-Yorker-than-hell* rent was due somehow formed part of the regular landscape of life.

My stomach bottomed out for the third time that morning as I watched Nicole prepare to walk away from our two-bedroom in Brooklyn.

"I don't have the money," I croaked, my mouth desert dry. "I...there's no way."

Because there wasn't any way. I was a fresh transplant from Kentucky, less than six months under my belt and just enough cash each month to make ends meet. I didn't have a spare month's rent saved up. I didn't have *anything* saved up, unless my hopes and dreams could be converted to currency somehow. I pressed a hand to my forehead, wishing I hadn't opted for the belted dress this morning. The pressure around my waist made me feel like puking.

"Jessa, trust me," Nicole called out after me as I stumbled down the hallway in search of fresh air or a hidden stack of money. "You'll find something! People always do in New York."

"What the hell do you think I'm gonna find?" I shouted as I gripped the edges of the sink in our too-small bathroom. My Kentucky twang sounded louder than ever as I stared at my reflection in the mirror. "A job as a stripper? Nicole, I'm too big for stripping!"

Nicole sighed loudly. "What are you talking about? Anybody can be a stripper these days. All I'm saying is put your ear to the ground. Make a post or two on social. At this price, you'll have a replacement for me in twelve hours."

"A serial killer replacement, maybe," I shot back, studying the familiar contours of my face as a way to ground myself. I'd calmed myself the same way as a teen, when my mom got too loud with her boyfriend of the week in the living room or the partying threatened to spill over and ruin my chill. I traced my hairline with my eyes, imagining a lead pencil tip following the curves. I drew my face in my mind's eye, imagining the scratch of pencil against paper as I reconfigured my own face and body as a fashion sketch. Drawing out my fantasy—via the perfect body, the perfect clothes, the perfect runway—was one of my tried-and-true methods of calming the anxious thrum in my chest.

But I could only hold off the anxiety for so long.

Rent was due in *four mother-cluckin' days*.

"You are underestimating the power of Manhattan," Nicole said in a sing-song voice as she continued to pack up her life and leave me in the lurch.

I squeezed my eyes shut and let out a sigh. "Pretty sure I'm not," I muttered to myself.

If anything, I underestimated the power of life to throw me curveballs right when I was on the verge of achieving anything. I wasn't in New York just for funsies. I was here to start putting together the puzzle pieces of my future. The puzzle I'd let others convince me I couldn't ever solve. The puzzle I'd even convinced myself I shouldn't solve.

I was here to get my fashion design certificate and finally make a go of my deepest and longest held secret dream: become a fashion designer for plus-size women, with a special focus on dresses that looked *amazing*.

My phone vibrated in the secret pocket I'd sewn into the side of my dress. I fumbled to extract it from its position against my thigh. The screen read JEREMY.

"Hello?" I tried to keep my voice level. Jeremy would know something was up at the slightest waver. As a very good and perpetually concerned big brother, he was excellent at sniffing out trouble.

"Jessa?" Jeremy's familiar baritone was calming, but the pause on the other end told me he was already on to me. "Everything okay?"

I gulped. "Sure. Why do you ask?" From down the hall, Nicole loudly zipped her suitcase. I looked back at my reflection in the mirror and imagined the pencil lines.

"You sound like something's wrong," he said.

"Well, this is just me!" My voice came out unnaturally bright. Slightly psychotic, even. "Just, you know, being myself."

"Jessa, it's time!" Nicole's voice broke through my pitiful attempt to keep it together. I let out an exasperated sigh.

"See, I knew there was something wrong," Jeremy said. "Did I call at a bad time? What's going on?"

"Nothing," I said, still committed to keeping up the ruse. I darted out of the bathroom, watching as Nicole rolled two wheeled bags to the front door of our overpriced shoebox. "Can I call you back?"

"All right, I'm leaving forever," Nicole stated dramatically with a little eye roll. She'd always been prone to theatrics, but then again, what struggling actor *wasn't*?

"Who's leaving?" Jeremy hissed.

"I'll call you back." I swiped the phone off before he could pester me anymore. My family loved to swarm like vultures on my New York adventure. Waiting for the first sign of rot so they could dive in to tear apart the carcass of my dreams. Well, that might have been a bit strong for Jeremy. But my daddy, mom, and older sister were licking their chops waiting for me to fail.

Any excuse to tell me to pack it up and head home.

And on days like this, I wondered if maybe they were right.

I was just biding my time until the vulture of New York came barreling toward me.

"Are you sure you want to do this?" I asked Nicole, holding out my arms for a hug. We'd grown close in our months together—as close as random passengers on the struggle bus in New York could grow, which was something just shy of family.

"Jessa, you will be fine. I just have enough sense to hang up my theater hat. You, on the other hand—you have too many designs you *should* hang up. Literally. On a clothing rack in the best boutiques in Midtown. I belong in Peoria."

"Peoria?" I spat.

"Yeah, Peoria. Illinois. I'll pay a third of what I paid here and still be able to afford cocktails on the weekend. I'll get a job serving tables—lord knows I've gotten lots of experience with that here."

Even though I hated her for leaving me, I also understood that this was the constant churn of the Big Apple, a churn that I could soon be victim to.

"Good luck, I guess." We hugged tightly, but briefly. When we parted, she offered me a sad smile.

"You'll be fine," she repeated, tucking her blonde hair behind her ear as though the motion guaranteed it. Then she rolled her things out of my life forever.

Once the door shut behind her, anxiety drilled down into my gut like an oil-seeking expedition. I pressed a hand to my forehead. This felt like a four-alarm emergency.

Jeremy called again, just as I thought maybe I'd pass out.

"Can you talk now?" he asked in lieu of a greeting.

"My roommate just moved out," I said past dry lips.

"Ohhhh shit bricks," Jeremy offered. "She was nice, wasn't she?"

"Very nice," I confirmed, "until that whole last-minute decision to move out of our apartment thing."

"Where is she moving?"

"Peoria."

"Peoria?"

"It's in Illinois," I said, as though I hadn't just learned it thirty seconds ago.

"Well look at you, Miss Geography. What's in that weird-soundin' city?"

"Lower rent, I guess," I grumbled.

"I know a place that has *real* low rent," Jeremy said, extending his drawl in the way that told me a fatherly lesson was around the corner.

"Oh, Jeremy, don't—"

"It's called *Oakville*. You heard of it?"

I heaved the most annoyed little sister sigh I could muster. "I do *not* need your sass right now."

"Rents are so low they're *free*, little sister," he went on, oblivious to my pleas. "You've got a nice twin bed with your name on it at my house. Besides, Louisville ain't too far from Oakville. It's an easy commute, and you can get plenty of that 'city culture' you like so much."

He was referring to the bed in his spare room I'd used briefly after breaking up with my ex-boyfriend Tommy. It had seemed safe until Tommy started showing up in the bushes of Jeremy's front landscaping nightly, tapping on my window with the rim of his Busch Light and begging me to forgive him. One of the downfalls of crashing with your brother in your hometown. Not only does everyone know your name and your history, they also know which window to peep through when harassing an ex-girlfriend.

But forgiveness was not in order after I discovered Tommy's lies and manipulation throughout the end of our relationship.

"That twin bed isn't a refuge anymore," I reminded him. "Way too close to Tommy for my comfort."

"Tommy has moved on," Jeremy said on the heels of a sigh.

"Has he?" I doubted very much that my ex-nightmare, who spent six months lightweight stalking me after I broke things off with him, would fully move on from any woman who had spurned him. If anything, he was spinning more complex yarns about why I was the bitch, or even the butch. He'd loved to accuse me of being a lesbian when I wasn't in the mood. Great guy, Tommy, 0/10 did not recommend.

"All I'm saying is that if things fall through in New York, you can always come home." Jeremy had said this to me no fewer than fifty times since I'd moved to the Big Apple, which equated to roughly two times a week. I appreciated the sentiment. It was at least better than what I heard from my big sister Tara, which usually sounded like "We know you can't hack it there, so why don't you just give up now?"

"Thank you, Jeremy," I muttered. "But let me at least exhaust my options before I tuck my tail between my legs, mmkay?"

"What are your other options?"

"I-I don't know yet," I spluttered. "But I'll think of them. Nicole reminded me that stripping is always an option—"

"*Jessa Walton.*"

I didn't dare mess with Jeremy when he used his dad voice. "I'm just saying—"

Shrieks on the other end of the phone interrupted me, which brought a smile to my face. I knew those girlish squeals.

"The girls are home?"

Jeremy sighed. "Some sort of teacher in-service day, I dunno. Had to call off work to pick them up."

"Why didn't Chelsea go get them? I thought she worked swing shift." I welcomed the digression from my own problems.

"She's been going into work early lately," Jeremy said.

"Well, tell Izzy and Hannah I said hello and that I'm *not* turning to stripping, so don't worry."

My older brother let out a long, exasperated groan. "How much do you have left in your savings?"

I swallowed hard. There had barely been a savings to begin with. I'd arrived in New York on fumes from my minimum wage job as a welding company's office assistant. As soon as I could escape, *I did.* All my accumulated funds had gone toward paying for fashion school and the triple rent—first month, last month, and a security deposit—required to get into my apartment. That was it. There was no wiggle room.

"I have..." What was the least frightening way to say *absolutely nothing*? "Enough to get by."

"So you have rent covered for next month?"

That was a hard no. "Ahhhh...well..."

"Jesus, Mary, and Joseph. You know what, Jessa? If you won't come home, I'm sending help. I'm calling Damian."

His words landed like a lead blanket. My hand shot out in front of me to put a stop to this suggestion, even though he wasn't here to see. "Hang on."

"What?"

"You can't do that," I said, my lips dry for an entirely different reason now. "We don't need to get the Fairchilds involved."

"Why wouldn't I? They're the best friends I've got, and they're two miles from where you're sitting. Jessa, you know they'd help you in a heartbeat. Why can't I call them?"

My chest began a slow throb that indicated a pending heart attack. Because the suggestion betrayed a truth so unsavory, I'd rather fling myself on a spear than face it head-on.

Not only was Damian Fairchild my older brother's friend, he was my high school crush. The guy had stalked my fantasies and stained my attempts to date anyone else in high school, lest Damian secretly be in love with me and take my dating to mean that I didn't truly love him, *which I did.*

And sure, I was a twenty-seven year old woman with enough curves to make a select group of grown men weep.

But when it came to Damian? I'd always be the goofy, overweight little sophomore he'd never more than glanced at.

"Well?" Jeremy prompted. My shocked silence must have worried him.

"Please don't call him," I said feebly, though I knew it would do no good. "It's so humiliating. I'm broke and struggling. He's rich and wildly successful. He probably doesn't even remember me. Besides—"

"Jessa, how could he forget you? He spent the entirety of his senior year at our house. Sitting on the same couch as you."

Everything inside me deflated. I hated how much I *still* enjoyed those memories of Damian and I watching *The Big Bang Theory* while Jeremy dicked off somewhere else. Sometimes, our elbows would brush, and I'd spend the entire weekend wondering what it might feel like to go to second base with him.

"I just don't want to be a charity case," I said slowly.

"You aren't a charity case," Jeremy said, a certain glee punctuating his words. "You're *family.*"

I couldn't deny it—he'd found his angle, the rationale that would puncture any attempt I made to deflect his help. I hated him for it as much as I loved him for it. Jeremy wouldn't let me flounder—I had to acknowledge that. Even though everyone in my family wanted me to skulk back to Kentucky like an unsuccessful raccoon after rummaging through empty trash cans, Jeremy would make moves to help me see this New York thing through. And his reaching out to Damian was technically help, even though the mere thought of it made me want to shrivel up and die of embarrassment.

"I'm gonna call him now," Jeremy announced. "Hang tight."

The phone went dead. I groaned so loudly that Nicole probably heard me on her way to Peoria.

Seconds ticked by with a walloping slowness. I paced every square inch of my apartment over and over. Of course I knew what the Fairchilds were up to. Everyone in Oakville—actually, everyone in greater Louisville—knew what the Fairchilds were up to. They were practically the Kardashian family of our area, minus the butt lifting and heavy makeup. Everyone had an opinion about them, too, but one thing was certain—nobody was more successful or more interesting than the Fairchild brothers.

My lowly little broke ass did not fit in their new world. And I did not want Jeremy to shoehorn me in there.

He called me back twenty-three minutes after we hung up, not that I had been counting. I could hear the smile in his voice. "Jessa, I've got great news."

I grimaced, preparing myself for whatever came next. "Yes?"

"They've got a job waiting for you."

I slapped my palm against my forehead. "Do they?"

"And guess who needs a confidential secretary?"

Please let it be anyone other than Damian. "Who?"

"Damian!"

I nodded, my gaze stuck to the curling edge of the linoleum in the kitchen. This was just my luck. Trace couldn't need me. Not even Axel. It had to be Damian. The one guy I'd barely been able to speak in front of as a sixteen-year-old. Sure, I'd grown and matured since then. But he'd outstripped me ten to one in every department imaginable. If I'd been the meek and unnoticeable sophomore back then, now I was even tinier in Damian's long shadow of accomplishment and world experience. From what I'd heard, the man had a private chef, and I couldn't even afford a bagel.

"Great." Even I could hear how devoid of enthusiasm I was.

"He said they've been looking for a new full-time hire. Jessa, you're gonna get benefits and everything, I bet. He said you can go on over today. Can you get to their building by three? I told him how your roommate just up and left, so he said he could fit you in last minute. Isn't that nice?"

My stomach cinched into knots. *Full-time hire. Fuck.* "So incredibly nice."

"Jessa, this is gonna work out great. We should have called him as soon as you got into town. But no, you insisted on doing things your way. Jessa's gotta do what Jessa's gotta do."

My eyes fluttered shut, something sick churning inside me. "All right, Jeremy. That's enough. Don't make me turn sour."

"All I need is 'Thank you, big brother, for being the best.'"

"Thank you, big brother, for being the most annoying. Now I gotta get ready for this interview."

We hung up, and I drifted back toward the bathroom mirror, tracing my face in imaginary lines. My fingers itched for an actual pencil. Truth was, I had nearly fifteen new designs scrambling to get out of my head. Between my weekly fashion courses and the part-time job I'd found at a diner five blocks west, I'd had just enough time to keep up with the coursework, make my half of the rent, and sketch out new ideas for myself.

But now? I didn't know how I'd keep up with a full-time job.

I'd come here specifically and solely for the fashion course so that I could launch my dream of becoming a fashion designer. But I couldn't get the certificate if I couldn't pay rent.

Frustration swallowed me whole, and I spent the rest of my afternoon mentally preparing to reacquaint myself with the Fairchilds. I'd last seen Damian in person at his graduation party, which was damn near thirteen years ago. Damian, Axel, and Trace had a joint graduation party at their mom and daddy's farmhouse, the old one they'd moved their parents out of as soon as they made their first kajillion dollars.

I still remembered the autumn cherry tree near their driveway, the tree that masqueraded as normal—with tire swing and normal green foliage—until September rolled around when the thing turned into a fiery piece of artwork sent from Heaven. And for whatever reason, that cherry tree was one of the earliest indicators that the brothers were destined to burn brighter and more beautiful than anyone else around them. After Deb Fairchild's extensive update one day in aisle two of the Sav-a-Lot about Damian's hunt for the perfect marble countertops for his third home, I knew the brothers preferred the finer things now. Which meant I had to look the part, even if I couldn't act it.

I thumbed through the dresses hanging on the rolling rack in my bedroom, sifting through the best thrifted dresses I had, as well as some of my own designs. I settled on a high-waisted black dress with a fifties vibe and set to giving my mahogany hair soft finger waves.

I gave myself a once-over in the full-length mirror hanging on the back of my door. *Here we go, Jessa. Let's find a way to make it work.*

The subway ride to the financial district was about as uneventful as New York could get—that is, stuffed to the brim with fascinating characters, random shouts, an unsurprising number of stinky armpits for late October with unseasonably warm weather. Halloween was right around the corner, which meant stray zombies roamed the subway, along with the occasional sexy kitten and grim reaper. Once I'd made my way to the Fairchild building, I took a moment to compose myself in front of the tall, black building.

You went to high school with these people. They're old friends. Nothing scary here.

No, nothing scary about being the brokest bitch in Manhattan kneeling in supplication before one of the gods of Wall Street.

Inside, the lobby gleamed with polished floors and expensive framed art. The elevator ride was hushed, reverent. On the twentieth floor, the reception area for Fairchild Enterprises bustled with activity, small groups of people gathered in intense conversations. A receptionist took my name, checked something on her computer, and then had me follow her. She deposited me in front of a closed door that read D. FAIRCHILD then strode away, mumbling something I didn't catch over her shoulder.

I drew a fortifying breath. Damian Fairchild was an actual billionaire now, one I'd gone to school with a lifetime and a half ago. This mortifying dynamic couldn't get worse.

I turned the knob of his office door and pushed it open, preparing the bright smile and enthusiasm I needed. The heavy door swung back to reveal a large office decorated in matte gray and black. Floor to ceiling windows overlooked the East River. Bookshelves lined the walls. A big wooden desk stood in the center of it all.

Damian Fairchild leaned back in his chair, his eyes pinched shut.

A brunette bobbed between his legs.

I gaped, my hand shooting to my mouth. I knew instantly what was happening, more from feeling it in the air than anything else. Damian's eyes popped open, and his drugged gaze slid my way. The woman between his legs didn't stop.

Every inch of my insides turned to cement. My eyeballs felt like they were seconds away from popping out of my skull.

Whatever mortifying dynamic I had been afraid of had just gotten infinitely worse.

CHAPTER TWO

"Jesus, Damian. Why are you in such a hurry?" Harper's disapproving blue eyes cut like diamonds as she adjusted the buttons on the front of her dress. She'd needed to undo half of them to arrange herself between my legs for the afternoon delight.

A delight I normally welcomed.

But Harper tried to delight me too often these days, tried to tie it to other things, like nights at my house and scheduled dinners. I didn't do that shit. Every woman I'd ever been with knew that, Harper included.

"I have an appointment." I dragged my hands down my face, my cock pulsing in my pants almost as hard as my heart hammered from the unexpected guest in my office. Harper hadn't even realized we'd had a witness. But every inch of my body had realized who was standing in my office, and I'd come harder than a fucking porn star after eight hours of foreplay.

And what the hell did that mean? I needed a second to figure it out. Harper wasn't hearing me, though.

"You're the boss. Just push it back." Harper's *duh* tone was well-earned. As the CFO of a big flavored-water company, she knew how my world worked. My excuse was too flimsy.

"Besides," she went on, "I want more of this." A devilish grin sprouted, and she snaked a hand down my chest, her fingers seeking the crotch of my pants. "You haven't been giving me enough."

"I'll call you."

Her minx's smile dissolved, and she grabbed for her purse on my desk. "You'd better."

Her confident strut toward my office door was enough to snag my attention. Harper commanded the attention of a *lot* of men, and she loved to remind me of it. But for some reason, like many single women out there, she only wanted the attention of the man who wouldn't give it to her.

Me.

She slipped out without another word, simply sending me a pointed look before the door clicked shut behind her. An avalanche of a sigh tumbled out of me, leaving truths littered on the ground around me.

Jessa Walton was outside my office—or maybe she was halfway across Manhattan by now, after seeing what she'd walked in on.

I'd fucking scandalized my childhood best friend's little sister, which only underscored the need for a confidential secretary. If I'd had one already, this wouldn't have happened.

And the most unsettling truth of all? Seeing Jessa Walton materialize in my office had been the hottest tug on the balls I'd ever gotten. Which was not the dynamic I wanted with my soon-to-be confidential assistant.

I was supposedly on the top of the world; if only the outsiders knew how precarious my perch truly was.

I snapped up the phone and called the front desk of the office. Felicia picked up, cooing a sugary, "How can I help you, Damian?"

"Who brought Jessa to my office?"

"Madison did."

"Tell Madison she's never to allow a visitor to enter a Fairchild office without permission."

"But Harper always does."

My stomach sank. The lines were blurring. I couldn't have that. "No visitor may enter a Fairchild office on their own, without permission. Remind the staff. If it happens again, there will be consequences. That's all."

"Okay." Felicia's voice sounded quivery now. "Am I in trouble? I—I—"

"You're fine, Felicia. But let's remember this going forward." I hung up the phone and then raked a hand through my hair. Each second that ticked by without acknowledging Jessa only allowed the awkwardness to multiply.

Fuck.

I pushed to standing and crossed the distance between my desk and the door in four big steps. I tugged the door open, straightening my back, pulling the icy, neutral mask into place. The mask I had to wear on Wall Street and in most of Manhattan. The mask that allowed me to get shit done without breaking down entirely.

Even though I was on top of the world, I sure didn't feel like it. Nobody had ever warned me it would be so miserable up here. So utterly uninspiring and stressful. Who could blame me for a midday blowjob to help me make it through?

Jessa sat in the guest chair in what should be my secretary's office, gnawing on the inside of her lip as her gaze bounced around the space.

"Jessa?"

She jolted and looked up at me and then glanced away. "Ahhhh, hi."

Right. So this was going to be awkward as fuck. "You ready to come in?"

"I don't know, are you?"

I bit back a grin. We hadn't seen each other in more than twelve years, but familiar energy thrummed between us. Jeremy Walton and I were ride or dies. We didn't talk nearly as much as we used to, but we had each other's backs for life. That's just how it was. Which meant I'd do whatever he asked when it came to his family.

Including hiring his little sister, who I'd been infatuated with during high school. But I'd also been too scared to ever make a move.

Thirteen years later, I was even less inclined to make a move, even though every single thing about Jessa had gotten better with age.

She surged to her feet, facing me with a straight back and the crystal, silver-blue eyes that had snagged me as a seventeen-year-old horndog and again as a slightly more mature thirty-two-year-old horndog.

"Come on in. We can...chat," I said, ripping my gaze from her figure. The black dress and fifties vibe she had going on worked a little too well. She was a pinup model in the flesh, with curves in all the right places. I'd fantasized only a million times back in high school about what it might be like to seduce Jessa Walton, but not wanting to cross the line with Jeremy had always held me back.

The air buzzed between us as she followed me into the office. I headed for my desk, rubbing at the back of my neck. "So listen..."

She cleared her throat, sitting primly in the visitor's chair. I came around behind my desk and leaned on it, pressing my palms against the surface. I dared myself to look her in the eye.

Her crystal blues were waiting for me, the blush of her high cheekbones serving as a strange knife to my chest. Looking at her this close after so long produced something far too warm and sinuous inside of me.

Dangerous. She was mahogany-haired danger wrapped up in the most beautiful and voluptuous package.

"Sorry for what you walked in on," I said, needing to get that shit out of the way first. "Probably made my case for why I need a confidential secretary so bad, huh?"

"Hey, it's your office, Damian. You do you."

I hefted with a laugh. "Right. Well, let's start over. What's up, Jessa? Long time no see."

She cracked a smile, her posture relaxing slightly. "Hey, Damian. I guess Jeremy filled you in."

"Yeah." I gestured to her. "You look..." *Stunning. Breathtaking. Like the woman of my dreams.* "Great. He told me you came to New York this summer, right?"

She nodded, dragging her tongue across her plump bottom lip. I couldn't look away as she traced the soft pink line there. "Got here in August. It's been a wild ride ever since."

I crossed my arms over my chest, unnerved by the way she watched me. Something sparkled in her gaze, as if she could see through the business veneer I'd been wearing for the past decade. In a way, it would have been easier if she were just a stranger off the street. I'd gotten comfortable wearing my mask. A little too comfortable, maybe.

And honestly, part of me preferred a total stranger for a job like this one. Someone who wouldn't catch my eye or stir up warm feelings—both of which Jessa had already done. But shuffling her to another department within the company wasn't an option right now. There was no other position open at Fairchild Enterprises, not since we'd pared back some positions and reorganized in the wake of the investigation. I wanted to help the Waltons out—and this was the one spot that needed filled.

"What have you been doing?" Jeremy hadn't gone into much detail. Just that she was chasing rainbows in New York, which to me sounded like she was drifting aimlessly until she found something that stuck.

"Just trying to make it work," she said with a laugh. "It's the city of dreams, right? Well, I've got a few dreams that I've ignored for too long."

"Jeremy says you're looking for a new job."

Her mouth opened, but nothing came out at first. "Sort of. My living arrangement has changed, so I need a higher salary."

I nodded. "What number did you have in mind?" It wasn't my style to discuss numbers before experience or responsibility, but I knew Jessa could do this job in her sleep. She'd always been the detail-oriented and driven little sister compared to Jeremy, and that alone was enough to assure me she could hack it.

Her eyes widened. "Um...sixty thousand a year?"

I laughed. "Come on, Jessa."

She deflated. "Fifty?"

"Wrong way. Aim higher. What do you need per month for rent?"

Her eyes turned into saucers. "Um...three thousand."

I did a quick calculation and nodded. "We'll start at 100k and review in three months. If you do a good job, we can go up from there. You okay with signing an NDA?"

The stars in her eyes were almost as beguiling as the flush of her neck. "Um...of course. Wait, are you serious about the 100k? You actually said that, right? Or am I dreaming this?"

"I really said 100k."

Her throat bobbed. "Like in US dollars?"

"We can discuss crypto if you'd rather—"

"No, no. Let's keep it real. None of that digital stuff." She rolled her lips in, a grin threatening to explode. "Can you say the starting pay again?"

"One hundred thousand dollars." Now I couldn't fight the grin either. "Simply because this job is what we might call...full-time *plus*. We start at eight in the morning, and sometimes you'll need to stay late. Things crop up, late meetings are scheduled, and we have business dinners and other events. My brothers and I are going through something right now which can be time-consuming on occasion. Maybe you've heard?"

"The investigation," she said softly.

The acid twist in my gut returned, the one that accompanied me every day when I woke up and every night when I went to bed. I swallowed the sensation, tucking it back into the recesses of my mind and body. If I didn't, I'd crumble on the spot.

The U.S. Securities and Exchange Commission's fraud investigation was one of the most devastating turns of my life. The only thing that surpassed it was losing my biological parents at age seven, and then losing my younger sisters to the foster system and then sex trafficking during my late teens.

Bad always followed the good. The universe had massive pitfalls in store for me, which meant I needed to tread carefully. That included keeping romance at a solid zero. Because that feeling when you met someone and your heart skipped a beat? That was called arrhythmia. That shit would kill you. It was better to stay away from all potential threats.

"It's brought its own sort of workload to our lives," I said. "But beyond that, you'll mostly be responsible for my direct schedule, sitting in on meetings, preparing reports, running errands as needed..."

"So basically your bitch?"

A laugh rocketed out of me. "That's not the technical term, but sure."

"For 100k a year, I will be your bitch, Damian Fairchild." Her coy smile paired with the husky lilt of her voice had my cock stiffening in my pants. I squelched the curiosity that sprouted to life inside me, the urge to toy with this thread.

"Great. Now, being my bitch does have rules," I went on. "It might not seem like it after what you saw, but we run a tight ship here when it comes to our staff. We're fair, but we like things a certain way. I know we go way back, but here, you're just part of the Fairchild team. That's how it has to be."

She nodded effusively. "So what you're saying is I need to keep it a secret from the rest of the staff that you and Jeremy came in last place in flag football every year during middle school, right?"

"No need to go sharing my middle school dirt, Jessa. Besides, if you start that, you don't want me to retaliate," I teased. But as soon as the words came out of my mouth, I wished I hadn't said them. The warm grin that blossomed on her lips was a hard yank into the past, and I didn't have time for a distraction like that.

"Fine. We keep all Lipscombe Public Schools incidents to ourselves, and nobody gets hurt."

"Deal." I caught her silver-crystal gaze for a moment before reminding myself to barrel forward. The clock was ticking. I had too many things on my to-do list, and too many thoughts about Jessa that I wanted to ignore. We needed to wrap this up and move forward under a new dynamic: distant and professional, employer and employee.

A soft rap at my door had me looking up. Trace's tall, boxy frame entered the office a moment later.

"Wow! Jessa Walton, is that really you?" Trace's good-natured baritone didn't betray an ounce of the tension that we Fairchild brothers had been living for with the past few months. And to be honest, I still wasn't sure how deep I planned to let Jessa get into the family bullshit. She'd be my confidential secretary, but that didn't mean she needed to know *everything*.

"It's me! Good to see you again, Trace. How are things?"

"Oh," he said, tapping a rolled-up sheet of paper against his closed fist, "it's going. I'm sure you've heard about...everything."

"I've heard about some of it, for sure. But I want to help you guys however I can."

"I appreciate that, Jessa. How're Jeremy and Tara and your folks?"

Jessa shrugged. "Everyone's the same. For better or worse."

I knew through Jeremy that their mom had gone into rehab for heroin again this year, a habit she'd started when Jessa hit freshman year of high school. Which meant her mom would be over on the *worse* end of the spectrum.

"We should get Jeremy up here sometime," Trace said. "You can show him around, we'll wine and dine him. It'll be great."

Jessa snorted. "Good luck. I think that man is allergic to crossing the Kentucky state line."

"I could get him up here," I blurted. "Trust me. With how much Jeremy loves pizza, I'd get him here."

Jessa giggled, covering her mouth with her hand. "You might be right about that."

"Let's pencil in a Jeremy kidnapping then," Trace said, unrolling the paper in his hand. He came up to my desk and passed it to me. I scanned it while he continued speaking. "Meanwhile, you should look into this, Damian. Fundraiser for Teens 4 Tech. We should probably get our names behind a big donation here."

The fundraiser was happening the following weekend, and the whole premise focused on getting computers and coding skills into the most underserved areas of New York City. It was a mission so beautiful I was upset our own charity wasn't already doing it. This shit was near and dear to my heart—especially the coding part. And with my own code hanging in the crosshairs of the SEC investigation, I saw Trace's point.

"We should donate, and we should *go*." I set the paper down, my gaze sliding toward Jessa. "You ever been to a fundraiser in Manhattan?"

"I, uh..." She swallowed hard, looking between Trace and me. "I haven't had any funds, so..."

"Let's consider this your first assignment," I said. "We'll all go. You can take notes in case we ever need to do something like this in the future."

Trace's brow lifted appreciatively. "Now there's an idea."

"And afterward, you'll probably have a better idea if this job is a good fit for you," I told Jessa, looking her up and down as furtively as I could. Appreciating the enticing swell of her chest, the tantalizing dip of her waist, the ruffles over her hips that begged me to give them a little tug.

Jessa had been finishing her sophomore year the last time I'd seen her, too young at the time and too off-limits because of her brother.

But now? She was all woman, pure curves and style, with a gleam in her eye that had me ready to throw my office policies aside.

"Sounds like a plan." She pinned me with a toothy smile, one that sent my belly flopping.

"Great." I crossed my arms over my chest, reminding myself of the *real* plan: get Jessa to employee status ASAP, where I wouldn't dare fantasize about her, be tempted by her. Because my life had zero room for romance or anything more than the occasional blowjob. "Welcome to Fairchild Enterprises, Ms. Walton."

Ms. Walton. That's how it needed to be from now on. That's how it needed to *stay.*

If we were anywhere else, she'd be my first pick. But here, inside the walls of Fairchild Enterprises, I could have her no closer than arm's length.

CHAPTER THREE

JESSA

Pinch.

Ouch.

Pinch.

Ouch.

Pinch. I grimaced through the third round of reality-checking. It still hurt, which meant that I was *most likely* still not dreaming about my current life in New York. You know, the one where I was on the Fairchild payroll, had my own desk outside of Damian's office, and was striding around wearing sensible black heels like I belonged there.

I smirked to myself, casting an approving eye over my brand-new desk space. Three days into the gig and I felt equal parts capable and terrified that everyone would figure out what a fraud I was. *Hired because of my big brother! Just an old family friend with no experience!* I'd only recently discovered that it was forbidden to refer to north or south in this city. No, no—it was *uptown* or *downtown.* How could I possibly fit into a place where I'd referred to midtown as *north* only two months ago?

"Jessa, here are some customer profiles you'll need to look over, get acquainted with." Francis jolted me out of my desk layout as-sessment—the cute fake cactus *really* brought the whole thing together—as he laid down some papers. "Pay attention to anyone with a *Jr* behind their name. This means they have *lineage.* The Fairchilds are very interested in lineage, but not for the reasons you'd think." He clicked his tongue, setting more papers in front of me. "This is a list of expected attendees for the coding fundraiser Damian is planning on attending. Tasks like these will soon become yours, but for now, I'm showing you what I'm doing so that you can learn who to schmooze before you go."

I blinked a few times at the papers raining down on my desk. "Schmooze?"

"Yes. These events are horribly boring and there's only a fifty-fifty chance of good food. You'd think, being in a culinary capital of the world, we could count on better food. But alas, even some scallops taste fishy in New York City."

"That sounds so profound," I murmured.

"It is," Francis concluded, dropping another set of pages in front of me. "Now this document is a detailed list of Avoids."

"Avoids?"

"People we need to avoid—in person, in theory, in writing. People who have scorned or betrayed the Fairchilds. Things like that. I've put this together so you can get up to speed, and quickly. Making mistakes with the brothers is not recommended."

My brows had been continuously furrowing during his rundown, and now they were simply sewn together. "Why not?"

His dark gaze rooted me to my spot. "Listen, I know you're new here, but the Fairchilds expect a certain...caliber. Time will tell if you have it or not."

His words left my tongue sticking to the roof of my mouth. Clearly, word had not gotten out that Damian and I had known each other in our previous lives. I was firmly in the Random New Hire file. I didn't mind.

"Well...that's good to know. Thank you."

Over Francis's shoulder, I saw Axel coming down the hallway, his head turned sharply as he talked with someone behind him. I hadn't spotted Axel during my interview on Thursday or my first day on Friday; now on Monday, it seemed like I'd been waiting to say hi to him forever.

Francis started saying something else, but his voice drifted away as Axel spotted me from down the hall. His eyes lit up, and he strode my way in a perfectly tailored dark gray suit, a dog with a dark, glossy coat loping alongside him.

"There you are, Jessa! Welcome to Fairchild Enterprises."

I could practically feel Francis's hackles rise. "Oh. Do you two know each other already?"

"Axel!" I held out my arms, and he gave me a loose hug. He seemed taller since the last time I'd seen him, beefier, too. All the Fairchild brothers had sharpened and blossomed under the influence of wealth and success. "It's been forever."

He smiled down at me, pinching my arm like he always used to. "Little Jessa Walton. Really never thought I'd see you up here."

"Welp, here I am. Jeremy sent me. I'm the Walton ambassador," I said with a laugh.

"Meet Zero," he said, sweeping his hand toward the handsome pup at his feet.

"Aww, it's a pleasure to meet you, Zero." I offered my hand, which Zero sniffed inquisitively before I got a friendly lick.

"That's how many concerns he has around you, since he knows you're in the trust circle." Axel beamed down at his dog.

Francis cleared his throat. "So this is a Kentucky connection, I take it?"

Axel draped his arm over my shoulders and grinned over at Francis. "Kentucky through and through. We've gotta take good care of Jessa, Francis, or else her big brother will come beat me up."

Francis laughed, but it was hollow. "Noted."

Damian strode down the hallway next, his hands stuffed into his pockets. His moss green eyes registered mild curiosity as he approached Axel and me. "What's going on here?"

I swallowed hard as I took him in. The sixteen-year-old in me still fangirled every time I saw Damian up close, especially now that he'd lost the glasses he'd always worn during high school. Dark stubble lined his jawline and above his lip—elegant scruff. His big, plump lips were the stuff of fantasies; mine, specifically. I had wondered no fewer than eighteen thousand times what it might feel like to touch those lips with my own. He dragged his tongue across his bottom lip, as though he could hear my thoughts, which sent heat to my core like a lightning rod.

"Just saying hello to our old friend Jessa," Axel said.

"She needs to get back to work," Damian said curtly, then his gaze dropped to Zero. "Hey there, buddy." He leaned forward to smooth his hand over Zero's head.

Axel sent me a look that said *get a load of this guy* and removed his arm. "Fine. But Jessa, if you need anything, especially a break from this guy"—he jerked his thumb in the direction of Damian—"you know where to find me. My office is right down the hall. And you'll be meeting my girlfriend Cora soon too. I have a feeling you two are going to get along great."

I smiled at him, basking in the warmth from his greeting. That's what I had expected from the Fairchilds. It wasn't at all what I had gotten from Damian.

But it was fine. He'd made the employer-employee boundary clear. No big deal.

Well, okay, maybe just a tiny deal.

Axel waved and headed away. Damian slipped into his office, the door clicking shut behind him, leaving only his *delicious* cologne lingering in the air—something woodsy and refined and *feral* all at the same time—and Francis's heavy stare.

"So how long have you known the Fairchilds?"

I swallowed. This felt like a trick question. So much for starting with a blank slate here. "Um...since...middle school? I guess?"

"Hm." He surveyed some of the sheets on the desk again, his jaw flexing. "Wasn't aware of that history."

"They're practically like brothers," I said.

Francis fixed me with an inscrutable look. I couldn't tell if this was a good or bad piece of information to share. "Just be aware that whatever you think you know about them from back home, it's different here on Wall Street."

I nodded, not entirely sure what he meant. "Yeah. That makes sense, I think."

"Get settled in. I'll keep you up to date." He offered a brief smile and flitted away, the sheen of his dress pants snagging my attention in the bright light of the hallway.

I looked around at the quiet reception area outside Damian's office. There weren't too many people who came down this short, dead-end hallway, beyond Francis or the brothers. I liked that aspect of it—there wasn't a ton of foot traffic. It could just be me and Damian, tucked into our own little corner.

I listened for some sign of life beyond Damian's door. Everything was cool, calm, collected here. But more than that, it was *fancy*. There were espresso machines in practically every office pod. The break room featured only the most expensive brand of bottled water, the kind I had very specifically never purchased because *who pays that much for water?* The carpets lining the hallway looked like they came from some sort of Fanciest Rugs 'R' Us custom-order magazine, all silver-threaded and patterned.

This was ten leagues above the last job I'd had, the diner gig I'd quit Thursday evening after an excessive amount of apologizing to my former manager.

I couldn't deny it. I was *thrilled* to be here.

But a small part of me tugged at my metaphorical arm saying *but wait...this isn't what you came here to do.*

I tried to push the thoughts away as I clicked through screens on my new company laptop. The keys were nearly silent as I typed out a quick email to Francis, acknowledging I'd gotten the Avoids addendum. My desk phone rang—I knew it was Damian because of the red light that signified which line the call came from.

"Damian Fairchild's confidential secretary," I cooed in my sugariest voice. "How may I help you?"

He snorted through the phone. "Are you always going to answer like that?" His voice sounded gritty this close to my ear, something caught between sex voice and just-woke-up. I clenched my thighs together. I could barely look at him without fangirling, and *hearing* him was proving to be just as difficult.

"I'll answer however you want me to," I said, and then realized how suggestive that sounded. Heat crept into my cheeks.

He paused, and the vacuum that stretched between our words became deafening. "Hmm. I'll think about that," he finally said. "Did you see the email that just came through?"

I refreshed my inbox and a new email pinged. He walked me through something regarding his upcoming schedule. Once I'd figured it out, he said, "Great. Talk later."

"Ahh, wait," I blurted. It was Monday. Which meant rent was due. My only plan forward was to just artfully dodge my landlord until my first paycheck landed...whenever that was. "I forgot to ask. Uh...when is payday?"

"Mmm, next Friday, I think. Though you might not fall on that cycle. I can find out for sure."

Anxiety spiked inside me. I couldn't dodge paying rent for another two weeks. "Okay. All right. That's uh..."

"What's wrong?"

"It's just that, uh, my rent—"

"When is it due?"

I swallowed hard, feeling every inch the pathetic, broke loser that I truly was deep inside. "Today."

"What's the exact amount that you need for your landlord?"

I told him the number, down to the cents, working my teeth over and over my bottom lip as I reminded myself that soon I'd be making six figures and these issues would be a thing of the past.

Except in earning six figures, I'd create another issue: neglecting the whole reason I'd come to New York in the first place.

A different anxiety sprouted this time, a deeper, more wrenching kind. The type of anxiety that came when I turned away from that whisper of intuition inside me, the guiding voice that had urged me to come here in the first place. The voice I'd ignored for my five years at Tommy's side, withstanding his gaslighting and abuse, telling myself that staying with him, staying in Louisville, was the best thing for everyone.

I was halfway through my fashion certificate course. I *had* to finish. Which just meant I'd do whatever it took to both work this job *and* finish my certification.

Damian cleared his throat. "Send me your landlord's information when you get a chance."

"What?"

"His number, or cash app account. Whatever you use."

"You...you're going to pay it?" I stammered.

"Sure. Just until you get on your feet."

Warmth spread through me, and tears pricked my eyes. First a six-figure job, and now *this*. "Damian, you are *too* kind."

"It's nothing. I promise. Consider it a hiring bonus. And speaking of company perks, the fundraiser gala this weekend..."

"Yes?" Excitement prickled to life inside me. I was itching for a chance to see a real-life New York City soiree.

"Do you have anything to wear to a black-tie event?"

At home, I had three finished dresses that would be perfect, and one that I was halfway finished designing. The chance to premier *any* of them in an upper-class setting would be a dream come true. If even one well-connected woman asked me where I'd gotten my dress...this was the sort of thing I dreamt about with each stitch.

"Actually, I do! I have a few different dresses I'm thinking about."

"Well, I'll give you some money in case you need anything else. Remember, this is a highly formal affair. Don't be shy about buying what you need."

I couldn't think of a single thing I needed as it related to this formal affair. The only thing I *needed* had to do with this man and my naked body. The image of that brunette buried between his legs sizzled through my mind. Truthfully, that image was *branded* there. It might never disappear. I needed *me* to be the one between his legs. Heat scorched through me again as I felt the blush make its way to my cheeks. Thank God Damian couldn't see me having naughty thoughts about him.

"I won't," I finally said.

"Great." The line disconnected, and I slowly hung up the phone. This felt like an alternate dimension. I pinched my forearm again. *Ouch.* Still painful. Still probably not a dream.

Damian's door opened a moment later, and before I could even suck in a fortifying breath, his sturdy frame was at the side of my desk, sliding a credit card across the surface.

"Here," he rumbled, his mossy green gaze sliding over my face like a caress. And then he *winked.* "No spending limit."

Damian retreated into his office, leaving me in a pleasant cocoon of his expensive cologne, hints of musk and earth wrapped around me like a blanket. A sigh escaped me and my eyes fluttered shut.

I had Damian's credit card. He was paying my rent. And he'd fucking *winked* at me.

According to my vagina, we were in love and close to getting married.

My cell phone buzzed from on top of my desk. An unknown number had sent me a text, but from the way my stomach pitched, I knew it was Tommy. He crept up every so often from a new number, one that I hadn't blocked, just to remind me that he was still breathing and wishing the worst for me.

"Heard you're a slut for the Fairchilds now. Doesn't even surprise me."

I swiped through the motions to block that number, so repetitive I could have done it in my sleep. Then I deleted the text and turned my phone face down.

Tommy was a reminder that I'd come to New York for myself. Despite what he or anybody else thought about it, my life was my own. And I wasn't here to waste my time thinking about Tommy's opinions. I wasn't here to waste my time on *men*, either.

Not only was Damian my boss now, he was *taken*. He had a brunette who showed up in his office to *service him*, a woman who probably oozed rank and power and big fat acronyms behind her name.

But more than that, I wanted no ties to any man. My adolescent heart would always want Damian, but my adult heart needed independence. Success.

A future all my own.

At the end of the day, I was lucky that Damian and his plump lips wanted nothing to do with me.

Because I only had time and attention for paying my bills and getting my fashion certificate. No matter what.

CHAPTER FOUR

DAMIAN

564.

The number ran through my mind on repeat. A lot of numbers of did. It was part of the way I processed the world. But this number in particular perplexed me.

564. The number of dollars Jessa had spent on my personal credit card. In other words, absolutely nothing.

It was chump change. It was laughable. What the fuck had she bought when I'd given her no spending limit? A pair of designer shoes from the bargain bin?

Not knowing made me nervous, especially while I milled around this fundraiser nestled in an art gallery, flanked by my brothers, and waited for Jessa to show up. She needed to look the part, and part of me was a little too concerned about whether she could pull it off.

But if she were any other secretary you wouldn't fucking care.

She'd clocked her first week at Fairchild Enterprises uneventfully. She did as she was told, asked questions, arrived and left on time, like the good little sister she was.

My fingers tightened around the tumbler of whiskey in my left hand. I was so close to convincing myself that adding her to the team could be a normal, regular occurrence in the office. That it wouldn't disrupt anything. That she could become part of the background blur of daily life. A potted plant one scarcely notices. A potted plant with arms—and ridiculously hot dresses. Okay, a potted plant with a few too many curves.

I cleared my throat, tipping some more whiskey into my mouth as I completed my tenth furtive scan of the arched doorways to the gallery. Strange, kinetic art blobbed across the centerpiece wall. Metal sculptures dotted the large room, both liquid and graceful in their abstractness. Jessa still wasn't here, and she should have been. Trace chatted with people to my right, while Axel and Cora were deep in conversation to my left.

"Well Damian, as you know, has plenty to speak on in that arena." Trace's conversation drifted my way as he turned, roping me into his conversation. He stretched out his arm, gesturing to a man with a beard that could only be described as a chin strap. "Damian, this is Franco Serpetti."

I drifted through the introductions and ensuing details—tech start-up looking for knowledgeable advisors, and would I be interested in acting as one?—and excused myself as graciously and quickly as I could with a quick promise to assist in any way at all. I passed along my card.

"My email is on there. My secretary Jessa will get something set up," I told him, fighting the urge to start scanning the room again at the mention of her name. Where was she? And why was I so eager to see what dress she'd have on tonight?

My skin prickled, heat zipping from head to toe. Behind me, Axel crooned, "Oh, Jessa! There you are. I've been dying for you to meet Cora..."

Everything inside me went taut, a rubber band ready to snap. I turned to find Jessa beaming at Axel and Cora like they were the most fascinating duo in the world.

And all I could see was her.

Jessa. She became the focal point of the room, sucking up every ounce of my attention and available oxygen in a form-fitting, off-the-shoulder, black lace gown. Big pearl earrings dotted her ear lobes, her glossy auburn hair framing her face in soft, elegant waves. My hands balled into fists as I drifted closer to her without even deciding to.

Her work performance might have been routine, but her presence hardly was. When Jessa was around, the air buzzed, which did not seem remotely sane or normal. The other thing that did not seem sane or normal was how much I fucking wanted her. Was this some sort of high school attraction gone awry? Maybe I'd truly lost my mind amid all the stress of the past couple years. Whatever it was, I didn't want it in my life.

I could control this.

"Cora's been out at the Hamptons house this past week," Axel was saying as I stepped closer. Cora grasped Jessa's hands in her own, leaning forward for a fake kiss on the cheek. The delight in Jessa's face was impossible to miss. Jessa was meant for this—these ballrooms, the ritual of fundraising, all of it.

"It's such a pleasure to meet you," Cora gushed. "And can I add you look stunning! Where did you get this dress?"

Jessa's cheeks went pink. Her throat bobbed. "I, uh...I made it myself."

This was news to me. Impossible news. I sipped my whiskey, pretending to look around the room, feigning focus on anything that wasn't this conversation I wasn't a part of. Axel slung his arm around my shoulders, bringing my head close to his mouth.

"Are you going to pick your jaw up off the floor, or should I?"

His cocksure smile was begging for someone to slap it off. I'd happily volunteer. "Fuck off."

"Just curious. Because if you don't plan to, Jessa might get the wrong idea about her new boss."

I elbowed him in the ribcage. *Hard.* "There are no ideas for her to get. Can you stop harassing me? You are the last person to talk about workplace ethics."

Axel's grin turned devilish. "Listen, just because I'm enacting a hostile takeover of Margulis Realty doesn't mean I don't have workplace ethics. Are you going to tell Jessa that you used to be in love with her in high school, or should I do that too?"

I sent him the most lethal look I could muster. It only made his grin spread wider.

"The way you're looking at me tells me I'm going to have to."

"Shut the fuck up," I warned him. "If this is your definition of stress relief, it's fucking annoying already."

Cora suddenly turned toward us, reaching for Axel. Her mulberry grin jostled us out of our quiet argument. "Axel? Can you get one of my cards out of your pocket for me? I don't have any left in my handbag."

"Of course, sweet cheeks." His face was pure mischief as he rummaged through his inside breast pocket.

"What were you guys talking about?" Cora inquired.

"Just some unresolved issues from Lipscombe High." Axel winked at Cora and Jessa. I delivered a stealthy punch to his lower back which made him cough abruptly. He produced the business card a moment later.

"I'm gonna fucking kidnap you and send you on a helicopter to the Bermuda Triangle," I warned him once Cora and Jessa were wrapped up in conversation again. "You are being the ultimate douche-scraper."

"Tell me," Axel said, "is douche-scraper an implement one uses to remove douchery, or is it a sky-high building of douchery?"

"It's a sky-high building of douchery," I clarified for him, practically hissing into his ear. "One of the ultra-tall ones. You know, the buildings that only get approved because of the shady-ass contractor."

Axel nodded sagely while Trace sent both of us a judgmental arched eyebrow. "What are you guys bitching about?"

"Nothing," I told him.

"Trace, tell our brother how many times we caught him staring at Jessa like a lovesick fool our senior year of high school."

"Fifty-two times," Trace reported. "An average of once a week during the calendar year."

I rolled my eyes. "You guys clearly have nothing better to do than to flip through our old yearbook and make up stories."

If there was any doubt that I needed no one else in my life beyond my brothers, here was my proof. Between Axel and Trace, I had my hands more than full. I had the essentials: my closest family, the mingling of work and pleasure on the weekends, and the knowledge that I was doing good for people. My work was my atonement for my past failures. I was helping kids, even though I hadn't been able to help my own little sisters.

A painful wrench in my chest left me gulping for air.

"Hey, you need another drink?" Axel asked me. "I don't think we're getting our ladies back anytime soon." He tipped his head toward Cora and Jessa, who were currently fawning over the details of Jessa's dress.

Our ladies. That was a joke. Jessa would never be my lady, because I'd never have *any* lady. Not long-term, at least, and not any time soon. Not when I had the beast of the SEC investigation over my head and I had to figure out which exciting new way my life might begin to deteriorate when I was least expecting it.

"Whiskey," I told him, handing off the empty glass. Axel took Trace's order as well and then slipped into the crowd, heading for the bar. Really, we knew he wanted to mingle too. As the social butterfly and chameleon, mingling was Axel's specialty. My job at these events was to simply remain alive and blinking until it was an acceptable time to leave. Trace fell somewhere in the middle: sociable enough, but he was a homebody at heart.

"Gosh, I haven't even made it over here to say hello!" Jessa's sweet voice wrenched at my insides again, my thighs tensing. I tipped my head in her direction.

"Welcome, Jessa." Trace leaned in and gave her a loose hug. Her cheeks flushed as she looked over at me. My palms itched, wanting to extend the same, but I couldn't. Not with the line I'd drawn in the sand. She and I were to remain boss and employee. That's the only way that made sense.

"This place sure is fancy," she said, smoothing her hands down the front of her dress. "So many fantastic outfits here tonight." A handbag dangled from one wrist—something simple and silver. When her eyes swung my way again, I caught the same glint of silver in her eyes. "Are they carrying shrimp around on a tray?"

"The appetizers are good tonight," Trace said.

"How much do they cost?" She nibbled at her bottom lip, looking around the room. A waiter approached, a tray balanced on his palm.

"Nothing," I told her. "The food is included in the cost of the ticket. Have at it."

"I can just take one? They aren't orders?"

"All for you," I reassured her, unable to fight a grin.

Relief flooded her face, and she pressed a hand to her cleavage as she intersected the nearest waiter. "Excuse me, sir? Could I bother you for a sample?"

The black-tie waiter paused in his rounds as Jessa plucked a cocktail napkin and one perfect, recently-shelled shrimp off the tray. Her eyes were wide as saucers.

"This looks *fresh*," she said. "Not at all like the little pink things you get from the Sav-A-Lot."

"Those are bonafide Gulf shrimp," I told her, unable to pry my eyes off her as she nibbled at it. She licked her lips a moment later.

"Oh my god. The sauce is spicy. My mouth is on fire already."

I signaled for another waiter, grabbing whatever drink was on his tray. A champagne flute. I lifted it in her direction. "We have this on standby if it gets too hot."

She giggled, took another bite, some of the sauce smearing on her lip. "I'm ruining the fancy event ten minutes in, aren't I?"

She had no idea how cute she looked. Dolled up to perfection, delighted by one spicy shrimp. I couldn't help but crack a grin. "Luckily you're allowed to eat at these things."

Jessa took the last bite, moaning appreciatively. *That* wasn't what I usually heard at events like this. I flexed my jaw, watching as her tongue swiped out over her juicy pink lip, lapping up the orange sauce.

"Okay, I think I'm ready for that drink now," she said with a laugh. I handed it over to her, gobbling up the display as she daintily lifted the rim to her lips, pinky in the air, and sipped.

"You're a natural," I commented, finally able to rip my gaze off her face. She'd always been too easy to look at, to get lost in. I could have spent the next two weeks watching her lick orange sauce off her damn lips. "You ready for work now or do you need some more shrimp?"

She wilted ever so slightly. "I shouldn't. If I eat another, I'll eat thirty more. And then I'd still need dessert on top of that. Damian, I'm in New York City—I need to eat like a supermodel."

"It's not as glamorous as it might sound," I told her. "It's mostly celery."

She huffed. "I can't do celery. It's like biting water with hair in it. So yeah, I better get another shrimp." She swooped toward the nearest waiter, plucking another shrimp from the platter, more confident and experienced than the first time around. "So much for the supermodel diet. That idea lasted five seconds."

I watched as she polished off the next shrimp with an appreciative moan. I hated how much I enjoyed this. "You ready?"

"Never. Not when there're so many tempting appetizers around me."

I bit my lip, fighting the smile that threatened to overtake me. Jessa rummaged through her handbag, producing a sleek tablet. I surveyed the room, discretely waving over another waiter. His tray held stuffed mushrooms, and I suspected Jessa would enjoy those too.

"All right. Let me just get out my brand-new tablet so I can take notes," she murmured as she turned it on, swiping through screens. "My new boss just got it for me, ain't he a peach?"

"He's some type of fruit," I returned, "but not sure he's a peach."

"Oh, is he a fruit?" Genuine curiosity swarmed in her eyes as she looked up at me. "I didn't take you for the fruit-pickin' kind."

"Maybe a tomato," I offered, seeing where she was going with it and wanting to steer it back to clarity. Even though it shouldn't matter to me if she got the wrong idea. In fact, it would be *better* if she got the wrong idea. "Acidic. Powerful. The base of whatever dish you're putting together."

She blinked a couple times, nodding. "That sounds about right."

The waiter approached with his tray of stuffed mushrooms. I nodded toward Jessa. "What about these?"

Her eyes lit up and she plucked one off the tray. "Damian Fairchild, are you trying to distract me? It's my second week on the job and I still need to prove myself. My tomato of a boss might fire me if I don't."

I couldn't contain the grin this time. It was too easy with her, with the back-and-forth, the jokes, the whimsical way we could sit here and say nothing and everything all at once. I couldn't remember the last time I'd done this with anyone other than Trace or Axel.

I plucked a mushroom off the tray for myself. Our gazes met and we popped them into our mouths at the same time, watching each other as we chewed.

I hadn't seen this woman in over a decade until last week, but now, it felt like no time had passed at all. Even though there was a ravine the size of Kentucky between us, filled with unknown life events and experiences, I still felt like I *knew* her.

The familiarity made my skin prickle. I didn't like it. Couldn't have it.

Not when I'd spent the last decade of my life keeping to the shadows. Things were safe there, unattached and lukewarm. No new people, no new love.

I had enough love in my life. And I didn't have room for more.

I cleared my throat, straightening my back as I set my sights on the nearest person of importance. It didn't matter who. I just needed to direct the conversation away from anything that threatened to tug at the armor that protected the softest parts of me.

"You'll probably be hearing from that guy over there."

"Who, the one standing next to the most phenomenally beaded dress I have ever seen in real life? That must be so heavy. I wonder how they fastened the beadwork."

I cracked a grin and pointed out the man Trace spoke with earlier, giving her an uninspired rundown of my interaction with him earlier. After that, I pointed out all the biggest names in the room—some of which made her gasp, particularly the well-known names like Spike Lee and Tina Fey.

"There are so many celebrities here," she murmured, a hand pressed to her chin. "I should have worn something designer."

I blinked a few times, glancing down at her dress. Her cleavage was the first thing I noticed—luscious, pearlescent, completely fucking bitable, *dammit*—but I yanked my gaze away before my thoughts could careen too far. "Did you really make this dress?"

She nodded with a sad sigh. "I should have gone with Givenchy, though."

"It's a nice dress."

"Nice? See, you gave me your credit card and I was coming to this function and—" She sighed again, returning her focus to the tablet in her hands. "I'm breathing the same air as Tina Fey. That's all that matters."

My fingers tightened around the tumbler of whiskey. I had more questions about the dress. And a lot more words to describe the dress, all of which were much stronger than *nice*. But I wouldn't give in to them. I focused on the clamor of the room around us, the din of voices and far-off champagne bottles popping open. I took a deep breath to clear my head. It was hard to stay focused around Jessa. She was far too warm and inviting.

"Hey. I made the donation." Trace jostled my shoulder, filling my vision suddenly.

"Oh, you guys donated tonight?" Jessa asked innocently. "More than just buying the tickets?"

Trace nodded, jerking his head my way. "It's all this guy. Supporting the hackers of the next generation."

I smirked in his direction. "It sounds so uncouth when you say it."

"How much did you donate?" Jessa asked him. I braced myself for his answer—and her reaction.

"Three hundred thousand," Trace replied.

Jessa blinked several times, swinging her gaze my way. "Oh, is that all?"

This time, I couldn't help the laugh that rocketed out of me. Something about the jaunty look she'd given me coupled with the air of insanity behind her words.

Axel joined us a moment later, something wild lighting up his face, as usual. "Guys. There's someone we need to scout tonight. Her name is Roxy Windham, and she's very interested in finding a new wealth management firm. Not only that, she's hacker friendly. I've made contact, but we need to seal the deal. I told her we'd send the ambassador."

The ambassador usually meant Francis. But tonight, that meant Jessa. She looked up at us with wide eyes.

"I take it that's me?"

"All you have to do is go introduce yourself, get her most important info, and woo her a little," I said.

"Woo her a little?" Jessa repeated.

"Chat about whatever seems relevant," Trace offered. "Find a shared interest, something to talk about..."

"I'm pretty sure she'll realize within ten seconds that I'm a nobody from the sticks, but okay. Let's do this." Jessa expelled a fortifying breath and straightened her back. "Where am I heading, boys?"

Axel helped guide her to the target, and the three of us watched as she drifted through the crowd, headed for Roxy.

"She'll do great," Trace murmured. I furrowed my brow and nodded, perplexed by my inability to look away from the sashay of her hips.

"Well, we've shown our faces, made our donation, and we're scouting a new client," I said, making a big display of checking my smart watch. "I think it's time for me to leave."

"When the party's just getting started?" Axel asked, feigning incredulity. "Yeah, that sounds on brand for Damian Fairchild."

"Hey, I'll cut loose at a party when it's my *own*," I clarified. Not like I needed to. My brothers knew well enough just how hard I could party when I wanted to. What they didn't know anymore was how much self-medicating I did when they weren't looking.

Drinking or smoking myself to sleep was now the norm. I wasn't proud of it, but it was a natural conclusion of this clusterfuck of a situation I was in. And I needed to get a head start on winding myself down for the night.

Axel smiled out into the crowd. I followed his gaze, finding Roxy watching transfixed as Jessa told some story in her typical gregarious, contagiously warm fashion.

"I think Jessa is nailing it," Axel murmured.

"Great. Even more reason for me to head out. She's got it handled."

"Sure you don't want to head down memory lane?" Axel nudged me obnoxiously. "Steal that kiss you never could under the bleachers?"

I turned to him, trying my best to puncture him with the daggers in my eyes. "Remember what I said about the Bermuda Triangle."

And I was serious. I'd hire the cartographer necessary to deposit his ass there and have him never return. I hated their ribbing about Jessa only because there was a kernel of truth to it, which they knew. They were my fucking brothers, after all. The whole thing was aggravating. The only thing I knew to do was walk away.

Deep down, a part of me wanted to snag Jessa and run far away from the party, take her someplace where we could just sit. Catch up. See what happened. And I couldn't afford to give that part of me a chance to act.

A third had joined Jessa and Roxy across the room, a well-dressed oil exec who came to all these things. Tall, dark hair, and a winning grin beaming down at Jessa. She touched her chest as he said something that prompted a blush to bloom. The knot in my gut cinched tighter.

The worst thing about having Jessa in my orbit was knowing that she'd be scooped up in a heartbeat. And it could never be me doing the scooping.

I downed my whiskey, handing the empty glass to the nearest waiter. "I'm out. Tell Jessa if she asks."

"Go tell her yourself," Axel shot back.

I narrowed my eyes at him again. "Bye, douche-scraper."

He laughed, pulling me into a hug. "I love you, you freak. You know that, right?"

I hugged him tight, slapping my younger brother's back. "Love you too."

It was me, Axel, and Trace against the world. That's how it had been since my teenage years. And that's how it was going to stay.

Introducing—or taking away—anyone else would disrupt everything, and God knew I couldn't handle that.

The only way to keep everything together was by making sure nothing changed.

CHAPTER FIVE

JESSA

My eyes burned as I sat on the subway Monday morning. The dark features of the subway tunnel flashed past the windows at a startling pace, far too quickly for my un-caffeinated state. Most of my morning commute was underground, but occasionally when the train came up for air, I'd see fascinating snippets of life: brownstones and park chess games; clusters of schoolkids and cerulean backpacks; best friends with heads tossed back in laughter, cigarettes tight between fingertips. I blinked rapidly, trying to conjure some bit of clarity at seven a.m., but nothing came. It was too early. The sun was too bright; the stench was too real. The sound of the wheels on the tracks threatened to lull me back to sleep as we clickity-clacked our way through Brooklyn, headed for the Financial District.

Another week was beginning at Fairchild Enterprises, which meant another week of hanging on for dear life to my fashion course.

A yawn burst past my lips, unsanctioned. I capped my mouth with a hand. I'd spent every bit of Saturday and Sunday catching up on my coursework, preparing things for the week, catching up on designs. I was determined not to fall behind. Which meant I'd work a hundred hours a week between my two obligations if I had to. As long as I could make it to my classes on Monday and Wednesday evenings without giving Damian any reason to suspect I wasn't giving him $100,000 worth of dedication, I'd be fine.

That was all that mattered.

My phone buzzed with notifications from social media. I'd kept them turned on ever since leaving Tommy, because he loved to surprise me, post-breakup, by sharing embarrassing photos with the world—like that "oopsie didn't mean to post and tag you in that" intimate picture that I'd shared with him and him alone. Even years later, I was always on high alert.

I scrolled through my feed. I'd been tagged in a photo from the event on Friday evening. My heart swelled as I took in the scene. Trace had posted it, a candid photo of the sprawling party. In the picture, I was mid-sentence, gesturing toward Damian, who watched me with his trademark serious look, plump lips on display. I melted for the hundredth time as I took in that broad-shouldered man in his perfect black suit, his chestnut-and-dark blond hair swept back in the perfect mix of formal and loose enough to fist. Not that I would ever be fisting his hair, of course. Damian had made it plenty clear that anything beyond business interactions was a laughable impossibility.

My gaze drifted to Axel in the picture, who was leaning toward Cora, gorgeous people crowded all around them. Between the beautiful gallery and the black-tie affair, it looked like I was living the dream in New York.

The smile I wore made my cheeks hurt as I drank in the photo. I wasn't sure if this was the technical definition of success, but it was sure something. It at least *looked* successful, even if some things looked more perfect than they really were. For example, this picture didn't hint at the patterning mistake I'd made that meant my dress swished too much against the floor on only one side of the dress—a total design error that I couldn't wait to tell my professor about.

And the other thing this picture didn't hint at? The fact that Damian had ghosted me within a half hour of my arrival.

No, he wasn't obligated to stay at my side all night or hunt down yummy snacks like the stuffed mushrooms or hold my champagne while I ate spicy foods. Those were just the things I *wanted* him to do while I pretended he was my date, even though he'd never be caught dead linked romantically with someone like me.

But what had I really expected? Damian could be icier than Antarctica, a trait he didn't hesitate to reveal as time went on.

I basked in the surreal fanciness of the photo for the rest of my trip. By the time I'd stepped onto the platform and breezed my way through the subway station, it was 7:50 a.m. Perfect timing. I wasn't fully caffeinated, but the adrenaline from seeing my first near-debutante outing featured on social media *and* making it to work on time after slaving away on fashion all weekend was a close second place to a shot of espresso.

And wasn't I just living the New York life? I couldn't fight the grin. I'd never felt so giddy.

My life had changed dramatically, thanks to Damian. Even if he would never press those pouty lips against mine, I could at least admire him from afar for the rest of my time at his company. That would have to suffice, at least until I found some other introverted tech genius to fall into unrequited love with.

My phone vibrated with an incoming message as I surged into the gleaming lobby of the Fairchild building. I reviewed my phone dully—as any New Yorker would. A commonplace occurrence in my fancy life, with this fancy job, attending fancy events.

But my grin faltered once I saw who had messaged me. It was my sister Tara. Which meant something unpleasant lurked around the corner. My stomach knotted in anticipation.

TARA: Wow. Just saw the party pics from yr wild wknd in NYC.

The grin fell further, lead weights at the corners of my lips.

JESSA: It was a work event. Mostly boring.

A total lie. I'd been enchanted by every moment of that evening from start to finish. But I couldn't let Tara know that I actually *enjoyed* something.

TARA: How much are they paying you?

I didn't want to answer the question. I didn't even want to be asked the question. I'd confided in Jeremy about my new salary out of sheer excitement after I'd started, but he knew better than to share that with Tara.

Didn't he?

I swallowed hard, pocketing my phone as I reoriented myself. I'd missed the elevator going up, thanks to Tara. *Shit.* I headed for another door, hitting the button, as more people gathered in the waiting area. I tapped out a reply as the numbers of a different elevator ticked downward.

JESSA: Standard salary for this type of position in the city, nothing crazy.

Except going from roughly $22,000 per year to six figures was *fucking crazy.* Even I couldn't fully believe it.

TARA: So, what are you making with the Fairchilds? $20/hour or something?

My stomach didn't just pitch downward, it got on a high-speed elevator to hell. I made more than double that. My average hourly wage was a number that would make Tara choke. But everything about New York made regular people choke: the traffic, the salaries, the sky-high rents, the sheer number of hot dog stands. Tara couldn't understand. She'd never even left northern Kentucky.

I ignored my phone and boarded the next elevator that opened. It was 8:02 already. I was officially late. Nervousness wrenched my stomach as I stared at the ascending numbers, tucked behind ten other people. When the doors opened at the Fairchild Enterprises level, I strode purposefully to my desk at the back of the building.

I spotted Trace heading down the hallway to the conference room, and he jerked his head into a nod.

"Morning, Trace," I sang out. "I'm late today, don't tell my boss, okay?"

He cracked a grin. "He's late too. What a coincidence."

His words hinted at something I only wished could be true: that we were both late because of the other one. But that wasn't true, and would never be true. Not when Damian kept me at an arm's length and had perfect-cheekboned Harper in the wings. I'd planned to ask him where she'd been that night at the fundraiser, but he'd disappeared before I could probe even slightly. Which just seemed like confirmation that he'd been rushing off to meet her somewhere.

At my desk I drew a deep, cleansing breath as I set my purse down and surveyed the quiet area. Damian's door was closed though maybe he was already in the conference room. The air felt crisp and inspiring inside Fairchild Enterprises, somehow, though maybe that was just an extension of how I felt about the brothers.

From day one, they'd always seemed destined for greatness, possessing some otherworldly essence about them. Sure, that might have been my unrepentant schoolgirl crush lending them some of that celebrity status, but the truth was plain to see. All these years later, *they* were the ones on top of the world. Nobody else from Lipscombe Schools, nobody in Oakville itself had gone even half as far. And as far as I could tell, Damian lived and breathed helping people—including lost dreamers like me.

I drew another deep breath. No more daydreaming about Damian. It was time to work.

TARA: ????? Forget how to text?

I frowned down at my phone. No more of this conversation with my sister, either. At least not during work hours. I unpacked my lunch, my essentials bag, my sketchbooks for downtime, and put everything in its rightful place—which also included the phone going into my desk drawer. But before I hid it away, I fired off a quick response.

JESSA: At work now, can't chat.

TARA: Must make a lot if you can afford new dresses n shit

JESSA: I didn't buy that dress.

TARA: So you're just gonna leave mom to rot, huh?

My eyes drifted shut, guilt taking an insidious lap inside me. Our mother was in rehab for the third time. Third time was the charm, she'd promised. Tara expected me to be waiting at the exit, open arms and a smile at the ready. Because according to her—and most of my family—my rightful place was in Kentucky. With family. As the youngest child, with no children or husband, it was my duty to pick up the pieces of my mother's life without fail, without complaint. Tara fucking *hated* that I'd moved to New York instead.

So much for stowing my phone at work.

JESSA: She's not rotting. She's getting the help she needs.

TARA: So where's your $$ for this month?

JESSA: I already sent it to you.

TARA: If you're making $20/hour you should pay more. This shit ain't cheap. You got three kids to raise too, or is that just me?

Tears crept into my eyes, blurring the edges of my vision. It was always the same old cycle. I wanted out, but I couldn't find the escape hatch.

JESSA: I'll send what I can after my next paycheck.

TARA: Pretty sure the woman who gave you life needs the help more than your wardrobe. Act right, Jessa.

Her words landed with the finality of an axe blow, and I shoved the phone into my desk drawer, chin trembling. One tear escaped, and I swiped it away before anyone could see—or even feel—that I was crying at my desk.

I drew a shaky breath, staring at my computer screen but seeing nothing.

It wasn't fair. None of it felt fair. But Tara's words brought the guilt crashing back over me, a sticky-sour avalanche of fears and doubts. Who was I to deserve this life? What right did I have trying to do better, do something new, when the rest of my family struggled so badly?

Maybe her words were just a reminder to pack up this silly fantasy and go back to where I was needed. New York didn't need me. But Kentucky did.

I could feel the perma-frown on my face as I scrolled through my inbox.

All I could do was get lost in my to-do list. If nothing else, I needed to earn this six-figure job, and I intended to at least make the money I—and my family—required. I waited until I could see past the tears once more, and then I got to work answering emails, checking appointments, researching clients. By nine thirty, there was still no peep from Damian. That's when I remembered to check his calendar—ugh, anxiety always derailed my common sense—and realized he was in a meeting until ten with his brothers and Francis.

When the admin tasks failed to keep the tears at bay, I pushed away from my desk and strode down the hallway. I wasn't entirely sure where I was going, only that I needed to go somewhere. As I passed the open door of the break lounge, I spotted a head of glossy dark hair.

Cora Margulis. Axel's *absolutely wonderful* girlfriend who'd I'd met—and fallen in love with—Friday night.

I stared at her through the doorway, wondering if our friendliness from the fundraiser would carry over into the office. She'd mentioned being in town sporadically from her perch in the Hamptons, which made me think this was more of a social call than a bona fide work appearance.

"Hi, Cora!" My voice sounded unnaturally chipper. Whatever cool points I'd collected for making my own dress withered in the air between us as she slowly turned, eyes widening.

"Jessa!"

Phew. At least she'd remembered my name. Cora came toward me, her arms outstretched. It took me a moment to realize she was angling for a hug. I surged forward, and we embraced like the oldest of gal pals. My heart thumped as her fruity perfume wafted over me.

"So good to see you," I gushed.

"You too." She stepped back, looking me up and down. "Tell me, is this another one of your creations?"

I swallowed the last bit of my sadness from Tara's guilt trip and looked down at my dress, smoothing the front of it. It was a simple A-line cream and black design that I'd made at the start of the course. "It sure is. One of my favorites. I didn't intend it for work wear, but it seems like it's up for the job." I looked over her outfit then, noting the bold colors and blocky design. I could think of at least a few designs of my own that she might like in that style. "I'm still glowing from that party. I've never been to anything like that."

"They're a dime a dozen in this city," Cora said wryly. "But they can be a good time in the right company. And I think you have the right company."

I laughed, but it trailed off quickly. "It's great working with old friends. Even though Damian is...you know..."

Curiosity furrowed her brows, and I clamped my mouth shut. *Shit.* I'd been aiming for small talk and instead landed near shit talk.

"He's what?"

"Just such a serious genius," I blurted, adding a small laugh that I hoped didn't sound forced, or insane, or both. "He left so quickly, I didn't get a chance to see what he's like away from the office." God, I hoped I sounded even remotely normal and not like a lovesick ex-teenager who'd been in unrequited love with that man for something like fifteen years. "You know, when we're here, it's all work."

Cora nodded sympathetically. "That's true. He haunts this office like a ghost sometimes."

"But it's fine. He's such an amazing genius, he doesn't need to waste time chatting or hanging out with me after all these years, you know?" I was just rambling now, desperate to make her understand how much I wasn't complaining about my literal boss. "Besides, I'm sure he's got his hands full between the business and all his philanthropic work and the investigation, not to mention his girlfriend..."

The curiosity on her face etched deeper. "Girlfriend?"

"Yeah, that brunette that was visiting him the day I interviewed," I said. "I didn't catch her name but, you know, they're together."

Her brows lifted and she nodded, looking toward the conference room door. "Wow. That's a new one. I don't think I've ever known him to actually put a label on things with anyone."

The further I dug this hole, the harder it would be to scramble out. I needed to shut up. But I needed to be graceful, too.

"Well, it just seems like he's been so stressed since I started."

Cora heaved a sigh, nodding gravely. "That's definitely an effect of the investigation."

Francis had done an excellent job of filling me in on every sordid detail about the SEC investigation, and it was no wonder Damian was stressed. "I just want to do something to pick up his spirits, get him to loosen up a little bit. Do you have any suggestions?"

She tilted her head back and forth as she thought. "That is a sweet question. I wish I had a better answer for you. Honestly, I think what Damian would like most is a bottle of whiskey and being left alone in his room."

I laughed, even though the last thing I wanted to do was leave him alone. I just didn't know how to get him to want to be with *me.*

And I wasn't supposed to be trying. So that ended that.

"Still the same as when he was a teen," I said. "Except for the whiskey."

Cora laughed, her gaze dancing over my dress again. "You know, this dress reminds me. I really loved the one you wore on Friday. I'd be interested in one like that myself, honestly. Do you ever take custom orders?"

My mouth parted, unsure if I wanted to focus on my excitement or gratitude first. So in lieu of either, nothing at all came out except for one tiny squeak.

Cora laughed. "Was that a yes?"

"I've never been asked for custom orders before," I forced out. Actually, that was a lie. My high school bestie, Joni, had asked for a custom order once, but that was before I knew what the hell I was doing, and she loved me enough to wear the tank top I'd made her even though it came out looking like a trash bag.

"Well, I'd be happy to be your first client," she said sweetly. And she meant it—I could tell. Cora was the type of woman I'd only seen in magazines and on TV. That type of classically gorgeous, prim and proper beauty. But up close, she was magnetic. Warm and personable, the most beautiful acquaintance I'd probably ever have in my life.

Getting my designs on a woman like her would be a dream come true.

"I have so many designs, too," I said. "Notebooks and notebooks of them. I've only made a few come to life so far, but I could probably give you a different dress of the week for the rest of your life if they all became real."

Cora's eyes lit up, and she grabbed my wrist. "Can I see them?"

"My notebooks?" The squeak was back.

"Yes. I'd love to see your design process. You've got some real talent, Jessa. It's obvious to anyone with a set of eyes."

My throat tightened and I looked away. Talent didn't mean much in my family. But Cora's encouragement was sorely needed, a cool gulp of water after wandering the desert that had been my home life the past decade or so.

Still, I was scared to believe it. I might have found the courage to pursue my certification, but that didn't mean I'd make something of it. It just meant I had the bravery to start something. Starting had nothing to do with finishing, or even succeeding.

But maybe starting had to be enough for now. I could figure out the rest later.

"Well, I suppose I could show you..." My words turned into mumbles.

Her eyes lit up. "Could you bring them to the penthouse tonight? We could look at everything, have some dinner, relax. What do you think?"

My mouth parted, no words leaping out. This was the platonic girl version of Netflix and Chill. Something like Notebooks & Gush. But really, I saw this for what it was: a chance to make a friend. It was so hard to meet people, which was ridiculous considering how many of them lived in this dang city. But Cora wanted to see my designs, and she wanted to do it in a place Damian called home.

How could I say no?

"I'd be honored," I blurted.

"Oh, this is excellent!" Cora squeezed my wrist again, her eyes sparkling. "I honestly can't wait. I have a feeling I'm going to like what I see."

My mouth flapped uselessly as I processed the comment. A virtual stranger believed in me more than a single soul in my family. How did that make sense?

As if on cue, the snarky voice of my older sister floated through my head, the words she'd said to me the day before I left for New York: *This is so stupid, Jessa. You'll see it soon enough.*

But I couldn't sit in that for long. The door to the conference room across the hallway opened. The first one out was Axel, his face drawn, lips a thin line. He stormed down the hallway, not even glancing at us.

"Uh oh," Cora murmured. "I better go see what's up."

I nodded, watching as she floated away after him. Damian exited the conference room next, followed by a man I'd never seen before, and then Trace. Francis beelined toward me from the conference room, his mouth turned downward.

"Jessa," he began, the tone of his voice leaving no room for confusion. "You need to pay extra attention to Damian today. The brothers received some difficult news, so be attentive."

My mouth went dry. I couldn't imagine what *other* news could be waiting for them. "What was it?"

Francis lifted a finger and shook his head, which made my stomach pitch to my toes. "Not now. Damian will fill you in when he's ready."

CHAPTER SIX

DAMIAN

The air of my office became sepulchral and stagnant as the three of us stared at each other, saying nothing. We'd all practically fallen into our respective chairs the moment we were behind closed doors.

"He says he's a blood brother of yours," Axel repeated after an eternity of staring and thinking and processing. His gaze slid like a boulder over to Trace. The office was so quiet I could actually hear the throbbing of my own head.

"He has to be lying," I said. "There's literally no other option." I wanted that to be the truth so badly. We couldn't handle another explosion like this. Not when life as we knew it was already crumbling.

A man named Ian Fairchild had turned up during our regular Monday meeting and claimed he was Trace's biological half-brother. No amount of scoffing or judgement or questioning could deter him. He'd been completely fucking convinced, which only made this whole thing weirder. More curdling. More *uncomfortable*.

Silence descended once more. Trace's eyes flitted between me and Axel.

"Right, Trace?" Axel pinned Trace with a stare.

Trace cleared his throat.

Axel didn't move.

Something deep inside my gut started to pulse.

"I'll start doing the research." It didn't even need to be said. I'd have a full report on the man within an hour, and then we could start piecing together the details. But a lot of things weren't adding up. Ian had come from Kentucky, all the way to *New York*, just to visit us at Fairchild Enterprises and inform us he was Trace's long-lost brother.

Why the fuck hadn't he called first? And why now? Did it have something to do with the investigation?

"I don't know who that guy is," Trace finally said, expelling a deep breath. He ran his palms up and down the arm rests of his chair. "Never seen him."

"He kind of looks like you," Axel mused. "Maybe he *is* telling the truth."

I gritted my teeth. I'd thought the same thing but didn't want to admit it in front of Trace. They had the same gray-blue eyes as our adoptive father Gary...which was probably just a coincidence.

Because there was no fucking way Trace had a secret biological brother.

"Sounds like we've got our first extortionist," I said loudly, trying to drown out the anxieties screeching inside my head. "We were overdue for one anyway."

Nobody laughed. It wasn't funny. No matter what the truth behind this guy was, it wouldn't be funny.

"I gotta go," Axel said, checking his watch. "Let me know what you dig up on Ian, okay?" He sent a dark look to Trace and me before heading out of the office. Trace came to standing then, working his jaw back and forth.

"Let me know, too." He jerked his chin in my direction and disappeared wordlessly, the door shutting softly behind him.

And then it was just me, myself, and the overwhelming swarm of anxieties.

My gut roiled as I got down to work. Each new twist and turn in my adult life looked different, but it all felt the same when it hit—an acid nut in my belly, or sometimes my chest, that took me right back to the beginning of our current trajectory.

The night my biological parents died. Becoming the eldest Haynes at the ripe old age of eight. I was the one who had to figure out the path forward. Navigate through the storm. Protect Axel, and our little sisters Kaylee and Jordan at all costs.

I gritted my teeth, desperate to escape the negative churn of my brain. Sometimes it felt like I'd never let myself off the hook. And why should I? I'd failed two of the most important people in my life. I'd been a kid when our parents died, but that didn't matter. They'd been *babies*. I'd had some understanding of the world by that point, and it had been my responsibility as the oldest to take care of the others.

My chest tightened the way it always did when I went down this path. Ian showing up was a hard shove into the failures of my past, a road I hated to travel but found myself on nearly every day. I needed to switch into hyper-focus mode, the only escape I knew besides drugs and alcohol.

I reached for my headphones, turned on the best death metal on my playlist, and sank into ultra-productivity mode. This workaholism was 100 percent responsible for all of my success in the tech sector. I knew how to sit down and crank out code for twelve hours on end, and it was all thanks to the insatiable need to turn off the obsessive, irrational part of my brain. This skill would serve me well as I hunted for dirt on Ian.

I began collecting information immediately, gathering everything of note into one organized document that I could present to my brothers as a recap. The most interesting bit of information? *Fairchild* had only been his last name for the past year. Previously, he'd been Ian Keller. This reeked of a shoddy con job already.

A movement beyond the computer screen pulled me from the depths of my concentration. My door was open and Jessa stood in the doorway, her mouth moving, though all I could hear was the heady thrum of bass drums.

I tugged my headphones off, instantly annoyed to be back in the real world. Down there, in the relentless pulse of oblivion, I could fucking breathe.

But not up here.

"Sorry to interrupt," she said, her cheeks turning pink. "I called a few times, but..."

"Yeah. I had my music cranked." I tossed the headphones onto my desk, looking over the most recent bit of information on my screen. I had to focus on that, because if I looked at Jessa, a different type of tension threatened to consume me.

The woman was built like an hourglass with a circulatory system. She apparently only knew how to select dresses that accentuated every luscious curve. And it wasn't that I tried to notice; no, I simply *had* to notice. It was my body's prime directive to notice Jessa Walton. It had been that way since high school. There was something about the slice of her collarbone, the curve of her cheeks, the sway of her hips that fucking yanked at my eyes and forced me to watch.

I couldn't *not* see her and every last detail about her. And I couldn't afford to get distracted, because of my current reality and this current arrangement. So I needed to stare at the screen a bit longer.

She stepped closer to my desk. "Can I interest you in some donuts?"

My stomach rumbled in response, even though I tried to glance disinterestedly at the tray she held in her hands. Frosted donuts, coated with red and orange sprinkles, dotted the silver tray. I blinked a few times, weighing my best response.

I could send her and her sweet, thoughtful delivery away...or...

"What is this?" I snapped.

"Just a late-morning donut delivery," she said, with the sweetest *duh* tone. Now it was impossible to look away from her, and all I could see was the dark red stain of her lips, the black and cream pattern stretching across her breasts. She was professional, elegant, entirely off-limits. My fingers curled into a fist beneath the desk. "To get us in the Thanksgiving spirit."

When I didn't answer, she stepped closer. "Come on. Don't you want one?"

There was a strategy behind her words, though I wasn't sure what it was. I stared at the white frosting.

"These were your favorite in high school," she said, which finally broke me. I deflated slightly and nodded.

"Yeah, I'll take one." My stomach growled even louder this time. I usually didn't eat breakfast. Hell, I sometimes didn't even eat lunch. I wasn't very good about taking care of myself beyond daily caffeination and working out.

The grin that lit up her face brought a smile to my own lips. She set the tray down on the corner of my desk and clapped her hands together.

"Great. I'm dying to try one too. These are my second-favorite kind, but I'll make an exception for you, Damian. You pick first."

I grinned, swiping up one of the thick rings. I could already tell it was going to be incredible, just from the sponginess of the donut, the indentation of my fingers. Jessa picked one as well, and we shared a conspiratorial smile.

"On the count of three," she said. "One...two...*bite*!"

We took big chomps at the same time. Her eyes fluttered shut as she chewed.

"Dear lord above," she moaned, "I must have been good to deserve a donut of this exceptional quality."

I laughed as I tore into the donut. This hit the spot and then some.

"It's really good. Thanks for sharing."

She shrugged, sending me a coy smile. "How could I not? So tell me, now that we're here, anything I should know from the meeting?"

I could feel my grin fall a few notches. "No. Nothing urgent."

She nodded, licking a speck of glaze from the corner of her mouth. I didn't plan on telling her about Ian, even though part of me wanted to. Jessa always provoked that in me. Hell, she probably provoked that in most people. It was one of her natural talents. She was so contagiously warm, she could make friends wherever she went, prying deep dark secrets out of someone's heart within minutes.

My goal was to stay unattached. Unaffected. Invulnerable. My secrets were the only things I could control. Jessa wasn't getting them from me.

"I need to get back to work," I blurted, reaching for a napkin on the tray. "Appreciate you bringing these in."

Even I could hear the clipped, all-business tone of my voice. Jessa's chin dipped and she stared at the uneaten donuts on the tray.

"Are you sure you don't want any more?"

"I'm good. Thanks."

She gnawed on the inside of her lip. "Do you feel okay?"

I appreciated her question almost as much as I resented it. "I'm fine. We need to get back to work."

In truth, I was desperate for the warmth she brought with her. I just couldn't stand to want it. What I was going through demanded clarity, detachment.

I needed to stay away from *everyone*.

Jessa collected the tray and offered a small smile before heading back out to her desk, shutting my door behind her. Alone in the silence of my office again, I reminded myself that keeping Jessa in the employee file was for the best.

It sucked, but it needed to be done.

I sank back into the productivity zone, gathering more intel on Ian Fairchild. He'd been born in Louisville and was six years younger than Axel. His birth certificate listed a Raina Keller as the mother, but no father was listed—*convenient*. It just didn't make sense that my adoptive father could be Ian's father too. This had to be a case of some ancestry DNA sample gone awry. Maybe Ian had sent in his blood and gotten a ping for Gary Fairchild, when really it was one of our uncles instead. Who knew? Something like that made way more sense than my adoptive father actually stepping out on our mother. There was just no way he'd cheated on her during our adolescence.

No way at all.

Ian Fairchild also had a brief jail stint on his record, due to cocaine possession. That had been two years ago. And who didn't have a random wild night with cocaine here or there in their early twenties? Nothing screamed delinquent, even though the whole thing screamed *scam*.

A message from Axel toward the end of my workday tugged me back to real life.

AXEL: You got dinner plans? Cora and I are doing dinner and drinks upstairs tonight. You gonna join?

My shoulders slumped as I noticed the time. I'd eaten one donut before noon, and now it was almost four thirty. I sucked at this.

DAMIAN: I might make an appearance. What's on the menu?

AXEL: Same as always. Whatever is the most delicious, decadent, and expensive.

DAMIAN: I kinda just want some mac and cheese.

AXEL: Jesus, you are still 15 years old, aren't you?

DAMIAN: Make it fancy if you want.

AXEL: Fine. I'll tell Butch to make some fancy Kraft shit.

A liter of coffee, one donut, and some mac and cheese. My personal trainer would be having a conniption if he knew about this. Luckily, he would never know, because I'd pared our visits down to the bare minimum required to keep a semblance of a six pack. Okay, so most days it was a four pack. With the state of my mind these days, sometimes even seeing my trainer was too mentally taxing. Maybe I really was the raging introvert Axel had always accused me of being.

It didn't matter. Nothing mattered but forward motion. Finding a way to quiet the buzz inside my chest. I finished up as much work as I could by six p.m. Jessa sent me a message through our internal messaging client: *See you soon!*

That was odd. Why hadn't she said tomorrow? Though tomorrow was technically soon, at least compared to next year. I frowned, clicking through other screens. I *wanted* to see her soon, as much as I wanted to see her in every possible way, most of which were not sanctioned or allowed by the brick fortress of my heart. But there would be no mingling. No sweetness. I couldn't afford to let her in even an inch. Sharing donuts in my office was already a slippery slope, even if she didn't know it.

I tacked on an extra hour of work, just to crank a few things out and find my level again. By the time I wrapped up, I knew dinner would probably be almost ready upstairs. And that's how I preferred it. Work. Work some more. Work a little bit more. Put in the requisite socialization and eating. And then disappear into my room for more planning, stewing, and then finally, drinking so that I could quiet the thoughts enough to sleep.

Rinse and repeat. Every day.

I soared upward in the private elevator between our office suite and the penthouse. When the silver doors slid open, the clamor of voices was the first thing to greet me. Onions sizzled on the stovetop, the popping of oil taking me back to one of those pristine childhood moments, back when everything felt like a puzzle with all its pieces correctly aligned. Something deep inside me unclenched as I took in the smells of cooking and the sharp cuts of Axel's laughter from the other room.

"Welcome home, Damian," Butch rumbled as I walked through the kitchen. "You've got a fine ass mac and cheese heading your way."

A pot burbled with water nearby. I grinned over at him. "Thanks, Butch. I need it today."

"Comfort food, huh?"

I nodded. I needed comforting in a couple different ways by my count. A feminine laugh wafted through the air, making my forearms prickle as I headed for the conversation. That didn't sound like Cora.

I knew who it was before I even rounded the corner into the great room. My insides froze. It had to be Jessa. I'd know that laugh, that sweet tone, anywhere. Maybe I was just repressing myself so much I was conjuring her from thin air.

"Damian!" Axel's voice boomed through the room, and he held up his hands to welcome me. He and Cora were on one leather couch...and Jessa was on the other.

The track lights from above illuminated her in stark clarity, but she glowed with something otherworldly too. Her mahogany hair glinted auburn, her easy smile sending a jolt through me. She looked at me like I was the exact person she'd been waiting for, the perfect fourth to round out the crew.

Warmth spiraled alongside familiarity, followed up with the hot zing of desire. Everything about this woman acted as a magnet for me. *Fuck.*

"Hey, guys," I said dully, setting my briefcase down on the nearest armchair. Zero was tucked into a dog bed in the corner. He lifted his head briefly, then settled back into his comfy spot. I stuffed my hands into my pockets, suddenly unsure how to navigate this situation. I desperately wanted to treat Jessa like the old friend she was—and possibly a lot more. But I couldn't. I'd drawn the line in the sand myself. "Where's Trace?"

"No idea," Axel said with a frown, his hands dropping. "But dinner's almost ready, and we know Butch it gonna knock it out of the park."

"I invited Jessa over to show me some of her designs," Cora said, gesturing toward the coffee table, where a big sketchbook lay open.

"Cool," I said, unnerved by the tempest that awaited me on the other side of that comment. I jerked my head toward the kitchen. "I'm gonna check on dinner."

Jessa's face fell ever so slightly, which I tried really hard not to notice. She swung her head back toward Cora, who wore a fixed smile.

"Butch has got it," Axel said, waving his hand in the direction of the kitchen. "Pour yourself a drink. Stay awhile." He paused, sending me a look edged with something I didn't often see from him. A command. "Come on."

We stared at each other for a couple seconds, but it might as well have been an hour. I knew what he was doing as much as he did. He wanted Jessa and me to be together in the same room, like some adult version of a high school hookup.

But Axel would be disappointed.

However cute and warm and alluring Jessa was, there was no room left inside me for someone like her. And as my secretary, there was even less room for my usual status quo of one-and-done or every-so-often.

So what was I left with?

I had to walk away.

CHAPTER SEVEN

JESSA

"Ooooh, now this one..." Cora's voice was a purr, her eyes wide as she thumbed through my designs.

My head spun. Not only was I in the Fairchild *penthouse* surrounded by exotically shaped furniture and hand-carved columns and so much fucking marble I could hardly fathom what it cost to furnish this place, but one of the most influential women in the country was actively thumbing through my designs, enthralled and excited by what I'd drawn.

By what I, Jessa Walton, little ole nobody from Oakville, had come up with.

And to top it all off? My high school crush and boss sat just a few feet from me, tipping a tumbler of whiskey back and forth in his hands, looking every inch the off-duty billionaire he was. He'd loosened his collar and rolled up his sleeves during small talk, which had very nearly impregnated me right here in his living room. No, that was impossible. The man didn't even want me here—that much had been clear in the dour look that washed over his face when he spotted me in the living room.

He'd barely said two words to me after asking me how I was and what I thought of the place. Now he simply sat in the taupe leather armchair, watching us without really seeing us, brooding and moody as hell.

Which was also sort of hot, in its own annoying way. Because I would have given anything to know what was roiling behind those moss green eyes.

"Jessa, you need another?" Axel asked me, popping to his feet. Cora and I sipped on white wine, and I'd drained my glass. Whatever they had seemed expensive, because I was buzzed off a single glass. Usually the six dollar bargain bin wine took at least three glasses to get me good and warm. I nodded happily, eager for more of whatever they had to offer—this penthouse experience, this companionship, this luxurious slice of life.

"Thanks, Axel," I called out as he took our glasses to the wet bar near the huge windows overlooking Manhattan. Damian sipped from his tumbler, his gaze flitting to meet mine only briefly.

"Jessa is a fantastic clothing designer," Cora said, sending a smile my way, then looking back at Damian. "Did you know that?"

"I didn't," he said.

"Not fantastic," I said quietly. "Just learning."

"You're headed for greatness," Cora said, squeezing my shoulder.

I fought the smile that threatened to consume my face. Her support still felt so strange, so foreign. My design work was a secret I'd barely admitted even to my closest loved ones. Now she was outing me...with pride. She had no idea how much it meant to me. My throat tightened, and I surged forward, wrapping her in a quick hug.

"Thank you," I whispered. "For believing in me." A laugh fluttered out of her, and she rubbed my back. I sat back in my seat, pressing a hand to my heart. "It means a lot to me, is all."

"Awww, would you look at that." Axel returned with our glasses, shimmering with freshly poured white wine. I received mine with a big smile.

"Now that we've been refreshed, I think we should keep looking," Cora said with a big grin. She dove back into my designs, making comments about the small details along the way. I loved the conversation and her attention to my craft, but Damian's presence sizzled on the periphery. My entire body prickled with awareness, though I was sure I had to be imagining his attention.

Axel approached Damian and the two started their own conversation in hushed tones. I tried so hard to be a part of both conversations, but I couldn't. Cora was *too* excited about the lace details on the dress I'd worn to the fundraiser last week.

She flipped another page. I looked behind me. Damian shook his head at Axel, the two clearly in the middle of some brotherly battle, and then he stood. Zero perked to life, trotting over to stand by Axel.

"Oh, you're just gonna walk away?" Axel goaded Damian. I was too curious not to watch. Damian flipped off his brother and headed for the kitchen.

Axel cackled as he absent-mindedly pet Zero's head. "Come on. Come back."

"I'm busy," Damian called over his shoulder. "You can come with me if you want."

Axel heaved an exaggerated sigh and followed Damian. "Excuse me, ladies," he said to the both of us, though Cora hardly noticed. Zero returned to his dog bed with a sigh.

"Are they fighting...?" I asked Cora. A grin curled at her lips.

"Hardly. Axel just loves to needle him."

"About what?"

"Everything, mostly."

A laugh shot out of me. That summed it up nicely. I watched Axel and Damian retreat, pausing in the doorway between the kitchen and the hallway to argue a bit more. It was the most I'd seen Damian's lips move since I'd started working with him. And I was mesmerized.

"Don't you think?" Cora's voice snapped me back to reality.

"I'm sorry, what was that?" I turned toward her again, heat creeping across my chest. I'd been caught staring at Damian—how embarrassing.

"I said you'd do well to enroll in fashion school, don't you think?"

I swallowed hard. I didn't want to tell her I was already enrolled in a fashion course. I didn't want her to know, because I didn't want the brothers to know. I couldn't have anyone doubting my dedication to the job. I needed the money so badly, I was too scared to do anything to jeopardize it.

"I've considered it," I said slowly, wondering if this was considered a white lie or an outright lie. My course didn't equate to a fashion *degree*. And I *had* considered it. "I might have to get some savings under my belt first."

"Mmm, that makes sense." She tapped at her lips, flipping to another page. "But maybe it would just be redundant. You seem to have a handle on the back end of things pretty well."

That was thanks to the fashion certificate course. My chest went hot again. I hated lying, fibbing, or any manner of hiding a pulsating truth. But it just seemed unwise to talk about something that occupied up to thirty hours of my life each week while sitting next to the woman who had likely fired plenty of people for not performing adequately.

"Thank you," I said.

Axel came back into the living room. Without Damian. "Butch said dinner is almost ready, so we should head into the dining room. And just so you know, Damian won't be joining us."

I frowned, collecting my sketchbooks. "That's a shame."

"He needs to decompress," Axel said, sipping some more whiskey. "That man is constantly decompressing."

"Like you aren't the same way?" Cora asked wryly.

"I decompress in my own special way," Axel said with a mischievous grin. "With you."

I laughed, hating how my mind immediately went to *I could decompress with Damian if he needed.* But no. He had that beautiful, brunette businesswoman waiting for him. He didn't need a wannabe like me.

I followed Axel and Cora into the dining room, where the table was already set with square black mats, gold charger plates, and perfectly folded linen at each place. The table was set for six.

"Are others joining us?" I asked as I sank into an open seat, watching as Butch brought out plates two at a time.

"Just us tonight," Axel said. "Trace has disappeared since Ian showed up."

"Ian?" I asked, not missing the sharp look Axel sent Cora. His brows knit together.

"Damian didn't...tell you?" he asked.

I looked between Axel and Cora, who watched me with serious looks. "No. He didn't. Is this something I should know about?"

Axel sighed, barely perceptibly. "He'll probably tell you tomorrow. Don't worry about it."

But it was hard not to worry about it, especially when it was clear something major had happened during that meeting this morning. And who the fuck was Ian? My concerns drifted away once Butch placed my plate in front of me. It was a downhome delight, the black plate filled with all the best things: steak, potatoes, and mac and cheese. But it didn't look anything like my plates from back home. The steak sat atop microgreens, and exciting, brightly colored lines slashed across the plate, unknown sauces I couldn't wait to sample. The mac and cheese looked like it came from a magazine shoot, speckles of pepper artfully arranged on the top.

"This is amazing," I said. Butch only smiled.

"Wait until you try it," he said, slinging his hand towel over his shoulder as he disappeared back into the kitchen. I blinked over at Axel and Cora, who were removing their silverware from their napkins.

"There's no way Damian can't have this," I said.

Axel only grumbled.

"He hasn't eaten all day," I went on. "He had one donut, and only because I basically forced him to. Should I call him?"

"He won't answer," Axel said.

"Then I'll take the plate to him." I looked over at Damian's place setting. The mac and cheese steamed lightly, but it wouldn't for long. The man needed to eat, and he needed to eat while the food was in peak form. "Where did he go? I don't mind."

Cora's smile was somewhere between pitying and sweet. "You don't have to chase him down."

"I promise it's not a bother." I pushed up from the table, determined to see this through. Damian might be old enough to feed himself, but clearly he wasn't able to focus enough to actually do it. That's where I came in. I could see where I was needed, where I was most helpful. And someone needed to remind this man to *eat*. "Now where is Jessa's Delivery Service heading?"

Axel watched me with an amused grin. "He's working out. Remember the tour earlier? Head to the back of the penthouse and hang a right."

I nodded, repeating the instructions to myself. The tour had been brief, and I'd been too awestruck to retain much. This was the type of place you could actually get lost in.

"Got it." I swooped up the plate and silverware/napkin bundle and hurried off, unsure if this was regular ole friendliness or wine-fueled insanity. Cora was probably right—I didn't need to chase him down inside his own house.

But what if I wanted to?

My footsteps fell quietly on the polished floor as I headed into the moodily lit caverns of the Fairchild penthouse. Lounge furniture lined the hallway, facing the floor-to-ceiling windows. One thing I'd noticed about this place was that you could pause nearly anywhere and just take in the view. Maybe that had been one of the most important things for them. Lord knew this view was worth whatever price tag they'd paid.

At almost seven p.m., Manhattan was already wrapped in the soft blanket of another autumn night. The endless sparkling lights and skyscrapers beyond the thick panes of glass stole my focus. I stumbled, nearly pitching forward. I gasped, steadying myself, staring at the plate of food.

Keep it together, Jessa. You're the one who keeps it together.

It had always been that way. I was the one making sure my mom woke up on time to get work after her late nights partying. I was the one who'd written my ex's resume so he could get the job he wanted.

Now I was the one bringing dinner to the man who couldn't remember to eat.

Light angled out into the hallway from under the workout room door. From out here, I could hear the muted undertones of Damian's workout—the clank of weights, the breathy grunts. I swallowed hard, steeling myself for whatever I might see on the other side, and pushed the door open.

A wall of mirrors was the first thing I noticed.

And then Damian himself, straddling a bench, facing the mirrors, his broad chest on full display to me. All the air in my lungs evaporated as I beheld him. His chestnut hair was mussed and sweat-stained, and I could not physically force myself to look away from the ripple of his shoulders. He wore only red gym shorts; his stomach crinkled as he bent down for a bottle of water. As he did, his gaze found mine in the mirror.

"Jessa."

He could barely disguise the silent *oh, shit* in front of my name. I forced myself to smile, approaching on wooden legs. The testosterone in the room was so thick I could barely breathe. Or maybe that was my own attraction to this man, slowly squeezing my neck until I couldn't inhale.

"Damian. I wanted to bring you dinner." I swallowed again, my mouth totally dry. God, why was I doing this again? "Axel told me you didn't plan on joining, but that's ridiculous. Look at what Butch made." I stepped closer, showing him the plate. "You can't not eat this. It's practically a sin."

His jaw flexed as he watched me, his gaze sliding to the food. Then he looked away. "Have you eaten?"

I shook my head. His gaze was on me in the mirror. "Not yet."

"Why don't you go eat?"

"You haven't eaten all day. I know you haven't. I got you to swallow one little donut and that was it. Now you're in here burning all these calories. You need a homecooked meal."

The start of a smile curled at a corner of his mouth.

"Seriously, it's not right to miss out on a meal this good. Look at this crazy bed of microgreens, Damian. Jeremy would flip his shit if he saw this and you're just gonna act like it's not piping hot in front of you?"

His expression softened. He met my gaze in the mirror again, then slowly turned to face me for real. The width of his chest stole my breath again—when would it not?—and he reached out for the plate.

"You're probably right."

I handed it off, feeling slightly victorious. Okay, a lot victorious. "I am right."

His smile widened by an inch, crooked and glorious in its genuineness. "You tend to be right, don't you?"

My heart raced, though I couldn't say why. "That sounds like a trap if I agree."

"I've known you for over two decades. I'm just speaking based on experience," he said, his gaze washing over the plate of food in his hands.

"I'd like to think I'm usually right," I admitted. "Maybe not about everything, but I'm at least right about the fact that a genius like you needs to eat some damn protein if he wants to keep changing the world."

He laughed softly, but it sounded sad.

"And listen," I went on, that white wine still blazing through my veins. I took a seat next to him on the bench press, since clearly I was no longer making rational choices. I'd brought the man gourmet mac and cheese during a workout session. Who did that? Drunk women who needed any excuse to see their personal hottest man in the universe, that's who. "I'm right about something else."

"What's that?" His gritty voice scraped over me, and when he tilted his head to look at me, heat shot to my core. Suddenly I was lost in the moss green abyss of his gaze. We were two feet apart, but we might as well have been humping. This was just as erotic as hanging out with him on my father's couch back in the day.

"I'm right about the fact that you should tell me what's bothering you," I said, trying to keep the snappy, lighthearted air I'd come in with. But it was hard to keep my bearings; I felt like I was wilting under the intensity of his gaze. I could read so much in his stare. But who knew if it was actually there?

Damian opened his mouth to respond, but I barreled onward. "I know you got some hard news today. Axel and Cora even confirmed it. You can tell me, you know. I want to help."

Damian's jaw started flexing, but his gaze didn't waver from mine. He finally shook his head, looking away. "You can't help. Sorry."

A sigh rocketed out of me. "And why not?"

"You don't need to get into it."

"Don't you think I can handle it? I'm supposed to be your secretary. How can I do my job if I can't handle it?"

Damian's silence filled the air between us. All I could hear was my heart pounding against my ribs.

"I've been working for you almost two weeks. Am I not doing a good enough job?" I asked, my cheeks heating up again. This was the scariest question I could have asked him, because I desperately wanted to be doing a good job for him. I *needed* him to be satisfied with my work at Fairchild Enterprises. Literally everything else in my life depended on it now.

His eyes drifted shut and he crumpled a little. "Jessa—"

"It's hard to tell, since you hardly speak to me."

Damian's chin lowered, his gaze hardening. "You're doing a great job. But I warned you at the beginning. Work is work. I'm not your friend. That's how it has to be."

"So what about now?"

"What do you mean?"

"Well, we're not at work. In here, I'm just your old friend Jessa Walton." My heart hammered so hard I thought I might pass out. I had not planned on *any* of this coming out right now, but even I couldn't deny how much the workplace distance bothered me. "Right? Let me help. You know I can."

A grunt escaped him, and he rubbed at the ridge of his eyebrows with his free hand. "I can't. It's better if we keep our distance. I'm not going to budge on that."

Disappointment rippled through me, hot and effervescent, utterly consuming every inch of free space inside my body. "I don't understand why you gave me the job, then. It seems like you didn't want to."

Damian pinched his eyes shut, shaking his head. "It's not that—"

"Should I find a different job?" I asked. The words coming out of my mouth shocked even me. I was drunk and rambling. Oh lord, I'd regret this tomorrow morning. I already knew it. "I don't want to be a burden. I don't want to prevent you from having someone who can actually do the job you need."

Damian frowned at the floor. "You need to trust me when I say it's better for us to keep that professional distance. Okay? That's all I need from you."

My brows knitted together, his words landing like a slap.

"It'll be better for everyone in the long run," he said, pushing to his feet. "If you really want to be my friend, don't be my friend."

Damian stormed out of the workout room, carrying the plate of food. I watched him go, my head spinning from the unexpected turn the past ten minutes had taken. The wall of mirrors reflected my red-cheeked confusion. I sat stewing in my own arousal and confusion.

I wasn't ready to give up on him yet, though.

I'd known this guy since grade school. He needed a shoulder—that much was obvious. And he was in denial of how much he needed that shoulder.

I needed to get to the bottom of this, and there was only one person who could help me dig deeper: my brother.

CHAPTER EIGHT

DAMIAN

Mornings were always hard for me.

First of all, they were harbingers of another day. I didn't normally care about "another day, another dollar," but mornings were the threshold of opportunity across which unexpected surprises and unwelcome guests entered. Most days had some combination of the two. Not only that, mornings required me to be sociable, which I also resented. It took me at least three hours to ready myself for the general public. And even then, it wasn't guaranteed I'd land well with my audience.

But the worst part about mornings was that they set the tone of the day ahead.

And if I didn't get that tone just right, well...let's just say the entire rest of the day tended to fucking blow.

It was eight a.m. on Wednesday, approximately forty eight hours after I'd met the supposed 'long-lost bio brother', and I was praying for no further unexpected surprises or unwelcome visitors today. Sunlight streaked through the slatted blinds of my bedroom, casting dreamy patterns on the gray carpet as I located my business slacks du jour, one of the last pairs hanging in my closet. I scowled at my room as I buttoned my pants and slipped on a dress shirt.

My bedroom was a fucking mess, because it was my last safe haven in Manhattan. It was larger than the apartment my brothers and I originally rented in Chinatown; hell, this bedroom was larger than most starter apartments on the market. I scooped up a pile of dirty clothes; I kept meaning to send them to be washed. My phone cord that had been missing for the last couple of days was revealed, and I picked that up too with a grunt.

I hated mornings so much, I spent most of my nights awake and avoiding daylight. And last night, I'd had a bit too much to drink. *Again.* I knew I needed to stop this, but it was hard to find the motivation to do so. Not when I had so much to stress over.

My phone vibrated in the pocket of my dress pants. I heaved a sigh, steeling myself for whatever was about to start my day. *Please don't be an explosion. Please don't be some other new secret relative.*

I grabbed my phone and looked at the screen. Jeremy. Not what I'd expected. I swiped to answer, curiosity pumping through me.

"Hello?"

"Hey, buddy. How you doing?"

I tucked the phone between my ear and shoulder and continued my quick clean-up session of the room. I liked to think I wasn't a slob, but this floor begged to differ. "Just heading into work. What about you?"

Jeremy laughed. "Another day in paradise, right?"

I'd imagined paradise a hell of a lot different from this. Which was ironic, because plenty of people saw my life from the outside and probably assumed I *was* living in paradise.

"Hey listen," he went on, "I don't want to hold you up. I just wanted to check on Jessa. Like, I want to make sure she's working out for you."

My gut started the slow squeeze. This wasn't boding well for setting a good tone for the day. "Why do you ask?"

Jeremy sighed. "Well, she sent me some messages yesterday that kinda got me thinking..."

Fuck. I rubbed my forehead, images from Monday night coming back to me. I'd stayed up late drinking Monday and Tuesday night precisely to *erase* those images from my mind. Her relaxed and laughing in my living room, flanked by Axel and Cora, was an image I couldn't let myself get attached to. It fulfilled something too deep, too intimate, inside of me. And I knew better than to hope for anything beautiful like that. Not with a potential prison sentence hanging over my head. Jessa's warmth and bubbliness didn't fit into my life, and I needed her to get the message ASAP.

"I'm just worried she's crashing and burning, you know?" Jeremy went on. "Like, you'd be honest with me, right? Don't sugarcoat it cuz she's my sister. Give it to me straight. I need to know."

I cleared my throat, unsure where to begin. Jessa's work performance was fine. It was her interpersonal performance that needed work; she excelled a little too much in that department.

"Well, how can I say this..." I started.

"Oh, God. I knew it." Jeremy tutted. "You know, I was worried that this situation with Mom was gonna affect her. Being so far away and all, she tries to act tough, she really does, but I know it's been hard for her."

I blinked. I knew their mom had been in and out of rehab, but my memories were fuzzy. All my brain power was actively in use worrying over the SEC investigation and whether or not my entire future was ruined.

"The last I heard...she was in rehab?" I ventured.

"Yeah. Been there for almost two months. She'll be sprung soon if she keeps up the good work. We're hoping she'll be ssettled in a halfway house by Thanksgiving. But nobody knows where she's gonna go after that. Tara wants Jessa to come back to Kentucky and stay with our mom. Live with her, keep an eye on her, you know? But with Jessa being up there...it's just been a little tense."

"Does Jessa want to go home and help?" I asked, fear ping-ponging through me.

"I think part of her does. The part of her that still loves her mom. Tara thinks she can convince her to come back. But those two butt heads like nobody's business. Always fighting about splitting the bill for rehab and who's gonna pay for the groceries once she's out and all that shit. I give what I can, you know? I make good money for me and mine. But it's harder for Tara. She's got three kids and that deadbeat husband of hers. Personally I think she's just hoping Jessa's gonna be the sugar mama for our own mom. A mama sugar mama." Jeremy laughed. "Is that a thing? I've never heard of it if it is."

I bit back a smile. You could wring gossip and news out of Jeremy like a wet washcloth. Took hardly any work at all. But now I knew a lot more about what was happening back at the Walton homestead. I'd purposely avoided diving into that whirlpool, because I knew that the deeper I dove, the harder it would be to get myself out of the water.

And Jessa's waters were far too warm and inviting.

"Dang, Jeremy. I'm sorry about all of that. But listen, I can tell you one thing for sure. Jessa is a doing a great job. She's not crashing and burning." I really meant that. I picked up one last stray set of dress pants from the floor and tossed them in the laundry basket. Then I straightened my back in front of the mirror, looking myself over. "She's an asset to our company. I have no plans of letting her go."

Jeremy heaved a sigh of relief. "You have no idea how happy I am to hear that."

"She's been great," I told him. "Honestly."

"Just keep an eye on her for me, would ya?" His concern still rang deeply. "She needs a friend in New York. That's why I'm glad she's got you."

My gut cinched tighter, forming the knot I'd been trying to avoid starting my day with. Too late. Jeremy would never know how deeply and unsettlingly ironic this request was. Two days after I'd asked Jessa to *not* be my friend. My eyes fluttered shut and I shook my head at the heavens.

"You got it, buddy," I told him.

Because I was nothing if not a rescuer.

We said our goodbyes, and I faced myself down in the mirror a final time. I wore my standard work attire: Prada dress shoes, Gucci dress pants, button down shirt that had been tailored to perfection. I ran a hand through my longish hair, enjoying the way it settled, mussed but exact.

My exterior needed to gleam, because my interior was a lot like this bedroom. Fucked up. A mess disguised as put-together. Hiding too many secrets.

If I truly let Jessa in as a friend, she'd unearth all of them and more.

That didn't sound like a wise idea to me. But I'd figure out how to both honor Jeremy's request and keep Jessa at arm's length later. It was too much for this early hour.

"I guess it's time," I said to my reflection. The best approximation of a pep talk I had these days. I left the bedroom behind, closing and locking the door on my secret mess, the four computers, the ten back-up drives, the empty bottles and glasses littering my shelves like a ransacked bar. My eyes hurt when I blinked. Every cell of my body craved a type of rest I didn't know how to obtain. I needed something I couldn't even name.

And all I knew how to do was keep moving forward. Keep the train moving along, in the safest way possible. No disruptions. No disturbances. Nothing new. Because everything else in my life depended on it.

I wove my way through the empty penthouse. I hadn't seen Trace since the meeting in my office after Ian dropped the scam bomb on Monday. Axel had left super early with Cora, as usual. Down at Fairchild Enterprises, everything was bustling and bright. A little too bright for my taste, to be honest. I nodded and forced smiles where appropriate. Of course everyone had to be chipper and alert at this time of the day. I braced myself to see Jessa as I wound through the suite. I hadn't exactly been nice to her in the gym yesterday. Who knew what she'd told Jeremy?

I rounded the corner, the dark sweep of her hair the first thing that caught my eye. Her back faced me, and her juicy ass was the *second* thing I noticed. She wore a waist-cinched dress that showcased every delectable curve of her body. I knew without knowing just how heavenly she'd be undressed—thick thighs that begged for me to get between them, breasts she could barely contain in her dresses and blouses. Fuck, I was half-hard already. This was not a good start.

"Jessa."

At the sound of my voice she turned, looking startled. Pearl earrings stood out against her dark hair, and her winged eyeliner had been drawn to perfection. My heart thudded a little harder in my chest.

"Oh, Damian. Good morning. You scared me."

I checked my watch. "Yeah. I'm a little late today."

"It's okay. No judgment." She brushed a stray hair away from her face, nibbling on her bottom lip. She didn't meet my gaze again, and instead rummaged through papers on her desk. Things had been weird since what happened in the weight room Monday night. Strained, even. I saw her open sketchbook near the edge, showcasing the bare bones design for a flowy dress. It was the first time I'd seen her notebook since meeting up with Cora in the penthouse. Personally, I was curious to see what was in there too, but I'd never allow myself to ask.

Jeremy's words came back to me: *She needs a friend.* He thought I would be that friend for her. I couldn't go all the way to true friend status, but I could throw her a bone. I could loosen up. Maybe.

"Everything okay?" she asked after I'd been standing there a moment.

"Yeah. I was just realizing you've never worn the same dress twice." That was the most diluted, PG version of the truth knocking around inside me, which was that I would fuck her for a week straight if I could convince myself it wouldn't ruin me.

Her brows lifted. "Wow. Is that a compliment?"

"Just an observation. Though your dresses are wonderful." Even more wonderful would be taking them off her body.

She touched her chest with her free hand. "Well goodness gracious. Thank you, Damian. That might be the nicest thing you've said to me since I started working here."

Okay, so maybe I had inadvertently been a bigger dick to her than I'd planned on. I could make it up to her a little without letting her in all the way.

"I'm honestly surprised you noticed," she went on.

"Of course I notice." How could I *not* notice someone like Jessa? I'd practically fallen in love with her on sight during my sophomore year, which had been awkward because she'd been in eighth grade. But there was something about her face, or her essence, or—I don't know, her fucking soul?—that spoke to me. Always had. Still did. And maybe it always would. "I just don't say everything that occurs to me," I added after a moment. "The world needs less talking. Fewer opinions."

She smirked, her gaze washing over me appreciatively. "Well, I wouldn't mind if you shared *your* opinions a bit more often. They're worth hearing."

"I don't know about that. I've got a few unsavory ones."

"You've always been the smartest one in the room, wherever you go. How could I not want to hear your opinion?"

This prompted a smile—a genuine one, at that. "Aw, Jessa. Are you trying to warm my parched and blackened heart?"

She wagged her finger at me. "Don't give me any of that tortured villain stuff. There's nothing parched or blackened about you, Damian. You're as soft as the day is long."

That one made me laugh. "Soft as the day is long, huh? I'm not sure if I should be ashamed or proud of that."

"Be proud of it. Even if you are a bit brooding. But the smartest ones are always the broodiest."

This felt a lot like a roast, in the best way possible. My tongue found the inside of my cheek, and I crossed my arms, tilting my head at her.

"So I'm soft and brooding. Is there anything else you'd like to label me with before I start my workday?" I was laughing as I said it, and I wanted to take a picture of the grin she flashed me so I'd never forget she could look at me like that.

"I think that's it for now," she said sweetly.

"For your information, I'm not brooding. I'm just...thinking a lot. There's a lot on my mind."

"That's the definition of brooding, sweetheart," she said in a singsong voice.

The temptation to indulge in this sweet back and forth was too great. I was a goner. I had to dive head-first into this conversation.

"Don't call me sweetheart," I warned her. "You saw my muscles, didn't you? Nothing sweet about those guns."

A laugh popped out of her, and she covered her mouth with a hand. This was just like old times. My heart pounded, waiting to see how far this could go. Somehow, space had shrunk between us, and I was at the edge of her desk, leaning closer to her. I wanted more of this. I wanted it so badly. Teasing Jessa, being on the receiving end of her sweet digs, filled a hole inside me I fought to ignore on the daily.

"Careful, Damian. It seems like you're trying to be my friend right now, and that isn't allowed." She pursed her lips, challenging me with her gaze. "Unless you had a change of heart?"

I didn't get a chance to respond. Francis came up then, looking severely confused. His brows furrowed as he looked between us like he'd caught us sacrificing virgins in broad daylight.

"Well hello," he said with distaste.

I stepped away from her desk, the veil of our reverie collapsing around us, like a ghost abandoning the sheet. We'd been a breath away from linking hands and skipping off to kiss under the football bleachers. We'd gone too far.

And now that we'd recoiled from that warmth, the air in the office felt extra chilly, as if I'd been stripped of a whole layer of clothing. But I needed to ignore that, because Francis had saved me, allowed me to see that I needed to stay focused on my priorities, which did *not* include getting lost in dreamy banter with a plus-size pinup model like Jessa. This was my own fucking workplace. What in the fuck was wrong with me?

"What's up, Francis?" I crossed my arms over my chest, trying to clear the haze. I told myself he hadn't seen us flirting, because we *hadn't been flirting*. We'd just been talking. Like two humans tended to do.

"I can't find Trace," he said with a sigh, clutching some files to his chest with a cock of his hip. "He missed his eight a.m. check-in with me, and I need him to get his signatures on these contracts. I've been calling, but just get voicemail. This is very unlike him."

I blinked a few times, wracking my brain for answers. "I haven't seen him since after the meeting Monday. He hasn't answered your calls?"

"Not a one," Francis said. "And I tried about fifteen times."

"Shit. Okay." I ran a hand through my hair, thinking of next steps. "Let me do a little digging. I'll let you know what I find, okay?"

Francis sent me tight smile. "I was hoping you'd say the magic word: *digging.* Thanks, Damian." He headed back down the hallway. Jessa was back to nibbling on her bottom lip.

"Do you need me to do anything?" she offered.

"No, I've got it. I'll let you know if I do, though." I retreated into my office, shutting the door behind me. The cool air was a much-needed reset as I grappled with the conflicting feelings of Francis interrupting me and Jessa and the fact that I'd engaged in that conversation with Jessa in the first place. I'd only meant to throw her bone and ended up throwing her my entire being.

Why did she make it so easy to forget my resolve to resist her charms?

I expelled a breath and sat in my chair, pulling out my phone. I called Trace on speaker while I started up my laptop. It clicked over to voicemail after ten rings. I tried calling again immediately—same outcome. He wasn't answering anytime soon.

I called Axel next. He picked up on the second ring.

"You heard from Trace today?" I asked as I clicked through screens on my computer, navigating to my GPS tracker. I didn't use this unless absolutely necessary. I could track anyone at any time based on their cell phone. My brothers knew it and were okay with it. None of us had anything to hide.

"No," Axel said. "I thought it was weird he didn't show up for dinner Monday night, but I just figured he was at his Tribeca apartment. And come to think of it, he didn't fucking answer my texts yesterday either."

"Francis just said he missed their eight o'clock."

Axel groaned. "So, what are we looking at here—a kidnapping to add to the roster? Life hasn't been exciting enough recently? I swear to god, if Trace got kidnapped—"

"He hasn't been kidnapped," I said with a laugh. "I just pulled him up on the tracker. Want to take a guess where he is?"

"Sleeping on a bench in Central Park?"

"Because that's so on-brand for Trace Fairchild," I countered. "No, you doucheknob. He's at a very specific apartment in Harlem."

"Ohhh." Axel knew as well as I did what that apartment in Harlem represented for Trace. The same thing Harper represented for me. A sanctioned and well-deserved respite from the stressors of daily life. Trace's on-again, off-again fling was apparently on-again.

"Still, though," Axel went on. "I'm pissed. We're supposed to be dealing with this fucking Ian Fairchild bullshit, not dicking off to go get laid."

"Let the man get laid," I said. "You're always the first one to go after that yourself. Trace can't do the same?"

"Fine, fine," Axel grumbled. "It *is* the best stress relief. It's the only way I'm staying fucking sane now, I'll be honest."

"Good for you," I said in the best chiding tone I could muster.

"Don't give me that attitude," Axel shot back. "To be honest, it sounds like you need that stress relief more than anyone. Isn't Jessa available for stuff like this?"

I groaned, dragging my hands down my face. "That is so fucking inappropriate, dude."

"Haven't you at least thought about it?"

"Of course I've thought about it," I hissed, snatching up the phone and taking it off speaker. I knew the walls of my office were thick—I'd designed them that way—but I would take zero chances.

"You were so obsessed with her during high school," Axel said with a laugh. "I thought seducing her would be the *first* thing you'd do. Before the interview even."

My chest went tight. "She's on our fucking payroll, Axel. I would never even consider it now. She's in a different category altogether."

I wanted this to be true so badly. Maybe repeating it to Axel would make it so. But I thought about Jessa nightly, especially now that I had firsthand knowledge of how relentlessly hot she'd gotten. I could craft odes dedicated to her ever-evolving array of dresses or the constellation of freckles across her cheeks. Just the memory of her sweet laugh as she gave me shit about being *soft and brooding* sent warmth spiraling through me. I didn't even want to admit how many times I'd imagined pushing up one of those dresses—specifically the lacy black one from the fundraiser we'd attended—and finding that sweet heat between her legs. I'd gotten off to the memory of her image more times than I cared to mention since she'd started here.

Which was why I needed to make sure that line between us stayed firm.

I was liable to cross it if I let my guard down even an inch.

"You *think* she's in a different category," Axel said. "But she's not. I see the way you look at her. You're just as smitten as ever."

I scoffed. "It doesn't matter. Even if I was smitten, I'd never do anything."

"Not even if she walked naked into your office right now?"

I paused. I'd do so many things to that woman if she walked into my office naked. But I needed to be stronger than that. Smarter.

A hookup with Jessa would never be possible. I knew through Jeremy she'd dated her last boyfriend for almost six years. And before him, one other long-term boyfriend. She wasn't a woman who fucked around. And that's all I had time for.

As far as I was concerned, Jessa was a stop sign with legs.

"I'd make sure she knew not to wander the office naked," I replied. "In whatever form that message took."

Axel laughed. "Sure. I'll let you act pious. But we both know the truth. You're as dirty as they come, Damian."

I grinned as he gave me shit before we hung up. As I dropped my phone to the desk, a new message popped up.

It was from Trace.

The four little words staring back at me made my stomach bottom out. And if there had been any tone set for the morning, this message blew it to smithereens.

We need to talk.

CHAPTER NINE

"Ohhhh, shit bricks. Shit bricks." I wove through the dense crowd, clutching my tote bags dangling from each shoulder as I ran. The doors of my train were about to close, and I *could not miss this ride*. Everything inside me tensed. This was the outcome of leaving work fifteen minutes late. Missing this train would make me miss half of tonight's class.

With a yell, I launched myself through the crowd. The doors had just started to close as I slipped between them. Sweat dotted my temples, and I stood with my chest heaving, looking out at the platform with winded victory.

"You made it," someone at my side said dully.

"Yes!" I pumped my fist, grabbing one of the poles as the subway lurched into motion. I might sweat the entire way to the Garment District, but I'd been victorious. I now had a shot at making my class on time.

I smiled to myself the whole ride, buzzing with satisfaction. Not only had I clocked another successful and productive day at Fairchild Enterprises, now I was slated to clock a productive evening making strides toward my fashion certificate. It was hard, but I was making it work. Even if I slacked on my coursework a little.

My phone vibrated from inside one of my tote bags as the train approached my stop. I fished it out once I'd crossed the platform and was heading up the stairs to the street.

DAMIAN: Hey. Have you left the office?

I frowned down at the message. This was odd. I waited until my feet hit the sidewalk before I typed out my response.

JESSA: Yeah. What's up?

When Damian didn't text back immediately, thoughts of his message vacated my brain space altogether. After all, tonight's topic was pattern making—my *least* favorite part so far—and I needed to start refocusing on design.

That's what I was here to do, after all. I hated that I had to remind myself of it after getting caught in the captivating Fairchild web.

Anxiety thrummed under my skin as I spotted the deli I normally stopped at. But I didn't have time to stop for a sandwich today, even though I knew I'd be starving within the hour. These sessions were three hours long, and the pattern making class threatened to be grueling. I'd be home after eleven, which meant dinner tonight would consist of popcorn out of my purse.

After another city block, I remembered I hadn't heard back from Damian. I headed for the edge of the sidewalk, right up against the wall of whatever building occupied this block, and dug out my phone, which had gotten buried at the bottom of my purse.

DAMIAN: Where are you?

He'd sent the message ten minutes ago.

JESSA: Just out and about. Is everything okay?

I sent the message and continued my trek to my class, nibbling on my lip as I wove through people on the sidewalk. It wasn't normal for Damian to text me like this outside of work hours. Especially not after a full nine hours at the office. And *especially* not to demand to know my whereabouts.

Anxiety spiked as I crossed another street. I wanted to get to the class as much as I wanted to know what was going on with Damian. I pulled out my phone, just in case I missed a notification. As I glanced at the screen, I miscalculated the distance between me and an oncoming pedestrian. My tote glanced against them, knocking me off balance. I stumbled, and my phone flew from my hand onto the curb.

"Sorry," I called out over my shoulder but got nothing in return.

"Shit shit shit bricks," I muttered under my breath as I scurried after my dropped phone. It lay on a small pile of browned and crusty leaves, the last round of fall still on its way toward decomposition. My screen reflected my face on a black, silent screen—with a brand-new crack at the top edge. I sighed, tapping my foot as I attempted to tun it back on.

But the clock was ticking, and my phone wasn't turning on. I tried again, failed, and decided to forge onward. The hustle and bustle of hoisting my totes, arranging my dress, trying to revive my phone and making sure I hadn't forgotten anything consumed the rest of my trip, until suddenly I was a half block from my class.

When my phone began vibrating in my bag, I realized it must have come back to life somewhere along the way.

"Hello?" I pressed the phone to my ear as well as I could with the ten pounds of sewing paraphernalia dangling from my arms.

"Did you get my messages?" Damian demanded, something foreign and twisted in his tone.

"Uh, yeah. Well, I mean, no." My flat slipped off my foot as I crested the curb, and I swore softly, pausing on top of sewer grates to wriggle my foot back into it. People flowed around me like water bypassing an enormous rock in the river. "I was about to check again. I lost signal—"

"Listen, I need you at the office."

I swallowed hard, looking up at the big block letters that spelled out the name of the building this class was in: *RICHARDS*. Class started in ten minutes. I was *here*, and I needed to go to class.

"Is everything okay?" I asked, lingering by the front doors. A few classmates I recognized glided into the building, sending me smiles. "What's going on?"

"I'm calling an emergency meeting," Damian said, his tone leaving no room for disagreement. "I already sent the car to your apartment. It's en route."

I squeezed my eyes shut. *Fuck.* It wasn't that I didn't want Damian to know about this fashion certificate course, but, well, I didn't really want *anyone* to know about this fashion certificate course unless they absolutely needed to. Until I had some semblance of a future in fashion already secured, so I didn't seem like even more of an idealistic failure than I already was.

"Damian, I'm not home right now."

Silence. Then he snapped, "Then where the fuck are you? I'll re-route."

I nibbled at my lip, glancing inside the doors. A few of my classmates had gathered there, admiring each other's clothing. "I'm in the Garment District."

"What are you doing there?"

"It's like...a night class."

"What?"

I sighed. "I have a life you know."

He grunted. "I'll have a car there in twenty. Text me the address. I'll see you here."

The line went dead. I frowned down at my phone. A few choice retorts balanced on the tip of my tongue, but I swallowed them. Something seemed to be seriously amiss, so I'd save the comebacks for later. But he'd hear about this. Especially since I was ten feet away from my classroom, and desperate to not fall behind or fall out of grace with my professor.

Damian had said twenty minutes. I at least had time to explain myself to the professor. I sent Damian the address and then darted inside, waving a quick greeting to my classmates gathered by the doors, and headed for the large warehouse-style room that served as classroom, runway, and incubator. The murmur of conversation and the dress forms lined up along the far wall sent a wave of calm through me. I loved these classes; I loved being here. Part of me never wanted this course to end.

But there was no way in hell I could afford another term without keeping the job that paid the bills. I pushed the familiar anxiety aside, the money worries and the future woes. I knew them too well; they were as familiar to me as the smell of cigarette smoke in the morning, my mom stumbling bleary-eyed and hungover through the kitchen.

"Mr. Mitchell?" I stepped up to our dapper and refined instructor, who had once told the class that we should all find our unique fashion hill and die on it. He rummaged through a briefcase at the large desk at the front of the room. Gray dotted his temples and streaked his neatly trimmed beard. He mentioned famous fashion names as easily as my friends back home mentioned McDonalds.

"Jessa! Your dress is on point today. Excellent use of patterning in this design, whoever made it. What can I do for you?"

I relished the warmth of his compliment before launching into my bad news. "Thank you. That means a lot coming from you. I want you to know I did prepare for tonight's pattern making class. But something has come up—an emergency—" I was assuming as much, based on Damian's bizarre messages. "And I have to leave."

Mr. Mitchell's face fell—more than I expected. His brows knit together. "Okay. First of all, I hope everything is okay. But tonight's class is the foundation for the subsequent lessons, Jessa. How can we make sure you get caught up?"

"I'll be here early next Monday," I blurted, without even considering what that would entail. If I came early, I'd have to leave work early. And Damian had only *just* found out that I did anything outside of work hours. I nibbled on my lip. "Or, you know, stay late on Monday, too, if that helps. Or I can do extra work between now and Monday? Uh—"

"Early on Monday will work just fine." The perplexity on his face softened, and he offered me a smile. "Good luck with whatever you're going through."

I could have hugged him for that. Instead, I covered my heart with my hands and sent him my biggest smile. "You're such a peach, Mr. Mitchell."

"So are you, Jessa." He winked, and I rushed out of the classroom, relieved that I was still in Mr. Mitchell's good graces. It felt wrong to be tearing myself out of the classroom as everybody filed in, noisy and excited for the lesson to come. But Damian needed me, and he was bankrolling this whole New York experience now. What else could I do?

I paced the sidewalk outside the building, transferring all my anxiety about the missed class to what might await me at the office. They'd never sent a car for me, so I wasn't even sure what to expect in the next five minutes. Half of me was disappointed they hadn't sent a helicopter, but where would it have landed? I inspected the building behind me, imagining the logistics of an emergency helicopter landing. I'd probably have to go to the roof—that made sense. Unless helicopters could land in traffic? While I was staring up at the building, a horn beeped behind me. I turned to find a sleek black SUV at the curb, hazards flashing.

The passenger window rolled down. From the driver's seat, a man in a black suit leaned closer. "Jessa Walton?"

I nodded, my mouth going dry. My gaze bounced off the mirror-like reflection of the paint job, the enormous chrome wheel wells, the likes of which I'd only ever seen inside car showrooms. The driver tipped his head toward the backseat. "Hop in. Damian is waiting for you."

"D-do you mean…" My voice wilted as I pulled open the door to the backseat, half expecting to find Damian waiting in the back, head propped against his fingertips, watching me like a hawk. But the leather backseat was empty, and the cool air smelled fragrant and pure. Like they used an ionizer, which I wouldn't put past them.

Once we were in motion and I had discretely rubbed my palm against the entire length of the backseat, I said, "Thanks for the ride. I hope it wasn't a bother."

The driver smiled. "Not a bother. This is what I do."

"What's your name?"

"Legs."

"What?"

"Legs," he said again, tapping his thigh. "Like your body part." His Brooklyn accent was in full swing now, and I smiled to myself. I loved how every day in the city felt like an adventure. And on really special days, like a trip to a foreign country.

I suspected Tara and Jeremy would never understand this sort of thing or why I loved it so much.

"Should I even ask how you got that name?" I asked with a laugh. "Or is that your legal name, the one your mom gave to you?"

"Just a nickname," Legs said with a knowing grin. "And you'll hear the story someday. But not today."

I blinked rapidly, staring out the window as the Garment District bled into Chelsea on our way to Lower Manhattan.

"This is certainly a nicer way of moving around the city," I said after a few moments. "This car drives like a dream. I feel like we're in a cloud."

"The Fairchilds are very particular," Legs said.

"Is that a good thing or a bad thing?"

"It's a *them* thing," he replied with a laugh. "Not good or bad. Just who they are."

Questions sprang to life inside of me, at least 70% of them relating to Damian. But no, I wouldn't grill his poor driver for information. Well, not *that* hard, at least.

"So how long have you been working for the brothers?" I asked.

"'Bout three years. Mostly with Damian, though. Each brother has his own driver, but we all go where we're needed."

"Ah, so you mostly just cart around Damian and his girlfriend, huh?"

Legs chuckled, though it was hard to tell if it was an *oh yes, the love of Damian's life* sort of chuckle, or an *are you crazy, they just broke up last week and he's so single and ready to mingle* laugh. I hadn't seen any afternoon delights on Damian's schedule, nor had his brunette business goddess come around the office since my interview. So that meant she had to be slinking around the penthouse afterhours.

And Legs would be the one to know.

"Exactly," Legs said.

Well, it was as close to a confirmation as I'd get without asking Damian directly. I frowned out the window. I wasn't sure why it mattered—Damian wasn't interested in me, I had no shot at a man like him, *and* I was his employee. What was I actually hoping for? That my high school crush fantasies would suddenly come to life?

I spent the rest of the car ride calculating how many years after Damian graduated I spent still thinking about him, imagining the ridges of his biceps in those cut-off shirts he'd always wear at the horse farm when I stopped by to drop something off for the family. That boy could wear the shit out of some blue jeans. He'd existed as the man of my dreams for so long after he left my daily life—his knowing smiles, the soft laughs, the way I could just sit at his side and feel accepted. Those qualities were mere bonuses on top of the facts that his green eyes were *still* my favorite shade of green and his jawline paired with his plump, kissable lips were the stuff of cover models.

By the time we reached Fairchild Enterprises, I was back to my natural state, which was hot and bothered for Damian. I took a deep, cleansing breath, thanked Legs for the ride, and hopped onto the sidewalk.

The tantalizing scent of a grill greeted me. I sniffed, following the scent to the next building over. A gyro stand had popped up, and my rumbling stomach guided me toward the ordering window.

"Hello. What a delicious looking setup you've got here," I cooed as I looked over the big menu board. Lamb gyros with tzatziki sauce sounded perfect. After all, who knew how long this meet-up would last? "I'll take your classic gyro please."

The squat woman behind the counter rang me up, which was just enough time for me to change my mind. Because what if Damian wanted one too? That man never ate. I needed to make sure he was clear-headed. But if Trace and Axel were up there too... "Actually, I'll take four, please."

I handed her money, watching with a smile as they wrapped meat, tzatziki, and veggies up in soft pita. She handed me a heavy bag containing four foil-wrapped gyros, and I hurried into the Fairchild building, my shoulders weighed down with the food bag and my class totes.

It was after-hours inside the Fairchild office suite, so the lights were low as I stepped off the elevator. The entire floor felt hushed and half-asleep. I headed for my desk, figuring I'd find Damian in his office. Before I could take three steps, a sharp voice broke the silence.

"Jessa. Over here." Francis's head poked out from around the corner down the hallway. He tipped his head toward the hall that led to the conference room.

Shit. I'd forgotten to bring food for Francis. I swallowed hard, clutching my bag of food tighter. I could offer him half of mine.

Or maybe someone else wouldn't be hungry, and Francis could share with them. I was so excited for this gyro though. Thoughts clambered over each other as I headed for the conference room, wracking my brain for a gyro solution. How had I forgotten about Francis?

I rounded the corner into the conference room, straightening my back. Here went nothing.

Francis closed the door behind me, and at the table sat Axel and Damian, faces drawn. Tension pulsated through the air.

My tongue stuck to the roof of my mouth. I looked over at Francis as he took his seat on the other side of the table.

"Hey, guys," I offered a bright smile. If nothing else, I would diffuse some of this tension. "I have a surprise for y'all."

Damian's gaze flicked my way. Axel lifted two fingers in a mini salute.

"Where's Trace?" I asked. "I'll wait until he gets here, I guess."

Something snapped in the air, heavy and electric. Damian dragged his hands across his cheeks and Axel's frown turned into a scowl.

"Trace won't be joining us," Axel said, in a sharp tone I'd never heard from him before. "He's no longer part of the family."

CHAPTER TEN

DAMIAN

We'd gotten the news four hours ago.

Once Trace had slunk out of his Harlem getaway and back to the office, Axel and I had known something was seriously wrong.

Trace hadn't even been able to meet our gazes, his knee bouncing wildly as he told us what had kept him holed up in Harlem.

He wasn't surprised by Ian's appearance. He'd been expecting the half-brother allegation.

He'd known since senior year of high school that our dad had fucked around on Mom. He'd known since we were seventeen and never said a damn thing.

More than a decade of silence on something so important, so crucial, and I couldn't stop thinking *why?*

"Gyros," Jessa said, dropping two big totes from her shoulder and then opening up a plastic bag on the table. "Food to fuel...whatever is happening here."

I was so preoccupied with my own thoughts, I didn't react. But on the inside, somewhere deep inside, I chuckled.

"Francis, I have a gyro for you too," Jessa said, sending a pointed look at Francis. "So don't think I forgot about you."

"I already ate," Francis said, but his eyes were on the foil wrap as she brought out four packets.

"Well, you are by no means obligated to eat. But if anyone is hungry, which"—her gaze found mine, warmth and understanding there—"I suspect some of you are, then you have a meal here waiting for you. Bon appetit."

"Thank you, Jessa," Axel said, clearing his throat as he reached for one of the gyros. "That was sweet of you."

Sweet was an understatement. Sweet was what Jessa was on her bad days.

Jessa pushed one of the gyros toward me across the table. "I figured you haven't eaten since noon, as usual."

I accepted the food, hating how right she was. Just the sight of her had loosened something wound tight inside of me. "You know me too well."

She winked at me, which sent the corners of my mouth curling into a smile. How was that even possible? I was in the middle of a personal crisis, yet Jessa could still make me smile. I furrowed my brows, jerking myself back to the situation at hand.

Trace had kept a secret from Axel and me for over ten years.

He'd essentially lied to us...for a decade.

And because of this, we could all be damned sure that Axel would never speak to Trace again. It didn't matter how many times Trace explained his side or rationalized his decision. It didn't even matter that I sort of, kind of understood why Trace hadn't said anything.

Axel would never get over it. That man held a grudge longer than Medusa kept her enemies petrified.

And now, in the blink of an eye, our unshakeable family was fractured.

Anxiety sizzled through me like water on a hotplate.

"Now," Jessa said with a sigh, arranging her dress around her as she sat back in the leather chair opposite me at the table. "Somebody catch me up?"

Axel cleared his throat. I gestured to him, so he knew that he could take the lead. I didn't have the energy to rehash this again. I'd spent the last three hours keeping Trace and Axel from killing each other. Axel had a way of saying ridiculous shit when angry, and Trace had a way of punching when provoked. As the perpetual middle brother mediator in the Fairchild clan, I always put aside my own reactions in order to prevent theirs from ruining everything. And mediation was as much of a drain on me as leaving an air conditioner turned on with the front door open.

"Ian Fairchild showed up at our office Monday," he said, then ran his tongue over his top teeth. "He claimed to be a biological half-brother to Trace, which we all thought was bullshit. Well, when I say we, I mean Damian and I. Turns out, Trace knew the truth and kept quiet. Ian *is* his biological half-brother. Our adoptive father Gary stepped out on our Mom during our school years. Trace discovered it our senior year in high school and never thought it was important enough to share. And now we have the mother of all liabilities breathing down our neck and a very conspicuous breach of trust ripping apart the family."

Jessa blinked, her gaze bouncing between Axel and me. "Oh, is that all?"

Another grin threatened to bubble to the surface, but I tamped it down. "That's all," I deadpanned. "Nothing major."

She sent me a wry look, resting her chin on her fingers. "And we're positive Ian is who he says he is?"

"I did some digging," I said, and Francis nodded vehemently in approval, "and I can confirm Ian is who he says he is. He was born in Louisville to my father's mistress, eight years after Trace was born, right after Axel and I joined the Fairchild family via foster care. Ian's mother moved away, and Dad kept in touch with his secret family sporadically through the years. Ian says he never knew much about our dad and was always curious why he could only come to visit for a weekend here or there."

"So your dad kept a *secret family*?" Jessa whispered forcefully.

Axel expelled an annoyed burst of air and popped up from his chair. "Exactly. One that Trace fucking knew about, and he never said a damn thing to *anyone*. How wrong do you think that is, Jessa? On a scale from one to ten."

She blinked rapidly. "Uhhh…"

"There's no wrong answer, unless the answer is anywhere from one to eight," Axel replied.

"So a nine or a ten," she said.

"Exactly," Axel said, clasping his wrists behind his back as he started pacing the far wall of windows. "That asshole knew and didn't say a thing. About a secret family, no less. What else do you think he's keeping secrets about?"

"Axel," I started, swiveling in my chair to send him a stern look.

Axel looked at me with wild eyes, like he had been all evening. "What? Am I wrong?"

"Just shut up," I said quietly. "Let's not beat the dead horse, okay?"

Axel grunted and turned toward the windows, his jaw flexing. "The horse isn't dead. It's alive and well."

I sighed, looking back at Jessa. "I was really hoping this whole half-brother thing would blow over, but it's looking like it won't. So we need to strategize. We don't know how much of a liability he could become."

"What could he do to you guys?" Jessa asked. "I mean, he's nobody. You guys are powerful. He's got nothing on you."

Francis chuckled sarcastically from the head of the table. "Oh, sweet child. You know so little."

Jessa's gaze darkened as she looked at Francis. "So he could sell a made-up story to the tabloids. Big deal."

"He could do a lot more than that," I said quietly. "Unfortunately, it's part of our job to imagine the worst-case scenarios." Lord knew I was more than adept at doing that. "But just to give you an idea, Ian could wield his last name as leverage in the media. He could approach business partners as some sort of unsanctioned liaison. He could drag us down even further, possibly more than we want to even contemplate during the SEC investigation."

"He connected the dots to find us," Axel said as he stared out at the city, which was rapidly becoming bathed in dusk. "What's to stop him from connecting dots that don't even exist?"

"Okay," Jessa said, holding up her palms. "I get it. Tell me what I need to do, and it's done. Even if it includes arranging for Ian's untimely demise."

This time, the chuckle erupted out of me. I squashed the grin and looked over at Francis. "Can you go over the list of tasks?"

Francis nodded, pulling out his tablet. While he organized himself, Jessa reached for her gyro. During the recap, I'd forgotten entirely about the food. *Again.* For the millionth time in my life, Jessa licked her lips as she slowly unwrapped the gyro. I couldn't stop watching her.

"Okay," Francis began, settling into his seat as he peered down at his tablet. "It'll be best to start with a list of priority tasks."

Jessa nodded, pausing to swipe open her own tablet before lifting the partially wrapped gyro to her lips.

"Admittedly," Francis went on, "there are still some things that need to be figured out. For example, how public are we going with the secret family knowledge?" He swiveled to look at me and Axel. "Do we want to be the first to announce or keep it under wraps?"

"Under wraps," Axel bit out. "Our mother doesn't even know."

Jessa gasped softly. Another wave of disappointment crashed through me. Every cell in my body wanted to do anything other than deal with this right now—infidelity ripping apart a family. Now we had to figure out how to handle this suspicious half-brother *and* find a way to bring the topic up with our mom.

If I'd had any spoons left in the emotional cupboard, this turn of events mangled them in the garbage disposal.

I rubbed my forehead. "I think the best path forward is keeping a tight lid on Ian until we either get a better picture of his potential connections or the SEC thing blows over." The chair creaked as I leaned back in it. "Ian could be a real threat based on any number of potential links. What if someone working against us has planted seeds with Ian already? His gaining entry to our world could just be another way for someone else to hurt us."

Jessa's mouth turned downwards. "Someone would do that?"

Francis sighed again. "Don't be so naïve; it's not a good look."

She glanced sharply at Francis. "Excuse me?"

I looked between the two of them. The stress wasn't helping the situation, but Francis didn't need to be acting like this on Jessa's first brush with Wall Street drama. "She's not naïve, I promise you. But this is her first experience with some Grade A Wall Street shit, so cut her a break."

Francis smirked, returning to his tablet. "Shall we continue?"

"Priority tasks, please." I steepled my fingers, focusing on my fingertips as Francis began reading down a list. I needed to focus on my fingertips, because each flinch or sigh from Jessa across the table yanked at my attention.

But it didn't quite matter what I did. My gaze slid back to Jessa, watching as she lifted the gyro to her mouth and took a bite. Her teeth sank into it at the same time sauce squirted out, landing right on the front of her green and white dress.

"Oh noooo," she moaned, setting the gyro on the table.

"What is it *now*?" Francis asked, looking up from his list.

"I'm sorry. I don't mean to interrupt. I just—" she sighed, dabbing at the spot with a napkin. "Can y'all excuse me? I've gotta go try to keep this from staining."

"Send it to the cleaners later?" Francis said, the *duh* tone unmistakable.

"I can't," Jessa corrected sharply. "I need this dress for Monday."

"You're wearing it again so soon?" Francis asked, disgust tugging at his lips. "Not a good look. You're in Manhattan, dearie, you need to act like it."

"No, it's just—" she sighed again. "I need it for something else. I can't have this stain on it." To me, she looked supremely apologetic. "I'll be right back. I gotta go try to fix this."

"Wait," I said, pushing to standing. "I've got something upstairs that could help." The words were flying out of my mouth before I could think better of them.

"You do?" The way her eyes lit up made my chest warm. I jerked my head toward the door, urging her to follow.

"It's in the penthouse. Let's take a dinner break, guys." I twisted to look at Axel and Francis. "We need the break."

Francis grumbled his agreement, and Axel nodded morosely. Jessa hurried behind me as I led the way out of the conference room, our footsteps falling softly on the carpeted hallway.

"I'm so sorry Damian," she said. "I feel like I just hijacked that whole thing."

"It's not a problem." I stuffed my hands into my pockets, my mind racing faster the further we moved from the conference room. My thoughts were turning to static now. All I could feel was how close she was behind me. Nobody else was here. "I think we needed that meeting to be hijacked, honestly. So thank you."

We came up to the elevator at the far end of the building, the private one that led to our penthouse. I swiped my keycard and pressed the button, looking over at her as we waited.

"You should have brought your gyro so *you* could eat," she said.

"I'll eat when we get back. Gotta deal with this emergency first."

She smirked. "Hardly an emergency, considering what you guys are going through. But if my professor finds out I ruined my project..."

The information sizzled through me. A million questions sprang to life. "Is that the night class you mentioned?"

Her shoulders slumped. "Yeah. This dress is my project." She fanned out the bottom of it, looking down at herself, allowing me a gracious glimpse of cleavage. I balled my hands into fists in my pockets. "I'll die if I stained it. I'm in my late twenties, Damian, why do I still need a bib to eat?"

I laughed as the elevator door opened. We stepped inside and I swiped my keycard before hitting the button labeled P. "Don't feel bad. We all need a bib sometimes, at least when tzatziki sauce is involved. Or someone to remind us to eat in the first place."

She sent me a warm smile. "You've got a lot on your mind."

"Yeah, well, you didn't sign up to be my mother." I crossed my arms over my chest, my head growing cloudy as we zoomed up to the penthouse. Every inch of my body knew how the next steps should go: alone time in the penthouse, laughter and wine, one amazing night in my bedroom—or probably the guest room, based on how I'd left the room that morning. My heart thudded with a desire so pure, so intense, that I felt lightheaded trying to keep it at bay.

"I'm not being your mother, just being a friend." As soon as the words came out, she rolled her lips inward. "Which, I'm not supposed to be doing, so..."

Her words seeped into me, reminding me of all the conflict and confusion since she'd started. I'd been trying so hard to protect myself, but at what cost? The elevator doors slid open, revealing the side foyer of our penthouse. We stepped off the elevator.

"I know it's confusing, Jessa." I cleared my throat, unsure of what I was trying to say. I pinched the bridge of my nose, opting to drop the thread altogether. "Follow me. I think we've got some top-notch shit in the laundry room."

I strode down the hall, the half-finished conversation sizzling in the back of my mind. My forearms prickled from how close we'd been in the elevator; from how badly I wanted to make all the wrong decisions.

Our laundry room was more like a hallway, a long, narrow room with multiple washers, dryers, racks, counters, and baskets. I headed for the closet right inside the door.

"Wow," Jessa murmured. "I didn't see this part on the tour."

"Welcome to the laundry tunnel," I cracked, rummaging through the boxes of crap I looked at maybe once a year.

"Do you still do your own laundry?" she asked.

"Sometimes." I found the spray bottle I'd been hunting for. "When I've got my shit together enough to remember, that is. Which means it's probably been...months."

She cocked her head. "Those basic things just slip under all this stress, huh?"

My shoulders slumped. Here she went again, with the damn insight and tenderness. The way she looked at me told me she *saw* me. Like she was looking inside my body with an X-ray, reading all my innermost thoughts and worries.

"To say the least," I replied, turning the bottle over in my hands. "Let's get this on before the stain sets."

She looked down at her chest, then back up at me. The splotch sat right between her breasts. "I should get it...right?"

My hand tightened around the bottle. *Do not suggest she take the dress off. That is unnecessary. You just want to see her naked. Stop it, Damian.*

"Um..." I fought for a moment to remember how to form words as I stared at her breasts. I hoped it looked as though I was formulating a plan of action. "We can do this together."

"Don't fall in," she cracked.

Like that wasn't precisely what I wanted to do. Not just into her cleavage, but into all of her. I wanted to dive so deeply into Jessa it scared the fuck out of me. I must have sent her a stern look because she bit her lip.

"Sorry, I know that's too far into friend territory again."

"Slide your hand underneath," I instructed her. "Then I'll spray it." *And then I'll run far away from this situation.*

She did as I said, and I doused the stain in the spray. She nibbled on her lip as she watched. "You don't think it'll discolor it, right?"

"It shouldn't. I've used this on fancy shirts before and never had a problem. We'll let it sit then we'll wash it out."

She nodded, pressing a hand to her forehead. "Sorry, again."

I was still standing so close to her, far closer than needed. But hell if I could pull myself away. My gaze washed over her, taking in all the spectacular details. The flecks of blue in her eyes, the wispy hairs lining her face. The lightest smattering of freckles across her cheeks, like she'd tried—and failed—to cover them up with makeup.

"I should be apologizing." I didn't know if it was the proximity, or the stress, or what, but I needed to get these words off my chest. "I'm the one who ripped you from class. You wouldn't have stained it if I hadn't brought you here. Just another thing I need to make up for now."

She blinked, pulling back slightly. "Oh? What else do you have to make up for?"

I narrowed my eyes. "Come on. Like you don't have a running tally by now."

"I don't, Damian. I'd love to know what you think you have to make up for."

I swallowed hard. I spent late nights cataloguing all the ways in which I didn't stack up, the ways in which I'd failed. I had my running tally on Jessa's behalf, as well as a longer one for my entire life. "I know how much of a dick I can be."

"Ahh, so you do realize." She tutted, her grin nearly ear-to-ear. She leaned in again, the coyness emanating from her so alluring that I nearly fell head-first into a kiss with her. "So what's the plan for making it up to me? I'd love to know."

"Do you have any suggestions?"

"Well I'm not looking for a chocolate gift basket here, Damian."

I laughed. "So that rules out my first idea."

"I don't know, my ideas might not fall on the right side of the friend line," she said with a wink. I knew this game a little too well. And there was no one I wanted to play it with more than Jessa.

"Who's keeping watch on that line anyway?" I asked.

"I thought that was your job," she shot back with a challenging lift of her brow.

It *had been* my job, back when I was still in control of my desire. Back when I could lie to myself about how attracted I was to this woman. But now that she was inches away from me, looking at me like I was the only man in the entire world, I couldn't care less about the fact that I was supposed to be keeping myself away from her.

"We're in the laundry room, Jessa," I said, turning the bottle over and over in my hands. Because if I didn't, I was liable to grab her by the waist and press her flush to my body. "The line only exists downstairs."

"And in the gym?" she prompted.

My heart rate picked up as I realized she'd probably been aware of my struggle to do the right thing since the beginning. "I think the line has been totally erased in all areas of my penthouse."

"Now I'm *really* curious what your plan is to make it up to me." She cocked a hip, every part of her body challenging me. Luckily, I knew how to rise to the occasion.

"I'd have to take you off my payroll to answer that question," I said smoothly.

Her eyes went wide, a blush coming to her cheek. I could have kissed it until it went away—or it grew even brighter. "So in order to have all my high school fantasies come to life I'd have to quit, huh?"

Now I was the one to blink in surprise. A laugh escaped me. "Wait, what?"

She clamped a hand over her mouth. "Just kidding."

"High school fantasies? Let's circle back to that part."

Her blush grew as she covered her cheeks with her hands. "We don't need to circle back."

"Jessa, you're blushing. We need to circle back." I could have needled her like this all day. Or at least until it finally led us into the bedroom.

She groaned, looking up at the ceiling. "I hate my cheeks."

"I'm a pretty big fan of them." I didn't even care anymore that I was officially crossing the line. The line I myself had drawn. I reached for a different spray bottle. "Let's rinse this stuff off while you tell me more about these high school fantasies."

"Damian, I'm so embarrassed," she said, fanning herself. "I was such a geek back then, and I—"

"You were fine," I assured her. "Though you're lucky seventeen-year-old Damian didn't know about this."

Her eyes went even wider. "Say what?"

"There was a time that I was pretty sure Jeremy was going to hate me for life because of what I wanted to do with you," I admitted with a laugh. Inside my head, my mind was rioting. Why was I saying this? How had we gotten this deep, this fast? Yet I couldn't pump the brakes. Not even a little bit.

Her throat bobbed, and she clamped her hands over her mouth again, looking up at me with saucers for eyes.

"You're kidding."

"I'm not."

"I would have *died,* Damian." She started fanning herself again. "I would have died and gone to Heaven."

"You were too young, anyway." I lifted the bottle, and she slid her hand beneath the fabric again as I doused the spot. "You were a sophomore, I was a senior. Then I went to college and became properly distracted."

But that wasn't the whole truth. The distraction was temporary. And now that she was back in front of me, within arm's reach every day, I could barely control myself.

She nodded, the blush fading. But her chest still rose and fell heavily. And I was inches away from cinching my arm around her waist and never letting go.

"Yeah. Those high school crushes never last, huh?" she said.

I disagreed. My infatuation with her had lasted longer than any other romantic relationship in my life, much to my dismay. But I didn't want to admit *that.* It seemed somehow sad. After all these years, after so many women in and out of my life, why was my high school crush still the one that had sunk the deepest?

"Here. Dry this off." I reached for a dry hand towel behind Jessa. "I think you narrowly avoided a permanent stain."

She clutched the hand towel to her chest, her gaze searching my face. We'd opened a can of worms here, and I knew better than to think we could stuff them back in. Which meant I needed to retreat. Because anything with Jessa, or anyone else for that matter, was a non-starter.

Anything beautiful I had a chance at creating would surely end in flames.

My entire life was proof of how misery followed on the heels of beauty. I'd lost two sisters; my passion project was probably going to send me to prison. What misery awaited me on the other side of a fulfilling relationship?

I didn't want to find out.

"Damian—" she started, but rustling from the kitchen interrupted us.

I tipped my head toward the door. "I'm gonna go check that out. If you're ready, we can go back down."

I took a gulp of air as I strode out of the laundry room, feeling like I'd both crossed multiple lines *and* saved myself from something perilous. How could one simple stain removal be both victory and failure?

I crossed the threshold of the kitchen, finding Trace at the island, his palms pressed to the surface.

"What are you doing?"

Trace's dark brows were pinched toward the middle of his forehead. "Just deciding if I want to stress eat or stress drink."

"I'd go with stress eat first," I said. "Followed by stress drinking."

He hefted with a humorless laugh. "Thanks for the tip."

I tapped my knuckles along the counter as I approached him. "Axel's down in the board room with Francis. We're crafting our strategy."

Trace's jaw flexed as he stared at some unknowable point in the air. "Shouldn't I be a part of that?"

"I don't think so," I forced out. "Not right now, at least."

He swung his dark gaze my way. Brokenness shone back at me. A rawness that stole my breath. "What should I have done differently, Damian?"

The question was a gut punch. Now, as we were all thirty or older, hindsight was more than picture perfect. "You should have told us then. When you found out."

"Dad asked me not to," Trace bit out.

"That was wrong of him," I said softly. "That was too much for a kid to keep quiet about, to carry alone."

"But I did it," Trace said. "And after a while, it just didn't seem necessary to detonate everything over a little detail I wasn't even sure was true."

"A little detail." Now *that* was funny. This little detail had the potential to upend everything. Most importantly, our family. The one thing I'd thought was rock solid and unshakeable.

Yet again, proof that good was always followed by bad. Even the surest bets in life were susceptible to complete and utter failure. When would I learn?

"Hey, guys." Jessa's soft voice behind me caused me to twist around.

The sight of her there, wringing her hands together, nibbling on her bottom lip as her gaze darted between us, that damp spot on her dress in full view, sent a shock wave of warmth and tenderness through me. I wanted to gather her into my arms and never let go.

"Hey, Jessa." Trace waved, but it was tired.

"Why don't you head back down without me?" I tipped my head toward Trace. "We need to talk about a few things."

She nodded. "Of course. Do I need a key to operate your fancy elevator or...?"

I cracked a grin, deciding to escort her to the elevator, even though it *didn't* need a key to go down. I pressed my hand to the small of her back without even thinking, guiding her out of the kitchen. "Let Axel know I'll be back soon, okay?"

She nodded as we approached the private elevator. I pressed the button and the doors slid open. I searched her face for some sign that whatever threshold we'd crossed earlier in the laundry room wasn't going to make things weird.

"I'll be down soon," I added, knowing that in my alternate fantasy life, this was the part where I'd lean in and kiss her.

Kiss her.

Kiss her.

Kiss her.

Jessa stepped into the elevator, lifting a brow. "So I *didn't* need a key for the fancy elevator?"

I shook my head. "Not to go down."

The doors slid shut then, hiding her knowing smile from view until I was staring at my own reflection in the polished metal. I ignored the thumping of my heart and went back into the kitchen.

"What were you two doing up here?" Trace asked.

"She had a tzatziki incident," I said.

"Is that a euphemism or…"

I narrowed my eyes at him. "No. And besides, what I'm doing up here with Jessa is the least of your concern. Even though it was just stain removal."

Trace looked like he didn't believe me. "Sure. Now, let's just cut the crap. Let me come down there and strategize with you guys."

"I *really* don't think that's a good idea."

"I'm part of the fucking business," he said forcefully, stepping closer. "I'm part of the fucking *family.*"

"I'm not trying to cut you out," I said. "But I know how fucking mad Axel is right now. If you go down there, nothing is going to get better or advance. It will just grind to a halt. And you know it too."

Trace grunted, flexing his hand into a fist repeatedly. "He can't stay mad forever."

"You think? Trace, he might not ever talk to you again." Emotion pinched my throat unexpectedly, and I looked away. "I'm not lying about that. He's angrier than I've ever seen him."

"Are you that mad at me too?"

His question caught me off guard. I was so used to being the mediator, I barely remembered that I had my own opinion. I swallowed hard. "I am. But I also get it. So I'm...I don't know. I'm caught in the middle. That's what I am."

"True to form," he muttered.

"Listen, it's probably for the best if you go back to Harlem tonight," I told him. "Or maybe your place upstate. If Axel even comes back here tonight, I think we all just need some time to cool off. You know?"

Trace's jaw flexed as his gaze settled on me. "You're gonna kick me out of my own house now?"

"Not kicking you out," I said. "But you gotta admit, some space would help things. You dropped a big bomb today. And you can't fault us for needing some fucking time to sort through the rubble."

"What rubble is there?" Trace demanded, pounding his fist on the island. "You guys know everything there is to know. What more can I say?"

"You can say nothing," I said. "That's what we want. Let us be pissed. We thought we were a team. That we were moving through life with the same set of data. But you had different data, and chose not to share it with us." I jabbed my finger at him. "That's the fucking rub, Trace. If it looks and smells like betrayal, what the fuck do you think it is?"

He scowled. "I never betrayed you guys. It was the fucking opposite. I worked my ass off for my entire life to be loyal to us. To our family. To keep this shit together."

I waved away his words. We weren't getting anywhere, and there was too much waiting to be figured out downstairs. "Please. Give us some fucking space."

"You'll fucking get it," Trace spat. "Don't worry."

He stormed out of the kitchen. The space between my ears throbbed as I headed for the elevator.

My entire life, my family had been a mountain—the landmark that guided my efforts and grounded me to the earth. First as a Haynes, then as a Fairchild.

But now?

My mountain had cracked. The rift had formed.

And the last bit of solid foundation in my life had officially split in two.

CHAPTER ELEVEN

JESSA

Priority tasks. Action tasks. Care tasks. Personal tasks.

I was drowning in a sea of tasks. Thank God I had a tablet, desktop, company phone *and* my personal phone. Otherwise, I might not have been able to stay afloat with *so much to do* in the Fairchild world.

I'd gotten to work extra early the next day, since our late-night meeting ended with approximately 127 new items on my to-do list. Priority items 1 through 78 included the rapid planning and execution of a brand-new Programmer's Ball that the brothers wanted to host to begin repairing their post-investigation reputation via fundraising, donations, and transparency. It was a noble cause, one that I was eager to work on, but the date Axel and Damian had chosen for the event scared me.

One month from now.

It didn't leave much room for error—or anything else, for that matter. Damian had already handed me a draft version of the invitations they planned to paper Manhattan with, which, pending booking one of the venues I'd call today, would roll out by eight a.m. tomorrow.

This wasn't just breakneck speed. This was a liquefying to-do list for little ol' Jessa Walton.

I flitted around my office space, getting ready for the day. Damian wouldn't be in for at least another half hour, and I was planning what I might surprise him with today on the food front. We could call that a *nourishment task*, since a good portion of my day was spent thinking about what might go into his mouth.

Like maybe my nipples? My eyes fluttered shut, and I shook my head. No, that wasn't helpful at all. Not after what happened in his laundry room last night. Or his brief touch on my lower back, which had sent a surge of moisture straight to my panties.

I wasn't proud of how sensitive I was to Damian's nearness. It was embarrassing. But the man had essentially admitted that he'd had a crush on me at least once in his life, which was the green light for my body to start acting even more insane when it came to this man.

If he'd crushed on me once, maybe I had a shot now.

Jessa, quit being crazy. He has a girlfriend. Legs basically confirmed it. Besides, 17-year-old Damian having a crush on you does not equate to 32-year-old Damian being even remotely interested in you.

I sighed, looking at his closed office door. To make things worse, I missed him, which was just further proof that I was living in an unrequited love bog that I needed saved from immediately.

Focus on work, Jessa. If he wouldn't put my nipples in his mouth, then he'd put a bagel in his mouth. I'd quickly amassed a list of interesting delivery options in the neighborhood, and today's selection was going to be a bagel smorgasbord, complete with an interesting array of jams, jellies, cream cheeses, and more. I wiggled in my seat with excitement as I set up the details, scheduling the delivery for ten a.m. That seemed to be the time that Damian really came to life, which seemed like the best time to surprise him with a bagel tray.

Once breakfast was ordered, I got to work on my to-do list. Some tasks were easy, like verifying availability of their preferred venues and checking in with the company's lawyers. I tried to knock as many of those out as I could first, so I could feel preliminarily victorious.

As always, I had my sketchbook open on my desk, ready to receive fresh lines in whatever design I was working on whenever I had a spare moment. Today it was a miniskirt my instructor wanted us to develop, even though a thing like this would hardly cover one of my ass cheeks.

Around 9:40, my phone buzzed with an incoming call. I peered down at it, my belly knotting when I saw Tara's name on the caller ID.

I contemplated not answering it. I was plenty skilled at avoiding her calls. But not answering had just as many risks as answering.

I picked it up right before it switched to voicemail. "Hi, Tara."

"Hey! You actually picked up."

I tucked the phone between my ear and shoulder, instantly annoyed. "What's up?"

"Just wanted to let you know the latest."

The knot in my belly turned to stone. "Hopefully good news?"

"Mom got sprung from rehab. She's in a halfway house now."

The news settled over me in the same way sludge coated the river bottom. I'd been through this song and dance too many times. I knew better than to rush to excitement. Knew better than to even hope for the best.

"Okay..."

"It's actually the second halfway house," Tara went on. "She was in one for a couple days before we found out it had roaches."

"Oh, jeez." I nibbled on my bottom lip as she spoke.

"Yeah. Unfortunately, this new place is a little bit more expensive than we had planned."

The belly stone now began to slowly twist into something else altogether. "Yeah?"

"We need some more money to make this halfway house payment," Tara said. "Jeremy and I already pitched in. The rest is due today."

My heart started racing, a sure indicator that a heated conversation lay ahead of us. I looked around the office. There were too many ears in the hallway for me to finish this conversation here. I turned the knob of Damian's office, double checked that it was still empty, and slipped inside.

The lingering scent of his cologne instantly soothed me. It was a warm hug as I waded through the cold, unpleasant waters of this conversation. I drew a fortifying breath and continued.

"So how much are we talking?"

"Five hundred."

I swore under my breath. "*Tara.*"

"*Jessa*," she retorted.

"Shit bricks. How much does this place cost?" I demanded.

"We had to pay first and last month's fees," she hissed. "You'd think you'd be willing to pay any price for your mother's health, though."

"It's not that," I told her. "I'm tapped out, Tara. I just sent you two hundred a week ago."

"Right, which was for your regular portion of her living expenses," Tara said. "This is something else. Rehab let her go early, and the halfway house had roaches. You think I wanted this to happen?"

"N-no, I just—" I stammered, unable to quickly and articulately express how insane this was. "Tara, I don't have it."

"How can you not have it?" she demanded. "You make the most of anyone in this family. What the fuck you spending your money on?"

"I live in one of the most expensive cities in the United States," I shouted. "My rent is more than your entire salary. What do you want to hear, Tara? I pay rent, credit card bills, class fees. Not to mention materials for the course. Sometimes I like to eat, too. And that's on top of paying for Mom's rehab and everything else."

"Oh, boo-hoo. Cut the crap, Jessa," Tara shot back. "Your little sob story about cost-of-living expenses isn't gonna work on me. You think all that's expensive, try having three kids. Besides, I know how much you make."

"Excuse me?"

"Jeremy told me what you make. You're making six figures out there and can't even spare five hundred for the woman who gave you life? You're fucking pathetic."

Emotion tightened my throat, and I squeezed my eyes shut. This wasn't right. But I didn't know how to make it right. "Don't say that, Tara. You're being a bitch."

"I'm the bitch?" Her raucous laughter sent anxiety sparking under my skin. "Yeah, I guess keeping our mother alive qualifies me as a bitch."

"Don't be such a goddamn martyr," I hissed through gritted teeth. "I pay my dues for that woman. You can do what you want, but in the meantime, I need to wait until my next mother-cluckin' paycheck."

"Oh, your next paycheck, huh?" Tara's laughter this time dripped with sarcasm. "I sure wish I could tell my kids to just wait to eat until the next paycheck. Wouldn't that be so much easier? You're fucking swimming in cash, Jessa, and you have the balls to tell me to wait? Get a fucking clue, you self-centered brat. No wonder Mom started using drugs when it was just you two left in the house. I wouldn't have been able to put up with this shit either."

The line went dead, and I stared at the phone through a veil of tears. I turned around and gasped. Damian stood in the doorway, concern etched into his features.

"Is everything okay, Jessa?" he asked.

Something about his broad shoulders, the familiar lines of his face, or the way he was looking at me like he wanted to hug me landed the final blow to my self-control. Whatever it was, the tears broke through the barrier. I covered my face with my hands.

"It's fine," I said, my chest hitching with a sob.

Damian's arms were around me, wrapping me in his thick and deliciously warm embrace. I melted into him without even thinking about it, grabbing my own wrist behind his back and nestling into the most perfect and secure spot against his chest. The tears instantly vanished, but I had no intention of moving. Ever.

"Do you want to talk about it?" His deep voice rumbled closer to my ear than it ever had before. Goosebumps flared over my entire body, head to toe. He had to notice.

I shook my head. And then I thought better of it and nodded.

His body shook with laughter. "So, that's a yes and a no?"

I couldn't speak yet. Not when I was buried in his perfect embrace, wrapped up in the woodsy musk of his scent. My heart raced for completely different reasons now, and I knew my grace period on this hug was quicky expiring.

I drew a deep breath, pulling myself away from him in one big burst, even though every cell of my body wanted to stay right there.

"I'm so sorry," I whispered, dabbing at my eyes. "I didn't mean to cry."

"It's okay." He shrugged. "We're just passing the intense-life-moments baton. Today's your day. Yesterday was mine."

"Tara just told me that my mother started using drugs because of the stress of living with a selfish brat like me," I said quietly, my gaze dropping to the floor. "She was angry because I can't send her five hundred dollars by the end of the day. My mom had to unexpectedly enter a new halfway house because *reasons*, and..." I threw my hands out to my sides. "And here we are, as always. Running in circles around my mother's addiction. She always makes me feel like every aspect of it is my fault. But I still send money, even though deep down, I don't want my mom to see a dime of my money after what I had to live through with her."

Tears pressed at my eyes again, and I rubbed my forehead. "Good morning, by the way," I added with a laugh. "Sorry I was in here. I just didn't want anyone to hear my conversation."

"Don't worry about it. Whatever you need is yours." He leaned against the edge of his desk.

But what if what I need is you? I looked over at him and wondered if he could see the question in my heart. "Thank you, Damian. You've been nothing but generous, and I promise you, it's been life-changing."

"Tara's always been a bitch, hasn't she?"

"To put it mildly."

Damian stepped up to me, grabbing me by my arms. He searched out my gaze. "There's no way in hell you were the cause of your mother's addiction."

I nodded, getting lost in his mossy gaze. "Thank you. She says it because she knows it hurts me."

That hadn't even been the worst part about what she'd said. Tara calling me a self-centered brat had been the worst. Because she knew what had happened under my mother's roof. She knew which one of Mom's exes had forced himself on me and the ways I begged for things to change.

But no. The do-gooder teenager was the brat, the one who'd forced the adult to use drugs. *Sure.*

The whole thing made my blood boil.

An alarm broke the comfortable silence between us—my phone. It was 10 o'clock. The bagels were here.

"Oh my god." I slapped my forehead, more than ready to shift gears for the day. "The delivery is here."

"What delivery?"

"Breakfast, silly!" I winked at him. "Wait here. You're gonna love what I got for us today."

Damian looked genuinely amused as I headed out of his office. I beelined for the reception desk, where I found the delivery driver with my order. I returned to Damian's office with three large paper bags.

"Okay, so this might be more than I was expecting," I said, heading for the long table to one side of his office, which I'd started using just for these occasions. I unpacked the brown paper bags, laying out all the elements as I discovered them: everything bagels, plain bagels, cinnamon-raisin bagels. Cream cheese and smoked salmon. Raspberry chia jam. Sweet chili jam. Lavender jelly. With each new item I revealed, my *ooh*s and *aah*s grew louder.

"Hot damn, Jessa," Damian murmured once it was all laid out.

"I think we need to invite a few more people to partake," I said with a laugh. "Maybe I went overboard."

Damian stood so close to me I could feel the heat pouring off him. I so badly wanted to reach out and grab his hand, or maybe have him touch the small of my back again. I glanced over at him, wondering if he suffered from even an ounce of the same lunacy. But he was entranced by the bagel spread.

"It's perfection," I said with a sigh. "Even though nobody back home can ever find out how much we spent on bagels today."

Damian laughed. "Your secret is safe with me and my credit card." He reached for an everything bagel and then contemplated the cream cheese selections. "You think she'll ever come around?"

"Who, my sister? Never." I reached for the lavender jelly, wondering how that might pair with an everything bagel. "She reminds me every week how I should be back in Kentucky taking care of mom because I'm the unmarried and childless one who needs to repent for the sin of being alive. According to her, I'm doing nothing with my life. But to me, I'm *saving* my life. I was going to die if I stayed in

Kentucky even another week—from boredom, from lack of fulfillment, from..." My voice dried up. The ghosts of my past were real there. Not just what had happened with Mom's ex-boyfriend, but what went down with Tommy, too.

I had plenty to run from. Plenty that I never wanted to think about again.

Damian nodded. "Yeah. Some people won't ever get it."

"And it's okay if they don't," I added, licking the edge of the plastic knife I'd used to spread the jelly before tossing it in the waste basket. *Damn* that stuff was good. "But I don't want to be made to feel like a bitch for going after what I want and need."

Damian's gaze was heavy on me for a few moments. Then he looked back at the bagel spread. "Not everyone is going to agree with your decisions. Sometimes even the people closest to you."

"Well, if I've learned one thing, it's even those we call family aren't necessarily the closest ones in life. Nor are they the ones looking out for your best interests." I took a bite of the impossibly soft bagel and moaned. "And this bagel rights every wrong in the entire world."

Damian's soft grin was the stuff of heartthrob posters. "Better than the celery diet, right?"

I scoffed. "Don't mention that water with hair as I feast on this perfection, please."

We shared a warm smile, heat spreading through my chest. I loved this man. *Still.* I'd loved him since we'd been peripheral friends throughout our school years. I loved him throughout the years as a distant acquaintance. And I loved him now as his old-friend-turned-secretary.

It was real, human love. But it was also passionate, unrequited love.

And dammit, I wished this shit would go away already. But with moments like these, I was a goner. If he touched my lower back again, I'd be ready to exchange vows.

I distracted myself by loading up another bagel while my every-thing-lavender masterpiece with one bite taken out sat off to the side. "I'll let Axel and Cora know there's a smorgasbord in here if you want."

"And Francis," he added.

I sighed, rolling my eyes. "And Francis."

As if on cue, Axel waltzed into the office, his eyes widening as his gaze landed on the spread. "Wow, guys. Really holding out on me, aren't you?"

"I was just about to call you and tell you," I said sweetly.

"Sure, sure. Listen, Damian, we've gotta take a quick crosstown trip. Just you and me and however many of those bagels you can fit into your pockets."

"Stuff your own damn pockets, Axel." To me, he added, "I guess I'm leaving. Let me know if anything crops up today, okay?"

Axel loaded up a plate of bagels and the entire jar of sweet chili jam plus the plain cream cheese, and the two left the office. I wished for a sweet caress or an arm squeeze on his way out, but Damian kept his hands to himself. I heaved a sigh and straightened my back. After an emotional morning, it was time to get back to work.

Hours drifted by, fueled by internet research and everything bagels. Around two o'clock, the click of heels coming down the hall yanked at my attention. I perked up, thinking it might be Cora. But a different brunette rounded the corner, staring down at me.

I tipped my head back, trying to place this face. I recognized this woman. Smartly dressed, perfect chestnut waves, a sharp gaze that promised to crack a whip if I spoke out of line.

"Hello," I said. "How can I help you?"

"I'm here for Damian," she said with equal parts sweetness and condescension. She clutched a handbag against the front of her body. "I'm his two o'clock."

I mechanically turned my gaze to my computer. Why was everything inside me jamming up, like I'd never worked a day at this job before? I clicked aimlessly around the desktop, trying to remember how to open Damian's appointment book. And that's when I saw it.

2:00: Harper Bennett

Pieces clicked into place, showing me the larger picture. I knew why I recognized this lady. She was the woman who had waltzed out of his office on the day of my interview, the woman with her head between his legs. *Damian's girlfriend.*

My mouth went dry. "He, uh…" I pretended to focus hard on the screen, struggling to piece together a sentence. "He's not in…right now."

She cocked her head, her smile growing wider. "What was that?"

"He's uh…gone. Totally gone. Out of the city entirely," I said, which I knew wasn't true. Damian had only gone across town with Axel. But I couldn't make my mouth get the memo.

"That's impossible," Harper said. "We had something on the books. He never cancels."

"I'm sorry. He's out of the office, and I don't know when he'll be back." I offered my best approximation of a detached customer service smile. "I can take a message for you though, and I'll see if he's interested in rescheduling. He may have found your services no longer necessary, or—" Judging by the confusion etching itself across Harper's face, I was crossing a line and needed to reel it in. "Or maybe there's some other reason that we don't know about yet."

"Trust me," she said succinctly, something lethal glinting in her gaze, "he's interested in rescheduling."

"Ma'am, I can't do that until he returns."

Her chin lowered, something in her tone sharpening to a lethal edge. "Do you know who I am?"

"I, uh…" I swallowed a knot in my throat. I felt backed into a corner. "Of course I do. You're the person in the 2 o'clock slot for today."

Awkwardness throbbed through me as I braced myself for her response. *Why are you doing this?* Everyone in Damian's contacts had a brief summary attached for information at-a-glance. Even if I *hadn't* spotted Harper giving Damian a blowjob the day of my interview, I would have been able to play along given the fact that her summary clearly included "VIP with Privileges." If only I'd played the subservient customer service role from the start, but no, I had to let my jealousy figure in.

"Ms. Bennett," she said sharply. "You may call me Ms. Bennett."

"Ms. Bennett," I said slowly, "I'm sorry to be the bearer of bad news. But Damian cancelled your appointment, and I have no further information at this time. I'd be happy to take a message, as I said. What's the nature of your business? Are you a supplier for the firm?"

My heart thumped like a bass drum as I awaited her response. *Jessa you are going to be in so much trouble.* Though I was being professional, secretly I hoped this conversation would push them toward breaking up, which made me feel like a villain. I wrung my hands under the desk as her nostrils flared.

"No message at this time. I'll handle this." She sent me a plasticized smile and turned on her heels. Once she was out of sight, I slumped back into my chair, letting the horror of what I'd just done wash over me.

Not only had I white lied to Damian's probably-very-powerful girlfriend, I'd also let jealousy get the best of me.

And for what? I groaned inwardly. Of course she'd say something to him, especially if they were dating. So maybe I just needed to avoid Damian until it all blew over. I could ask to work from home for the next week. While I considered the logistics of such a request, Damian sent me a text that made my insides freeze up.

DAMIAN: There's a dinner tonight I want you to attend. Can you make it?

There went my plans to avoid Damian for the next week. There was nothing I wanted more than to attend anything, at any time, with Damian. But that warred with my very real need to catch up on my homework, and my newer, more urgent need to not look Damian in the eye until I could assess the damage from lying to his girlfriend.

I swallowed hard and typed out my response.

JESSA: You know it. I'm there.

CHAPTER TWELVE

DAMIAN

I checked my watch for the billionth time that evening. It was still 7:01 p.m., like it had been for the last hour. My knee bounced wildly beneath the table as I resigned myself to more waiting and scanning the crowd.

Doing what I did best. Searching the place for any sign of Jessa.

"You need another wine?" Axel leaned closer to me, jerking his chin toward my drained glass. "Carménère, right?"

"Sure. Actually, let's just get a bottle. Jessa will probably have some too." She would be here any minute; I could feel it. I'd told her to meet us at 7:00 at the Monaco Lounge, which didn't explain why I'd been searching for any glimpse of her for over twenty minutes. When she got here, I'd be able to relax. And hopefully, with some wine, she could relax too.

And then maybe we could both relax together. Back at the penthouse.

Francis checked his watch from across the round, white-linen–covered table. "She's laaaate," he said in a sing-song voice.

"Give her a minute." I didn't love the rivalry that had cropped up between Francis and Jessa. I wasn't sure if I felt like the father they didn't want to share or the boyfriend they both laid claim to. At work, I had no favorites.

But off the clock, I only thought, saw, and wanted Jessa.

I hated how true this was becoming, how thoroughly she infiltrated my thoughts. I'd ignored Harper's texts that afternoon because I didn't want to think about her yet, even though occasionally a new one arrived. My phone buzzed again, signaling yet another message. I peered at my phone, which I kept below the table.

HARPER: I thought we had something here? Was I wrong?

OK, that last text signaled something at the brink of explosion. I opened the thread, catching myself up on what I had been avoiding all day.

HARPER: Just stopped by your office for our afternoon delight, but you cancelled on me? Or was your new secretary lying?

HARPER: She asked what the nature of my business was, which tells me you haven't even briefed her on what we have going on.

HARPER: Don't waste my time if you'd rather not see me. I don't have time for that shit. Neither do you. So what gives?

HARPER: I thought we had something here. Was I wrong?

I groaned out loud, pocketing my phone once more. I did *not* want to handle that right now.

"What's wrong?" Axel asked.

"Just some texts from Harper." I raked through her messages in my head, specifically the one about cancelling and the possibility of my secretary lying. That was interesting, to say the least. And it made me wonder if Jessa had embellished the truth somehow.

Or maybe she recognized Harper and didn't want her around.

This possibility scorched through me, acting as a breeze to the red embers of my desire. I'd been permanently half-hard since hugging her in my office that morning, and more than desperate to get her alone somewhere, somehow. Even though I knew I shouldn't, I wanted to dive back into her warmth. Seeing her in tears, in need of a hug, had broken down one of the last standing walls inside my mind and heart. I couldn't keep acting like she wasn't the gorgeous, sweet, inviting, hilarious, and genuine beauty that she was.

But you should if you want to keep yourself safe.

"Harper was in today," Francis said, smiling up at the server as she brought the newest round of drinks. "She didn't look very happy."

"Because I forgot about our meeting," I said, reaching for my new glass of wine. I started the scan for Jessa again. It was 7:04.

"Haven't seen her on the schedule much anymore," Axel murmured with a shit-eating grin on his face. "She used to come at least once a week…"

"Yeah, well, we've been busy," I said, sipping my wine.

"Harper is a catch," Francis said, sipping at his wine. "You two are so cute together."

"Hey, y'all!" A bright, feminine voice yanked at my attention, and I nearly broke my neck turning. It was Jessa. Lord almighty, it was finally fucking Jessa. "Sorry to keep you waiting. I went to the wrong restaurant!"

Her laughter was like a fresh breeze as she tugged off some black gloves that accented her dress. Even though it was the same one she'd worn the office today, a deep slate blue piece with black buttons down the front, the new accessories made the look entirely different. She wore a floppy black hat, and a boxy handbag hung from the crook of her elbow. All of the air in my lungs evaporated as she tugged a gray jacket off and sat down, looking and feeling like a totally different person than the woman I'd been lusting after since morning.

"How is that possible?" Francis asked. "There's only one Monaco Lounge."

"What can I say?" Jessa shrugged, setting her handbag on the table before she eased into the seat between Francis and me. "I'm a New

York newbie! Plus the front doors of the next place over are *right* under the Monaco Lounge sign."

"I like the hat, Jessa," Axel said. "How was the rest of your day?"

"Oh, it was great. Had a few too many bagels though. The buttons on this dress are liable to pop off any second, so take cover, y'all."

I ran my thumb along my bottom lip as she spoke, unable to focus on anything that wasn't Jessa. Her pink lips. Her winged eyeliner. Her easy smile and the tiniest hint of those freckles. Her gaze finally swung my way, and something flashed in her eyes.

Fear? Or maybe it was desire.

Whatever it was, I intended to get to the bottom of it. Along with a couple other things.

"I got you a glass of wine," I told her, gesturing to the Carménère waiting for her. I lifted my glass, encouraging her to do the same. "To excellent staff who can handle anything when the bosses are gone."

Okay, maybe I'd said that on purpose. That same fear flashed through her eyes again, and her throat bobbed. The four of us clinked glasses.

Jessa's worried gaze met mine as she sipped at her wine. Then she set it down, popping another bright smile on. "So, what's on the agenda tonight?"

"We are simply thanking you both for a job well done," Axel said, gesturing at Francis and Jessa. "We know how stressful things have been lately. We wanted to wine and dine you two. Make sure you don't slink away with all our secrets."

Jessa laughed. "The secrets I've learned so far haven't been *that* exciting."

Axel recoiled in mock horror. "Are you saying we're boring?"

"Well, no. But I really thought you billionaires might have some crazy sex dungeons or at least some very questionable art that the internet would love to pick apart."

Axel sent me a smug look. "You haven't shown her the sex dungeon?"

This was the last thing I wanted to talk about in front of Jessa. Any reference to sex reminded me that I wasn't having it with Jessa, and I desperately wanted that to change.

"Listen, all sex dungeons aside, Axel and I are really glad you two are on our team. So thanks." I lifted my glass again, something hot and urgent pulsing through my veins. The more alcohol I drank, the harder it was to keep it under wraps. Or maybe that was the goal?

"A surprise employee benefit night," Jessa said with a laugh. "I'm always down for that!"

A server came a moment later to take our orders. I watched Jessa as she ran her finger down the board menu, mouthing words to herself. The things I wanted to do to her...I made a fist with my hand and pressed it to my mouth, trying to focus on anything that wasn't Jessa or her spectacular style or the curve of her breasts in literally every outfit she wore. I'd been fantasizing for weeks about spreading those luscious thighs open with my knee, filling the space between her legs with my shoulders and then my head. I could only imagine how sweet she'd be down there; I'd make sure she was dripping wet before I did anything. I'd find her clit and pinch it so, so softly and just watch what happened on her face. A shiver ran up my spine.

Seeing Jessa dripping wet was my new life goal.

"Damian?" Axel's voice cut through the dense fog of my desire. I looked over at him, trying to keep my face as neutral as possible.

"What?"

"I asked if you saw that email from our attorney today."

"Oh, uh..." Fantasy images of my head buried between Jessa's legs flashed through my head again. I wasn't sure if I needed more or less wine at this point. Though I suspected keeping my mind off Jessa for the rest of the night was a lost cause, regardless of how much wine I had. "I missed it."

Axel caught me up to speed while I sank back into my thoughts. Thank God Axel was the gregarious one, because it gave me the chance to sit back and observe. I watched as Jessa fiddled with the clasp on her bracelet damn near the whole evening. The way she lifted her shoulders and cooed whenever Axel said something sweet about Cora. The way she'd glance over at me as if she was checking on me, searching out my gaze. A visual hand squeeze.

Dinner came and went, though I could barely focus on the food. The pulsing between my ears—between my legs, actually—was getting more raucous by the hour. Just as our plates were cleared, Cora showed up, which resulted in big hugs from both Axel *and* Jessa. The five of us chatted amicably for a bit, before Francis excused himself to go "find the gays" as he put it.

And then there were four. Wine arrived for Cora, and the women were instantly engaged in their own conversation. Axel smirked over at me, leaning back in his chair.

"Everything okay? You've barely said ten words tonight."

I shrugged. "I've got nothing to say."

"I don't believe that."

No, it wasn't the entire truth. I had plenty to say, but none of it was appropriate for dinner conversation. And I wasn't entirely sure it wouldn't scare Jessa off. Sure, she'd had high school fantasies about me. But that meant nothing about her fantasies *now* or whether I was included in them.

I had a suspicion that her interaction with Harper told me everything I needed to know.

While Jessa and Cora chatted, Axel quietly ordered dessert for Cora, who had been at a different dinner meet-up elsewhere in Midtown. I tacked one on for Jessa, too. When the crème brûlée arrived, Cora pressed a hand to her heart, looking over at Axel like he was the most perfect man in the world. The smile on his face said it all. These two were so deeply in love I was surprised they could still function.

Jessa's mouth turned into an O as her crème brûlée arrived next. She sent me a pointed look. "Is this for us?"

And here we were. Two couples, at least seemingly.

"It is."

She rested her chin in her hand and batted her eyelashes at me. "Do I look like a lady who needs dessert?"

"Nobody said anything about needing it." I leaned closer to her, wetting my bottom lip as I caught a whiff of her sweet perfume. "The question is...do you *want* it?"

Her eyes fluttered shut. "Hmmm. Always."

She made it too easy to travel down the path of temptation. Sitting with her here at this table, tucked into the back of the restaurant, shielded from the clamor and commotion of the world, felt like a full-fledged fantasy. I relished the thought of what *this* could feel like—having Jessa at my side, seamlessly melded into my world, my inner circle. Only Jessa could ever be the woman who looked at me with hearts in her eyes when I ordered crème brûlée, the woman who made ordering dinner hard because I couldn't stop imagining pinching her clit.

Fuck. Jessa had me crazy already. And we'd only hugged once.

She cracked the caramel crust with a spoon. "Come on. You have to take at least one bite."

"Okay." I reached for the second spoon, letting her scoop out her portion before I dove in.

Her appreciative moan came a moment later. "Oh my god."

"Good, huh?" I couldn't fight the grin as I took my own taste. I loved trying new foods with her, the way she was so adventurous and noisy about it. If we did ever end up together, I'd insist that we spend at least two months of each year traveling to new places, trying new foods. I had a suspicion Jessa would like that idea, too. Excitement pulsed through me, and I tucked the thought away for later.

The four of us finished up our desserts, trading comments and feedback as we slowly savored the perfect caramel and custard. It was almost ten by the time we'd drained the last bottle of wine and were ready for the check. Axel took care of that part while Jessa set her napkin aside and stood.

"I better get going," she said, slipping on a gray jacket. "It's so late, and I've gotta call a cab."

"No, you don't." I waved away her words. "I'll take you." I texted Legs, letting him know we were on our way out.

"You really don't have to," she said. "I live, like, a thousand miles away from here."

"It's just Brooklyn. And it doesn't matter. I have a car and a driver, and you don't need to take a taxi."

I caught the secret look Axel and Cora shared as I pushed my chair in. Cora was perched on Axel's lap as he finished up with the check. "Good night, guys," I told them. "Excellent dinner as usual."

"Goodnight." Cora waved her fingers at us, the grin on her face all too knowing.

"Are you coming back to the penthouse tonight?" Axel asked with a wink.

"Of course," I said, thankful Jessa had already started for the door. "Don't be a fucking weirdo. I'm just giving her a ride."

Axel gave me an exaggerated wink, and I flipped him off before following Jessa out of the restaurant. Outside, the November night air was cold enough to cause Jessa to cross her arms over her chest. I fought the urge to wrap my arm around her and suggest we go turn on the fireplace at my penthouse, maybe turn on a crappy movie and test out the faux bearskin rug a time or two. That wasn't what a man trying to stay on the distant and unattached side of the line would do. Hell, I wouldn't have even suggested that with Harper. But here with Jessa, the idea was practically all I could hear.

My car pulled up a moment later, and I paused, wondering if I'd gather the courage to send it away—at least to get me another half hour with Jessa.

"Is this Legs again?" she asked.

"Yes," I admitted with a laugh. My conviction wavered, and I pulled open the back door for her. No Bearskin & Chill tonight. And probably not ever. We'd shared crème brûlée—that was enough for my scarred little heart.

"Do I get the story of his name this time or do I have to log a few more rides for that privilege?"

"You need to complete a minimum of ten rides before you'll receive that story," I teased, watching as she stepped up into the back seat of the SUV. The flex of her calves snagged my attention as she scooted across the leather so I could join her. Once we were safely enclosed in the vehicle, my internal clock began ticking.

We had roughly twenty minutes before we hit Jessa's apartment. Twenty minutes to figure out if she felt the same as me, dissolve her walls, kiss her fucking face off, and fuck like rabbits.

Totally doable.

Because that's all it had to be: a drunk one-off. At least that's what made sense to my drunk brain. If I couldn't agree to anything sustained or deep with Jessa, then why couldn't we just fuck once? It made so much sense here in the darkness of the car, as the lights of Manhattan flashed past our windows.

"Thanks for the ride again, Legs," she said, leaning toward the front seat. I caught the curve of her hip in the golden city light streaming in through the window. I wet my bottom lip, fingers curling from the urge to palm that curve for myself.

"Anytime, Jessa. You're one of my new favorites to drive around."

"Oh yeah?" she asked in that good-natured, sociable way of hers. "And why's that?"

"Well, you're just a sweetheart," Legs said, his Brooklyn accent almost garish in the quiet car.

"Oh no, *you're* the sweetheart, Legs," Jessa gushed. "Now tell me, who's your *least* favorite to drive around? Don't tell me it's Damian, either, because that's a given."

I laughed despite the dig. "I'm not even mad, because you're probably right, Jessa."

She reached back and swatted my knee. I caught the smile on her lips.

"Nah, I can't say that," Legs said.

"Okay fine, don't tell us the worst ever, but just give me *one* person you didn't like driving around. Come on, I need the gossip to stay alive. I'm like a gossip vampire."

Legs laughed, scrubbing at his chin as he thought. "All right. I got one. That Harper lady."

His words landed like a blow, though he couldn't have known how timely his comment was. I clenched my teeth as Jessa turned to me, nodding.

"I had an experience with Harper today for the first time," Jessa told Legs. "She made it very clear that I was to only call her *Ms. Bennett.*"

"Yeah, she pulled that same shit with me too," Legs said with a laugh.

"She's not always like that," I said, though I wasn't sure why I was defending her. Maybe to preserve their good opinions of *me.*

"No judgement, Damian," Jessa said, lifting her palms. "You do you."

The mention of Harper opened a necessary doorway. The question burned on my tongue for at least thirty seconds before I found the courage to speak. I looked over at Jessa, who stared quietly out the window.

"Hey." I leaned toward her in the backseat, keeping my voice low. She turned to me, and in the darkness, I could tell we were much closer than we otherwise would be in daylight, where the stark clarity of our better judgement would add a few extra inches for good measure. Her knee brushed mine as she leaned back against the seat. "I gotta ask you something."

"What is it?" Even in the dimness of the back seat, I could see the vibrancy in her eyes. My entire body buzzed at our nearness. I inched my hand closer to see what I might find.

"Be honest," I said.

"Okay..."

I cleared my throat, looking to the heavens for some form of support before I launched into this. I wasn't just going after something I wanted. I was forever adding a new layer to our relationship history. A new layer that could potentially not end well, given our work context. But to hell with it. I was too drunk to care right now.

"Did you lie to Harper today?" I blurted. "About my meeting with her."

"Oh God." Jessa pressed her hands to her face. "I've been waiting for you to bring this up."

"You knew I would?"

"I figured she would reach out to you and tell you." She started playing with the clasp of her bracelet again. "I'm so dumb. I'm sorry. I-I-I just...I don't know, I got flustered. I thought I was helping cover for you, and then I realized I'd said the wrong thing, but I just wanted to run with it..."

"You asked her what the nature of her business was." I couldn't keep the smile off my face as I said it. That was a power move, plain and simple.

"Well, I didn't know who she was." Jessa crossed her arms and looked out the window.

I chuckled, leaning closer again. "You knew who she was. Every single person in my contacts comes with a summary."

The truth sizzled between us. Besides, Jessa had walked in on Harper giving me a fucking blow job in the middle of the afternoon. How could she not remember that?

"I'm sorry, Damian," Jessa went on, uncrossing her arms to fiddle with her clasp again. "Should I call her and apologize or something? I knew she wasn't happy when she left, but I—"

"No." I grabbed her wrist when she lifted it to fiddle some more. I pressed my fingers against her skin, easily finding her pulse. She inhaled sharply, and I caught the confusion in her eyes in the flashes of city lights.

"You don't need to apologize." I squeezed her wrist, bringing it down between our legs. The thrum of her pulse calmed me and told me she was just as intrigued and possibly aroused as I was. "It was an innocent mistake, right?"

"Yeah." She nodded emphatically. I swiped my thumb back and forth over her wrist, desperate for more, but unsure how to get it. "It was a mistake. I thought I was protecting your company, I don't know. You guys fight so hard to uphold the integrity of what you do, I just wanted to do the same. And it didn't seem like a good idea to tell her you'd just forgotten about your...appointment."

Did this even make sense anymore? I couldn't tell. Even through my drunk haze, I could tell that Jessa was genuinely apologetic for what had happened. Though she'd misread entirely what I was looking for here.

"I'll make sure Harper goes on the VIP list," Jessa barreled on. "Sorry, *Ms. Bennett*." She couldn't hide the sarcastic lilt from her voice that time. "I mean, this is my learning curve, right? Now I know how important she is."

Fuck. She was misreading this altogether. The car slowed to a stop.

Jessa gasped. "Oh, this is me."

Disappointment crashed through me. I released her wrist, feeling a lot like the main character in some chaste Victorian drama. Here I was, limited to touching wrists, when the passion pumping through me demanded nothing less than Jessa's legs in the air and my absolute suffocation between her thighs.

"Sleep tight, Jessa," I said, because there was nothing else to say. I was dying to take it further, but there was still that part of me that knew better.

I shouldn't go there with Jessa. So I wouldn't.

No matter what.

CHAPTER THIRTEEN

JESSA

On Friday, Damian wasn't in the office.

I'd gotten a curt message from him around nine that simply said "Working from home today." Which meant he was thirty stories above me, probably in his pajamas, eating leftover bagels sent from Heaven. I was half-tempted to ask if I could join him, but after what had happened the night before on the drive home, I also knew that I needed some more time.

Like the length of the weekend, to be precise. That was the exact amount of time needed (seventy-two hours) to fully recover from his warm, passionate wrist grab. Only after all those days apart would I be able to think of things other than his lips covering various areas of my body come Monday morning.

I'd even used his comforting hug in his office as masturbation material over the weekend. My desperation knew no limits.

But on Monday, I got the same message from Damian. "Working from home today."

This seemed odd, but who was I to say anything? The man had earned the right to work nude from his bed if he wanted to.

I just very much wanted to join him, even though I was positive *Ms. Bennett* would not approve.

After what I'd learned from Legs and my encounter with Damian in the car, it was decided. He had something with Harper, and I needed to lay my childish fantasies to rest. Even though his surprise crème brûlée had made me think we might be getting married, that was not the case. High school Jessa needed to lie down and go to sleep. Forever.

I spent most of Monday switching between productive work mode and being mortified for being so asinine. Axel strolled up to my desk around four thirty, holding a sealed envelope in his hand.

"Hey, Jessa. Could you do me a favor?"

"Of course, Axel."

"Take this up to the penthouse?"

"Sure." I took the hefty envelope from him. "But why can't you go?"

He sniffed, looking away. "Trace is up there. And this needs to go to Damian."

I nodded slowly, beginning to understand just how serious the rift had gotten between the brothers. Uneasiness spread through me. I'd only ever known the Fairchild brothers to be solid. This new development felt unnatural and bizarre, as if science had suddenly discovered that gravity wasn't real.

"Of course. I'm almost done for the day, so I'll just wrap up here and then take this up before I leave, if that's all right."

"Sure. And here, you'll need this in the elevator." He tossed me a key card with a wink. "Just get it back to me another time, okay?"

I clutched the key card in my hand, nodding. "Thanks, Axel. I appreciate it."

"And make sure Damian's okay while you're up there. He's been going through something the past couple of days. I think you'll be able to snap him out of it."

Well, if that wasn't equal parts cryptic and intriguing, I didn't know what it was. I stuffed the card into one of the pockets I'd sewn into the folds of my dress and hurried to finish up at my desk. Now that I had the green light to visit Damian, I didn't want to delay another minute. We hadn't seen each other in almost four full days, which was too much.

All I wanted to know was if Damian felt as desperate and insane as I did.

Fifteen minutes later, I was packed up and heading for the penthouse elevator like I owned the place. Had *Ms. Bennett* ever used this elevator? I sure as cluck hoped not. I swiped the card just like I'd seen Damian do, then pressed the big P button. The elevator soared upward, smooth and silent, coming to a gentle rest thirty stories above. The doors slid open, a pair of male voices reaching me.

Anxiety snaked through me, and I clutched the envelope to my chest. Even though Axel had asked me to do this, it didn't mean Damian was expecting me. I identified the rumble of Trace's voice. Luggage wheels clicked over the tile floor. I left my work bags near the elevator door and headed deeper into the penthouse, following the sounds of conversation. A moment later, I found Trace and Damian standing at opposite ends of the living room.

Trace had two pieces of rolling luggage at his side. And Damian, in a sleeveless T-shirt and shorts, looked like he was carrying the weight of the world.

Damian's gaze swung my way, and something inside him crumpled. I could see it. He squeezed his eyes shut, dragging his hands down the front of his face and turned away from me. Trace looked over, the smile he sent my way only a flicker on his face.

"Hey, Jessa."

"Trace, it's good to see you again." I stepped forward, hiding the envelope behind my back. "Are you going somewhere?"

"Taking some time away," he said simply. Then he nodded toward the front door. "I better leave, or I'll miss my flight."

"Can I ask where you're going?"

"Bali," he said. "I'll see you guys later."

Trace headed for the front door, the wheels of his luggage click-clacking over the floor. Damian rolled his head in a slow circle.

"Hey, Damian. Long time no see." I glided his way, something deep inside me feeling better now that he was so close, like some final piece of a puzzle had clicked into place. "Everything okay?"

He shook his head, avoiding my gaze. "I don't know."

I set the envelope down, assessing his posture. His shoulders looked bunched, like he'd been in full stress mode since our dinner last Thursday night.

"You're so tense," I murmured, reaching for him. As soon as my hand made contact with the heat seeping through his shirt, I realized my mistake. But despite my pounding heart and the moisture in my panties, I couldn't stop it. I ran my hand over his upper back. "Do you want a massage?"

Damian turned to me head-on, the full brunt of his masculinity washing over me. Normally he was in tailored suits and dress shirts, but now he was every inch the brawny farm boy I'd fallen in love with during high school. His biceps bulged, freed from the constraints of his dress shirts. The scent of his cologne hit me harder today, or maybe it was just the intensity of his gaze. Something was different today. *Way* different.

"Do you really think that's a good idea?" He stepped closer to me, something in his tone sounding dangerous. Feral. He seemed to loom over me, gobbling me up with his gaze, his energy, his intentions. But I had to be imagining it. Sure, we'd crossed some kind of line that night in his laundry room. But it hadn't gone further, because he had *Ms. Bennett* waiting for him.

"I think it would be a great idea for you," I said, nervousness pushing me to babble. "You look really tense, so loosening up those shoulders would probably contribute to your overall well-being. Besides, you missed two days at the office, so something must be wrong." I brushed a stray hair from my face as I went on. "Speaking of which, why weren't you in Friday or today? I was worried about you."

"Because I have to keep myself away from you, Jessa," he said, reaching for my hand. He picked it up gently, turning it palm-up. "The more I'm around you, the harder it is to convince myself not to proposition you. And I really don't want to proposition someone on my payroll. Even though I've wanted to proposition you since I was seventeen."

I blinked a few times, letting the meaning of his words sink into me. And then again. And then again.

He traced lazy lines across my palm, watching me with the most deliciously destabilizing intensity.

"Ummmm," I started, as though I had anything to follow up with.

"Tell me I shouldn't," he said, stepping even closer. My fingers brushed his chest, and he pushed his thumb across my palm. "Tell me I shouldn't, and I won't."

"I can't tell you that," I whispered, my voice nearly sticking to my throat. "But you said it yourself: you can't proposition someone on your payroll." I blinked rapidly, trying to see or think or function at all with him this close to me. It didn't seem possible to continue living in a world where Damian's heat wasn't wrapped around me, where his skin wasn't touching mine. "I mean, that's what you want, right?"

"Past tense. Wanted," he growled, jerking me closer to him. His hands slid over the top of my ass, crushing me against him.

My eyes fluttered shut as the hard expanse of his chest found my breasts. Oh dear lord. It felt better than I'd ever imagined to be pressed up against him.

"I mean, even if we both wanted to fuck each other senseless, we can't. Right?" Where I found the breath to speak, I didn't know.

He dipped down, his breath hitting my earlobe. A million pinpricks of pleasure skated under my skin, and I almost died perfectly happy in that moment.

"You tell me," he breathed against my ear.

"Right," I whispered, forgetting entirely why any of this was a bad idea. Harper blinked through the back of my mind suddenly, reminding me. Damian was taken. And I had no intention of mucking around inside someone else's mess. "So I should go," I said, my voice barely working.

"Where are you going?" Damian licked the tip of my earlobe, and I collapsed against him.

"It's uh...I...um..." Was that his *penis* I felt pressed against my hip? My heart raced so quickly I thought I might pass out. This was every fantasy come true and then some.

He still wasn't mine. Nor would he be, when the haze cleared.

"Yes?" Damian nuzzled the side of my face, and I tipped my head so he could do it again, more freely, possibly for eternity.

"The uh...what do you call it? The...class..." My eyes drifted shut as his stubble scraped against my cheek. I squeezed my legs together. "The class that I'm in or whatever."

"Oh, your fashion course?"

"Mm-hmm."

Damian rummaged around in the folds of my dress, lifting up the front portion of it. Then he wrapped his fist in it and tugged, pinning me against him.

My panties were soaked.

"Are you off the clock?" His voice was sex and grit.

I nodded helplessly.

"Then there's no employer-employee issue in the way. Just give me half an hour. I will personally inspect this dress from head to toe for your class, then I'll deliver you wherever you need to go." He cinched his fist even tighter in the fabric of my dress. "Now can I fucking kiss you?"

All the air whooshed out of me in one breath, and I nodded, succumbing to my fate. I was powerless to stop whatever was happening. I didn't want it to stop, judging from the river flowing between my legs. Maybe I could just have this one taste. This one try. I'd deal with whatever came after, including the Harper mess.

"Please," I croaked.

Damian descended on me, capturing my lips in a kiss that froze time. Everything else around us ceased to exist, the world itself shuddering to a stop as I finally found out just how soft and perfect his plump lips were. I moaned, my knees feeling wobbly. He tightened his hold on my dress, diving in for another kiss, his tongue pressing at my lips.

I opened my mouth to receive him, and our tongues tangled together. Damian loosened his fist and pushed his hand up over the curve of my hip. Up the front of my dress, over the swell of my breasts. He left a permanent trail of goosebumps wherever he touched me, his hand stopping below the heavy curve of my left breast. My nipples turned into hard points beneath his potent touch.

Damian was hungry. And he knew what he wanted. He squeezed my breast hard enough to make me whimper, and then his hand snaked up along my chest until it was planted at the base of my neck. He rooted me there, like he controlled me, his fingertips digging into the softness of my neck. When he broke the kiss, he looked drugged. Gone. Completely fucking lost in the passion.

Just how I imagined I must look.

"You're a good kisser," he said, a grin curling at his lips.

"You...don't even know...how good you are." Talking was still hard. We needed to keep kissing instead.

He hooked his arm around my back, more parts of our body touching, which meant more of my skin erupting into goosebumps. Being locked in his embrace felt so good, so divine, that I couldn't even comprehend it. My brain shorted out trying to make sense of it all.

"We wasted a long time," he said, dipping down for another kiss. But this time, it was soft. A feathery peck. One that made me push up onto my tiptoes looking for more.

"I always knew you'd kiss like a dream," I murmured. My body sighed with relief as he blessed me with another deep tongue kiss. His grip around the back of my neck tightened, and my core wound up like a coil.

"Come to my bedroom," he growled between kisses. His lips drifted from my mouth across my cheek, back to my earlobe. The hand he'd planted at the base of my neck drifted around to the front of my chest, down slowly over my cleavage. His warm touch felt like healing. A hot stone with medicinal properties. Everything inside me throbbed, wanting more of this touch. More of him.

But his request was a big one. I'd only ever had sex with two men in my life. Damian could easily be the third. But not if I was the other woman.

Clarity made tiny steps through me, dousing some of the embers of our makeout session. But only for a moment. Once Damian's fingertips pushed underneath the fabric of my dress and drifted toward the edge of my bra, all reason flew out the window again. The man was mere seconds away from cupping my breast, and there was nothing I wanted more in this life.

"You've never seen my bedroom," he went on, his tongue flicking out against my earlobe again. "The tour was incomplete."

His fingers plunged deeper, his pinky finger nearing my areola. My eyes drifted shut. If this was heaven, what would going all the way be?

I might actually die.

The front door swung open suddenly, a movement I barely noticed around Damian's square shoulders. I gasped, stepping away from him, the intrusion feeling a lot like a bucket of water dumped over our steamy affair.

Damian twisted to look toward the front door. Trace's voice boomed out a moment later.

"Don't mind me, just forgot a few things," he said, his footsteps scuffing across the tiled floor as he rolled his luggage back inside the house. I tore myself even further away from Damian and sat on the nearest armchair, covering my face with my hands.

What are you doing?

What have you done?

Damian didn't bother to respond to Trace, who hurried through the living room and disappeared into the depths of the house. Damian watched his brother go and cleared his throat, adjusting his gym shorts. That's when I noticed the thick ridge of his arousal. My mouth parted, and I took another glorious glimpse before I buried my face in my hands.

You're about to sleep with a man who is taken. Jessa Walton, what has New York done to you?

"Come on." Damian offered his hand, tipping his head toward the other end of the house. "Let's go."

"Damian, I can't." My voice came out trembling and weak, no doubt a combination of the nearly fatal arousal pumping through my veins, combined with the stress of a one-night stand with my taken boss. "Are you kidding me? You're with someone."

"Jessa—" he started, his face crumpling.

"I don't care how perfect, or sculpted, or surprisingly possessive you are," I said, waving my hand at the complete package that he was. "I don't care that it would be most definitely the best sex of my life. Not like there's much to compare it to, trust me. So let's just say you win by default and save ourselves the trouble of turning me into the other woman."

His shoulders sank. "It's not like that."

"That's what all womanizers say," I snapped.

His gaze darkened, and he crossed his arms. "I'm not womanizing. But you and I both know there's something here. Why not see where it goes?"

I pressed a finger to the center of my forehead, feeling like I could burst at any second. The problem with seeing where it went was that our end points were different. He wanted it to lead to the bedroom. I wanted it to lead to forever. And given how long I'd known this man, how strongly I'd felt about him throughout my life, there was no chance I wouldn't fall in love.

Actually, scratch that. I already was in love. *Hell.*

The realization spread through me like piss in a cold stream.

I loved Damian Fairchild, and messing around with him would only break me in the long run.

"I don't have the energy to see where it goes," I finally said, daring to meet his gaze. "Don't get me wrong. I want to see where it goes. But I also don't want to see where it goes."

He hefted with a humorless laugh. "That's not confusing at all."

"You have to understand," I said, making my voice lower as Trace emerged from the far hallway. He muttered something to himself and then disappeared into the house again. "You have a situation here with Harper. And I am allergic to situations."

His mouth formed a thin line and he watched me heavily. I could see the wheels turning. The haze of arousal receding. The calculating clarity returning to his green eyes.

"Yeah. You're right." His voice sounded flat, and he nodded, looking past my shoulder.

Silence fell between us. I swallowed hard, realizing that I needed to either leave or go back on my word and kiss this man until the sun came up.

"I'm gonna go," I said, more as a test. I took a few steps away, watching Damian carefully. Checking to see if he'd fling himself at me again. Or maybe he'd sink his fingers into my neck again.

Goosebumps flared, but nothing happened. He stood watching me with his hands on his hips, standing a defiant distance away.

"Your envelope is over there," I said, pointing to it. Then I pointed to myself. "My dress and I are leaving."

A grin ghosted his lips. "Bye, Jessa."

I waved. And then I bolted.

I needed to be smart. Being smart meant keeping myself out of sticky situations with active girlfriends. Being smart meant keeping my head down, doing my job, and getting my fashion certificate.

That's what I'd come here to do.

Nothing good could come from falling in love with—or messing around with—a man who was taken. Since I'd already failed on one of those fronts, I needed to hold the line on the other one.

No matter how hard it would be to say no to those perfect, kissable lips.

CHAPTER FOURTEEN

DAMIAN

Working from home today.

I considered making that my new auto-responder, so I didn't have to send the same message every morning to Jessa. Because as Tuesday came, and then Wednesday, I realized I was in a very uncomfortable predicament.

I needed to keep myself away from Jessa as a precautionary measure, while every particle of my body craved her presence.

But I wouldn't give in again. She'd found me in a moment of weakness. Her tenderness had split me in two, and I'd taken the bait. But not again.

Aside from the text I'd sent her Tuesday morning that simply said "I'm sorry," I only reached out for work matters. And I truly was sorry. I was sorry it hadn't gone further. I was sorry that I had every intention of kissing her again the next possible chance I had.

Mostly I was sorry that I wasn't really sorry at all.

But it was for the best. *For the best. For the best.*

I had Harper on stand-by, and that arrangement made way more sense. Harper was the safe choice. The non-threatening one. Harper was the woman I could say no to, the woman I didn't crave, the woman who wouldn't upend my safety or stability.

It was better that Jessa assumed Harper and I were more serious than we were. She didn't need to know I hadn't seen and had barely spoken to Harper since the day Jessa came in for her interview.

I'd felt like a spinning top for the last two weeks. Partly, it was how my personal life continued to crumble, with the secret brother and subsequent split with Trace. Jessa had a way of restoring calm amid an active hurricane. And realizing that I had an extra shoulder to lean on—someone who wasn't Trace or Axel—was perhaps the most disorienting of all.

My circle had accidentally grown bigger. And that scared the shit out of me.

"Are you in here, you hermit fucking recluse?" Axel's voice boomed through the penthouse, which he had returned to now that Trace was in Bali. I lifted my hand in a wave from the dining room table, which I used as one of my work setups during the day. I loved working in my bedroom, but it was more geared toward intense late-night work-a-thons. Out here, bathed in daylight and cityscapes, I felt more like I was in my office.

The only thing missing was Jessa.

"What can I do for you?" I asked. I hadn't bothered to put a shirt on yet, and it was three p.m. That was one of the benefits of working from up here. I popped into the gym for reps on the bench press more than normal. Every time I caught myself fantasizing about the creamy smoothness of Jessa's breasts, I headed into the gym. I'd be ready for a bodybuilding competition in a week.

"This work arrangement isn't going to last forever, is it?" Axel said, a whine to his voice. He propped his hands on his hips and assessed the situation at the dining room table. "You're really inter-rupting my flow when I have to take the fucking elevator all the way up here just to run something by you."

"You know there are these things called telephones," I murmured. "You could try using one of those."

Axel pulled a face at me. "This is why we built out an entire office suite, my dude. So we could take ten steps instead of one hundred and ten."

"I'm just helping you get your steps in for the day," I offered, clicking through screens on my laptop. "Keeping you fit and active."

"Thank you for your concern," Axel said, patting his waist through his button-up. "Your insistence on working from home is really going to take my fitness routine to the next level."

I ignored his sarcasm and focused on my inbox. "So did you have something real to run by me, or did you just come up here to complain about how I'm up here?"

"Mostly the latter," Axel grumbled. He headed to the window, stuffing his hands into the pockets of his dress pants. "Actually, I think we need to call Dad."

His words landed like a hammer. We'd been putting this off. All of us, really. Trace had assured me that he wasn't going to talk to either of our parents until he was back from Bali. But that meant that Axel and I had some decisions to make. Some awkward conversations to have. Some possibly life-ruining words to spell out.

I heaved a sigh, abandoning my work as I leaned back in my chair. "You want to do it now?"

"I want to get it *over with*," Axel clarified. "So yeah, I think we should just do it now."

"What are we even going to say?"

"I don't fucking know. But if we just accept the idea that it's going to be messy and not fun, then I think it's nowhere but up from here," he said.

"I think there's considerable room to go down from here," I pointed out.

"You're probably right," Axel conceded, "but let's just do it." He clapped his hands, then brought out his cellphone. "We ready?"

I smirked at the phone. "Are you sure we should do this over the phone?"

"What's the other option? Show up at our parents' house like a couple of merry messengers? With a singing telegram about our father's secret family? No, Damian. We're calling."

It was hard to argue with Axel. Most times it was just easier to let him have his way. I nodded and readied myself for whatever the other side of this conversation had in store for us.

Axel swiped through the phone and made the call on speakerphone. It started ringing a moment later. He sank into the chair next to me, and we both leaned closer, staring at the inert phone.

Our father answered a moment later. "H'lo?"

Axel glanced my way, doubts crowding his blue eyes. "Hey, Dad. It's me and Damian. You got a second?"

"'Course I do, sons. What's going on?" The phone rustled on his end, and I could imagine him reclining on his favorite brown couch. He'd had that thing for way too long, and he even insisted on moving it after we built him and Mom a brand-new house in the country. He'd rejected any number of offers to buy him a new recliner. He only wanted that ratty old thing.

"Hey dad," I said softly. "You hear that Trace went to Bali?"

"No, I didn't. Where on earth is *that*?"

"It's in Indonesia," I said. "Really close to the equator. Famous for the beaches and coral reefs and stuff."

"What'd he go there for? Other than probably to catch a bikini contest or two on the beach," Dad said with a gritty laugh.

"He needed some time to think," I said, knowing that Axel would rather not even mention Trace's name—or his plans—during this conversation. "Something pretty wild happened recently and we need to talk to you about it."

"Well, all right," Dad said in his slow drawl. "Let's see if you can shock me."

That's what he always wagered: *see if you can shock me.* Only when we told him we'd bought our first helicopter did he admit that he was surprised. Not even hearing that we'd met the president of the United States shocked him, since he'd claimed *Anyone could meet that old codger during a rally.*

This might finally be the thing to shock him.

"Someone named Ian Keller recently showed up at our office building, Dad." Axel glanced at me, his jaw flexing. "He says he's our half-brother."

The silence from the other end of the line stretched long and cavernous.

"You there?" I ventured.

"Yeah, I'm here," Dad said.

"You know who Ian Keller is?" Axel asked. "Though he goes by Ian Fairchild now."

"I do," Dad said.

Axel's face crumpled, reflecting what I felt in my own body. Part of me had been hoping that it could still turn out to be a scam, even with Trace's confirmation, the secret he'd held for over a decade, and the fact that Ian's background checks had been rock solid.

I'd still been foolish enough to hope for a miracle.

"Is what he says true, Dad?" Axel pinched at the bridge of his nose, grimacing. "He says you're his father."

A long, resigned sigh escaped our father, and then the phone rustled. "Let me take this damn thing off speakerphone."

Axel and I exchanged a look. Dad's soft breaths were all we heard for a minute, then the slamming of a screen door in the background.

"Ian's not lying," Dad said in a hushed voice. "I'm just sorry he came all the way to New York to drop it on ya like that."

"Dad." I hefted with a despairing laugh. "Were you ever planning on telling us?"

"There's never been a right time."

Axel pinched his eyes shut. "What do you know about Ian?"

"He's a firecracker," Dad said, sounding sad. "Book smart like Trace, but rougher around the edges. His mother wasn't doing too well during his school years. I tried to be there for him when I could, but...it was too hard, with the three of ya."

I swallowed a knot in my throat. "Does Mom know?"

Dad heaved another resigned sigh, and I knew the answer wasn't going to be pretty.

"Just tell us," Axel said, pressing his palms together, resting his chin on his fingertips, as if praying for the best.

But didn't he know better by now? The best was relative. There was only bad and then less bad.

"She don't know," Dad hissed. "And I'd like it to stay that way."

Axel let out a low whistle. "You've gotta be fucking kidding me."

"Axel, there's no good in telling her about it now," he said.

"I think there's plenty good in telling her," I added, sharing a concerned look with Axel. "This cat is out of the bag. There's a good chance it will hit the papers eventually. That's not how she should find out. Trace knew and kept your secret, and if he'd just told us... How could you ask him to do that?"

Dad sighed again. When he spoke, his voice cracked with emotion. "I just wanted to keep everything smooth and stable for y'all. No disruptions."

"Well, you created a pretty big disruption anyway," Axel added.

"We could have handled it," I told him.

"Could you? Those early years with all three of ya, they were tough. I'm not lying. You two came into our lives, and I thank God every day that you did, but we were breaking our backs to make ends meet. And the transition was rough for everyone, even without that. Don't you remember?"

I did remember. It took me years until I could let my guard down fully with the Fairchilds. Our year bouncing between foster homes produced double the amount of damage and distress. Deb and Gary and Trace had done everything right with us—a safe home, warm meals, lots of love and understanding—but it still took Axel and I a while to soften up.

And then once we were settled with Deb and Gary, financial pressures mounted. Axel and I shoveled shit for spare change. Trace did the same until he found a local business that needed bookkeeping help under the table, which gave him his start with finances. He was fourteen years old keeping the books for the Sip n' Suds, a car wash and ice cream shop in one. We'd all worked hard to make ends meet.

"I never intended to step out on your mom. But it happened, and I live with this guilt every day. I had a weak moment. We'd just taken you two in, and the stress was eatin' me alive. I wanted an escape."

I knew a thing or two about stress relief. But it was different, coming from my foster father turned adoptive dad. The Fairchilds were a beacon of stability in my life, the rock I'd leaned on after my biological parents had passed, leaving Axel, Kaylee, Jordan, and me unmoored and lost at sea.

And now even that was crumbling.

"You gotta tell Mom," Axel said in a raw voice. "You tell her or I will."

"Axel," Dad started.

"He's right," I added. "You can't keep it from her. Not anymore. If Ian came all the way up here, what's to say he's not on his way to your house next?"

There was some commotion in the background. It sounded like Mom talking.

"Boys, I gotta go," Dad said suddenly. "We'll talk later."

"Did we shock ya?" Axel asked.

"I'd say you did."

The line went dead. Axel and I shared a long, heavy look.

"Well, let's mark that off the to-do list," I finally said, once the silence had grown too suffocating.

"Clearly we were the ones who were raised right, back when we were Hayneses," Axel muttered, looking down at his hands. "Trace kept that secret for how many fucking years? Just like Gary."

"Don't start," I said.

"I'm starting," Axel warned.

"You would have said worse shit about Cora six months ago, and look at how things changed once you get the full story," I reminded him. "Do. Not. Start."

Axel's frown turned into a scowl. "Don't rope Cora into this."

"I'm just keeping perspective," I said. "You're so quick to throw Trace under the bus. He's all but moved out of the penthouse because of you. He's halfway across the world because you don't want to run the risk of running into him. But he lives and dies for us, Axel. Just like Dad does. Regardless of whatever you think about the fucking mess they made."

It was complicated. And yes, I was confused and upset. But I wanted a shot at my only remaining family coming back together some day.

"Dad needs to do the right thing," Axel said, pushing to his feet. "Then we can figure out the rest."

"Agreed." I leaned back in my chair, the air whooshing out of me. The conversation had left a sick knot in my gut, one that didn't seem close to loosening anytime soon. Axel squeezed my shoulder before he headed toward the kitchen, in the direction of the private elevator that led directly to our office suite.

"You didn't answer me before," Axel called out as he meandered through the kitchen. "You plan on coming back to the office anytime soon, or do I need to install a vacuum tube from my office to this dining room?"

"The tube would probably work best for now," I said wryly.

"Everything's still good with Jessa, right?" He paused, turning to look back at me. He loved playing matchmaker with us, which I resented as much as I appreciated. And I knew that our pseudo double date at the Monaco Lounge last week had satisfied him on some haughty, brotherly level.

"Just fine," I said, probably too clipped. I didn't want him to know how fine things had gotten on Monday afternoon. Or how fine they would become the second I was alone with her again.

"You two should come to this Friendsgiving party with me and Cora next week," he said.

I shook my head. "Not happening."

"But you said things were fine."

"Fine meaning...stable." Except that was a lie. The push and pull between Jessa and me was the most unstable thing I'd ever experienced, simply because I could not convince my heart and my cock to stop reacting to that woman.

He tapped his knuckles against the countertop as he wound his way through the kitchen. "Just marry her already, will ya?"

I rolled my eyes, though he couldn't see me. "Says the man who swore off marriage entirely until two months ago."

"You just gotta find the right one," Axel said, his voice growing fainter. "And when you find the right one, everything changes."

I waited until I heard the ding of the elevator and the whoosh of the door before I allowed myself to relax. I didn't need Axel's love or romance advice. Not even a little bit. The love and romance life was fine for him, but I knew better than to jump into those waters. I could only ever dip my toe.

Because what happened if I went all the way with her, to girlfriend status and beyond? Anxiety started a slow pulse beneath my skin, bad outcomes popping up in my mind like mosquitoes on a humid night. I didn't trust the world. I didn't trust any of it. If I fell into marital bliss like Axel wanted, it would only set the stage for something devastating to follow. I'd seen this play out in every phase of my life so far. From Kaylee's death to the SEC investigation and now my Dad's decades-old secrets.

Diving into happiness paved the way for new pain. And I didn't have it in me to handle any more pain.

CHAPTER FIFTEEN

JESSA

Thanksgiving came and went. I spent the day holed up in my apartment, eating pumpkin pie I'd snagged on sale from a nearby bodega, while I worked on designs and watched Hallmark movies. It was never too early to start sappy Christmas movies, and now I had nobody to judge my choice of feel-good escapism where the brooding hero *always* chooses the bubbly beauty during that random weekend she's trapped back in her hometown.

Besides, I needed the palate cleanser. My current situation with Damian wasn't so feel-good. No, it was a mix between angst-ridden and desperate.

I wanted the man so badly I could disintegrate. But I refused to enter into anything that turned me into The Other Woman.

When regular office hours resumed, Damian worked from his penthouse for another mother-cluckin' *week*. Which meant it was now December and I hadn't seen this man since *last month*.

Not like I was supposed to care. I was getting paid. Doing my job. Focusing on my studies again. This was what I wanted, right?

No. I wanted Damian, almost no matter the cost. Even just having him sitting inside his office, twenty feet from me, seemed like a better alternative to not seeing him or being near him.

It made me feel insane. The truth of my revelation pounded through me harder every day that went by without him—I loved Damian Fairchild. I'd loved him for almost fifteen years.

And there wasn't a damn thing I could do about it.

Though he might want my body, he didn't want the whole package. And I didn't want to dole out pieces of myself like a sample tray of cheese cubes in the supermarket.

My days went by in a state of mild sulking. Damian's occasional check-in emails kept me mostly sane and reassured that he was alive, especially as we continued planning for the Programmer's Ball. Now that we had a venue nailed down, I'd gone to town on decoration planning—including crafting a new dress just for that night. And it would obviously match the room, because hell if I wouldn't be able to say once in my life *the carpet matches the dress.*

I might have been having a little bit too much fun plotting the particular details of this party Damian intended to throw. I also loved that it gave me an excuse to pester him, which I did freely, since it was the only way in I had.

By the next Monday, a full week after our *indiscretion* in his penthouse, I was about to unravel from how badly I wanted to repeat that make out session. I'd spent no fewer than eight total hours with my hands shoved down my panties, remembering the way he'd kissed me like he was starving for me.

I'd probably use that twenty minutes as masturbation fodder for years.

I believe this was what they called *#killingit.*

A late-twenties near-virgin getting off to the memory of the way her boss had fisted her dress. Insert eye roll here.

I spent the majority of the subway ride into work Monday morning tweaking a roommate wanted ad I'd convinced myself I needed to post. Sure, Damian paid me more than enough to afford the apartment on my own. *For now.* But what happened if things didn't work out with Fairchild Enterprises? What if I parted ways simply to finally, at long last, pursue fashion? I needed to have my ducks in a row, and right now, my ducks were halfway across Brooklyn and heading for Jersey.

I stared at my phone as I added commas and swapped out *sooo excited* for *eager*. I was determined not to find a serial killer. I'd give this roommate hunt a fighting chance. Every applicant would be highly vetted. Hell, I could even ask Damian to run hacker-style background checks on them. That was something he could do while he worked from home and kept his indignant distance from me.

I needed to be prepared for the day I couldn't afford rent again. And lord almighty, I just hoped that my future roommate would be somewhat normal.

I pressed Publish on my ad just as the subway reached my stop. I could hear the voices of Tara and Jeremy inside my head, asking me what the actual hell I thought I was doing, soliciting a stranger to live with me in New York City when I had a free place to live back home.

I'd done it once before, and it had led me to Nicole. Aside from abruptly moving to Peoria right before rent was due, she'd been fine. I had faith it could happen again. And maybe this time, the new roommate wouldn't run screaming to Illinois after a few months.

I hefted my work bags, hit the platform, and made my way to Fairchild Enterprises like I did five days a week. I smiled to myself as I basked in the early morning hullabaloo of Wall Street. So many suits, designer heels, immaculate hair styles. Today, I wore a form-fitting pencil skirt I wasn't too sure about. I hadn't designed it myself, but I'd found it on a discount rack and fallen in love. My ruffled blouse barely contained my breasts, and my bra strap kept slipping down. I looked good, but I felt wildly uncomfortable, and that was already breaking my cardinal rule of fashion.

Maybe that was the fashion hill I was going to die on. That or *only find dresses you can go to a buffet in.* Because I hated clothes that didn't allow for the expansion of one's gut after a meal.

My heels clicked over the shiny floor of the lobby in the Fairchild building. On the twentieth floor, I made my familiar winding route through the office suite to the back, where my desk and Damian's office sat.

Today, his office door was cracked.

I set my things down quietly, more hopeful than I wanted to admit that maybe he'd be joining me this week.

I took a few moments to listen for his voice or any rustling. Our area was totally quiet, except for the distant laughter of some of the receptionists down the hall. My hope started to deflate, and I began unpacking my things: today's lunch, my work tablet, my notebook, my design sketchbook.

I adjusted my bra strap no fewer than six times during the first half hour of my workday, keeping vigilant watch over Damian's office. At just after 9:30, soft footsteps shuffled down the carpeted hallway.

Damian strode into view, looking at some papers in his hand.

I froze, suddenly unsure. Did I pretend last Monday hadn't happened? Did we continue as normal, boss and employee? Or maybe I should lead with a joke about our make out session...

"Morning, Jessa." He jerked his chin in my direction, meeting my gaze for the briefest of moments. Then he slipped into his office, closing the door softly behind him.

My breath whooshed out of me. That had been normal. Casual. Completely fine.

I should have been okay with that.

But I wasn't.

I lasted ten minutes before I picked up the phone to call Damian with the first genuine question I could think of. It was about the event, so I needed his opinion.

"Damian," I whispered into the phone, though I wasn't sure why. Like if I spoke too loudly, it would force him back to working in the penthouse. "I need your input on something."

He paused. "What is it?"

"Colors."

"Aren't you the color expert?"

"Not when it comes to computers," I said. "Ten seconds. That's all I need."

The line went dead, and a moment later, his office door opened. He watched me suspiciously, like this might somehow turn out to be a prank. I swiveled in my chair to face him as he approached, giving him my sweetest smile. The difference in height put me at a very particular vantage point, which I tried not to notice as he stepped up.

But it was hopeless.

I'd spent most of the previous week imagining that thick ridge beneath his gym shorts and what I would have found if things had gone further last Monday. I might never be able to see Damian without thinking of that—the moment when I realized, without an inkling of doubt, that Damian wanted *me*, Jessa Walton, plus-size aspiring fashionista. A shiver raced up my spine, and I forced myself to refocus on the plot—I mean, task—at hand.

"I'm finalizing details for the Programmer's Ball," I said, gesturing toward my computer screen. "And I need to make sure I'm not making a programmer faux pas."

He narrowed his eyes. "What do you mean?"

"Well, you computer nerds have a world all your own, right? I wanted to do a white and Tiffany blue theme for the decorations"—I pointed out the images of the centerpiece designs I had selected from a *very* upper crust store—"but I wanted to make sure this shade of blue was okay. Like, maybe this blue means something in hacker world. Like how pink is for breast cancer? Or maybe it's the same shade as the 'blue screen of death' I've heard about." I watched him innocently, hoping he wouldn't see through my very flimsy façade.

He looked at the screen. "Actually, aqua has a really specific meaning in binary code."

I blinked. "It does?"

He nodded gravely. "It's related to the dark web."

My eyes widened, and I gasped, looking back at the screen. "Oh my god." And here I thought I was just inventing excuses to be at eye level with Damian's junk.

"You've gotta change it." He shook his head, turning back to his office. "Lives are at stake. Everything could crumble if you choose that blue."

I narrowed my eyes at his retreating figure. "Are you serious?"

I caught the flash of his shit-eating grin before he closed his door on me. "Deadly."

I bit back a smile as I swiveled back to my desk. Clearly that had not worked as planned. Though what was I hoping for? That he'd pin me to my desk and press those soft lips to mine again?

Actually, yes. That was exactly what I was hoping for.

The whiff of a normal interaction with him felt like the warmest blanket after a frigid winter stroll. I drew a deep breath, noting my rapid heartbeat, the goosebumps on my forearms, the overwhelming relief that pooled inside me.

I whiled away the rest of the morning, hanging onto that one thread of normalcy. Damian didn't emerge, and I could think of nothing else pressing enough to pester him about. When he opened his door before lunchtime, I popped to my feet, ready to somehow bump into him and coax something more from him. He was looking at papers in his hand again, and I used his moment of distraction to step in front of him. His hip brushed my backside and I turned abruptly.

"Oh, my goodness," I said, maybe a little too eagerly.

He stepped aside. "Sorry, I—"

"No, no. My fault. My big ol' behind just got in the way." What was I doing? I was ten seconds away from brushing my breasts across his arm, only to say *Oh, lordy, these tatas got loose again!* I was looking desperate.

Damian didn't respond; he only offered something resembling a pained grimace and headed down the hallway. My shoulders sank. I so badly wanted to replicate Monday evening, even as I knew that replicating Monday evening was the worst idea of my entire life.

I hated this conflicting vortex as much as I loved it. Which just started the whole dang cycle over again.

Lunch came and went with my boring deli sandwich and four ounces of cheese puffs. It was my attempt to balance extravagant meals out on the town with figure-friendly food choices. But once I'd eaten everything, I was left *waiting* again. For some glimpse of Damian. For any acknowledgement that what had happened in his penthouse was real. For a sign that maybe he hadn't already moved on and forgotten about his brief attraction to me.

It was driving me crazy. Pushing me to new heights—or maybe depths—of desperation. When he finally waltzed back down the hallway later that afternoon, far too many hours after lunch, I had to look away. The way my heart seized just from seeing him felt like a warning. I was already in too deep...and we hadn't even started.

"Jessa," he said, his bored rumble sending heat straight to my core, "these are for you."

He had a folder in his hand, which I took from him—and promptly dropped.

"Oh, mother cluck it," I muttered.

"It's fine," he said, bending to pick them up just as I leaned forward. Our heads bumped, and a giggle erupted out of me. I wasn't even *trying* to be awkward; it just came so easily to me.

"Sorry." I rubbed at my head. He quickly collected the papers, sizing me up before he handed them over.

"Can you come into my office for a second?" he asked.

My heart rate picked up. "What for?"

His jaw flexed. "Just want to chat."

Anxieties spiked as I nodded, following him into the office. He shut the door gently behind him, his gaze stuck to the floor.

"Is everything okay?" I nearly whispered, afraid of what might be on the other end of this conversation. Maybe he'd had second thoughts—possibly third and fourth thoughts—about what had gone down in his penthouse. Maybe he'd be forcing me to put in my two weeks' notice right here and now. Oh lord, was I facing termination because I'd run out of the penthouse? That didn't even seem possible—but given all the other surprise shit attacks in my life, I didn't feel confident.

He still hadn't let go of the doorknob, seeming lost in thought. Then his green gaze traveled up my body, finally resting on my eyes. My heart flung itself at my rib cage, over and over again, intent on escaping.

"I just want to clear the air." He straightened his back, shoving his hands into his pockets. "I made things weird, and I'm sorry."

Relief flooded me, and I almost collapsed. I pressed a hand to my forehead—*you're fine, he's apologizing, this is a pleasant surprise*—and then popped on a breezy grin. "Nothing to be sorry for." After all, he'd made my life just by revealing that he was attracted to me. That he actually *wanted* me. I felt like I could die happy now. Except I wanted so much more from him before that time came.

"I think I have too much on my plate these days," he said, his gaze back on the ground. "And maybe it's making me a little...blind."

"Blind?"

"I'm not seeing things clearly like I used to. And after talking to my dad last week, I realized that maybe the stress from everything going on is making me act...out of line."

I stepped closer. "How is your dad? Did you talk to him about Ian?"

Damian's green gaze met mine, and there was so much anguish there. "I did. And it's as bad as we thought, Jessa. He's had the secret family the whole fucking time and just never thought it was the right time to tell Mom."

Everything inside me crumpled. I took another step closer, reaching out to touch his arm. "I'm so sorry, Damian."

He looked at where I touched him, and I took my hand back.

"Sorry," I muttered. "I'll keep my hands to myself. But just know I'm hugging you in my head."

His jaw started flexing, a distinct glint returning to his eye. The same glint I'd seen in his penthouse. The air went tight between us. "That doesn't help things. Then I'll just imagine you touching me and I'm back in the same spot."

"What spot is that?"

"Talking myself off a ledge, trying to convince myself to keep my hands off you."

Goosebumps prickled across my forearms and thighs. "Well, if it helps, I'm fighting the same battle, Damian."

He walked closer to me, and everything inside me went taut, expectant. "Then remind me why we're even fighting it."

My voice came out a whisper because he'd stopped mere inches from me. Heat poured from him, mingling with the woodsy scent of his cologne.

"Because you're taken. And I'm not doing messy." I swallowed hard, reminding myself to stand my ground. "I've had my share of messy. That was one promise I made myself after I left Oakville."

He stepped closer again, which caused me to stumble backward. He caught me at the waist, his forearm sturdy against the softness there.

"Let me make one thing clear, Jessa." He wet his bottom lip, his heated gaze darting back and forth across my face. "There is no mess with me." Then he paused, his grin spreading wide and devilish. "Unless you count the mess you'll leave behind once I'm done putting my face between your legs."

My breath hitched and everything inside me went prickly and loud.

"I'm not with Harper," he said succinctly. "I know it looks like I am. But the truth is, she was a fling who didn't get the memo. She wants more; I don't. End of story. I've already told her she is no longer welcome in this office now that you've drawn the line. Does that help?"

I could barely even breathe from the impact of those words. I was both so horny I could dissolve and so in love with this man I wanted to cry. All I could do was nod.

"It's very evident that I can't control myself around you," he went on in a low growl, cinching me tighter against him. That thick ridge was back, pressed right up against my hip. "Look at us. All I wanted to do was apologize."

"I love your version of an apology," I forced out past dry lips, every inch of my body arching toward Damian for more, more, more. He dipped down, his lips finding the curve of my neck.

"I don't want to make things weird again," he murmured, his lips brushing against my neck like a feather. "But I can't stop myself."

"Please don't stop," I breathed, tilting my neck as his mouth drifted higher. I needed those kisses again as much I needed air. "Your mouth is the only thing I can think about anymore."

He chuckled softly against my jawline, then brushed his mouth against mine. "The only thing?"

I nodded, getting lost in his gaze. "I mean, I thought about it for fifteen years before this. But now I'm thinking about it a lot more."

"I could give you some other things to think about," he murmured, rocking his pelvis in a slow circle against me. The ridge of his cock was trapped between our bodies, and my head dropped back. This was pure bliss. How could I survive being within ten feet of this man without touching him?

"I'm open to thinking about whatever you'd like me to think about," I said, dissolving into laughter as he placed small kisses over my cheek.

He drew a deep breath, cinching me tighter yet again. He had me in an unshakeable embrace, and there was nowhere else I wanted to be. He could have squeezed me until I died and I'd still want more.

"Why don't you think about this?" His lips left soft kisses along my jawline, his tongue darting out to trace my bottom lip. "We make each and every high school fantasy come true, then we get to work on the adult ones."

I wilted in his arms, but his thick forearms supported me.

"I think that's a great idea," I forced out. "When are you going to kiss me again?"

He looked down at me with so much tenderness that I felt cartoon hearts shooting out of my eyes. He dipped down, capturing my lips in a kiss that froze time. He kissed me deeply, with so much passion I thought I'd drown. Over and over and over again.

By the time we broke for air, my panties were a mess. Maybe he'd been right. That was the only mess I'd have to worry about with him.

"We can have fun," Damian murmured, capturing my chin between his thumb and forefinger. "That's all I want."

The pull of his gaze tugged me back under again, and I was lost, swimming in the enchanting waters of his attention. "Yeah?"

"A good time. With *you*."

I nuzzled my face into the crook of his neck, relishing the warmth and woods I found there. "So what does that mean?"

"You know what it means." His fingertips dug into the flesh of my hips, and I was suddenly desperate to take my clothes off.

"Date nights, movie nights, fancy soirees…?" I smoothed my hand over his chest, loving the look of my maroon nails against the silky threads of his dress shirt. It was a sight I could get used to.

"Whatever feels good." He kissed my forehead. "No strings attached."

"Oh, so not like…wedding bells and babies and cheesy family photo albums." I tried to laugh it off, but inside, disappointment quivered.

Damian's smile looked sad. "I'm not made for any of that, Jessa."

I begged to differ, but how could I let him know that? In his arms, I was putty. If he wanted a good time, that's most certainly what he'd get.

But now that I knew what he expected, there was no way I could give him everything he wanted.

My heart was at stake, and I was far too in love with this man to ever go all the way with him. Not when he was looking for *right now*, but my eyes only saw *forever*.

CHAPTER SIXTEEN

JESSA

Saying no to Damian's cocktail bar invitation later that day seemed wrong. But it was Monday, and I had class that evening, dammit. Damian's lips would just have to wait.

My entire body buzzed as I finished out the workday. Now that we'd crossed the line and planned to stay on the other side, everything around me felt foreign and fresh. Every glance with Damian vibrated with intensity and depth. As I left for the day, I could feel his eyes on my backside until I rounded the corner at the end of the hallway.

This certainly made the workday more fun.

My phone vibrated with an incoming text moments later.

DAMIAN: So what about after class?

JESSA: Class goes until late. I don't even get home until 11pm!

DAMIAN: So you're saying you should come to the penthouse right after.

I mulled over my response as I drifted along the busy sidewalks on Wall Street and all the way down to my subway station. I couldn't lie—I *desperately* wanted to go to the penthouse afterward.

But doubts nagged at me, like small tugs on the corner of my dress. *Look here. Don't forget about this. Listen, this is important.*

Going to the penthouse afterward would lead to sex. I knew it. He knew it. That's what we wanted.

But I didn't want what came *after* that. I didn't want to become his next stand-by…the next Harper. The woman who wanted more from him and had missed the memo.

The anxieties that slithered through me acted as cold water on the fire he'd stoked in his office earlier that day. While fucking Damian Fairchild was one of my lifelong dreams, I was terrified to actually do it.

He'd ruin me. I didn't need to go any further to know it, because I was already halfway there.

JESSA: Let's plan for another night. Promise it'll be soon.

I needed to buy time to figure out my approach. Fooling around with Damian on the sidelines was all fun and games, but we needed to be smart. We needed to protect our hearts—well, mostly mine. It seemed like Damian didn't have to worry about protecting his. And I didn't want to become just another notch on his big-city bedpost.

So I added one more thing to my to-do list: *Figure out how to tell my boss and long-time crush that I don't want to have sex with him because I'm in love with him and sharing that with him without the promise of a relationship afterward will physically kill me.*

Easy peasy.

I went through the motions of my evening on autopilot: hop on the subway, emerge in the Garment District, grab a light dinner for later, trudge five blocks to class. I entered the noisy chatter of the classroom, a smile drifting onto my face. I was thankfully feeling not just caught up but *ahead* after having to miss a whole class the week Ian showed up.

I took my favorite spot, the second stool in the row of seven facing the center of the classroom. A large worktable stretched in front of us, just the right amount of space for us to cut fabric, take measurements, and sketch endlessly. Three of these tables faced Mr.

Mitchell's primetime spot at the center, so all students could get a good view of what he demonstrated to us during class. Behind him, over twenty dress forms lined the wall in a neat row, only a few odd ones leaning forward drunkenly.

"How is everyone today?" Mr. Mitchell's voice boomed over the commotion of unpacking and chitchat. I unpacked my bags as my classmates called out their responses: *Ready for patterns. Dressed to kill. Tired but fashionable.* Mr. Mitchell's face lit up as he heard each new response.

"Great. So we're all in a good mood and ready to turn in our quarterly portfolio."

His words landed like a wet towel to the face. I scrunched up my face, looking down at my notebook.

"As a reminder, these portfolios constitute a full quarter of your final grade," he went on.

I blinked rapidly, my brain growing noisy as I rummaged through my things. I didn't have my portfolio ready. In fact, the brown leather binder was at my apartment, half finished and fully forgotten. I'd known that it was due at some point this month. I just had...forgotten.

Panic seized me. Maybe Mr. Mitchell was wrong. I flipped through my planner, scouring my dates to see where I'd written the portfolio due date. But as my gaze washed over the month of December, I saw no quarterly project due date in there. I fumbled for the class schedule, desperate to find the mistake. It wasn't due today. I wasn't tanking my first big project. *I wasn't.*

"You can leave them here in the basket on my desk," Mr. Mitchell went on. *Shit shit shit.* I dug out the syllabus, scanning the dates printed there.

And there it was.

Today's date. *Quarterly portfolio due.*

Mother cluuuuuuuck.

The weight of my disappointment crushed me, stealing my breath and sending my head tipping toward the ceiling. How on earth had this happened? Of course, I knew immediately.

It was Damian.

It was Fairchild Enterprises.

It was my infatuation with the man who'd only very recently started to kiss me after I'd been wishing for said kisses for fifteen years.

It was because I'd allowed myself to get swept away.

My throat tightened, and I watched as everyone filed to the front of the classroom, dropping off their portfolios in a big metal basket at Mr. Mitchell's desk. I didn't know what to do. I didn't even know what I could say to him. I'd had the date in my possession, and I'd missed it. I wasn't just unprepared, I was woefully blind. And now my ineptitude was going to cost me my grade in the biggest, most important move of my life.

I hadn't saved all my money and left my family behind only to miss my first major project. What on earth was I doing? I fought tears as I thumbed through the pages of my planner, trying to distract myself with something. Anything. Once everyone had turned in their projects—except for me, of course—Mr. Mitchell got on with the day's lesson. I could barely concentrate for how loud my internal voice was screaming at me, berating me for this failure.

How much money are you going to waste on this shit? Spoiler alert—she fails at the end anyway.

My internal voice sounded just like my sister. I could hear the sarcasm inside me, as much as I could feel it sinking into my bones. Imaginary Tara knew best how to break me down.

This is a fucking joke and you know it. You had one main project to turn in and forgot about. What kind of fucking idiot does that?

This was a fool's mission, and my sister had known it before I did because she knew me best. I was just a starry-eyed fool. The idiot who had all the tools at her disposal and still forgot to write down the damn date.

You should have just stayed in Oakville.

I beat myself into the ground as class went on, barely able to focus and keep the tears at bay. It was the longest hour and a half of my life before we took a break. I spent the entire fifteen-minute break crying in the bathroom stall, choking back my sobs so nobody would hear me. After freshening up, I returned to the classroom, still dejected and upset but smiling, to withstand the final hour and a half of class.

I wasn't just stewing on my complete failure as a student and New York transplant. I was also figuring out what I was going to say to Mr. Mitchell after class. I needed to address this screwup. I might be a small-town idiot out of her element in the ocean of New York City, but I was going to turn in my project and get these points, mother cluck it.

By the time class ended, I no longer wanted to cry as much, so that was a plus. Students gathered their things around me and began heading for the door. Once I had my bags on my shoulders, I approached Mr. Mitchell's desk.

"Thank you for another amazing class," I started, popping on a bright smile.

"It's my pleasure," Mr. Mitchell said.

"I just wanted to mention that I, uh..." I paused, clearing my throat as my gaze dropped to the stack of portfolios on his desk. "I actually didn't bring my portfolio today."

I tried to remember all my practiced responses as Mr. Mitchell's brows knitted together. "You didn't?"

"I forgot it at home," I blurted, which was the condensed version of the eloquent and emotional speech I had planned during the second half of the class. "I'm so sorry."

He leaned back in his chair, crossing his arms. "Is there any way you could drop it off tomorrow?"

I blinked. Tomorrow was...*tomorrow*. And I had at least two days' worth of work left on that portfolio. *Shit shit shit.* "Well, you know, actually, Mr. Mitchell..." My throat tightened again, and the tears were back. "My project wasn't quite ready. I'm so sorry. I mixed up the dates; I thought it was due Thursday. But it's almost done, and I promise I'll have it at the next class. I'll even get here early."

A long sigh escaped Mr. Mitchell as he looked me over, his jaw working back and forth. "I didn't expect this from you."

My shoulders sagged. "I feel like an idiot."

"You've been so good about the assignments."

"I know it probably doesn't help, but I recently started a new job and it's been...a lot. Time-consuming is an understatement." My voice was nearly a whisper. "I'm trying my best, but I've been distracted. I'll do better."

Mr. Mitchell nodded slowly, his chair creaking as he leaned forward. "Bring it Thursday. I'll expect your best work. But you'll automatically lose 10% of your grade for being tardy."

I swallowed the knot in my throat, nodding rapidly. "Of course. I understand. That's no problem."

He offered me a small smile. "And I hope your new job goes well."

"Thank you, Mr. Mitchell." I brought my hands together as though I was praying. "You are the best. And I can't wait for you to see my project."

I raced out of the classroom, my mind whirring with thoughts. In my head, I began reorganizing my schedule over the next two days to accommodate the work I needed to crank out. It could be done. It would be hard, but it could be done.

And I was going to do it.

Step one involved tonight, and I'd stay up until one in the morning if necessary to get the head start I so desperately needed. If I could finish the final designs required for the portfolio tonight, then I could spend the next two days fine-tuning and tweaking the entire thing. *Excellent.* I reached the subway station and sank onto a seat on my train before allowing myself to finally release a deep breath.

I had a plan, and it would work.

I checked my phone as the train lurched into motion. New work emails and bank account notifications awaited me. And some texts from Damian.

DAMIAN: Call me when you get home tonight. That'll shut me up.

I smiled down at the phone. Whenever I had plans that conflicted with Tommy's, he'd either sulk to the point of not talking to me for a full day, or he'd do whatever possible to sabotage my plans. Attempting a similar course in Kentucky would have resulted in my dropping out, I was sure of it. He'd only ever wanted me on his schedule. When my own life, wants, and needs affected his, all hell broke loose.

I still wasn't sure how we'd been together for five years. But I still thanked God daily that I'd managed to get away.

And now I had someone who respected my time. Someone who didn't go ballistic at the mere suggestion of pursuing a class on my own.

My smile lasted only momentarily, before logic and reason stepped in.

You don't have *Damian. He's not yours. He doesn't want anything serious. Remember?*

The smile morphed into a frown. This was going to take some getting used to. And I wasn't sure how well I'd do at it.

A half hour later, I hurried to my apartment complex, my door key at the ready so that I didn't spend even a second longer than I needed to on the barely lit sidewalk. When Nicole and I had first moved in, she'd had an unfortunate encounter on the street involving two guys and a knife. She'd escaped unscathed, but at the expense of her favorite designer purse. Ever since then, we'd proceeded with caution at nighttime. And every Monday and Wednesday had me hurrying with bated breath to reach the front door and lock myself safely inside.

These were the details I didn't share with Jeremy. He and Tara probably imagined worse things anyway, so why would I add fuel to the fire? Once I'd dropped my things and gotten settled in the living room, portfolio spread out on the coffee table, I called Damian on speakerphone.

He answered almost immediately. "There you are."

"Hello." I couldn't fight the grin. Dipping my toes in the water felt too good to resist. I could control the outcome here, while still seeing how the whole thing felt. This, at least, was safe. Separated by a city mile.

How deep could I fall if we were just on the phone?

"Did class run long tonight?" His deep voice was gritty, like maybe I'd woken him while he was just drifting off.

"A little. I had to stay after and talk to the professor because I missed an assignment."

"Hmm. That sounds like the start of a porno."

I laughed. "Well, not this time. Besides, I'm pretty sure Mr. Mitchell bats for the other team. The only thing he's interested in are the dresses I wear."

"We share an interest, then."

The blush hit my cheeks first then slowly spread through my body in the form of a deep, tingling heat. "I never realized you were such a fan."

"I could give you a top ten list of my favorites," Damian said. "If you ever need professional feedback, I'm your guy."

"Professional?"

"Scratch that. There would be nothing professional about it. Purely inappropriate and scandalous."

I grinned as I laid out my syllabus, followed by the designs I intended to include in the portfolio. "Well, then, I'm *extra* open to the feedback you have for me."

"Open, huh?" The phone rustled and his low chuckle felt equal parts sexy and dangerous. "Like your legs will be when I see you next."

I bit my lip, the flush in my cheeks spreading to my chest. Focusing on my portfolio might be more difficult than I anticipated. "That'll be at work tomorrow. Where are you going to open my legs?"

"In my office." His sexy rasp scraped through me. "Nobody will see us there. We'll be discreet."

"And what are you going to do once you open my legs?"

"I'll begin administering feedback."

I laughed. "Oh, it's to be *administered* now?"

"Yes, via my mouth and fingers." I could hear the smile in his voice. "And something else if you're lucky."

My eyes fluttered shut. "Damian Fairchild, are you telling me you want to have sex with me in your office?"

"That's only *one* of the things I want to do with you in my office."

"You are so naughty. I should have known, after catching you and Harper in your office."

"I never claimed to be a good boy, Jessa."

My palms went hot as I toyed with the confession dancing on my tongue. "Well, I *am* a good girl. Or at least, I try to be. But after what I walked in on...Damian, I can't lie, I've imagined doing the same thing to you ever since."

The gritty chuckle returned. "Doing what?"

"You know what."

"I want to hear you say it."

I swallowed hard. "Why?"

"Because of how hot it'll sound coming from your lips."

My entire face heated up. I covered my mouth with my hand. I had not imagined this happening tonight, not even vaguely. Maybe that's how naïve I was, calling Damian and expecting to chat about our evenings like a couple of Girl Scouts. I swiped up my phone and took it off speakerphone. I needed his sexy voice as close to me as possible.

"I've imagined sucking you off since I walked in on you and Harper," I said in a low voice.

Damian's appreciative moan only made the fire between my legs hotter. "I've imagined fucking you since you walked in on me and Harper."

Disbelief mingled with unchecked desire. I wanted Damian so badly I could hardly breathe, but it had never once occurred to me that he might have felt the same for me.

Was I dreaming?

"Just the thought of your pretty pink lips wrapped around my cock..." His laugh sounded strained. "I wish you could feel how hard I am right now."

I shifted on the couch. My panties were slick already, my nipples two hard points beneath the thin fabric of my dress.

"Where are you right now?"

"Sitting on my couch," I forced out past dry lips.

"Are you wearing the same skirt from earlier today?" he asked.

"I am."

He rumbled with appreciation. "Love that skirt. But I need you to change."

"Into what?"

"The green and white dress you spilled tzatziki sauce on."

I bit back a laugh, drifting toward my bedroom. "May I ask *why*..."

"No, you may not. Let me know when you're changed."

I tossed the phone onto my bed as I rummaged through my clothes rack, snagging the dress he'd requested. I shimmied out of my pencil skirt and blouse, hurrying to shrug the green and white handmade dress on. Once I was fully zipped, I picked up the phone.

"All right, Damian. Your wish is my command. I'm going back to my couch now." I sighed with contentment as I wiggled back into my previous spot.

"Good. Now bunch your dress up to your hips for me."

I smiled. "Why?"

"Just do it."

I did as he told me, my skin pebbling as the cool air hit the tops of my thighs.

"Spread your legs, Jessa."

My entire body was buzzing. This felt so scandalous, yet so safe, even as my rational mind still struggled to believe Damian Fairchild was speaking such sultry, dirty things to me over the phone. This was better than I'd ever imagined it could be. And we had barely done anything.

"Are you wearing panties?"

I nodded, then remembered to speak. "Yes."

"What color are they?"

I struggled to remember what color I'd chosen that morning. My entire body buzzed from his attention. "Burgundy."

"Take them off."

I breathed quietly as I followed his instructions. My pussy was throbbing at this point. Why hadn't I just gone to the penthouse like he'd asked? Now I was over here suffering this beautiful torture. "Okay." I squirmed on the couch, waiting for more.

"Sit down and cover your legs with your dress." His voice was so sure, so solid, like he'd done this a thousand times before. I, on the other hand, was the inexperienced newbie. Sure, I'd had sex plenty of times. But never with someone like Damian. Never with a man who ordered me to take my panties off in the middle of my living room.

I'd never even achieved orgasm during sex with a man. I didn't think it was possible for me. It sure hadn't happened with either of my exes.

"Now spread your legs, Jessa." His sexy croon only sent another surge of moisture between my legs, this time making my thighs sticky. "Spread your legs so wide. Open them like you'll open them for me tomorrow in my office."

My clit was throbbing now, and I pinched my eyes shut as I rode the sexy wave of his voice.

"I want you to touch yourself through your dress. That beautiful, handmade dress. The one that makes me rock hard when I see how it hugs your beautiful curves."

I followed the seam of my hip inward, down between my legs. My fingers pushed against the swollen bud of my clit, eliciting a small gasp.

"How does it feel, Jessa?"

"Amazing," I breathed, sinking back into the couch. I kept the phone pressed to the side of my head; I didn't want to lose any bit of the heat and grit coming through Damian's voice right now.

"Imagine me between your legs," he growled. "Staring down your juicy pussy. Your lips are swollen. Your clit is swollen. Everything is just begging for it, Jessa. I can fucking smell you from here."

I swallowed hard, rubbing quick circles around my clit as he spoke. My entire body was on fire at this point, electrified by the dirty words spilling from his mouth.

"This is what would have happened in the laundry room that night. And believe me, I plan to drown in your pussy juice, Jessa."

I squeezed my eyes shut, arching into my hand as I rubbed myself desperately, needily. "Oh, Damian."

"You sound breathless, Jessa. Is this turning you on?"

I laughed. "That's an understatement. I've never been this turned on in my life."

"Pinch your clit."

"What?"

"Squeeze it with two fingers. Do it."

I did as he said, and pleasure jolted through me, hot and electric. I cried out.

"Mmmm. There we go," he murmured.

"And what are you doing right now?" I managed to ask.

"Fisting my cock," he growled. "Imagining my head between your legs. Wondering if you'll scream when you come, or if you'll just moan. I'd give anything to have my fingers buried in your pussy right now, Jessa. I'm half tempted to fly down there in my helicopter right now."

I laughed. "Where would you land it? On the sidewalk?"

"I'd figure it out. But I'll wait until tomorrow. As long as you promise to let me know when you come."

My breath quickened as I sank into the sensations of my fingers rubbing my clit through my dress. "I promise. I'm so close, Damian."

"You have no idea how good it's gonna get, Jessa. All the different ways we're gonna feel good together." His breathing got heavier.

"Oh my god, Damian." My thighs got tense, my orgasm nearing. I could feel it building up inside my core, prickle by prickle. "This is a dream come true."

"How long have you been waiting for my cock, Jessa? Be honest."

I laughed in spite of myself. "Since I was fourteen."

"Fuck, Jessa," he said. "That long?"

I groaned, my fingers zigzagging back and forth over my aching clit. I was so, so close. "Maybe."

"So you're gonna really love it when I finally bury my cock into that tight little cunt of yours, aren't you?"

His words tore through me like a tornado. The orgasm rolled through me in a big, soft wave, electrifying every inch of my skin.

I cried out, arching into my hand, wishing for all the world that Damian were here. On top of me. Fulfilling all these dirty promises.

"Ahh, so she screams." Damian's chuckle was self-satisfied. Smug, even.

I took a few moments to catch my breath, my chest heaving from the journey we'd just gone on. My pussy still pulsed softly when I was finally able to speak.

"And what about you?"

"I'm waiting for you to send me a picture of what you look like right now."

I groaned, covering my eyes with my hand. "Damian, you can't be serious."

"Do it. Take a selfie."

I grumbled but I did as he asked. I sent it off, barely even looking at the picture from sheer embarrassment. I did *not* want to see my sex glow.

"Now look at your dress," Damian said. "Did you make it wet?"

I fanned out the fabric across my knees, spotting the damp spot from my pussy. My mouth parted. "Oh my God."

"You stained your dress, didn't you?"

I groaned again. "*You* stained my dress."

"Guilty," he said with a laugh. "Though it's *our* dress now." Then he grunted. "Your picture..." He was quiet a moment while I regathered my courage. When he returned, he let out a low moan. "That's all I need, babe. Those tits and that sex glow. I'm gonna come like a fucking rocket."

"Then where's my picture?" I ventured. I was only half serious. There was no way he'd send me a dick pic...right?

"I thought you'd never ask." I could hear the shit-eating grin through the phone. He was quiet for a moment or two, then my phone pinged.

My breath caught in my throat as I opened the incoming message.

Damian's dick filled my screen.

His glorious, fully hard, thick and perfect *cock*. Right there. On my phone screen. His hand gripped the base, giving me some idea of the thickness and length. The air in my lungs evaporated.

There was no way in cluckin' hell that would fit inside me.

"It's not gonna fit," I whispered.

"Oh, it'll fit. I'll make sure it does. I'll go nice and slow, babe. Don't you worry."

"And you're...jacking off? Right now?"

"I'm about to come." His voice sounded strained. "Thinking about the way you stained our dress while you were touching yourself. Talking to me. Hearing my words. Looking at your satisfied expression." He grunted. "I'm harder than I've ever been. All because of you."

My cheeks flushed again, and the heat zipping through my core had me considering round two. Damian grunted again, and then a rough groan escaped him.

"Did you come?" I asked after a moment or two.

"So fucking hard. And the next time I do, it's gonna be all over those beautiful tits of yours."

My mind spun. He'd gone from grumpy to dirty talker extraordinaire in the span of a week, and I couldn't even decide what was the most outrageous part about what was unfolding between us. Three days ago, I'd been certain he'd never noticed my breasts in his entire life.

And now he wanted to come on them.

Insert mind-blown emojis here.

We chatted for a few more minutes about nothing, about everything. He'd lost some of the sexy grit, but every so often he'd let slip an "Oh yeah?" that had my pussy clenching. He asked about my missed assignment, which led to an extensive discussion of which pieces I planned to include in the portfolio. Not only did he have opinions about what I should include, he even remembered specific details about some of the designs I'd worn to the office.

Part of me thought maybe this was a dream. Probably I'd fallen asleep on the couch and imagined this entire thing. A man who could both get me off over the phone *and* stuck around to hear about my portfolio project?

I hadn't even dared to dream that someone so perfect could exist.

But when we finally hung up and I was left alone in my living room, dress still stained, heart still hammering, I realized that if we were standing at the mere beginning of this *thing* between us...I was already screwed.

If I had any hope of saving myself from certain heartbreak, then this needed to be the *end*.

CHAPTER SEVENTEEN

DAMIAN

If there were a better coping mechanism than Jessa, I didn't know what it could be.

All of my worries melted away as I basked in what was unfolding between us. Sure, I was breaking all my own damn rules, but I didn't care. Not now.

The SEC investigation? An inconvenience I'd get through. Secret family discovery? Unfortunate but surmountable. All of the unknown disasters that waited for me down the road? Well, I'd just have to wait and see when I got there.

I was more jazzed about Jessa than I'd ever been about any hookup. Maybe it was because we'd known each other practically our whole lives. There was a closeness there I didn't often feel with…anyone. Jessa had known me during high school, which is generally the low point for computer nerds growing up in the South, and still somehow had a crush on me back then. The woman deserved a medal.

Scratch that. She deserved a never-ending fuck fest that I fully intended to give her.

I could barely sleep that night, but not for the usual reasons. The merest recollection of her voice as she came for me was enough to send me spiraling into fantasy land again. I even got to work early the next day—*that's* how fucked up Jessa had me.

But what could I say? I was a sucker for her curves, and I always had been.

She was at her desk as I rounded the corner. Her crystal silver-blue gaze snapped in my direction, a shy smile tugging at her lips as I approached. To be perfectly honest, she looked a little starstruck. And I was okay with that.

Maybe I was a little starstruck too.

I paused in front of her, unable to contain my grin as I took in her dress du jour: a boatneck maroon dress with ruffles at the shoulders. The material looked stiff, which presented a possible logistic complication. But that was okay—I'd find a workaround. I wanted to kiss her face off already, but that was a strict no-no where someone could see us.

"Morning," I said.

"Hi." She looked up at me dreamily, and we stood like that for too long, staring into each other's eyes.

I ran a hand through my hair. "You sleep okay?" My entire body pulsed with the need to get her alone in my office. But I wasn't the type of Neanderthal to just drag her there. Even though I was half-tempted to.

"Yeah, once I finally went to bed."

"Did you get the portfolio done?"

"Almost." Her smile widened. "I'll finish it tonight, for sure. What about you? Did you sleep?"

I shook my head. "Not so good. Had a lot on my mind."

"Oh yeah? Like what?"

"I'll have to tell you in my office." I winked, and a delicious blush crept up her neck. I wanted to bite it.

"Okay." She followed me when I started for my office. I pushed open the door, finding the cool, quiet space welcoming. The door snicked shut behind us, and I had her pinned to it a second later.

"That was fast," she whispered.

She was right. It wasn't even nine o'clock yet. But there was no time to waste. "Not fast enough for my taste."

I dipped down and snagged the kiss I'd been dying for since yesterday. I could taste mint on her breath, and a hint of her morning coffee. We made out fast and furious, knocking teeth, biting lips. I was hungrier than I'd ever been. My cock was hard and trapped against her hip. I traced the curves of her body through her dress, squeezing her thick hips, her juicy ass. I could have eaten her from head to toe. She moaned as I fucked her mouth with my tongue.

"Damian," she gasped a moment later, clutching her heaving chest. "You're gonna give me a heart attack if you keep kissing me like that."

"You want me to slow down?" I nuzzled her neck while I rocked my pelvis in a slow circle against her. "I can."

She drew a shaky breath. Then she shook her head. "No. I'll assume the medical risk. The kisses are that good."

I laughed through our kiss, gripping the sides of her face as our tongues met over and over. Now that she was here, in my arms, suctioned to my face, something deep inside me was satisfied. Calm, even.

Having Jessa in my arms just seemed right. And I didn't want to let her go.

When we broke for air, her silvery gaze looked drugged. Those kiss-bitten lips would be the star of my internal porno reels for years to come. Everything about Jessa was made from my greatest fantasies. She was my dream woman come to life.

Which made it even harder to pace myself. Keep things in check.

"You are too much, Damian Fairchild."

I tugged at the sides of her dress, slowly collecting the fabric in my hands as it bunched easily, higher and higher. "So you're saying I *should* slow down?"

"Noooo." She drew out the vowel, her gaze darting down between our bodies. "What is happening here?"

"Just a little team morale booster," I said, unable to hide my grin. "To start the day off right."

She lifted a brow. "Morale?"

"Mm-hmm." I had the fabric of her dress gathered at her waist, my fingers roaming freely over her exposed hips. Her skin pebbled where I touched her. Her eyes went hooded, her breath hitching as my fingers hooked onto her panties.

"After what we did last night," I said in a low voice, right against her ear, "I thought I should follow up. Make sure you got the message."

Her throat bobbed, and she clutched my arms. "Mmm, that's a great idea. You should check thoroughly that I got the message."

I smiled through another kiss. This wasn't just sexy. It was fun. It was also wild, since some part of me still saw me as the senior and her as the sophomore. Like Jeremy might come waltzing in any second.

But it felt right. And it felt way fucking better than I could have imagined.

I palmed the front of her panties, watching as her throat bobbed, her gaze glued to my face. I gobbled up the tiny details about her—the silvery glint of her eyes, the barely-there freckles cresting her cheeks, the delicious lips I could have kissed for a year straight without getting tired of.

She was beautiful. And she was finally, thankfully, *blessedly,* backed up against my fucking office door like God had intended.

I swiped my thumb over the silky crotch of her panties, grazing the tight bud of her clit. She cried out, knees wobbling, but I steadied her with a firm kiss. While liplocked, I snaked my fingers beneath the soaked crotch of her panties, finding the epicenter of all her heat and passion. My fingers found the slick folds of her pussy, so swollen and ready for me. My head spun, and I tongue fucked her again while I explored the juicy terrain of her pussy, cradling her clit between my index and middle finger as I moved my hand against her mound. She moaned through the kiss, arching her body against me.

"You like that?" I whispered hotly into her ear. I bit at her lobe as she nodded, thrusting her pelvis against my hand as I massaged her clit.

"So much," she said wispily, as if she were a thousand miles away.

I pinched her clit hard—hard enough that she cried out again—and then I plunged my middle finger into her pussy. She was pure heat and juice, the most divine combination. Everything inside me coiled tight, wanting to tear the rest of her clothes off, to fuck her right there against my door.

But no. I could go slow. I could take things step by step.

For a little longer, at least.

"Oh my god, Damian," she moaned, squeezing my arms like I was the last life raft in the ocean. I pumped my finger in and out, in and out, adding a second finger, watching the sexy emotions splay across her face. Her pussy squeezed against my fingers. I could tell she was close from how hard she was breathing, from how hard she rocked against me. I was even closer to saying *to hell with it* and fucking her like she clearly craved.

I ground my palm against her mound as I fingerfucked her, capturing her lips in another deep tongue kiss. There was so much more to explore on Jessa's body, but for now, I just wanted to give her a little taste of what was to come. So she would know how much fun we were going to have, now that I'd sent that employee/boss boundary to Hell.

Her head knocked the door as she arched toward me, her eyes pinching shut. "Ohhhh, Damiannnnn." She fisted the front of my shirt as her pussy clenched around my fingers. A long, shuddery moan escaped her, her pelvis jerking. I could see the orgasm rolling through her, rending her pretty features into an expression caught between ecstasy and pain. When she finally came back to earth, her eyes looked drugged.

"Welcome back," I said, and planted a kiss on her lips.

She blinked lazily, the most satisfied smile drifting across her lips. I wanted to see a lot more of that look.

"You're incredible," she whispered.

"Am I? You've hardly experienced a fraction of what I plan to do to you."

She laughed softly. "I've never gotten off like that before."

I blinked back my surprise, reminding myself that her ex was *Tommy March*. He'd never been the most attentive crayon in the box, which I was sure translated to disappointment when it came to small details like a woman's pleasure.

"Really? No man has ever gotten you there like that?" I nuzzled her neck, placing soft kisses along her collarbone.

She shook her head, a faint blush staining her cheek. "Actually, no guy has ever gotten me off period."

This time, I couldn't contain my surprise. I pulled back to look her in the eye. "Seriously?"

She laughed sheepishly. "So, you win the award, Damian Fairchild. And it took place in my boss's office. *On the clock,* even."

I grinned, diving back into that sweet corner of her neck I'd already come to prefer. "What's better than getting paid and getting off at the same time? That's my motto, at least."

She tilted her neck as my kisses drifted lower. Her hands ventured inward, between our bodies, traveling to find my thick erection trapped against her hip.

"But what about you?" she asked.

"I have a few ideas of what we could do." I tugged at her earlobe with my teeth.

She nodded, doubts crowding her gaze. She opened her mouth to speak but nothing came out. I could tell something was waiting there, vying for airtime.

"What is it?" I asked.

Her gaze dropped, and she started nibbling on her lip. "I-It's nothing, I...."

"Clearly there's something on your mind."

She ran a finger down the front of my shirt, tracing the outline of each button before moving to the next. "I-I don't know how to say it, I guess. I'm a little afraid of, uh, sounding like a...prude."

I smirked, my hands drifting back over the exposed expanse of her hips. "I just fingerfucked you against my door. You're not a prude."

She blinked rapidly, searching my face. When she spoke, her voice came out a whisper. "I don't think we can have sex."

The words didn't make sense at first. I tipped my head, trying to understand what she was telling me. "What?"

"I-I-I just don't think I can," she blurted.

"Like, you don't want to?" Question marks piled on top of question marks. Had I completely misread this situation? "Because I'm pretty sure physically everything checks out down there."

She breathed out a small laugh and swallowed hard. "Physically, I would *love* to have sex with you, Damian. Don't get me wrong. I've only been dreaming of it for practically my entire life. But if I do...how can I say this? I'm not a girl who just has fun. I'm a girl who falls in love. And if we have sex..."

She didn't need to finish her sentence for me to know what lay on the other side. Disappointment crashed through me as I absorbed her features, the anxiety slashed across her face, the way she struggled to hold my gaze.

"Don't hate me," she whispered, her brows knitting together as she searched my face. "I want to. But I'm terrified of what will happen if we do. Because I already know…"

"I don't hate you," I told her, stroking her hair, wanting to relieve the anxiety thrumming through her.

"And I don't want to make things weird, either," she went on.

"I get what you're saying. It won't be weird. We can have fun in plenty of other ways that don't involve that magical, mystical, delicious act of fucking our brains out."

Her chest shook with laughter, some of the tension dissolving. "Well, thank you."

"Besides, maybe you'll change your mind. And if you do, you know where to find me."

Truth was, the barbarian in me was rioting, slamming shit around and demanding to know when he could fuck Jessa properly. But I'd play by her rules. If she wanted no sex, I'd give her no sex…while constantly reminding her just how fucking incredible sex with me could be.

But she was right to be guarded. Because there was no way in hell I could give her what she was looking for. If sex meant she'd catch feelings, then I needed to see myself out. Except I couldn't pry myself away from her. Even when it was probably the best path for everyone involved.

"Maybe *you'll* change your mind," she said, poking my chest.

"About just having fun?"

"Yeah. Ever thought about having a girlfriend?"

I smirked. I hated this line of questioning almost as much as I hated when people acted so daft about what the CTO could possibly do in a business like ours. It all boiled down to the fact that people didn't understand who I was or how I operated.

I wasn't like most people. I'd come to terms with that. I was an introvert who needed death metal and solitude to function. Axel wasn't wrong about that. And I didn't buy into the traditional family setup.

I'd had the traditional family once, and it had been ripped from me with no warning, for no reason. A freak car accident on Christmas Eve left four kids orphaned and thrust into the foster system. I'd been lucky enough to find a stable, traditional family a second time with the Fairchilds...and now that, too, was in the process of crumbling.

Going anywhere near traditional family would only spell disaster. I knew it down to my bones. After losing both Jordan and Kaylee, I didn't deserve stable and long-lasting. Not when my two little sisters hadn't been able to even hope for the same. I'd been their big brother, their guiding light...and look where I'd led them.

The guilt didn't tear at me so much as constantly simmered in the background, infusing my daily life like failure-scented incense.

Bona fide romances were a non-option. Not with how much the business demanded from me. Not with this investigation hanging over my head. Not when I'd failed the two girls closest to me. Not when there was a consistent pattern of very bad things following any remotely good thing in my life. I had a million and one reasons why romance wasn't in my personal deck of cards.

But she didn't need to know all that.

"The full list of reasons of why I need to keep things casual would only bore you," I told her. "And besides, you're not my therapist. And if you were, then we couldn't date anyway."

Her smile softened. "Not even someday?"

"Jessa, it's not for me. I respect your boundaries, you respect mine. That's how it works, right?"

Her smile sank until it wasn't even a smile anymore. "You're right."

"Then it's all good." I leaned forward, ending the conversation with a kiss.

Because it would be...as long as we stuck to the limits that each of us needed.

CHAPTER EIGHTEEN

DAMIAN

Almost a week later, I was starting another Monday morning at the office a little too early, winding my way through the hallways and already imagining the sexy glance that Jessa would give me when I saw her for the first time that day.

"Damian! You're early...*again*!" Axel waved at me from down the hall that led to the conference room. "Just come straight to the conference room. Francis and I are here already."

I ground my teeth. I'd wanted to use my thirty minute grace period to catch up with Jessa in my office. We'd been "catching up" every morning and afternoon, and sometimes evenings. I'd given her thirteen orgasms in the past week. Not that I had been keeping track or anything.

And all of that catching up was without taking our clothes off. They were simply heated, lip-locked encounters against the back of my door or on top of my desk or in my executive chair, my fingers buried in her pussy, all of my attention focused on her pleasure. After all, she had a serious orgasm deficit to make up for.

It wasn't sex, and she wasn't my girlfriend. This was perfectly fine.

"Let me grab my stuff," I called out to him.

"Come on. Let's get started. I'm ready to fucking vibe." Axel jerked his head in the direction of the conference room.

I set my jaw. I needed to see Jessa first. "Your vibes can wait until I grab my shit and take a leak."

He made rapid circles with his index finger. "Come on, bro. Genius doesn't wait."

I rolled my eyes and set off for my office. Once I rounded the corner, Jessa's angelic beauty awaited me, peering at me from beneath thick, dark lashes. My heart skipped a beat as I watched the sly grin blossom on her face, the pink hinting at her cheeks. Today's dress was navy, which paired well with her crystalline gaze. By the time I approached her desk, my heart was pounding. We couldn't stop grinning at each other, an entire conversation flowing between us via only our eyes. What in the fuck was going on here?

"Good morning," she finally purred, once we'd been staring at each other for probably far too long.

"Did we just have three conversations with our eyes?" I asked.

She giggled, burying her mouth behind her hand. "I think it was four, actually."

"Well I'm glad we're all caught up," I joked, winking. "You sleep good?"

"Yeah...once I finally went to bed. I was up late doing more designs for my next quarterly portfolio. I'm not missing the next due date, so help me God."

"Good girl." I squeezed my hand into a fist, wanting to follow those words up with a lot more. But we were in plain view here; even though nobody was around, this was a hard line. No canoodling in public. No kissing or touches where other employees could see.

All fun stuff needed to occur behind my office door. Period.

"Why'd you have to say it like that?" she said with a little laugh, that blush returning.

"Like what?"

"With your sexy voice," she whispered. "Like you're gonna eat me for lunch."

I glanced behind me, down the hall. I dropped my voice. "Because that's exactly what I intend to do."

Her blush flared brighter, and she peeked up at me from beneath those dark lashes. "Like those strawberries you told me about last night?"

An honest-to-god belly laugh erupted from me. I'd confided in Jessa during our hourlong video call last night that I used to practice kissing strawberries as a teen. I'd never told anyone that, not even Axel or Trace. But she seemed to think it had something to do with how well I kissed her face off, so I couldn't even pretend to be embarrassed.

I winked at her again. "Axel is riding my ass to get to the conference room. I'll catch up with you later."

"Have fun," she said, watching me dreamily as I snagged a tablet from my office and headed for the conference room. I fought the urge to glance over my shoulder, to keep eye contact until the last possible second. I felt every inch the moony high schooler again. These were the sexy looks and the double entendres that eighteen-year-old me couldn't even have fathomed.

It was probably for the best that we were keeping the affair within the walls of the office. If I had her out in the open or up in the penthouse, there was no telling how fast I'd shred the rules.

Jessa made me hungrier than I'd ever been for a taste of something I'd never allowed myself.

I hummed as I wandered back to the conference room. Inside, Axel leaned back in his chair, squeezing a stress ball, while Francis frowned down at his tablet, swiping through screens.

"All right. I'm here early, *as requested.*" I took my seat across from Axel. Francis headed the table. I glanced at Trace's empty seat reflexively, my chest tightening as the truth washed over me again. Trace was on vacation indefinitely, he and Axel hadn't spoken for weeks, and what had always been an unshakeable trio was now missing our third.

It still didn't feel right.

"Coffee is en route," Francis murmured as he swiped and poked his device.

I hummed to myself as I fished my phone out of my pocket.

Axel sent me a sharp look. "What's wrong with you?"

I silenced my phone and set it on the table. "What are you talking about?"

"You're humming."

"So?"

Axel looked over at Francis, as though seeking confirmation, then swung his accusatory gaze my way again. "You're...happy and shit. Borderline pleasant to be around. It's weird."

I cleared my throat as I leaned back in my seat. "I can't tell if that's meant to be a compliment or an insult."

"The best lines are disguised as both, my brother." Axel sent me his most self-satisfied smile.

"Well, I don't know what the problem is. Should I not be pleasant?"

Axel narrowed his eyes. "I just want to know why. And I think I do."

The door opened, and I turned to see our office assistant Felicia bringing in our coffee. I smiled up at her as she set the tray of steaming espresso cups on the table.

"I'm always more pleasant after caffeine," I told Axel.

"It's not that. I think you're..." He sent me a pointed look, widening his eyes, lifting his chin in my direction. "You know." He repeated the look. I knew what he was getting at: that I was *getting some*. But he was wrong. I wasn't fucking anyone right now.

"What is that supposed to mean?"

He glanced at Felicia, offering her a polite smile as she retreated from the conference room. When the door closed behind her, his smile dropped. "You know what it fucking means. You finally took my advice."

"What advice?"

He lowered his chin, giving me his best deadly-younger-brother look. "Will you stop parroting everything back to me? It's so annoying when you parrot."

"I'm not parroting."

"You just did it again."

I turned to Francis. "Was there something on the agenda that required me here, or did Axel just want me here early to hassle me?"

Francis looked like he was fighting laughter. "I'm not sure my contract allows me to answer that question."

Axel leaned forward, pinning me with a look. "Don't act dense."

He was so easy to needle. "I'm not being dense; I'm just looking for a little clarity on why you insisted on disrupting my morning routine."

"Oh, your morning routine. Says the man who would sleep until noon every day if he could. See, that right there is all the proof I need. Something is different, and I know what it is." He crossed his arms triumphantly, leaning back in his chair. "You and Jessa finally hooked up."

Francis sucked in a sharp breath, shock registering on his face. "You're kidding me."

Neither of them needed to know what Jessa and I had going on. So I cleared my throat and turned toward my tablet. "Can we continue?"

Axel huffed but relented. I sipped my coffee, avoiding both of their curious gazes. We somehow managed to get back to business, but my mind lingered on what Axel had thrust into the spotlight. He could tell something was different about me.

Sure, I'd been enjoying my time with Jessa. And maybe that had translated into some overall behavioral shifts. But it didn't mean anything. It wasn't a big deal like Axel liked to pretend.

I was still myself—the same nerd who stayed up too late trying to solve the world's problems via code, the same stressed-out Damian who knew better than to get wrapped up in romance or flings with roots.

Nothing had changed. I'd only added a few extra sexy video calls per week. And Jessa and I had only spent *one* of those three video calls accidentally chatting about life for hours instead of getting each other off. I hadn't even drunk any whiskey to fall asleep that night.

Everything was fine.

The top of the agenda was the Programmer's Ball that Saturday.

"So listen." Axel steepled his fingers thoughtfully, staring off at a distant corner of the universe before he went on. "Cora and I are prepared to do whatever we can to help the image of the business, of course. I know you wanted us to open the event with a speech. But I wonder if you shouldn't make the speech yourself, Damian."

Everything inside my body rejected this idea, but he had a point. He must have seen me ready to disagree because Axel held up a hand.

"I know you don't like talking in front of crowds. But we want to repair our reputation, right? This is about transparency. What could be better than hearing it from the algorithm horse's mouth?"

"You have a point. But what about Trace?"

Axel's face dropped. "What about him?"

"If we're repairing reputations, then we need him there."

"No."

I toyed with a pen on the table in front of me. "Then what's our excuse going to be when he's not there?"

"Urgent business." Axel shrugged. "Unexpected flu. There are a million reasons he might have to miss an event. Francis will pick the most appropriate one. Speaking of which," Axel said, tipping his head toward Francis, "keep an eye on the headlines. I do *not* want this surprise brother leaking anytime soon. If at all possible, we need to discredit any potential info dump Ian might be gearing up to offer the media. Deleting any hint of a possibility that there's a surprise Fairchild family member out there will go a long way."

Francis nodded as he took notes on his tablet.

"Has anyone heard from Ian?" I asked.

"Not since his visit," Axel said. "I'm not sure if that's better or worse."

"And has your dad told your mom about Ian yet?" Francis asked.

"As far as I can tell, no," I said.

"Every day I wake up and wait for that phone call from Mom," Axel said. "Dreading it."

Axel and Francis and I switched gears then, returning to progress on the Programmer's Ball. RSVPs were rolling in, the keynote speaker had been scheduled, transparency stories were being printed and readied to hang at the event. Friday promised to be a stressful day, waiting to see how this transparency attempt landed, whether our reputation would implode or stabilize. If the SEC investigation cast a shadow over our methods, we'd work double time to shine a light onto our side mission of supporting future generations of coders even more than we already did.

We whiled away almost two hours there, a surprise fruit platter arriving. Based on the sheer number of strawberries, I knew who had sent it without even asking. I ate strawberries with a smile, already planning the ways I'd thank Jessa later with my "kissin' skills."

But once we finished our meeting and dispersed to our respective corners, the energy of our session fizzling away, Axel's words returned to me.

I *was* acting different.

Which meant this thing with Jessa was affecting me more than it should. More than I could handle.

And the whole point of this was to "have fun" only as far as it wouldn't disrupt, destabilize, or deny me the fleeting grip I had on my life now.

Maybe you need to take a step back.

It would be the smart thing to do. The right thing.

But as I made my way back to my office and caught Jessa half under her desk, swearing softly to herself, I knew taking a step back wasn't even remotely an option.

"Hello, have you seen Jessa?" I teased as I came up to her. "I think she may have been swallowed by her desk."

Jessa tried to sit up but bumped her head on the desk, which prompted a giggle fit. She sat on the floor, clutching her head.

"This is all because I dropped my ding-dang earring."

I offered her a hand, and she took it, coming to her feet. We were inches away then, smiles lingering, quivering on the precipice of breaking the rules again in view of the office.

"How was the meeting?" she asked, a little breathless.

"Intense. A little depressing. Mostly the same as usual."

She pursed her lips and tapped her chin. "You know, Damian. I've been thinking. We're going to start something new."

"What's that?" I drifted closer to her, unable to stop myself. How would we make it through the Programmer's Ball without tipping anyone off? The entire office would be there, not to mention a hundred cameras, reporters, and more. I could barely keep myself off her in the office—forget about the Rainbow Room where alcohol and excess flowed freely.

I was doomed.

"A sanity break." She beamed with a proud smile. "You don't get out of the office enough. We're fixing this. You need to take a stroll once in awhile. And I will be your accountability partner, because I too need a regular stroll, though for different reasons."

My gut instinct was to reject this idea. Somewhere deep down, I suspected I had a recessive vampire gene. Daylight and I didn't mix well, but the way Jessa talked about this at least had me curious.

"A stroll?"

"Yes. Like a walk. With your two legs. Destination: somewhere that is not this office, the elevator, your penthouse, or en route to a fancy dinner or gala."

It was hard to act annoyed when she looked so pleased with herself.

"Let's say you might have a point," I said. "Where would this stroll take place?"

"The High Line." The smile grew wider, which only made it harder for me to not kiss it off.

"That sounds like a good idea for someday."

"No. *Today.*" She cocked a hip. "Check your calendar, Mr. Fairchild. It's already in there. Are you ready? We're almost late for your sanity break."

My workaholic tendencies had me itching to craft a viable excuse. I just wanted to stay holed up in my office, mulling and stewing and stressing, like I always did.

But she was impossible to resist. Impossible to reject.

"What are *your* reasons for needing a stroll?" I was already pulling my office door shut, readying myself to leave.

"Part tourism, part exercise, part excuse to get out of the office." She sent me a wink, slinging a small but stylish backpack over her shoulders as she jerked her head toward the hallway. "Plus, I saw in some pictures that they have some autumn cherry trees there, which are my personal favorite."

"Oh yeah?" I smiled, recalling the autumn cherry tree in the driveway of the house where my parents used to live. "My mom and dad—"

"Had one at their old house," she finished for me with a conspiratorial smile. "I know. I've loved it for *years*."

This seemed like important information to tuck away. "What do you love about it?"

She shrugged, getting a wistful look in her eye. "They're so beautiful. It's like a surprise. They spend the entire year blending into their surroundings and then *bam*. Wild and crazy surprise out of nowhere."

"Reminds me of someone I know."

Her mouth parted as understanding shivered across her face. We shared a sweet and meaningful look.

"Plus, they remind me of home," she said with a shrug, like shaking off the secret compliment I'd given her. "We said good-bye under that cherry tree before you went to college. I'd have brought it to New York with me if I could. I love that autumn cherry tree."

I loved how she talked about the whole thing. The nostalgia mixed with the warmth and the admiration. "You make me want to go pack it up and bring it here just for you."

"Don't do that. I don't think the tree would like that much. I'll just go admire it someday when I get back around to Oakville in the fall." She sighed, clapping her hands together. "Now are you ready to maintain your sanity?"

Hell if I wouldn't snap up the chance to shift gears and get away with only Jessa. If we hadn't been in the office, I would have taken her fucking hand and kissed her the entire way out of the building. But instead, I followed her and imagined all the things we'd do when we got there.

The more I got of her, the more I wanted, which ran contrary to the blinking neon light in the back of my subconscious that read *This is only temporary.*

I didn't want to listen to the smart, rational thing for once.

I wanted to follow sweetness. Flirty-ness. Something that didn't feel fucking heavy.

I just wanted to follow Jessa.

CHAPTER NINETEEN

JESSA

It was 3:59 p.m. on Saturday, and I was pacing my apartment so quickly I thought I might pass out.

Actually, nearly everything made me almost pass out today. Whether it was pacing or bending or staring into space, it was a bit harder than usual to breathe.

There were a few reasons. Primarily, it was the Programmer's Ball. The first ever gala I'd planned was a mere two hours from beginning, and my anxiety was on a roller-coaster spiral inside me.

I was also wearing my newest dress design. It had been created with this event in mind—my dress was absolutely going to match the drapes, in a non-sexual sense—but more than that, it included Mr. Mitchell's latest challenge to us, which was to incorporate a corset.

My breathing had become shallower. Was it anxiety? Was it the corset? It was likely both, and I fought to focus on anything other than the fact that I couldn't get a deep gulp of air. Because that only made me want a deep gulp of air even *more*.

Damn this corset.

The design allowed me to cinch and tie it off myself and cleverly hide the strings, but I wondered if I'd overdone it. But the more I paced and thought about it, I decided it was my anxiety getting the better of me—*not* the instrument of torture wrapped around my lungs. Besides, this dress was too delicate to fiddle with the corset strings any more.

The Rainbow Room was an iconic location in New York, one that I'd both researched online *and* visited two separate times in person in preparation for this event. The planning process had allowed me to design my dress perfectly in sync with the venue. This silver-gray dress was dripping with beaded details to match the delicate, diamond-like curtains of the Rainbow Room.

My phone vibrated inside my handbag, and I fumbled to get it out. I was waiting for Damian to get here; he'd insisted on coming to pick me up so that we could arrive at the event together. I hadn't dared to object. There was nothing I wanted more than to arrive on his arm, even though that wasn't the normal thing to do for mere *coworkers*.

"Hello?" I answered breathily, this time due to excitement.

"You ready?" His deep rumble sent a jolt of desire through me. I couldn't get enough of this man. His voice. His lopsided smile. The way he touched me. Oh, the way this man touched me. He'd pushed his fingers inside me no fewer than one hundred times since we'd started this...*thing*...and I only wanted more. I wanted so much from him that it scared me.

"Of course I am. I've been ready for twenty minutes." My grin was already ear-to-ear, and I hadn't even spotted him yet.

"Open your door."

My heart skipped a beat as I rushed toward the door. He'd never come to my apartment before. I'd been afraid to invite him over, afraid of what might happen if we were left to our own devices in a comfortable space I called my own. It was the same reason our fooling around hadn't ventured out of his office. I knew what a late night at the penthouse would lead to. And I was still dumb enough to believe that I could keep myself—my heart—safe by following the rules.

When I tugged the door open, Damian filled the doorway, looking somehow beefier and more refined than when I'd last seen him. His moss gaze was electric as it swept over me, taking me in. My cleavage was more conspicuous than usual, thanks to the corset, and that's where his gaze lingered.

"Jessa," he said.

I swallowed hard. "Damian."

He took a predatory step toward me. A moment later, his arm was hooked around my waist, the woodsy musk of his scent washing over me, sending me into outer space.

"You look fucking stunning," he growled into my ear, his other hand tracing the front of my dress, over the beaded details hiding the ridge of the corset. His fingertips brushed the exposed skin of my cleavage, igniting goosebumps in his path.

"You don't look so bad yourself," I teased, checking out his formal attire. He wore a designer black suit with lapels accented in the shade of aqua we'd selected for the event. The laces of his dress shoes reflected the same color. Damian's longish chestnut tresses were slicked back at the sides. He was so handsome I wanted to combust. Luckily this corset would hold in any internal explosions.

We shared a long look, getting lost in each other's eyes. Even though we still had to play it platonic in public spaces, it was getting harder to keep the cat in our collective bag. Our trip to the High Line, an old elevated train track turned into a public park, earlier that week had been spent fully hand in hand. He'd even kissed me on a bench. Of course, the office staff hadn't been there—that's what I kept telling myself, at least.

But it was times like these when it felt like something had irreversibly shifted.

We spent a lot of time looking into each other's eyes. And it just didn't seem like something you did with a fling. I wouldn't know—I'd never had a fling—but deep inside, I could tell that this was serious for Damian. Serious like it was for me, too.

"How are we going to make it through the night?" he asked me, his lips already drifting along my jawline. "I won't be able to get three feet from you."

I giggled, tilting my neck so he could explore further. "We'll have to find a way. I expect we'll be thoroughly distracted."

Damian grunted, then he dove for a kiss. I dodged it, pulling away.

"We can't kiss tonight," I said, sending him my most serious look.

His brows drew together, the poutiest look creasing his face. "Why?"

A laugh burst out of me. "Oh my god. I've never seen you look so *mad*. Like I just told you that snack time was over."

"Well, you *are* a snack," he said, running his hands across the fabric of my dress.

"This lipstick *smears*," I told him, pointing to my ruby lips. "Tonight is too important to be looking like some whacked out sex goddess."

He sighed, squeezing my ass cheeks through the dress. "Fine. But we'll leave early."

The simple ass grab sent moisture to my panties. It didn't matter how many times this man had gotten me off within the four walls of his office. My body always wanted more and was capable of giving it to him.

But I knew as well as he did that our situation was unsustainable. I didn't just crave more Damian—I *needed* him. All of him. I needed him buried so deep inside me his dick would come out the other side. I wanted to choke on him. I wanted to let him bend, flip, and fold me however he saw fit. We were poised to create something magical together.

Something I wouldn't be able to walk away from.

That was the part that scared me.

"Let's see how the night goes," I told him, wrapping my arms around his neck. "If you're busy making important connections and raising tons of money, we should stay as long as we can."

He grunted, his gaze lingering on my cleavage. "You're right." He leaned forward like he was going to kiss me, then he caught himself. "Fuck, this is going to be hard."

As if on cue, I reached between his legs, seeking the hardness I assumed was already waiting for me. I found his half-hard dick and rubbed him through his dress pants. His eyes went hooded.

"Be careful tonight, Jessa." His voice had a warning note in it I hadn't heard before. "I've done a really good job of sticking to the rules. But when you look like this and we've been toying with each other like we have..." He wet his bottom lip, leaning closer to me. "There's only so much more a man can take before he completely fucking snaps."

His words sent an electric chill through my body. I wanted him to snap. I wanted us both to break in two and rejoin as one, something altogether new.

"I won't distract you," I said sweetly.

"Impossible. You distract me even when you do nothing."

"Well, that's a *you* problem, Damian."

His eyes went hooded again. "Let's just stay here. Come on, Jessa. We can have plenty of fun in your apartment."

I laughed. "Absolutely not. Now let's get out of here before I actually agree with you." I pushed him toward the door, my nipples like diamond points and my pussy screaming for attention as I shuffled out the door behind him. He wasn't wrong. We'd been existing in a little fantasy bubble at work, where the only acceptable activities were insanely hot makeout sessions and his fingers buried inside me. During our video chats, I'd watched him jack off, and he'd watched me finger myself, but we hadn't done it in person yet.

This was the slowest, most confusing zigzag to home plate I'd ever experienced. We'd only agreed to this to protect ourselves. But at this point, it seemed more damaging to *not* go all the way.

Damian and I swept into the waiting SUV like incognito celebrities. Legs awaited us with a smile and his Brooklyn greeting—"Heeeeey, there's our girl"—and then we were off. The flashes of the Manhattan skyline beyond the windows of the vehicle barely registered as Damian and I sank into our own private world. Thigh squeezes, meaningful looks, winking at each other until we dissolved into laughter. We were simultaneously mature, grown adults and teens on my father's couch again. I loved the way we could dance between these two worlds: the one we shared from having grown up together and the vast new world that stretched all around us as adults, foreign and limitless.

It struck me then, as we wove through the streets of New York, that Damian rooted me. He made it safe for me to stretch upward, outward, beyond. Not just in a financial sense, but in a grounding sense. We knew each other, we'd shared the same air growing up.

And by acting as my roots, he made it that much safer for me to fall even more in love with him.

By the time we got to the event, it was both the corset and Damian making it hard to breathe. With one last caress of my ass, Damian helped me out of the car. We smiled at each other, walking down the red carpet toward the main doors together, but not holding hands. We didn't need to hold hands, because every time he looked at me, I felt the tiny kiss he was giving me in his head.

Christ, I was head over heels for this man.

As soon as we swept through the main doors, it was go time. After the elevator ride to the sixty-fifth floor, I joined forces with the venue consultant, Meredith, to review what remained to be done. As we toured the Rainbow Room, I could barely see past the beauty and glamour to focus on the tasks at hand. Floor-to-ceiling windows looked out over the city, offering a legendary view of the skyline, the glittery, beaded curtains that matched my dress hanging halfway down the windowpanes. Two dozen tables dotted the huge room, each one boasting small glass vase centerpieces with white blooms spilling out.

"Almost everything has been set up according to the plan," Meredith said as we paused by the low stage at one end of the room, where Damian would make his speech and presentations would be held. An enormous chandelier hung in the center of the room, yanking at my attention with its billion pieces of glinting crystal. How could I focus on anything with this much opulence around me?

"But we still need to figure out where exactly to position the screen," Meredith said, gesturing at the flat screen which would showcase images featuring the brothers' positive impact on the community at large.

"Ahh yes," I murmured, tapping my chin pensively as I relished this feeling. *Belonging* in one of the most legendary spaces of New York. I'd planned this event. And now we were going to sit back and fucking enjoy it. "Let's have it in front of the podium as people arrive, and just before the presentations start, we'll move it out of the way."

We worked on finalizing a few more of the details. I glanced over at Damian on occasion, both because I was curious about what he and Axel were talking about so intensely and to see if I could catch another heated look from him.

But I couldn't catch his eye. He and Axel weren't just having an intense conversation now. They were looking at something on Axel's phone, shaking their heads. My stomach wrenched, though I wasn't entirely sure why.

Meredith and I went around the room assessing each area. With one hour to showtime, tantalizing scents wafted from the nearby kitchen doors. The menu was the stuff of my fantasies—Montauk scallops over wilted leeks, osso buco with creamy saffron polenta, to name a few items on the night's dinner menu. That didn't even cover the sweets—apple crumble souffle, blackberry cheesecake, fondue spilling from hidden spots, equal parts decoration and dessert. Every inch of me was desperate to capture this evening from every angle, along with every taste.

But every time I got too excited, I could hear the derision spilling from my sister's lips, echoing through my head like a scream in a cathedral.

Look at you. Flaunting all this wealth, having such a good time while the woman who gave you life is living in a halfway house infested with roaches. What a great daughter you are. You selfish fucking bitch.

Thanks, Imaginary Tara. She always knew how to knock me down a peg or ten. I wrung my hands, flipping between beguiled and regretful. Proud of myself and hating myself. This old familiar cycle that I was so incredibly tired of. And this corset only made breathing through the anxiety so much harder.

When I next looked at Damian, I could tell something was seriously wrong. He and Axel were reacting to...something. Axel pointed downward forcefully. I excused myself from Meredith, hurrying over to them as though pulled there by forces beyond my control.

Damian rubbed at his cheek as I approached. He looked at me, something intense swirling in his gaze.

"What's up, guys?" I asked suspiciously. "Are we ready to start this party?"

"No," Damian said with a frown. "This party might not be starting at all."

My stomach dropped to my feet. "What? Why?"

Axel cleared his throat, his jaw flexing. "A protest is forming at the main door."

"A protest against...us?" I squeaked out.

Damian nodded while Axel sighed. "It's some whacko Manhattan group. They've never targeted us before but...well, now they have."

The words still didn't make sense to me. "But...what are they even protesting?"

Damian and Axel shared a weary look. When Damian met my gaze, he looked haunted. "There were rumors that our business supports sex trafficking. It's completely batshit, but it's based on the fact that a company we acquired not so long ago *was* associated with trafficking. We bought the company so we could put a stop to it."

When I was unable to form a response, Axel spoke up. "They think they're saving kids. They're not. And now we have to figure out a way to get rid of them."

Damian looked sullen, the same stress lines eating at his face as when I'd started working at Fairchild Enterprises.

"There is no way to get rid of them," he muttered, swiping through his phone.

"Like hell there isn't," I told him. "Can't we call the cops?"

"I've got Francis on the line," Axel told us, phone pressed to his ear. "He's in touch with legal. We're exploring options."

"They're probably legally protected," Damian said, his jaw flexing endlessly. "As long as they're on sidewalks, I'd imagine it's fine. Probably all they want is to get attention and to block people from entering our fundraiser."

"Shit bricks," I muttered, nibbling on my lip as Damian's face went from sullen to dour. "There's got to be something we can do."

"Jessa, we might as well cancel," Damian said in a low voice. "If people can't come in, what's the point?"

"Well, the point is..." My gaze drifted around the room, over all of the carefully curated opulence, the diamonds dripping from chandeliers, the fresh blooms tumbling from vases. This needed to be enjoyed. The Fairchilds needed to get the word out. "The point is that this is a setback. It's not a dealbreaker. We can get through it."

"That's what you think," Damian said quietly.

"It's what I *know*," I told him.

"This whole night is about reputation damage control," he said, stepping closer. "What's more damaging to our reputation than an active protest about sex trafficking allegations? They've got signs, Jessa. They're not mincing words down there. They'll tank the whole thing before it even gets started."

His words sank into me, the gravity of his prediction feeling like the heaviest lead blanket. But I refused to surrender. They still had a fighting chance to turn things around, and I wasn't going to let go of it.

I blinked rapidly, struggling to see pathways through the dark roadblocks. His words hung heavily in the air between us as an idea slowly gurgled to life inside me.

"What if we go...down there?" I said.

"And do what? Join them?"

I shook my head. "No. But you and I could be, like, the welcoming committee. Showing our faces despite the protest." The idea was taking shape faster than I could spill it. "We could hire protection, so nothing happens. Bodyguards, whatever. And then we could stand out in front of the protesters and welcome each guest personally."

Damian watched me curiously. Axel seemed to be tuning in, phone still pressed to his face.

"It wouldn't be so dire. It would be more of a nuisance, really. And with us escorting each guest in individually, they won't even get a chance to be pummeled by whatever bullshit they're trying to say down there. We'd be the front-line receivers, let's say."

"You and Damian down there?" Axel asked, phone pulled away from his face.

"Yeah. Why not? I'm not afraid of some dumb protesters."

The corner of Damian's mouth started to curl. "Even protesters in New York? Jessa, it could get out of control. I don't want you to get hurt. I don't even want you near the potential of getting hurt."

"I won't get hurt," I said. "Because we'll have big, beefy bodyguards that you can hire in the next thirty seconds because you are Damian Fairchild."

He held my gaze, amusement swimming there.

"I like it," Axel said, pocketing his phone. "Francis is working on getting some beef here."

"Is that what he called it?" I asked Axel, who nodded.

"He would," Damian mused.

"Grade A, New York City beef," I told Damian with a haughty smile. "Now are you ready to mitigate the effect of this protest or what?"

The next hour was a whirlwind of logistics—calls from lawyers, contact with the NYPD, organizing security, and more. The hired beef helped keep the protesters at bay, while Damian and I personally presented the smiling faces each new arrival needed to feel confident about walking into a swarming cesspool of human trafficking signs and shouting.

We shook hands and distracted guests as well as we could. Eventually, the police decided that the protesters had made themselves enough of a nuisance, so they were forced to disperse. What few people lingered were more random bystanders and less organized mob.

None of that was fun to deal with in general, but even less so with a corset squeezing my ribcage like an anaconda.

On the sixty-fifth floor, I only made it through two scallops before I knew something had to give. I fidgeted in my chair as Damian stood at the podium, giving his speech about the future of coding technology and the fight to fund open access to education. I loved all his talking points—poverty-stricken teen finding solace in coding, lucking out with an encouraging high school teacher and tons of late nights researching, as well as the limitless possibilities that awaited our society if more teens were given more access to information like this.

It was all beautiful, truly. But I could not concentrate on another mother-cluckin' thing until this corset came off and burned in hell.

"All ideas were scandalous or rejected at one point..." Damian went on. The Rainbow Room was bursting tonight, every chair filled, some people relegated to standing on the fringes.

I took slow, measured breaths. I focused on fixed points in the distance. I even counted to sixty-three.

Nothing helped.

All I could think about was taking this corset off.

I sipped nervously at my pinot grigio, watching as Damian wrapped up his speech.

"Fairchild Enterprises might not be here forever," Damian said, his voice firm. "But there will always be a new need, a new challenge, a new urgent, life-changing request. I want there to be more answers than questions in the future. More ideas than problems."

Murmurs of agreement rippled through the room, and I was caught between teary-eyed emotion and breathlessness.

"Thank you all for joining us tonight as we find new ways to support innovation and adaptation. It means more to me than I can express. But it means the most to our great-grandchildren." Damian stepped back from the podium, smiling out at the crowd as the room erupted into applause. Tears filled my eyes as I clapped wildly.

Once the applause had died down, dinner continued, but the room maintained a high buzz of energy and conversation. Axel, grinning broadly, stood at a nearby table, chatting with a gray-haired man who looked like he was probably important. Damn near everyone here tonight was important, or at least rich in a serious way.

But focusing on individual guests didn't help things either. *I need this dress off me.*

I'd brought a back-up dress as a just-in-case, not thinking I'd really need it, or at least not until the end. But who could have known that the adrenaline of my first ever planned event and my first ever protest—both on the same night—would have caused my lungs to malfunction when constricted?

Damian stood across the room, deep in conversation with potential donors. Guests mingled, snagging plates at the buffet or clustered in small groups. Laughter and conversation rippled around me. This night was perfect. It was going off as well as I could have hoped, especially given the hitches.

The only issue was that I might not make it out alive.

Damian caught my eye from across the room and waved me toward him. I drifted over, ready with a smile as I approached a refined, older couple.

"I'd like you to meet the Bancrofts," Damian said. I eagerly shook their hands, gobbling up Mrs. Bancroft's elegance—the diamond brooch in her dark gray hair, the tasteful navy blue wraparound, the simple silver bracelets. "They are what I'd consider angels in the flesh."

Mrs. Bancroft laughed daintily, swatting away the comment. "Damian, don't start with that again."

"I'll accept it," Mr. Bancroft said. "I've always preferred a little air of the supernatural."

"Jessa has been working with us for the past month and a half," Damian said. "She's the one who planned this whole evening."

Mrs. Bancroft gasped, looking my way. "You did an amazing job. I haven't been able to get over the details. And your dress looks as if it was made for this event."

I couldn't stop beaming. I wasn't sure if Damian had meant to stroke my ego through meeting this couple, but I'd take it. "Thank you very much, Mrs. Bancroft. I hope you're enjoying your evening."

"Jessa is also a fashion designer," Damian went on, his hand finding the small of my back. "She did actually make this dress for tonight's party. Mrs. Bancroft has a few pet projects in the fashion industry, come to think of it. You two might want to chat sometime."

Mrs. Bancroft grabbed my wrist, searing me with a look. "You made *this* dress?"

"I did," I stammered.

"Incredible. I meet up with Anna about once a month. We'll have to see if you can't join us sometime."

The way Mrs. Bancroft said *Anna,* with the round vowel, made my eyes widen. "You mean, like...Anna Wintour?"

Mrs. Bancroft nodded. "Of course, dear."

I swallowed hard, not missing the satisfied look on Damian's face as Mrs. Bancroft and I exchanged contact information. After the Bancrofts drifted away, Damian's hand found the small of my back again.

"Did you eat?" he asked.

"Um," I began, thinking about the uneaten scallops. Thinking about how hungry I was just reminded me of how I couldn't eat, because of this damn corset. "Sort of."

"Didn't you like the food?" he asked, his gaze washing over the buffet tables. "I thought you'd chosen the menu. Did they mess something up?"

"Er, no, it's just..."

His face creased with concern. "Is everything okay?"

"Yes, of course. It's fine. I had a scallop, so—"

"Just one? That's weird."

I gulped. Okay, he'd spotted that there was something seriously amiss. I gnawed at my bottom lip. "Actually, uh..." I looked down, hesitant to lose this cleavage, but also desperate to take a full breath again. "Could we, uh, step out for a second?"

Damian didn't ask twice. He led the way toward the elevator lobby. When we'd reached the cool, moodily lit space, the clamor of the Rainbow Room through the arched doorway was some- how amplified—like a living, breathing postcard.

"What's wrong?" he asked in a low voice, stepping closer to me. He could get closer because nobody was out here observing us. We had a temporary pass, and I could feel the way his intentions had darkened. My skin prickled, expecting his hands, craving his touch.

Damian's hands found the corseted dip of my waist, bringing me against him in a short, forceful tug. My breath evaporated. Between this corset and this man, I doubted whether I'd make it out of this night alive.

"Somebody might come out and see us," I whispered, because I had no oxygen left.

"I don't care," he growled into my ear. Then he bit my earlobe, sending a jolt straight to my pussy.

I bit back a whimper, wilting against him. My breathing had quickened, which didn't seem exactly safe. Now I understood why all those Victorian heroines were constantly gasping and fainting. They were *dying*, and nobody knew how to get the damn corsets off.

"Damian," I gasped out, "I need to get this corset off. I'm dying here."

He paused, pulling back to look me over. "What do you mean?"

"It's so tight, and I need to change. Will you help me take it off? I'm worried I'll mess up the beads. Getting it on was easy, but I need a second pair of eyes to make sure I don't ruin this thing. I brought a backup dress."

He blinked. "You want to take your dress off?"

I nodded, unable to read him fully. I couldn't tell if he was upset or thought I was joking. "It's too much. I thought I could last the night, but I can't. And with the way I designed the dress, the corset needs to be fully laced in order for it to lie right on the shoulders. Oh, I really messed this one up. Let's just call it a learning experience."

But then his fingers curled into the softness of my hips, and I started to understand a little better. "And where are we going to take this corset off?"

"I don't know...the nearest private room?"

His chin dipped, his gaze darkening. That predator energy was returning. "And you expect me to be able to keep myself off of you while we're doing this?"

I laughed, wilting against him. "We can be good."

"So you're going to take this entire dress off, including the corset, and stand in front of me naked while you change into a different sexy dress? What is this, a test of my willpower?" He laughed, his hands seeking the base of my corset from the back of the dress. "I'm already certain I'll fail."

His meaning zipped through me. Maybe I wanted him to fail. Because this thing between us wasn't just one-and-done. We'd been flirting, connecting, practically dating for weeks now. Hell, the man had fallen asleep while we watched a movie via video chat one night. You didn't fall asleep on video chats with flings.

Maybe it was time to give in and let this relationship evolve to its next level.

"Come on. Let's find the perfect little private room in which to take your corset off and *not* fuck you senseless against the wall." He laughed, shaking his head as he kissed the top of my hand. "You know what we're walking into, right?"

My heart rate picked up again. The evil, sexy glint in his eye promised so much. It promised *everything*. And I wanted all of it.

"We're just doing a costume change and then coming back to the party," I told him. But my words were more of a test to see how serious we were about not crossing the lines we'd drawn. I was ready to erase it altogether.

"Where's the backup dress?" he asked me. "I'll go get it so you don't have to exert yourself."

I grinned so hard my cheeks hurt. "Now that is the most gentlemanly offer I've ever heard."

"I can be a gentleman when I want to be," he said, squeezing my hand. As we came into full view of the party, he looked down at me, seeming reluctant to let go of me.

"It's in my bag at the table," I told him. He brushed a kiss to my forehead before he took off; his absence felt like a gust of cold air as I measured my breaths and waited for him near the doorway. My gaze landed on Francis across the party, whose eyes darted between me and Damian. *Shit*. Had he seen us? The thought only prompted more stress, which made the corset feel even tighter.

Abort corset. Abort corset.

Damian returned a moment later with my bag, tenderness and fire in his gaze. We searched out closets, a greenroom, whatever made sense to snag some privacy while I completely disrobed. We finally stumbled upon a private bathroom with a padded bench and powder room inside. Excitement prickled through me as Damian shut the door and locked it with a soft *click*.

"Okay, Jessa." The low rumble of his voice rippled through me, sending moisture straight to my panties. His gaze washed over me like he'd already completely undressed me, yet he hadn't even laid a finger on me. "Where should we begin?"

I turned away from him, exposing my back to him. I gently moved my hair over my shoulder, so he could better see what he was working with.

"There's a clasp there," I started, my voice wavering a little. The air snapped with electricity as he stepped closer. He palmed the swell of my hips through the dress, and I could feel the possession there. I'd felt it in the ballroom, too, when he'd touched me during our conversation with Mrs. Bancroft. And I couldn't argue. If he wanted me, he had me.

I'd always been his.

"Mm-hmm." He pressed soft kisses along the top of my back. "The clasp."

My eyes drifted shut, relishing the feel of his lips against my skin. I'd missed his kisses in the short amount of time I'd had this lipstick on.

"Just be careful with it because I didn't sew it in super well," I told him, my voice sounding faraway as his kissed drifted down my spine.

"I'll be careful," he promised.

"Once the top is open," I went on, "Then I can unlace it from up front. I just don't want to ruin my clasp, or this dress."

"Mm-hmm." He dragged his tongue over the bumps of my spine. Goosebumps erupted everywhere. I'd never had anyone *lick* my spine before. But Damian showed me I barely knew anything about what true pleasure entailed. He'd given me more orgasms than I'd even given myself. And we'd barely even begun exploring each other.

The dress tightened around me briefly as he fumbled with the clasp. Then I felt it release and he tugged down the material covering the corset. A moment later, he spun me around, the base of the corset came loose and some of the pressure around my ribcage disappeared. A whoosh of air filled my lungs.

"Oh, mother clucker," I moaned. "That feels like heaven."

He loosened the rest of the corset, and the material spilled away from my breasts. They were unrestrained now, completely free. I held the front of the corset against me as Damian's mossy green gaze glinted with something feral. He pressed his forehead to mine, drawing a deep breath.

"Do you know how fucking mad I am that I can't fuck your mouth with my tongue right now?"

I laughed, but it didn't last long. His hands traveled up the front of my dress, pulling at the corset. The stiff material fell away and my breasts tumbled out. His big hands caught them, his thumbs finding the stiff peaks of my breasts. He let out a low groan.

"Fuck, Jessa." He massaged my breasts, lavishing them with heated touches, until he dove down and replaced his hands with his lips. He kissed every square inch of them, from the tops to the tips, coaxing my nipples into rock hard points. He took bites along the way, getting lost in my cleavage.

"You are so fucking beautiful," he growled, making one of my nipples disappear inside his mouth. "You have no idea how long I've wanted to do this."

I could barely speak. The feel of his mouth around my nipple was almost too much. I arched against him, needing friction, needing *him*. He snaked a hand down between my legs, seeking the V between my legs through the fabric of my dress.

"Do you need me down here, babe?" He watched me with a dark curiosity. I could see the ridge of his erection through his dress pants, and all I could do was nod.

"Please," I gasped out.

Damian backed me up against the countertop, urging me to sit on it, bunching my dress up to my hips as he did. My back hit the cool glass of the mirror as he eased my legs open.

"You know what I want to do," he said, his voice gritty and full of passion. He filled the space between my legs, that stiff ridge finding the expectant heat of my pussy. He rolled his hips in a slow circle, the tip of his cock nudging my clit. My entire body jolted, and I cried out. "Do you want it too?"

Again, all I could do was nod. My chest heaved as he rocked against me again, his lips leaving a hot trail along my neck as we pretend-fucked on the countertop. He pulled back, shaking his head.

"I can't do this without tongue fucking you, Jessa." He sank his teeth into the side of my neck. "I'll reserve a room. We'll go straight there." He sucked at the same spot on my neck, his tongue circling playfully. "Then I can fuck you properly, like I've been fantasizing about this whole time."

His words left me dizzy and wanting. Of course I'd go along with it. Of course I needed this too. Boundaries be damned.

"What do you think?"

My head hit the mirror as I sent up one last plea to the heavens. I'd agree to it, but I needed God or whoever else up there to make sure that I didn't get torn in two and tossed aside as a result.

Please, God. Let Damian be the one.

"Let's go," I whispered.

CHAPTER TWENTY

DAMIAN

I got Jessa into her back-up dress and into the elevator without laying a single kiss on her lips, which I thought deserved an award.

Every thump of my heart said the same thing.

I need this woman.

We left the party without telling anyone. Axel would probably be pissed, but I didn't care. Not when I could only see, taste, hear, or smell Jessa. Besides, the matchmaker part of him would probably be happy that we were finally hooking up, so I planned to use that to my advantage if he got his feathers ruffled.

I had a luxury room booked before our feet even hit the sidewalk. We stumbled three blocks, a mess of laughter and cheek kisses, drunk on nothing but this feeling of freedom and anticipation. Like we had everything ahead of us. Everything was within our grasp.

I hadn't felt like this in an eternity.

No, scratch that. I hadn't felt like this *ever*.

We checked into the hotel, and I had Jessa pinned to the corner of the elevator as it soared toward the twentieth floor, lavishing her neck with more kisses, grinding my cock against her lest she forget what awaited her. We had nothing—no clothes but her abandoned corset dress, no overnight stuff, no nothing. But it didn't matter. All I needed was her.

The door hadn't even shut behind us in the room before I had Jessa's face in my hands, kissing that fire engine red off her lips.

She was right. It smeared. *A lot.* It was the least of my concerns.

I kissed her lips until she looked drugged, backing her through the room neither of had even noticed yet. The backs of her knees hit the bed and she fell onto it, hair splaying out around her. I ran my hand down the swell of her breasts, down the middle of her dress.

"You're mine now, Jessa." My hand swirled over her mound, my thumb nicking the tight bud of her clit. She moaned, jerking her hips in my direction. "We did a great job playing innocent for the past few weeks, but that ends tonight."

She reached for me, tugging at my belt. "Please. End it now."

I didn't need to hear another word. I helped her sit up, and then I palmed her cheeks, our tongues meeting hot and familiar in the middle. I undid the zipper of her dress between kisses, leaving only her back-up bra and panties. I stopped kissing her long enough to undo her bra. It crumpled away, freeing those big, beautiful breasts.

This was my new favorite activity. Drowning in her tits. I gobbled them up like I had outside the Rainbow Room, burying my face in them until I couldn't breathe. While I asphyxiated in her tits, she undid my belt. My pants crumpled to the floor a moment later.

"Oh my God," she said with a little laugh. Then her fingertips smoothed over my cockhead, sending a jolt of pleasure so strong through me I almost buckled to the ground.

"Take all of it," I urged her, shoving my briefs down so that my cock sprang out, heavy and bobbing. Her eyes turned to saucers. I hadn't denied myself by any stretch of the imagination while we played our little game of *lines in the sand.* I had sometimes jacked off twice a day, just to survive all the times I'd buried my fingers in her pussy without a lick of relief on my end. But it had been a fun exercise in deprivation. A game I'd participate in willingly again, knowing that this prize at the end of the Rainbow Room was better than any pot of gold.

Jessa handled my cock like she was afraid of it. I could see the question written in her eyes.

"It'll fit," I murmured, my gaze riveted to her smooth, cool hands fisting the length of me. "I promise."

I bucked my hips as she jacked me off, fighting the urge to flip her over and fuck her from behind like I'd been imagining for weeks. Then she brought her lips up to my cockhead, taking the whole thing into her mouth.

"Ohhhh, Jessa." A gravelly moan ripped past my lips, and I could only see white for a moment. Maybe the deprivation game had gone on too long. I'd come like a rocket the second I pushed inside her. Which meant she needed to come at least once first.

She took another slow pull at my cock, her mouth velvet and juice. When she released me with a pop, I grunted and dropped to my knees.

"I need to switch things up, babe." That pet name kept escaping unsanctioned. But I couldn't control it at this point. "I'm gonna come so fucking hard the second I get inside you. I know how tight you are. How wet you get for me." I met her gaze as I tugged her panties off and tossed them aside. I pushed open her knees, finding that swollen slit waiting for me. "I won't be able to last a minute, so I want you to come first. Like always."

She laughed wispily. "Okay. If you say so."

I pushed her knees wider and urged her to recline on the bed. She complied, and I dove between her legs, finding the sweet, sticky heat of her arousal instantly. I bit and slurped and sucked at her clit, coaxing her nub until it was rock hard. Her pussy glistened, the bedspread damp beneath her. She moaned as I tongue fucked her clit, her thighs quivering around my head.

"You like that, babe?" *Fuck.* There it was again.

"Damian—I—I can't even—"

"Mm-hmm." I shook my head, my tongue flicking back and forth over her clit. Nothing would go inside her but my cock. I fisted myself briefly. I was so hard it almost hurt. Every inch of my body *needed* her. "You want this cock so bad, don't you?"

"I do," she breathed. "Please, just give it to me."

"What do you want me to do to you?" I stopped licking her pussy and pulled back, admiring the gleaming, messy folds before me.

She grunted. "You know what I want."

"Say it, Jessa."

She moaned, rocking her hips in a circle. "I want you to fuck me, Damian."

The swear word was poetry on her lips. My cock jumped with anticipation. "And where do you want me to come?"

She bucked her hips, searching for my lips, fingers, anything. But I wasn't ready to give her more yet.

"Inside me."

The suggestion sizzled through me. I hadn't even considered that.

"I'm on birth control," she added, sounding a million miles away. "Please, Damian. Fuck me. *Fuck* me like I need it."

I hissed as I dove back between her legs, taking a soft bite of her clit. She screamed, bucking against my face.

It was time. The woman had probably had ten mini-orgasms in the time I'd been between her legs, and besides, I couldn't wait any longer. I repositioned us so that we were fully supported on the bed, my hands denting the mattress around her as I nudged myself between her legs. We shared an intense look, every emotion swirling there, alongside the unknowns of what came after. I couldn't even think about anything but *this*. The satisfaction of finally claiming Jessa. I'd wanted her for so long. Not just since she started working for me, but since I'd first fallen for her back in high school.

But that was too mushy for this moment. For who I was. I silenced the thoughts with a deep kiss, and my cock slid into her slick folds until it hit just the right spot.

She opened her legs wider, hooking those thick thighs around me as I slowly flexed and rocked my way inside her. My cockhead slipped in no problem, but I eased the rest in gently, not wanting to scare—or hurt—her. She moaned through our kisses with every inch by glorious inch I sank into her. I buried myself to the hilt, and pleasure exploded inside me.

I filled every last centimeter of her pussy. With her stretched around me, I'd found heaven.

My head spun as I rocked against her, starting a slow but fierce rhythm. She wrapped her arms around my neck, clinging to me as I thrust against her. Her thighs clamped around me like she'd float away if she didn't hang on, and I loved the way our bodies fit together. The suction and seal of our skin. Drugged and blissed, I buried my face in her neck.

I didn't just need her now. I needed more of this *always*.

"Damiannnnn," she moaned, arching against me. "I can't believe it..."

I grunted, taking a soft bite of her shoulder. "What, babe?"

"How good...you feel..."

Her whole body shook as I drilled into her, over and over, her pussy a slippery vice that had me ready to come in seconds. Her eyes were pinched shut, head thrown back, as I fought back the urge to orgasm. Sweat prickled on my brow. I wanted to last as long as I could. I would have extended it forever, if I could have.

But I could only withstand so much of this velvety heaven. I wasn't a robot. I was merely an eternally horny man whose eyes preferred all the luscious dips and rolls of Jessa's body. I dipped down and kissed her on the mouth, then I moved my lips to each nipple in turn, fucking her as hard as I could. With her nipple between my teeth, I saw her unravel. Her pussy contracted in waves around my cock and her back arched, writhing and grappling against me.

I never came inside a woman as a rule. But with Jessa, I was ready to throw out the rulebook. I went off like a rocket, my cock pumping out round after round of my pleasure inside of her. A gritty, rough moan escaped me, everything going bright and then black behind my eyelids. My body jerked as the orgasm wound its way through my limbs, lighting up every square inch of me.

We kissed for a long time as our orgasms receded. My body buzzed in the pleasant afterglow, but I still couldn't rip myself off her. We were a smeared ruby-red mess, and I didn't care. I always needed just one more kiss.

After a while, once our kisses slowed and I had finally slipped out of her, we lay on the bed staring at each other.

Lost in each other's gaze.

Speaking volumes without a single word.

I grabbed her hand and kissed each one of her knuckles, while she just smiled at me.

If this wasn't pure contentment, I'd never find it in my lifetime.

And Jessa just smiled like she'd known all along.

I awoke with a jolt.

My chest heaved as I came to, sitting bolt upright and looking around the darkened room. I was immediately hyperventilating, trying to orient myself in the unfamiliar place. *Who? What? How?*

All I could remember was the grip of the nightmare around my ribcage.

The screams and the unknown depths of my subconscious. Kaylee's face, evaporating into the void.

"Hey. Hey, are you okay?"

Jessa's soft voice beside me brought me back to earth. I drew a deep breath, our surroundings finally sinking in.

We were in a hotel room. Jessa was beside me. And the clock at the bedside read ten a.m. My face dropped into my hands, and I could have cried.

It was ten motherfucking a.m., which meant I had slept a full night for the first time since the SEC investigation had started.

Jessa's warm hand swished back and forth over my back. "Did you have a nightmare?"

I nodded, unable to find my voice. I dragged my hands down my face and twisted to look at her. Her just-woke-up softness was enchanting. There was no other word. Her mussed mahogany hair, the sleepy yet sharp quality to her crystal silver blue eyes. My gut wrenched. Everything about this was perfect.

Perfectly heartbreaking.

"Fuck. Sorry if I scared you." The sheets rustled as I lay down once more, welcoming her into my arms. My heart still pounded, but I needed to act like it didn't. I'd gone from unconscious to hyperalert in three seconds. My nervous system couldn't keep up, and my mind ricocheted around like an out of control ping pong ball.

"It's okay," she said, nuzzling into my bare chest. "Did you sleep well until then?"

"Uh, yeah. Better than I have in..." *An eternity.* Because that's how long I'd been waiting to relax. That's how long my body had been desperate to unwind.

And with Jessa at my side, I'd finally managed it.

Just needed to add that to the list of things to unpack. For now, I'd ignore it.

She cozied up to me again, a happy sigh spilling out of her. I kissed the top of her head. "You sleep good too?"

"Yeah. I woke up about an hour ago."

"So you've just been staring at me since then, huh?"

"Only for a half hour, I swear." She laughed, tipping her head back to look at me. "It's been nice to just lie in bed. Besides, when I thought about getting up and brushing my teeth, I remembered...we don't have any toothbrushes."

"Oh shit. You're right." I twisted to grab my phone, firing off an SOS text to Legs. "I'll have it delivered so we don't have to leave our cocoon any sooner than we're ready."

The words from my own lips were surprising. Who the fuck was saying them? Damian Fairchild did not create *cocoons*. He created temporary sex dens that evaporated into thin air as soon as the orgasm hit.

Jessa made it hard to want to evaporate, though.

"This is a pretty great way to spend a Sunday," she said.

"Sure beats what I normally do," I told her.

"What's that?"

"Work and stress myself out," I said with a laugh.

"You never turn off, do you?" The question was soft. A blunt-edged probe. Normally I'd harden up at a question like that. Deflect, divert. But something about the softness of the morning and the warmth of her buried in my arms prompted me to open up.

"I don't," I admitted. "I can't."

She drew a breath. "What are you afraid will happen if you do turn off?"

That one landed less like a blunt-edged probe and more like a spear. I had a list of things I was avoiding through work. An entire thesis outlining what I hoped to achieve via endless dedication and devotion to my career.

"You want to go deep this morning, huh?"

She smiled sweetly. "Just making chit-chat."

It was funny only because she knew how full of shit that response was. "I'm turning off now, see? I can do it. I'm not afraid of it." But that was a lie. I was terrified of it. And as soon as the sweetness of this encounter ended, I'd need to be back on a mission.

"When's the last time you turned off?" She drew aimless, lazy patterns over my bare chest, right over the ribs that practically vibrated from how hard my heart slammed against them. It was like she knew and was trying to calm me down.

"I can't even answer that." I stared at the ceiling, groping for some sort of idea. It hadn't been months. It had been *years*. But how did you tell someone you had a problem and chose to ignore it?

"I guess that's how you and your brothers rose so high, huh?" Her designs drifted across my nipple, down the side of my ribcage. "You don't stop. You don't see anything but the finish line." Her finger paused. "What *is* the finish line?"

I laughed again. "Is this an interview or a counseling session?"

"Sorry." She sounded sheepish. "I'm just curious."

"They're good questions. I just try not to think about them too much."

"Why not?"

"Because I know what the answers are, and I don't like them."

She tipped her head back, searching out my gaze. "How could you not like the answers? You're on top of the world, Damian. You're one of the world's wealthiest, most powerful men. You have the power to do exactly what you want to in this world. You *are* doing it, regardless of what the finish line is."

"And despite all that, there are still the haters who will show up to shit all over my fundraiser. Still reporters out there desperate to find whatever dirt they can to trash my life. It's not the top of the world, Jessa. It's the bottom. Because the world is on my shoulders now, and it's a fucking burden."

My words hung loudly in the air, echoing through my head over and over again. I'd never said it out loud before. Not to anyone, least of all a woman I'd hooked up with. But Jessa wasn't just a woman I was hooking up with.

The truth was, all of it was a burden and I fucking hated it.

But I had to choose it. Over and over and over.

"Is that the double-edged sword of it?" she asked quietly, after an eternity had crawled by.

"I guess."

"You could walk away from it."

My body hefted with a humorless laugh, my heartrate picking up again. We'd drilled into the heart of my anxieties in no time at all. How had she known? It was like she had a magnifying glass and knew how to aim it at the darkest corners of my soul.

"No I can't. It's hard to explain. But I...I'm obligated to do this."

"Obligated?"

"Yes. I work as hard as I do, I aim as high as I do, I do all the things I do because of Jordan and Kaylee." My voice cracked, and I dragged my hands down my face again. Fucking Jessa last night had shifted something, and I wasn't sure if I liked it yet. I stared at the ceiling for a moment, letting the words echo inside me first. "They can't be here to live life, so I've gotta do it for them. I owe them. I have to succeed for them."

Jessa pressed up onto an arm so she could look down at me. I'd never seen her so tender, so soft, so cracked open. Something huge quivered between us. Something I wasn't sure I was ready to accept.

"Why do you say you *owe* them?"

"Because I didn't save them."

Devastation trickled down her face. "Damian, you couldn't have."

"I could have done more. I could have called more people. I could have hounded the detectives, the police officers. I could have fucking canvassed the country until I found them myself." I pinched my eyes shut, the familiar waves of regret and pain swimming far closer to the surface this morning. Fuck. We needed to turn this around, and it was too early to drink an entire fifth of whiskey, which was my normal coping mechanism when the thoughts got too loud.

"Coulda, woulda, shoulda," she said softly. "You were a kid yourself when your parents passed, and then you were just another teen in the foster system. There wasn't anything you could do."

"I wasn't just a kid the entire time, though. Axel and I were Fairchilds by the time we lost contact with Kaylee and Jordan, but I was still the head of the Haynes family. It fell on my shoulders as the oldest brother. I was seventeen, eighteen when Kaylee started showing all those concerning signs. I could have done so much more."

"And now you carry the weight of the world for them," she said sadly, tears swimming in her eyes. "When are you gonna put it down?"

I soaked in her pretty face, the tiny lines by her eyes, the sadness reflecting from me onto her. I shook my head, swiping my thumb across a spilt tear on her cheek. "I can't, Jessa. It will all be in vain if I don't fucking accomplish something in this sad and stupid world. That's why I built the algorithm the way I did, to funnel money from the world's 1 percent into the poorest, most forgotten communities. It's why I raise all this money for kids and education. It's why we started the charity. It's why we do it all. There's no reason other than supporting the most vulnerable, the most forgotten. So no, I can't put it down."

Her throat bobbed, and she studied something unknowable on my chest, nibbling on her bottom lip. When she met my gaze, the sheen of tears was still there. "Have you ever thought that maybe the greatest way to repay them would be to just...be happy?"

I shook my head, but she hurried to add more.

"What I mean is, all the good that you do is valuable. It means something. But what if the real reason we're here, the best way you could honor them, would be to just love your family and eat each other's cooking and say it was good?"

Now I had the tears in my eyes. I pinched the bridge of my nose and shook my head. This was too deep. Too much. And I'd reached my limit of fucking thinking.

"Nope, time's up. That concludes *my* therapy session." I had to switch gears, *now*. "If you aren't careful, yours is next."

She laughed. "I've got a few skeletons in my own closet, don't worry. You aren't the only one."

"Can I end this conversation with the promise of breakfast?" My heart was still pounding, but I was determined not to fall into my mental sinkhole like I did most mornings. Not when Jessa was here. She was too bright of a light to ignore. And all things considered, she'd been the only person who had successfully navigated me in *and* out of those treacherous conversational waters, other than Axel or Trace. "I'm thinking a full spread. Opulent everything. Diamond encrusted water glasses. Gold shavings on the toast. Because for once, I'm remembering to feed *you*, instead of the other way around."

She laughed into her hand, that familiar tenderness shining in her eyes. "Wow. This is a momentous occasion. I think that'll shut me up, yes."

"Excellent. Mission accomplished," I teased as I pressed a kiss to her lips. She giggled through the kiss. When we broke apart, I added, "I see how much you worry about me. How much you care. I know I can be an asshole most of the time. I'm trying to be better."

She froze, watching me with an unreadable look. "You...you've noticed that I worry?"

"I see everything, Jessa. Even when I don't want to. I'm a fucking owl, I just hide it."

She licked her lips, the aimless patterns over my chest starting up again. "It's how I treat my family. My found family." Her words sank into me for a moment. "Blood doesn't always care," she whispered. "But your found family will."

I scooped up her hand, pressing her knuckles to my lips. This time, we both had tears in our eyes. I knew a thing or two about found families. That included Trace and the rest of the Fairchilds. But for her, it was more important. Because she'd been let down by her blood family.

Something big and aching existed between her and her mother, more than just the drugs. "That 'blood is thicker than water' quote is bullshit anyway," I told her, swiping my thumb back and forth over her knuckles.

"What do you mean?"

"I prefer a different version I've read: *The blood of the covenant is thicker than the water of the womb.*"

She nodded, understanding washing over her face. "Ain't that the truth?" Her gaze drifted off, something fierce churning inside her. "The water of the womb betrayed me, Damian. There's no covenant with that woman." She glanced at me. "Does that make me a horrible person, to say that about my own mom?"

"Addiction is hard, Jessa. I don't think it makes you a horrible person to say that. And I think you have your own reasons for saying it."

Her throat bobbed again, and she nodded vehemently. "Oh, I do. Addiction is one thing. But she—" This time, she was the one to crack. The tears were back, and she dabbed at the corners of her eyes with a finger.

I couldn't even explain what was happening or how we'd arrived here. The only explanation was that we had to. We *needed* to, for reasons beyond my own understanding.

"Damian, I've never told you this, but when I was a junior in high school, one of her boyfriends pushed himself on me," she said in a low, trembling voice. She made sure to avoid my gaze. "He all but raped me. When I told my mom, she didn't believe me. Told me I needed a boob job so that my huge tits didn't distract him. And then she stayed with him for another year."

My heart cracked. I gathered her into my arms, squeezing her as hard as I could. "That wasn't your fault, Jessa."

"Thank you." She hugged me back just as hard, and when she lifted her head, that familiar determination shone in her eyes again. "I know that now. But I just can't reconcile the betrayal. Tara knows what happened, but she doesn't care. Jeremy is the only one who went to bat for me. As far as I'm concerned, the only people in my family are you and Jeremy and your brothers."

"Hopefully you don't see me quite like a brother..."

She dissolved into laughter, a much-needed break in the high-stakes conversation we trekked through. "No. Not a brother. But definitely part of my found family. The one I chose."

"It's an honor to be included," I whispered, gathering her into my arms again. She clung to me, burying her face in my chest.

"I'd do anything for you, Damian," she said. "It's always been like that."

I knew how true those words were for her. But an even bigger truth rose above it all. I didn't deserve it.

Just like I didn't deserve her.

CHAPTER TWENTY-ONE

I didn't make it back to my apartment until seven a.m. Monday morning. Damian and I hadn't been able to rip ourselves out of the hotel room until the last possible second, instead choosing to nest hardcore via endless movies, room service, and so much delicious, intense, meaningful sex.

We were wrapped up in each other from head to toe. Dreamy, floating, and oblivious to anything beyond our bubble. Leaving the SUV to return to my apartment that morning was actually hard—but I needed the day to myself. I'd requested a personal day to get caught up on schoolwork for that night's class. And more than that, after our invigorating getaway to our hotel, I was freshly motivated to finish my roommate hunt.

Applications had been rolling in since I'd placed the ad, but with everything going on in Fairchild world, I hadn't been able to pay much attention. Now that the Programmer's Ball was behind me, I was ready to make my selection.

Even though I was closer than ever to Damian now, I needed to have a plan that didn't rely on him. This whole boss/employee/lover thing could go wrong so quickly. I wanted to make my way in this city with my own two feet firmly on the ground. I didn't think

Damian would undermine that—but I sure could easily get swept away with him.

Besides, the truth bubbling inside was that while I loved working at Fairchild Enterprises, it wasn't where I wanted to *stay*. My heart was calling me in a different direction. I didn't know what the future looked like exactly, but I was slowly putting together the puzzle.

And this roommate was one of the key pieces.

I whiled away my morning with a pumpkin spice latte—one that Damian had delivered to my apartment—and schoolwork, interrupted only by sexy texts from Damian and back-and-forth emails with the final round of possible roomies.

I was treating this roommate hunt like something just shy of a speed dating round. I needed to quickly and effectively vet these people, and what better way than back-to-back meetings in a public place so they couldn't serial kill me?

In the huge pool of applicants, only three seemed remotely compatible. Despite asking for women roommates only, I'd received a shocking number of male applicants, which just further proved my suspicion that nobody actually read anything they found on the internet.

By noon, I had a nearby coffee shop designated as the meet-up point and three back-to-back speed roommate meetings beginning at five p.m. My entire body tingled as I awaited the evening. It put an extra pep in my step as I did my homework and worked on new designs. One of the most important takeaways from the weekend was the fact that corsets *should be avoided at all costs* and that as a designer, I planned to never incorporate one into my pattern, no matter the amount of cleavage it provided.

Maybe *this* was my fashion hill to die on. After almost dying *because* of the corset, I would gladly die on any adjacent hill that included condemning the corset to Hell.

Damian was on a roll Monday. Not only had he sent me a pumpkin spice latte, he also sent me lunch in the form of pho. The accompanying text read:

DAMIAN: I wish I could be there to watch you enjoy this. Hope it warms you up as much as the memories of our weekend together are warming me up right now.

I didn't stop smiling for a full hour after that message.

Everything seemed to be going right for once. I was sitting in New York City, advancing my fashion career, making rent on time, all while having life-changing, breath-stealing, toe-curling sex. My high school fantasies weren't just fulfilled, they'd been blown to smithereens. I hadn't even known that men like Damian existed—where sex wasn't just a pleasure-mission for the man, where my clitoris figured into 80% of the equation. I could barely think about it without getting hot and bothered again.

Focus on design. Focus on the roommate.

That's what today was for. And mother cluck it, I was gonna accomplish what I set out to do.

At five on the dot, I was tucked into my local coffee shop, nursing a decaf coffee and wondering if I still had time to hop in line again and get one of those lemon poppyseed muffins. Bean & Brew was the quintessential New York coffee shop—rich wood floors, fascinating murals on the walls depicting various stages of the coffee bean harvesting process, the standard array of hipsters and work-from-homers, trendy glasses and knit caps aplenty.

I fidgeted in my seat, waiting for this roommate hunt to begin.

The first potential roomie was Adalynn. She showed up ten minutes late and spent an additional ten minutes hassling the barista about a mistake on her drink. After she took her tip back out of the jar, I knew Adalynn probably wasn't the best fit for my next New York chapter.

Potential Roomie #2 was a student named Jessie. She and I chatted politely for about twenty minutes before the dealbreaker emerged—she wanted separate fridges, each with locks. No thank you. I didn't have the time or brain capacity for that.

As six crept closer and I awaited the final candidate to arrive, I was trying to stave off disappointment. I didn't have a back-up option yet, and I was damn near out of choices. But I held out hope—if not this round of potential roomies, there had to be someone out there who wouldn't shit on the wait staff and hide her leftovers under lock and key.

Kendra, my third interview, rolled in at six on the dot. She was pure blonde hair and sunshine from the second she stepped inside. I waved, knowing instinctively this was her, and Kendra's face lit up even more.

"Hello! Are you Jessa?" She swept my way, holding out her arms to hug me as though we were long lost friends finding each other again.

"Jessa, in the flesh. Kendra?"

"It's so nice to meet you." After a quick squeeze, we sank into armchairs that faced each other. Kendra took off a giant messenger bag she had across her chest, setting it down with a thud.

"Whatcha got in there?" I asked. "Sounds heavy."

"Oh, not much. Just some research for a story I'm working on."

I perked up. This was either a red flag or the start of something very normal. "Story? Research?"

She flashed me a conspiratorial smile. Her girl next door vibes had an interesting edge. "I can't reveal too much yet. But it's for my latest piece. I'm a journalist for *Big Apple Mag*. And someday, I'll be a famous one." I liked the go-getter attitude immediately. Her sharp gaze washed over me, almost like an assessment. "What about you? What do you do?"

"Well, I'm...a struggling Kentucky transplant," I said with a laugh. "Hopefully *not* a famous one someday."

Kendra laughed, arranging her bag near her feet before relaxing back into the seat. "Fair enough. But what would you *like* to be famous for someday?"

A breath whooshed out of me. "You certainly are a journalist, huh?"

Her eyes sparkled. "Sorry, am I moving too quick? I can get intense pretty fast. It's sort of my flaw."

"No, no. I'm the same way. I'm just not used to having it doled back to me."

We shared an amused smile. Despite the fact that I'd known her for seconds bordering on minutes, the ease I felt made it seem like I'd known her for much longer.

"So? Let's hear the answer."

"I suppose I'd love to be famous for my designs," I said, smoothing a few wrinkles in my leggings. "I design clothing. Mostly dresses for plus-size girls. Well, for any size, but I'm trying to make a name for myself in plus-size fashion, because why not pick the skinniest fashion center of the country to try it in?"

Kendra laughed. "Now that's an excellent mission statement. Why didn't you lead with that?"

The question floored me. But I knew why. I didn't share my fashion aspirations with many people because I wanted to avoid the laughter and derision that followed my dream around like hungry wolves.

"It's dangerous to tell the world about your passion, don't you think?" I picked at a spot on my leggings. "It's easier to just do it and then if it happens, great, and if it doesn't, well, there's nobody there to say *I told you so.*"

Except there were more than a couple people around to tell me *I told you so* if this didn't work out.

"Right. But sometimes, don't you think the magic of making it happen rests on shouting it out?" Kenda looked like she was caught somewhere between revelation and deep concentration.

"Is that why you introduced yourself as a someday-famous journalist?"

Her laughter felt like a breath of fresh air. "Exactly."

"All right. So this is an interesting way to start getting to know a potential roommate," I said before I sipped my decaf. "Most people start with *what did you study in school*, but not us. Oh, do you want anything to drink? I figured I should ask before we deep dive into another question."

"No, I'm fine. I brought this." She rummaged in her bag, pulling out a thermos. She set it on the wooden coffee table in front of her. "Do you want to guess what's in there?"

I blinked, looking at the completely normal, featureless thermos. "Kombucha?"

She tipped her head. "I don't touch that stuff. No, it's just water!"

We shared a laugh, which led to more conversation, more laughter, more fascinating tidbits that blossomed into tangents that led deeper into conversation.

Two hours later, the coffee shop had transitioned into serving alcohol instead of caffeine. As the room grew more boisterous and my stomach panged with hunger, I was ready to make the offer.

"Do you want to come back to the apartment to see it?" I asked her. "That way you can make a fully informed decision."

"Excellent idea." Kendra followed me out onto the sidewalk, lugging her bag full of notes and not-Kombucha-just-water. I soaked up the waning rays of late-autumn sun as we walked the two blocks to the apartment. My phone started blaring just as we stepped into the apartment building. I fumbled with my purse to find it and silence it.

"Sorry," I muttered, pausing at the base of the stairs. It was Damian. "I thought I had silenced it. It's just my..." What was he to me now? "My boss calling."

"Oh, where do you work?"

I fished my key out of my purse before leading Kendra up the staircase to my door. "Fairchild Enterprises."

I pushed the key into the lock and the door swung open. I walked inside, though Kendra didn't immediately follow me. She watched me with wide eyes from the hallway.

"For real?"

"Yeah, why?"

She stepped inside the apartment, drawing a deep breath. "Wow. I bet that's interesting, huh?"

"Yeah, I'd say so," I said, laughing nervously as she shut the door behind her. I couldn't tell if that was a good *for real* or a bad one. "They're interesting guys, with interesting lives."

"So you know them *personally*?"

I swallowed, nodding. "Yeah. I actually grew up with them."

Now Kendra's eyes were the size of saucers. Awe shone from her. "That is so cool. Wow, I just thought of like, two hundred questions I wanted to ask."

"Is that a good thing...?"

"I'm fascinated by them. I've been following all the news about them, of course. But I really love who they are, or who they seem to be, despite all the contentious shit going on. I don't know—they're kind of counter-culture icons in a way. I respect what they're doing in the tech and finance worlds, because they're representing the 99 percent. Not many people do that. You know?"

I nodded, emotion welling inside me. "Yeah. I totally agree."

"And, of course, it doesn't hurt that they're all, like, painfully hot," Kenda added with a laugh. "Any chance you could hook me up with one of them?"

"Trace might be single." The words reverberated strangely inside me. But it was true. Axel was hopelessly in love with Cora, and I was...*hopelessly in love with Damian.* "I'll see what I can do."

I showed Kendra around the apartment—it was a laughably quick tour—and by the end of it, I could tell she was ready to say *yes.*

"So what do you think, famous journalist?" I asked with a wink.

"I think you've got a new roomie, famous designer." She cocked finger guns. "I've got to go drop this stuff off at the police station. But I'll text you later and we can figure out details, okay?"

"Kendra, what on earth is in that bag?"

She waved off my question, clunking over to the front door. "That's a story for another time. After we've lived together for at least a week. See you later, roomie!" She sent me a bright smile before pulling the door shut behind her, leaving me in a pleasant cloud of accomplishment, mingled with the scent of her floral perfume.

Kendra was fascinating and strong. Just the kind of person I needed in my life.

And I had a new roommate.

My phone buzzed again. This time, it was Jeremy. When I picked up, I could hear commotion in the background.

"Hey there, little lady." In the background, more shouts. "Just your family calling, to make sure you're still alive in the Big Apple."

"Of course I'm alive, Jeremy. Sheesh. Don't you think the police would call you if they found my cold, dead corpse on the sidewalk?"

"*Jessa Walton,*" Jeremy hissed. And we were off to the races. I smothered my laughter as he started to officially pitch his fit. "How could you even say something like that? What is wrong with you?"

"You know, you might actually be speaking to my ghost right now," I said in a spooky voice.

"Good, because that means I can give you the ass whooping you deserve for saying the words 'cold, dead corpse.' My lord above.

You're lucky the rest of them didn't hear that. I know better than to put you on speakerphone. My lord."

"What's going on over there?" Shrieks of laughter pealed in the background.

"Just having a little cookout at Pop's, since it's randomly sixty-five degrees today down here. He says hi."

"Tell him hi back." My dad wasn't one for talking, but when he talked, it was usually profound. He'd only called me once, and that was the night I arrived in New York, just to make sure I hadn't been kidnapped en route. Jeremy was the official spokesperson for the family, in that sense. The only one who really communicated with me, outside of Tara's hateful messages and pleas for money.

"I told him we were probably calling you too early," Jeremy went on, "but he wanted me to check in. Are you at work?"

"No, I had a personal day today, actually." I bit back a yawn as I spread out on the couch. It was a cracked leather couch that Nicole had brought—and left—and it would be the first thing to go when I had a spare dollar to invest in updating furniture and decorations.

"A personal day, huh? What's that even mean?"

"I just needed the day off, lamebrain," I teased.

"And they actually approve you to take a day off even though you're not sick and it's not vacation?"

"Well, yeah," I admitted, stretching out my legs, rolling my ankles in wide, slow circles. "It's part of the benefits package."

"Oh, the benefits package." The phone rustled a little, and then things sounded different. "You're on speaker phone now, Jessa. Pops wants to hear this."

In the background, more shrieking.

"Are the kids playing, or is someone getting stabbed over there?"

"It's this dumb parachute game they bought," Jeremy muttered. His girls were nine and seven now, and of all the things I missed about home, I missed them the most.

"Tell them if they play their cards right, I'll bring them back even more parachute games from the Big Apple."

"I will *not* tell them that, thank you very much," Jeremy said.

"Is that Auntie Jessa?" Their excited voices grew nearer, segueing into unintelligible laughter and more shrieks as we greeted each other on speakerphone. I could just imagine their wild chestnut hair streaked with gold, their freckles glinting on cheekbones as they did for the whole Walton family. A few moments later, they had run off again, back to their game.

"So anyway, what were we talking about?" Jeremy began. "Oh yeah, personal time. So they pay you to just dick off at your apartment?"

I laughed. "I mean, sure, if you want to put it that way. But I needed the day to...catch up on some things." *And to recover from the insanely hot twelve hours of sex with your childhood best friend, Jeremy.* I couldn't even fathom telling him about what Damian and I had done. Jeremy would never believe it. Heck, I could hardly believe it.

"Jessa, I worked for my job thirty years and never had no damn personal day." My father's voice always sounded gruff, like he'd forgotten how to use it since the last time he spoke. "You either worked or you didn't get paid. You're living the dream, sissy."

My gaze fell at the nickname. I could hear the pride in his voice. The stark wonder. After thirty years making hourly wages as a heavy equipment operator, he probably saw my job like something out of a movie.

"You are, Jessa. People have been talking around here," Jeremy said. "They all know you work for the Fairchilds now. And hot damn if some of them aren't a little jealous."

"Nothing to be jealous of," I said. "Tara isn't there, is she?"

"No, she's coming later."

"Well, I'd be lying if I said I didn't enjoy this job," I told them. "It's great. I just..."

"What, you don't like making all those dollar bills?" Jeremy teased.

"It's not that. It's just hard to focus on anything else," I said with a little laugh.

"You like your job, you make great money, you know the owners." I could practically see my pops ticking off his fat, stubby fingers. "What else ya want? You got it all, Jessa. It ain't so bad to put some things on the back burner when you find a job like this."

His words jarred a cold resentment into me. I knew what he was talking about. It was the same thing everyone else thought I should put on the back burner.

"Well..." I began.

"Nobody would blame you if your end goal changed while you were there," Jeremy rushed to add, always the mediator. "You should keep going. See how far this takes you. After all, one of us kids has to be the breakout success, right?"

I laughed, but it came out weak. "Yeah, I guess."

"I'm proud of you, sissy." Emotion wrenched my father's voice. My throat went tight, and for a moment I had no air inside me. "Making six figures a year. Fuckin' incredible."

"Thanks, Pops," I finally squeaked out.

I couldn't deny how good it felt to hear that he was proud of me—that *anyone* was proud of me. But that feeling came only on the heels of the thing I didn't fully want to do.

Would anyone be proud of me for going after my goals?

The question weighed heavily inside me as we chatted more. By the time we hung up, I couldn't even distinguish the voice in my head from my father's.

Was it so wrong to follow the smart, practical thing?

It didn't have to mean that I was a failure. Maybe the smart thing would be to recognize a great opportunity and stick with it.

So why couldn't I do it?

CHAPTER TWENTY-TWO

DAMIAN

Jessa was allowed to have a personal day.

It didn't mean I had to like it.

Shit wasn't the same without her around. I tried to ignore the odd atmosphere, but it was impossible.

Even without her here, I was still humming. At least Axel wasn't around to give me shit. He and Cora were off doing some goodwill PR. We needed all the positive PR we could get, especially since that very-public protest outside of our fundraiser on Saturday.

We had to be careful. Any wrong step could be magnified and multiplied. Which was why we needed to tread more carefully than ever before.

We were walking on the most fragile and unforgiving of eggshells.

Most of the workday passed uneventfully, since I didn't have the combination assistance/distraction of Jessa outside my door and Axel wasn't there to interrupt me every half hour with some new idea or complaint. I thought I'd make it through the day unscathed and was plotting my best strategy for convincing Jessa to come to my penthouse that night when Felicia at the front desk called my office.

"Damian..." There was a bloated pause. "Ian is back, and he's asking for Trace."

My gut wrenched. "Did you tell him Trace isn't available?"

"I did. But he seems...I don't know. I thought maybe you should talk to him."

I did want to talk to him, but the questions I had in mind weren't the kind most people would be eager to answer honestly. Indecision roiled around inside me. On the one hand, I knew Axel would send him away without a second thought. But something told me Trace would have reached out, started a dialogue.

"Show him in," I forced out. My heart pounded as I awaited the inevitable knock on the door. This felt wrong somehow, like a breach of a contract I had with Axel. But my curiosity overrode all that. This counted as research.

A light tap sounded on my door a moment later. "Come in," I called out.

The door swung open, and in sauntered Ian.

Felicia offered me a small smile behind him before she shut the door, leaving Ian and me alone in my office. He wore an inscrutable smirk, the type that either hid anxiety or foreshadowed trouble. Loose jeans hugged narrow hips, a black T-shirt exposing scrawny arms. His longish, dark brown hair was mussed, greasy, as if he hadn't showered since the last time he swung by.

But for all the unkempt details of his appearance, his eyes were what made me wary. A raven-sharp gaze that looked just like Trace's intelligent and knowing gaze. Just like our dad's.

"You're back," I said.

"Just wanted to stop in and see family one last time before I headed home," he said, shoving his hands into his jeans. "Where'd Trace get off to?"

"A trip." Fewer details were better, until I could figure out who I was dealing with. "I'll let him know you stopped by. Where's home for you?"

"Louisville." He ran his tongue along his upper teeth as his gaze bounced around my office. "Unfortunately."

"What brought you up here again?" I leaned back in my chair, interlacing my fingers.

"Just some business." He shrugged. "Why do you ask?"

"This is pretty far from Louisville."

"Well, I've got business near and far. Just like Trace. Must be in our genes, huh?"

I narrowed my eyes. "Sure. What line of work?"

He shrugged. "General."

"Fine. So you finished up here and are headed back?"

"Duty calls." He shrugged.

I fought against the urge to roll my eyes. The cryptic responses weren't cute. They only ratcheted up my annoyance. "What did you want to talk to Trace about?"

"Just trying to get to know my brother. We lost a lot of time. I had to really dig to find you guys. My old man was secretive, until he just disappeared." The smirk was back. "He chose you guys, which I get. You three had a better shot at making it big, and look at you now. Makes me wonder what might have happened if he'd stuck around in my life, too."

I cleared my throat. I felt for the guy—I really did. But I couldn't play therapist for him. My priority was to protect my own—and my brothers'—interests. I leaned forward and pulled up the folder on my computer where I'd saved Ian's information.

"Well, it looks like you've done well for yourself," I said casually, scrolling through the information I'd gathered. I paused when I came to the information that had stood out to me. "You started a family this year. That's pretty big."

His face darkened. "Where'd you hear that?"

"Just some information I was able to pull up." I flashed him my empty but polite smile. "Digging, as you say."

Ian didn't say anything, his gaze fixed on the ground.

"Looks like you had a little girl a few months back. What did you name her?"

He sniffed, crossing his arms before he met my gaze. "It doesn't matter. Ain't even sure if she's mine."

"Ah. My apologies."

His smirk had morphed into a scowl.

I pushed the façade of polite conversation a little further. "So what was your favorite part of New York? Meet any interesting people while you were here?"

His gaze returned to mine, right back to cocky. "You could say that. There's all sorts of powerful, interesting people in this city. I had half a mind to take a job up here. Run away from Kentucky for good. Maybe that's another thing in the Fairchild bloodline, huh?"

I shrugged. "Could be. Or maybe it's just what a lot of kids from boring hometowns do."

"Nah, I think it's something I come by honestly." Ian stretched out in his arms, knuckles interlocked. "Something I share with my brother Trace."

My brother Trace. I didn't like how the words landed.

"That makes you my brother too," I told him.

"Not so much. We're, what? Step-brothers? If anything at all."

"Well it's family, right?" I'd never call this guy family, but I wondered if that's what his end game was: a biological connection. If that was all he wanted, I might be able to rest easy. No, scratch that: there was no resting easy for me. There was only resting slightly less anxious. "Your bio dad is my father too. We're linked."

He sniffed, his gaze sweeping back across my office. "I'm mostly interested in getting to know Trace. Where's he at, anyway? I'm not opposed to meeting him there."

"Out of the country."

"You could send me there." The nonchalant way he delivered the words sent up a red flag. "I got time if you got the plane."

"I don't think so. Besides, you said duty was calling you back to Louisville," I said. "Nice try, though. What do you really want, Ian?"

"I told you."

"We are very invested in a low-drama lifestyle," I said, lowering my chin. "When you start getting to know Trace, he'll tell you the same. If you hope to maintain any type of relationship with your blood brother, you should be prepared for what 'low-drama' means."

Ian scoffed. "What, you think I'm here to stir up some shit?"

"I don't know what to think. I don't have enough information either way," I told him, keeping my voice low and measured.

"Seems like you were able to find some information already," he muttered.

"I don't like to go in blind. I let the data tell the story." That was the truest thing about my life. I let data tell the story. Which was how I'd arrived here, twenty stories up. Analyzing cold, hard data. Even when it led to less-than-savory conclusions.

"Well, here's some data for you," Ian said. "I want to see Trace one last time before I head back to Kentucky. Brother to brother."

"You might have to wait for him to visit Kentucky," I told him. "He goes there frequently. I'm sure you two can meet up soon enough."

Ian's gaze grew dark in the same way Trace's did whenever he found a brick wall. Maybe that stubbornness *was* inherited.

"Maybe I won't be going back to Kentucky after all," Ian said with a sigh. "I like it here in New York. It's busy. Lots of opportunities. I might take an interview before I go, just to see what happens. They're looking for mail runners at this company nearby, Rossberg Aerospace. You heard of it?"

I schooled my reaction, making sure nothing leaked out. The mention of that name in my presence was one thing, and I thanked the Lord above that Axel wasn't here.

If Axel had heard that name uttered inside this building, in this context, with this stranger claiming family connection, Ian would never be allowed back in. Actually, he might never make it out.

Thankfully, I was the calmer type.

"You'll have to let me know how that goes." I tipped my head, watching him intensely for any reaction. "I've heard the Fairchild name isn't too welcome in those parts, so you might have a bit of a hard time rising up the ranks. Now, I have an appointment in a few minutes. It's time for you to go."

He sent me an inscrutable smirk again, coming to his feet. "Well, it was great talking to you, Damian. Maybe someday I'll call you brother, too."

"We can only hope." I stood, my heart pounding as I followed him to my office door. He waved before he sauntered away. I watched him disappear down the hallway, making sure he actually left, before I shut my door.

Rossberg Aerospace. Eli Rossberg's family business.

Axel would have flown off the fucking handle if he'd heard that name dropped in our building. And while I'd been able to tamp down my reaction, it still left a distinct and disgusting taste in my mouth. Like the tang of copper, warning me of a wound I had yet to discover.

He'd almost had me. Almost convinced me of his pure intentions, his genuine interest in connecting with his blood family.

But the mention of Eli's company blew all that out of the water. This guy had an ulterior motive. He wanted something. Probably money. But there was something more here, and not knowing had my gut cinching tighter and tighter every second that ticked by.

You knew something else was waiting in the wings. You were right.

You were right.

It always gets worse after something good.

If data ruled my life, then this was the proverb inscribed on the hallowed halls of my temple to data. It didn't matter what I did, how good I was, how much I tried, how many people I helped.

Good was always followed by bad.

And the higher I rose, the worse the bad got.

My stomach churned, knees feeling weak as my mind deflected this truth, hesitant to accept it.

I'd gotten something really good recently. *Too* good. Jessa Walton was the brightest good I'd ever let into my life, and I'd done it against my better judgment.

And really, I had known better. Yet I'd still let it happen.

My only recourse was to stem the flow before things ballooned too far in either direction. Because they would balloon. That much was certain.

Only time would tell how much worse things would get from here.

CHAPTER TWENTY-THREE

DAMIAN

Backing off was the best recourse.

But that needed to happen slowly. I couldn't rush into it. I needed to wean myself off Jessa, which meant inviting her over to the penthouse Tuesday night after work.

She came to work that morning prepared with her overnight bag, and once most of the office had left for the day, we both took the private elevator up to the penthouse.

I hadn't told anyone about Ian's visit. And I wasn't sure I wanted to. Axel would only get angrier at Trace, and I wanted to forget about the what-ifs and oh-nos.

The best way to disconnect was through Jessa. And if I needed to be backing off soon, that meant my time limit with her was approaching rapidly.

I needed to enjoy this while I could.

Up in the penthouse, I had dinner waiting for us, a menu I'd put together for Butch to prepare. Jessa's eyes went wide as we moved through the kitchen where Butch was hard at work over steaming pots and crackling oil in sauté pans.

"What is all this?" she breathed.

"Dinner," I said, grabbing her hand and leading her to the sideboard. The shrimp cocktail awaited us, as I'd specified that morning when Butch and I went over the plan. "Here's our appetizer."

I picked up a shrimp by its tail, winking at her.

She gasped, bringing a hand to her chest. She'd worn a high-necked black dress with a seventies twist and big earrings to match. Yet another dress to add to my favorites list, though the list was near bursting by now.

"Shrimp cocktail? Damian Fairchild, you dreamboat."

"In honor of our first formal event together," I said, dipping the tail in cocktail sauce. "When you were enamored by the shrimp being passed out by the waitstaff."

She grew still, watching me with a look so tender it almost tore my heart in two.

"You remember that?"

I laughed, taking a bite of the shrimp. "Of course I remember that. It was the cutest fucking thing I'd ever seen."

She blinked rapidly. "I didn't know you thought so much about me back then. You ghosted me that night."

I dropped my chin, searching out her addictive gaze. When those crystal silver-blues homed in on me, everything was right in the world. Like a jolt of calm. "I had to. I was trying not to fuck my new hire. Not to mention my childhood best friend's little sister."

The coy smile on her lips had me ready to take her to the bedroom. "I don't think Jeremy would be mad anymore. We're all adults."

"Maybe not mad. But it sure looks suspicious when a friend asks you to help out his sister and then you immediately start fucking her."

"That's a form of helping me," she said. "It's helped me *a lot*."

I grinned, wrapping my arm around her waist, bringing her flush against my body. "Oh yeah? I didn't realize you needed helped so badly."

"Very badly," she whispered. "All over my body."

If it weren't for Butch, we would have fucked on the dining room table. Instead, we spent the evening trading inside jokes and bites of shrimp. Dinner came and went with appreciative moans, fantastic red wine, and all the accolades to Butch. But once plates were cleared and the bedroom eyes were out to play, we quickly saw ourselves out of the dining room. There was only one thing on both our minds— getting back to my bedroom to continue *helping her*.

Because that, in turn, helped me. Helped me forget about my stress. Helped me forget about Ian. Helped me forget that this affair was supposed to be so much more casual and infrequent than it was.

But I couldn't care about that now. Not when I had Jessa's pretty face and sunshine freckles in front of me, her entire being the lick of a spring breeze. When we were together like this—lip-locked and stumbling around—I felt like myself, the Damian I barely knew how to access anymore, who played video games on the weekends and got excited about the future and didn't fester in a sour pit of anxiety.

In my bedroom, I had her dress unzipped before the door closed behind me. I helped her out of the gorgeous thing without breaking the kiss. By the time it hit the floor, my kisses were migrating south, past her collarbone, to the luscious expanse of her breasts. I held them in my palms as I kissed the tops of each, burying my face in her cleavage, getting absolutely fucking tit-drunk.

This was my favorite place to be.

She laughed, running her fingers through my hair. "You suffocating in there?"

"Not yet," I mumbled, nuzzling deeper. "Trying, though."

I guided her to the bed, unhooking her bra and then tugging her panties to the floor. I shucked my own clothes next, unable to look away from her for even a half second. Once I was naked in front of her, my cock reaching for her, I took her chin between my thumb and forefinger.

"I want you on top of me," I whispered into her ear. "I've been fantasizing about this for too long. Sit on my face, babe."

A nervous laugh slid out of her. "I'm too heavy."

"Try me."

She tipped her head as though this was a ridiculous idea. "Damian."

I climbed onto the bed and leaned back, gesturing for her to follow me. "Climb on."

Her eyes widened. "Oh, you're serious."

"Deadly." I flashed her a wicked grin. "Sit on my face, Jessa."

She looked at me as if I were speaking Mandarin but crawled my way as requested. "Damian, I don't know about this..."

"I do know about this."

"You're gonna pass out," she said, nibbling on her bottom lip as she straddled my chest, palms pressed hard against my sternum. "And then you'll die."

"No better way to go, if you ask me." I palmed the wide sweep of her ass cheeks, my cock pricking to attention.

"But I'll be the one who has to explain it to the newspaper," she went on, advancing slowly, as if I might change my mind. I would never change my mind. Her gorgeous pussy hovered closer, advancing upon me like the most delicious dessert. "They'll come up with some ridiculous headline, like *Death by Thunder Thighs*. I can't have that, Damian."

Her tightly trimmed pussy paused above my chin, her sweet scent making my mind fuzzy. Everything else fell away. All that existed was this luscious, swollen snack.

"Let's make a deal. We try it this once, and if I don't die, you promise to sit on my face whenever I ask."

She covered her face with her hands and laughed. "I can't believe you."

I smoothed my hands over her thighs, up toward the crease where her leg met her pelvis. "You don't have to believe me. You just have to sit on my face."

I tugged at her hips which elicited a giggle, and then she sank down, down, down. My face found the damp crease of her pussy, my mouth immediately capturing her swollen clit. I moaned into her, loving the weight of her around me, the sweet stickiness greeting my chin. She was slick and so, so turned on. I ravaged her pussy with my mouth, plunging my tongue inside her tight cunt as deep as I could go, then flattening my tongue against the nub of her clit.

Her hips started a slow circle above me, a great sign. She was loosening up, leaning into it. I dug my fingers into the tops of her thighs, gripping her so there was no question about whose she was or where she belonged. I shook my face back and forth as I ate her out, and she cried out, bucking against my mouth.

My cock jumped every time she bucked. I wanted so badly to sink inside of her, stretch that pretty pussy to its limit like we had before. But not until she'd fucked my face off. I bit at her clit—gently enough to be sexy, but forcefully enough so she could feel my hunger—then swirled my tongue around, back and forth, rinse and repeat.

Her thighs started trembling. I clutched her tighter, my tongue making a slippery pattern over her clit. She was bucking wildly now. Fucking my face like I'd wanted. I wrapped my arms around her hips, locking her against my face as I assaulted her clit with my tongue.

Her belly started to pulse. She cried out, louder and longer than I'd ever heard. And then the moisture hit my chin and lips. I moved my tongue to her pussy, tasting her, relishing her, lapping up every last drop of that incredible orgasm. Her chest heaved as she pressed against my shoulders, lifting off me.

"Damian," she breathed. "What...how the...are you..."

I sent her a devilish grin. "Still alive down here."

"Oh my god, look at your face." She swiped at my chin, but it only made me grin harder.

"Scoot back, babe. I'm not done with you."

I guided her back until her pussy met the thick ridge of my cock. I sucked at my teeth as the slick velvet of her cunt slid across me.

"Ohhh, Damian." Her eyes fluttered shut. I rocked my hips beneath her. My cock throbbed from wanting more, wanting all of her stretched around me.

"You're so fucking gorgeous, Jessa," I murmured, running my hands over her belly, up the soft dip of her waist. I gripped her hips, rooting her against me. "Do you even have any idea?"

Her head rolled in a slow circle, eyes fluttering shut. "Stop, Damian. When you say these things..."

"What?" I wiggled my hips into place beneath her, my cockhead finding her slick entrance easily. She sucked in a sharp breath and arched against me.

"You make it too easy to believe you," she finally breathed. "And to...to..."

Her sentence evaporated as I pushed inside her. She moved against me, resituating, allowing me to fill her. Her head tipped back, and a long moan came out. I dug my fingertips into her hips so hard I thought I might leave bruises. But she was mine.

I didn't want this to end. Because this felt fucking right in a way I couldn't explain, much less understand.

I ground up into her as she moved against me, our bodies forming a slick, desperate rhythm. Her breasts jiggled as I drilled up into her, and everything about her from this angle was pure erotic joy. I could have eaten her alive for how much I wanted her, how much I needed her.

A warning whispered through me, but I couldn't pay attention to it. Not when she was on top of me, riding me, a quivering mess of ecstasy and freckles.

We reached our climax together. I'd been beating back the orgasm since I first plunged my tongue inside her. She rocked her hips against me, and the hot friction did me in. I released my load inside her, pumping out pleasure that made my abs twitch with every round.

Jessa turned to jelly, collapsing on top of me, her lips finding mine in feathery, blissed out kisses.

I wrapped my arms around her and smiled. I wanted to relish this freedom in my chest and in my limbs for as long as I possibly could. This freedom that Jessa had helped me find.

The freedom that I knew could never fully be mine.

CHAPTER TWENTY-FOUR

DAMIAN

Our sexy reverie could only last so long.

I wasn't three feet inside the office the next morning, still sharing lingering smiles with Jessa down the hallway, when Axel called me to his office.

His grim expression resurrected all my old anxieties, the ones Jessa had helped lay to rest. They slithered back to life like the snake coaxed out of its basket by the snake charmer.

"Sit down for this one," Axel said, palms against the top of his desk. I sat in the chair facing him, already too sick with worry to speak.

"I didn't want to talk about this in your office," he said quietly. "I'm starting to wonder if there aren't spies on your side of the building."

"Spies?"

He sent me a heavy look. And then he pushed a copy of *Big Apple Mag* my way.

THE FAIRCHILD RIFT: A look into the infamous trio's growing tensions

I flipped to the feature article and read as quickly as I could. The article relied heavily on photos of Axel and me together and then solo photos of Trace—most notably, some snapshots of him in Bali recently. The article was equal parts unnerving and pure fluff.

"Great." My mouth went dry, and I dragged my gaze up to meet Axel's. "How do you think it leaked?"

"There's only one way," Axel said, looking grimmer than I'd seen him since we'd the press conference we'd held to defend our name against the sex trafficking allegations over the summer. "We explained Trace's absence at the fundraiser. He's been on vacation, and nobody would think twice about that. We haven't talked to anyone outside of our bubble about this. Someone in the office leaked it."

I worked my jaw back and forth as I toyed with this idea. I didn't want to accept it. Not by a long shot.

"Who on staff would talk to the press?" I asked him quietly.

"I don't know," he admitted.

"So you don't even have anyone in mind?"

"No," he said with a huff. "But the truth is that is could be anyone. Are you prepared to accept that?"

"I don't think I have to," I told him. "We vet everyone. They've all signed NDAs. This could simply be tabloid speculation." I so desperately wanted that to be true. And as I rode the coattails of my night with Jessa, I planned on believing it until it became true. "They put two and two together all the time. What's so different about now?"

Axel's jaw flexed as he watched me. "You think so?"

"I don't have any data to the contrary," I told him. "And until I do, I'd rather trust the staff that we so painstakingly selected."

Axel nodded, his gaze dropping to the desk. "I'm just skittish after the sex trafficking article. I don't want to have to hold another press conference about anything. Especially not when they're right, for once."

"We'll let this one go," I told him, ignoring the wrench in my gut. "It doesn't mean anything."

But deep inside my body, coursing through my nervous system, hid the knowledge that it *did* mean something. I'd just played the role of the mediator, the calm one, the problem-solver for too long to know how to let any of those anxieties surface.

If they surfaced, they'd kill me.

So they needed to stay where they could cycle and fester and kill me more slowly.

When Axel didn't look convinced, I added, "They're just obsessed with us because we're newsworthy right now. So yeah, any little expose they can get their hands on, they're going to run with."

Axel nodded again. "You're right."

I wanted to be right. I fucking hoped I was right. So I needed to act like I was right. I tamped down the stress and the anxiety the only way I knew how—master-level compartmentalization and intense focus on my computer screen.

But just to be sure, I tasked Jessa with doing a little research. I asked her to comb through company call logs and highlight all instances of outgoing calls to all phone numbers associated with *Big Apple Mag*. It would probably lead to nothing, but it was part of the due diligence I needed to perform in order to relax even a fraction.

I disappeared into my office for the rest of the workday. I needed to be productive, to make progress on digging ourselves out of this hole we kept getting pushed into. And I couldn't extricate the company from this quagmire if I didn't focus and work.

The work week melted away in this fashion. By Friday, I could tell Jessa was getting worried. She checked in with me almost hourly, and I responded, but the gentle questions she asked and the prompts to eat, come out of my office, join her for lunch all betrayed her worry.

But this was the only way I knew to keep it together—focus on work at the expense of everything else. Even my health.

Friday after lunch, Jessa came into my office looking sheepish.

"Damian? Are you still alive in here?"

I waved her in, tugging off the headphones I used to blast my death metal as I sank into my own world. "Of course. What's up?"

"Listen, I did a thing..." She started nibbling on her bottom lip and put her hands behind her back. "I hope you don't get upset, but...I booked us a little getaway."

I blinked, the words hardly making sense. "A getaway?"

She nodded. "Just tonight. Nothing crazy. But I had Axel help me set it up because I think it's pretty obvious that you need to, well...get away."

I tapped one earpiece of my headphones as the idea rolled around inside me. My immediate thought was to reject it. After all, there was too much to focus on here. Too many unknowns to imagine and respond to. I'd been getting carried away with Jessa, and I needed to apply the brakes.

But she looked so damn beautiful standing in my office, her hair pulled back in a slick ponytail. She wor black slacks and a black ruffled blouse today, one of the few times she hadn't worn a dress to work, and I loved the look all the same.

I'd missed her in my four days of ultra-focus.

And realizing that made me more anxious.

"I shouldn't," I told her. "I've been slacking recently."

She sent me an unamused look. "That's bullshit. I'm here with you every day, and you are perfectly on top of your to-do list. I would know if you weren't."

I drew a deep breath, intent on disputing her words, but nothing made it past my lips.

"Just try it out," she said. "We'll get out of the city. If you hate it, we'll come back. Simple as that."

"What's on the agenda?"

"One night in the woods."

I smirked. It wasn't my usual MO, but I'd do it if she wanted to. "Electricity included or no?"

"Of course. I'm not trying to go full survival mode. Look at me. Do you think I packed anything remotely survivalist? I have heels in my suitcase, Damian."

I hefted with a laugh. "Okay. Fine. Let's do it."

She pumped her fist. "Victory! And listen, we're driving ourselves, okay? I love Legs and all, but this is a trip just for us."

I held up my palms in defeat. "Whatever you say."

Jessa retreated with a big smile, and for a moment, things felt light again. After wrapping up a few things on my computer, I left my office to begin preparing for our getaway—whatever it would entail—and stopped by Jessa's desk. Her sketchbook was out, showcasing a half-finished design for what looked like a winter coat.

She looked up at me as I approached. "You heading to get packed?"

"Yeah. Hey, do you have that list from the call logs that I asked you for on Tuesday?"

She blinked a couple of times, then her eyes widened. "Uhhh...let me get back to you on that. After you go pack. Okay?"

I nodded and headed to the penthouse, catching myself humming in the elevator. I made quick work of an overnight bag and slung it over my shoulder. On my way back to my office, I realized I was ready for a getaway. Jessa was right. I *needed* it.

At her desk, Jessa worked on that bottom lip like it might try to escape.

"I'm ready."

"Good." She folded up her laptop and tucked it into her oversized purse, then grabbed a duffel bag from beneath the desk. "Let's jet."

"Why are you bringing your laptop?"

She shrugged. "Just in case I need to work on anything."

This was odd, coming from the queen of the getaway. The enforcer of work breaks.

"Come on," she said, hurrying me along. "I had Legs bring your car around. We're ready to get the heck away."

We exited the suite the requisite three feet apart, but from the way gazes lingered on us, I wondered if the entire office already knew we were together. After all, we'd canoodled in the hallway of the Rainbow Room. I'd given zero fucks in the presence of her corset—could anyone expect otherwise?—and I had to grapple with the very real possibility that all of my employees knew that Jessa and I were an item.

Did I care? Yes. Was I going to do anything about it? Doubtful.

Because when I had Jessa's luscious booty in front of me and all these curves begging to be touched, I had a hard time caring about anything that wasn't her. Even though the whole idea of being an *item* with someone drove me bonkers, when it came to Jessa, I just never seemed to get around to setting the record straight.

She felt too good. I wanted this reverie to last as long as it possibly could, until it inevitably came crashing down around me.

Once we were tucked into the elevator, I wrapped my arm around her waist.

"This was a good idea," I told her.

"I know," she said sweetly. "And we haven't even left the building yet. Just imagine what a good idea it'll be once we actually get there."

In the elevator, we kissed. Outside the building, we kissed. And then once I was in the driver's seat and she was smiling over at me like we'd been doing this together for years, we kissed again.

Jessa programmed the GPS and I drove. Within hours, we were cruising through the New York state forests, deep in conversation about New York seasons compared to Kentucky, the native residents who'd been forced off the land in both areas, whether or not the cinnamon toast of our childhoods qualified as adulthood dessert. That's what I loved about Jessa. She didn't mind meandering through the most winding conversations, and we were both delighted to see where they led. The hills and sides of the road were blanketed in the faintest layer of snow, providing a dreamy backdrop as we wound deeper into this unexpected Friday afternoon excursion up the Hudson Valley.

I didn't drop Jessa's hand in a hundred miles—and didn't even think twice about it.

Our getaway stretched on like this—effortless, laidback, completely fucking lovely. We checked into a log cabin that was equal parts rustic and luxurious, with bearskin rugs and enormous windows overlooking the sweeping hills of naked forests. We tried a new restaurant. We strolled hand-in-hand down cobblestone sidewalks, smiling red-cheeked at each other.

We spent every minute inside our cabin wrapped up in each other: on the bed, against the wall, in the shower, and even draped across a chaise longue at one point.

By the time we were heading back to the city the following day, I felt moderately refreshed. I'd enjoyed myself, that much was certain.

But the to-do list was crushing me again as new emails rolled in during our trip back south. Because I was driving, I couldn't tend to them, which only stressed me more. Jessa read out the subject lines of new emails as they came in. A forwarded email from Axel was one of the subject lines she read: *Some Solutions for the Leak*

"Is that a penthouse water leak or another media leak?" she asked.

I laughed but it dwindled quickly. "Take a wild guess. Speaking of which, talk to me about the call logs you pulled up." I squeezed the steering wheel, prepping myself for the inevitable disappointing news that she hadn't found what I'd been hoping was there.

A burst of air escaped her. She rested her forehead in her palm. "Shit bricks. I meant to tell you when you asked yesterday after lunch."

"What is it?"

"Damian, I didn't get a chance to pull them."

An annoyed burst of air escaped me. I didn't like any of those words, but especially sentences that started with "I didn't get a chance." Successful people *made* the chance. That's how it was in my world.

"When were you thinking of doing it?" I asked her, trying to keep the annoyance out of my voice. But it was impossible. Annoyance vibrated from every cell in my body. Stress gave me a thin trigger, and that comment had officially snapped it.

"Well, I was going to try to squeeze it in while we were away. But then I realized that wouldn't be very getaway-like. If I can find the time tomorrow, I'll do it then. But I need to get things set up for my new roommate, who's coming on Monday. So I think first thing Monday is more realistic."

All I could hear from her was *but but but.*

"Fuck." I squeezed the steering wheel again. "I needed that info for the work I plan to do this evening. And who's this new roommate?"

"Kendra. She's amazing. We met up last week."

"Why didn't you tell me about this before?"

She blinked over at me. "I didn't realize I had to update you about my living situation."

"You have a new person in your life that will be sharing your space, with access to your phone, laptop, sensitive documents." I held out a hand, gesturing at how obvious this was. "You don't think I should know about that?"

"I...I was going to tell you..."

"What's her full name?" I snapped.

"Kendra Finneran," she said quietly. "I swear I was going to tell you. I was excited for you to meet her. She's excited to meet you too—"

"So she knows that you work for us?"

"Of course," she sputtered.

An annoyed burst of air escaped me. All I could see was potential security issues. With this dark cloud swirling above me, everything looked like a threat.

"I'm sorry, Damian," Jessa said as she wrung her hands in her lap. "I haven't shared anything with her that's personal or confidential, I swear. And about the call logs, I would have done it sooner but I...I just forgot."

I shook my head. "How could you forget?"

"I don't know. I guess I was distracted when you mentioned it. You keep sending me these high priority tasks, there's just been a lot going on."

I rolled my neck in a slow circle, the annoyance festering into something else altogether. "Probably just sketching dresses like always, huh?"

A strange silence settled over the car. When I glanced over at Jessa, she watched me with a lethal look.

"What are you trying to say, Damian?"

"Nothing."

"Doesn't feel like nothing."

"I want to focus on what's important," I said, squeezing the steering wheel for an entirely new reason now. "That's always been the goal."

"And you think I don't focus on what's important?"

"I didn't say that."

"Sure sounded like it."

"I think you focus on plenty. And maybe that's part of the problem. If you forget something urgent because your focus is too divided, that sounds like a sign."

She sputtered. "How could you say my focus is too divided? It's only on you. All I do is think about you, your business, your happiness, your...everything. I'm in school for god's sake, and I neglect that so that I can focus on *you*."

"Actions speak louder than words, Jessa." It felt like such a cliché, but it was the fucking truth. "I asked you to do something important, something related to the shitstorm of my reality right now, and you didn't. That's on you."

She stared out the window, her mouth a thin line. "Yeah. Guess all those other things I didn't forget about just don't matter anymore."

"You knew this was a high-pressure job coming in, regardless of your school situation. We're dealing with something huge. I need those fucking call logs to figure out where the crack in my business is."

"You think I don't know that?" She looked over at me so sharply I could practically feel the implied slap on my cheek. "I spend every day, morning to evening, assisting you. Planning for you. Looking out for you. Feeding you. I've forgotten one task and you treat me like this?"

"I'm having a fucking conversation," I told her, grateful to see the city skyline in the distance. We were close, which meant an end to this discussion. "This is important shit that needs to be talked about. This is literally all that matters in my life—don't you get that?"

"Yeah. I get that," Jessa said, sarcasm wrenching her tone. "All you live for is work."

I shook my head, squeezing the steering wheel again. "What else should I live for? It keeps my life afloat. It pays my bills, donates millions to charity, plus supports over one hundred other people. Including you. Tell me again why I shouldn't live for this?"

"That's not what I'm talking about, Damian," she hissed. "Obviously you're doing good in the world. Your work is valuable. That's not the point."

"Then what *is* the point?"

"You don't *exist* beyond work!" The words came out on a shout, and we sat in the strange, echoing aftermath of her words for a moment before she continued. "You don't even remember to eat most days because of how much you work. What happened to balance? I had to drag you out of the office to take this break. Do you ever go on vacation?"

"Honestly, Jessa, you don't have to fucking worry about my vacation schedule. I don't even know what we're talking about anymore. You forgot to look at the call logs and somehow I'm the bad guy for not going on vacation?"

She huffed, crossing her arms. "That's not what I'm saying either. What I'm getting at is—there should be some balance. The type of balance where you remember to eat and actually enjoy life. Going after what lights you up has to be part of the equation, right? That's why I scheduled this getaway for us. For *you*."

I clenched and unclenched my teeth as I stared out at the road. "Every day of my life is spent doing things that don't light me up. Because I have to do them to keep everything afloat. Too many people count on me to let it go. And I need to succeed for the ones who aren't here. How is this even a question?"

She pressed her hands to the sides of her cheeks, staring out the windshield like the answer might be written somewhere. "It's not a question. It's just...an idea. Work is crucial, Damian, nobody is arguing that. But none of it matters if you don't enjoy life." She swung her head to look at me then, sincerity slashed across her face. "Kaylee and Jordan wouldn't want you to work yourself to death just because they aren't here. I'm positive of that."

I shook my head, emotion welling in my chest. But I was too good at tamping it down. I drew a slow, cleansing breath and stuffed it down into the recesses of myself, where I could deal with it later. After hours. When I had a whiskey in my hand and a bedroom to myself.

"I enjoy life just fine," I told her, but even I could hear the hollowness in my words. I hadn't been enjoying life, not until Jessa came along. But now I was realizing she'd yanked me too far off course.

"All of this shit is a non-issue. I'm just asking you to focus alongside me so we can get shit done."

"Yeah." She nodded, staring blankly out at the road. "You really seemed like you were enjoying life when I first started working for you."

"I don't need the fucking commentary," I bit out, frustration bubbling over inside me. "I need someone who's on my side. Are you on my side, Jessa?"

She glowered at me. "I can't believe you even have to ask."

"So I guess that's a yes."

"It's 'of course I am, numbskull'. The question is insulting. I've been in love with you since seventh grade and you're going to ask me if I'm on your side?"

Her words hammered through the air between us, and judging from the sharp intake of breath on her end, she hadn't intended to say them out loud.

"Just forget I said anything," she muttered, facing away from me.

I white-knuckled the steering wheel, trying to control the waves of emotion coursing through me. She'd kicked up too much dust, and I was choking, struggling to reorient myself. We didn't talk the rest of the way home, but the interior of my mind was raucous with thoughts and shouts.

She'd admitted she was in love with me. That added a whole different layer to the unfurling onion between us.

Because maybe you're in love with her too.

I couldn't go near the L word. Not with her. Not with anyone. Just having the conversation was just a reminder that I'd gone way too fucking far. I should have realized it when I opted for an upstate getaway in lieu of making headway on the leak in my inner circle. I should have known when I stopped caring whether employees saw me holding her hand.

Jessa is just a dangerous distraction.

I'd gotten lost in the sweet-smelling and attractive bog of romance, lured by luscious tits and a shared childhood. This argument was all the proof I needed to remind myself that the tits and sentimental past meant nothing compared to the road I knew I needed to follow.

Jessa and I were ill-matched. I needed someone who would leave me alone, not challenge me. Someone who would respect my need for work, respect my desire to hyper-focus on life as I knew it. I didn't need change. I needed unquestioning, silent support.

No, scratch that. I didn't need that. I didn't need anyone at all. When had I forgotten that? Truth was, I needed to take a major step back. Starting yesterday. I'd been an idiot to begin anything with Jessa in the first place.

But I'd be an even bigger idiot if I continued what we'd started.

CHAPTER TWENTY-FIVE

JESSA

There had to be some word in the English language for the awkward aftermath of an intense argument.

I was consumed by a tornado of anger, regret, and confusion. Heck, I was ready to invent this word myself. *Angretusion.* No, it would have to be much simpler and more elegant than that, since it would clearly be a word I'd need to use with frequency in Damian's world.

Because despite all my best intentions, words had been said. Emotions had flared. And now, things had changed.

Saturday afternoon we parted ways with scarcely a *bye*, then Sunday started *and* ended without a single word from Damian. So all that *angretusion* eventually just transformed into sadness, which I supposed should have been the fourth ingredient in that unpleasant cocktail of a word.

When Monday morning came, I had to drag myself into the office. I knew things would be weird at best, but the lack of contact had me on edge. I'd gotten so used to the new normal we'd created, the sweetness and the romance and the together-ness. What had started as "something fun" had become so much more. And now we were fighting like we'd been married for years.

That had to mean something. I just wasn't sure if it was good or bad.

I got to the office a little early—just so Damian couldn't question my *focus*—and got things ready for the week. And yes, I grumbled to myself the entire time. *How can he think I'm too divided? All I do is an excellent job for him. I forget one measly thing and suddenly I'm the worst employee he's ever had.*

I knew things were bad when I'd caught myself engaging in imaginary conversations with Damian all day Sunday as I finished pulling the call logs he'd requested, and then again on Monday morning. I couldn't deny it. This shit hurt. All the more so because his words held a kernel of truth.

I *was* divided.

I'd come here divided. My end goal was the fashion certificate, and this job was simply the means.

So there was another ingredient for the cocktail: humiliation. Because I felt transparent. I felt seen to the core for the dumb, naïve hick that I was. I'd stepped into Damian's world and less than two months later, I was floundering.

Why did you think you could hack it in New York?

You should just come home to Kentucky where you belong.

A vicious chorus of criticism ran through my head—Tara's voice, followed by Damian's. And each time I felt the itch to distract myself, to reach for my sketchbook, I stopped myself. God forbid Damian see me not 100 percent productive 100 percent of the time.

God forbid I try to advance in a direction of *my* choosing.

God forbid I go after what *I* want.

And above all the internal strife, there was just one question: *How had I ended up here again?* Not in an office job, not in New York City, but *here*—feeling like a small, meaningless annoyance. The one that dragged down everyone else's plans. Everybody's favorite letdown.

Tommy had excelled at making me feel this way. But it didn't start with him.

Quick footsteps interrupted my sulky morning. Damian came down the hallway, his neck bent, phone pressed to his head. He glanced up only briefly as he passed me, and then disappeared into his office, the door clicking shut.

I was left with nothing but the memory of his handsome face and the lingering scent of his woodsy musk.

I slumped into my seat. This wasn't just uncomfortable. This mother-cluckin' *sucked*.

I drew a fortifying breath and straightened my back. We could be adults. We could sort this out. I headed for his office. Before the door opened even six inches, I heard his gritty growl.

"Jessa, not now."

The words were harsh, but the tone was worse. I winced as though I'd been slapped and shut the door again, turning back to my desk.

Goodbye, good times at Fairchild Enterprises.

This felt exactly like when I'd started here, dealing with the moody, work-obsessed version of Damian, the one who couldn't spare a laugh or a smile. I thought I'd coaxed the real Damian back out, but he'd never truly left his cave.

After stewing and fretting for a half hour, I popped onto the office messaging app and sent Damian a message.

JESSA: Everything okay? You seem tense.

Ten minutes later, his response came.

DAMIAN: Yep, all good.

Things were far from all good, but at least those three words let me know where we stood: square one. He was pulling away again, reinstating that professional distance that was so deep we could both drown in it. I could feel it like a storm rolling in.

Damian was MIA most of the day, which meant he didn't even see Kendra when she bopped into the office suite, looking for the spare apartment key I'd promised her. She greeted me with a big smile, that same messenger bag across her chest, who-knew-what tucked inside.

"Hey, roomie. I've got my stuff all loaded up. I'm ready to move in."

I rummaged in my purse and found the key, passing it to her with a conspiratorial smile. "I'm ready for you to move in, too. Welcome to the crazy house."

"The *famous* house," she corrected me, pocketing the key. "Which requires a certain element of crazy to function."

Kendra left, and I was caught between two worlds—excitement for this new chapter of my life in New York and utter sadness over the Damian chapter most likely coming to an end. Because this had to be the end. How could it not be?

At the risk of proving Damian right about my commitment to his company, I informed him I'd be leaving fifteen minutes early for a personal reason and left the office right at 4:45.

Truthfully, I wanted to get a head start on the rest of my day and needed to swing by my apartment before I headed to the Garment District. Class was tonight, and I had so many thoughts knocking around in my head that I needed all the extra seconds possible to get past this Damian drama. He was all-consuming, and I needed to remember what my life felt like outside the bounds of his world.

I flitted through the Fairchild building and headed for the subway. I even caught an earlier train, and I relished in this strange feeling of not being rushed for once.

My heels hit the pavement outside the subway station, only a few people filtering up the steps alongside me. Darkness had already descended upon the city at the unbearably early hour of 5:30. This was late fall in the east, I supposed. The sidewalks were emptier than usual, so I kept my head down and beelined for my apartment a few blocks away.

But I'd barely made it a block when I felt an arm wrap around my shoulders. Strange heat sank into me, an unknown body pressed against me.

And then a hard, unyielding jab in my side.

"Don't scream," the man said into my ear.

Everything inside me went solid, my body full of exclamation points. The thing in my side was a gun. I heard the click of his weapon.

"Keep walking. Look natural. Just give me your purse and whatever cash you've got," he growled. "Do it now."

My fingers trembled as I reached for my purse. I handed it to him without breaking our gait, without even blinking. My voice had disappeared entirely, my skin full of prickles and ice. I couldn't even feel my legs.

"What else ya got?"

All I could do was shake my head. He nudged the gun deeper into my side, and I shook my head again. I couldn't form words—maybe he sensed that, because he unwrapped his arm and took off.

I kept walking to my apartment, like any change in gait or appearance might convince him to come back. Shell-shocked and wide eyed, I stumbled into my building, unable to fully process what had just happened. When I got to my door, I looked around dumbly.

What was supposed to happen now?

My knees shook as I felt around. I needed my key. But where was it? I realized I still had my tote slung over my shoulder, the empty one I'd carried my lunch to work in.

It also had my phone in it, and an extra key I'd grabbed that morning in preparation for Kendra stopping by the office.

A relieved exhale shuddered out of me, wracking my entire body. I could barely open the door because of how hard my hands shook. Had that man followed me? Had he watched me? Had he *been* watching me? Had he targeted me because he knew I was weak, because I looked vulnerable? The questions formed a logjam inside me, and the only thing I could do was slam the door shut and sink onto the couch.

And then the tears came.

I didn't know what I was doing. I just knew I needed to respond somehow to *being robbed.* I sat up and tried to think of what had been taken from me. I fumbled for my phone and tried to start a list, but I couldn't see through the tears. My credit and debit card both needed to be cancelled immediately, so I could start there.

I managed to look up the number for my Kentucky bank, but calling the number proved difficult. Nothing seemed to work right. Finally, I heard ringing at the other end of the line, and I tried to stifle my sobs.

"What is it, Jessa?"

The simple question caught me off guard. My mouth parted and I struggled to make sense of what I was hearing. That sounded like Damian.

"Jessa? Are you there?"

The tears returned, a sob hitching past my lips. "I'm sorry. I didn't mean to call you. I was trying to c-call my c-credit card company."

"Are you okay? What happened?"

"I'm fine, I'm fine." Another sob. "I got mugged, but I'm figuring it out." Tears blurred my vision, and I swiped to end the call. I couldn't talk to him right now. Not like this. I needed to get my shit together on my own.

This time, I managed to call the right number. Tears streamed down my face as I lay back on the couch and stared at the ceiling, listening to the dull hold music. Every thump of my heart reminded me of the feel of that gun in my side. I hadn't lost much—barely any cash. So why was I so weepy? The fact that the tears wouldn't stop only upset me more.

I'd cancelled my credit card and had moved on to my debit card when someone thumped at the door. I jumped in my seat, heart racing as I twisted to look that direction. What if it was that guy again? Had he seen where I lived? I covered my face with my hands, more tears escaping.

"Jessa, open up. It's me." Damian's gruff voice left no room for discussion. Relief flooded me, toasty warm and inviting, like a blanket straight from the dryer. I moved on shaky legs toward the door. He surged into my apartment the moment I tugged it open, his thick arms wrapping around me. The comforting scent of his woodsy musk enveloped me, and everything was right in the world.

"Are you okay?"

My face was smashed to his chest, every inch of me warming at the contact. My eyes fluttered shut, the tears drying up. This, right here—this felt so damn good. Damian was a salve. He was the most delicious remedy for any ailment I might face. I squeezed my arms around his waist and melted into him.

"I am now," I choked out.

His warm hand stroked the top of my head. "What happened?"

"I-I was just leaving the subway…and this man came up to me. He wrapped his arm around me." I swallowed hard, the tears returning, remembering the way the fear had slithered through my limbs. "He had a gun." The words were coming out in a whisper now. "He told me to give him my purse, so I did. He asked for more, but I didn't have anything. And then he just disappeared."

"Fuck, Jessa." His arms squeezed tighter around me. "I'm so glad you're okay."

I buried my face in his chest, relishing his solidity beneath me.

"I don't want you living in this neighborhood anymore," he murmured into the top of my head. "We've gotta find you a new a place."

"Damian, I can't afford a new place."

"Yes you can. I'll help. And no more subway, okay? Only my cars."

I pinched my eyes shut, feeling like I was dreaming. We'd gone from arguing to cold silence to *this*. I couldn't lie—I relished the attention. I could feel the tenderness radiating from him, the caring. The love behind his words.

Because that's what it was. He loved me, just like I loved him.

I'd known he loved me since we started having sex. He couldn't hide it, even though he probably wanted to. Even though he might deny it under oath.

"I'll get you your own driver," he went on. "Your own car."

"Oh," I said with a laugh, wiping at my eyes. "That won't look suspicious."

"I don't fucking care how it looks."

"Because all secretaries have their own Fairchild vehicle?"

He sent me a severe look. "Well this one will. End of story."

I laughed again, wiping up the last of my tears. I couldn't argue with him. I didn't even want to. But when would he see the truth of what we shared?

"You should lie down," he said, leading me toward the bedroom. In a few steps, we'd reached my double bed. The bed creaked as I sat on the edge, looking up at Damian's concerned face, his square jaw, the hair tumbling out from behind his ear.

"Will you lie down with me?" I said, almost pleading. He nodded, and I scootched back onto the bed, making room for him. We lay facing each other, looking into each other's eyes. This was my favorite activity—studying the worlds swirling inside his gaze, getting those brief glimpses of the torment and drive that fueled him.

I wasn't sure how long we lay there. Damian's hand drifted to my face to stroke my cheek. I scooted closer. And then his hand was on my hip, moving up to my waist. I didn't know who kissed who first, only that our lips joined together, propelled by forces beyond my control.

Kisses tumbled off our lips, more passionate than ever before. They almost hurt from how heavy the air was between us. How thick things had gotten after our fight. But the passion was undeniable and unstoppable. When I rolled onto my back, pulling Damian on top of me, he paused.

"Are you sure?" He searched my face. "If you're too upset..."

"I need this," I whispered, desire and urgency pumping through my veins. Having sex after getting mugged didn't strike me as a typical response, but it felt so right in the moment. I needed Damian's reassurance, his firmness. I needed him filling me, reminding me of his love. "I need *you*, Damian."

He took my face in his hands, covering my mouth with his. He eased on top of me, the heat of him sinking down to my core. He was hard already—I could feel his cock pressed to my hip—and he tugged my dress up until it bunched at my hips. He broke our kisses only to lean back and unbuckle his belt. The metal *zzzzip* of his zipper was next, and then he fished his cock out from his briefs and filled the space between my legs again.

There was something urgent here, as if we were operating on borrowed time. We didn't have a second to spare, and I knew this even without knowing the why. Damian pushed himself inside me, fitting himself into my slick channel with a ragged sigh.

Here. This felt like home. This felt like the resting point, the perfect union of passion and companionship and family and future. Damian was it for me. I knew it as he sank into me, just as I'd known it when I fell in love with him back in seventh grade.

That fact had never changed.

The only thing that had changed was that now I finally accepted it. I wasn't just a foolish girl in unrequited love. This man loved me back. This man would race across New York City to hold me. This man would offer up his fleet of vehicles to ensure my safety, office reputation be damned.

Damian rocked against me, pushing himself in and out as he showered my lips with kisses. All I could do was cling to him and take him. All of him.

Tears pricked at my eyes. He took a soft bite of my neck and ground up into me, just the way he knew I liked, and I tumbled over the edge, clutching his biceps as the orgasm wound through me.

He came a moment later, heat filling me and eventually leaking out onto my thighs once he pulled out. We shared that drugged out smile, the one that told me everything was all right. That we'd hit the reset button.

As Damian and I were cleaning ourselves up, my phone rang from the living room. I rushed to answer it, finding it was my classmate Veronica.

"Hey, Jessa, are you coming today?" Her voice sounded hushed, as if maybe she'd called from the back of the classroom. "I just noticed you're not here—is everything okay?"

I wandered back into the bedroom, where Damian was buckling his belt.

"I'm okay now," I said. "Thank you for checking. I didn't come because I was mugged on my way home from work today." Damian's brows drew together as I said the words. I could tell it pained him. "He made off with my purse, but that was it. I don't think I'll be coming into class tonight though. I'm just here at my apartment with my boyfriend, taking care of things."

"That's horrible. I'm so sorry! I'll tell Mr. Mitchell. Take care, okay?"

"Thanks, Veronica." I swiped the phone off and looked up at Damian. His face was drawn, and he stared down at the carpet.

My stomach clenched. I immediately knew what was wrong. I'd used the word *boyfriend*.

"Why do you have this face?" I asked, gesturing toward him. He dragged his gaze up to meet mine, the answer written there, though he said nothing. "It's because I called you my boyfriend, isn't it?"

"Jessa...we've talked about this," he started out slowly.

"What do you call someone who races across two boroughs during rush hour to console a lover who just got robbed?" I asked him, cocking my hip. "What do you call the man who offers a chauffer and car to a woman just so she can avoid the subway? Or who lies down in bed with her just because she asked you to?"

His gaze darkened.

"*Hookup* doesn't seem right. I don't think it's *sugar daddy*," I went on. "But *boyfriend* seems appropriate, don't you think?"

"I told you at the beginning," Damian said in a low voice. "I'm not made for that stuff. I *told* you."

"So you don't want to be with me?"

He hesitated. "It's not that. I like what we have going. Why can't we just continue it as-is? Without labels. Who needs labels?"

Hurt slashed through me. If Harper had been the fling who hadn't gotten the memo, what did that make me? The hopeful fiancée who missed a million of them? Humiliation lashed through me.

"I guess I misunderstood what we had going on," I forced out, emotion making my chest go tight again, but for different reasons this time. "Have you been exclusive?"

"Of course."

"So then why can't we call each other boyfriend and girlfriend?"

Damian shook his head. "Jessa, I told you at the beginning. This is my hard line—whatever feels good, no strings attached. Remember? I don't want to go past that. Now would you pack some things so we can leave?"

I lifted a brow. "To go where?"

"Back to my penthouse, so we can find a better apartment for you."

"So you're trying to take me to live with you temporarily, yet you won't even call me your girlfriend. That sounds like a few strings to me. Actions speak louder than words, Damian. Didn't you just tell me that?"

An exasperated sigh rocketed out of him. "*Jessa*. There's no chance at long-term with me. There never was. I told you this from day one, and you accepted it."

"But why?"

"Why what?"

"Why is there no chance at long-term?" The question came out on a whisper. I searched his face for some hint, some answer, but all I could see was conflict and tension.

Damian's throat bobbed, and he seemed like he was weighing his words. "Because it's not in the cards for me. I don't know how else to explain it," he finally said. "I don't deserve it."

"Oh, Damian." I touched his face, dragging my thumb over his cheek. "How could you say that?"

"Because it's true. It's too much after the way I failed my sisters. I just can't do it, Jessa. It's fine if you don't understand. But I've told you from the beginning what I can give you. And it's not long-term."

There was a hardness behind his eyes, a wall I couldn't penetrate, much less understand. And behind that: fear.

But I knew he wasn't lying. He believed it. And if he believed it, then it was true.

"I'll always do what I can do protect you. You're in my inner circle. But I can't give you what you want."

"And what do you think I want?" I asked him, emotion clogging my throat.

"You want it all," Damian said, something so fierce in his eyes that it was difficult to hold his gaze. "The getaways and the pet names and the labels and the happily-ever-after. I want to give that to you, I do. But I can't. There is no future with me. I'm either going to prison or I'm going to drag you down into whatever fucking curse surrounds me. You deserve better than that. You deserve better than *me*."

A single tear rolled down my cheek, and I sniffed, looking away. There was so much I disagreed with there. But I didn't have the words—or the energy—to fight him.

"Okay," I finally said. "I get it."

"Now let's go," he said, gently nudging me toward the door. I shook my head.

I couldn't just keep pretending at his side, playing the role of a devoted girlfriend while he kept himself apart. I didn't understand how he could lie to himself like that. Didn't he see or hear himself? Every move he made screamed *I'm Jessa's boyfriend.* The insatiable attraction. The thoughtful touches. The sweet moments. Damian was the safe, handsome caretaker who bent over backwards for his woman. For *me*.

But I deserved to be acknowledged. I didn't want to hide in the shadows or pretend my love wasn't real.

He'd promised no mess. But this was messier than anything else.

"I want to stay here," I told him.

"Please, Jessa—"

"No." I shook my head. "I need some time to think about things. I'll be fine, I promise."

Damian looked defeated. He pinched the bridge of his nose, looking like he was about to add something. Then he dropped his hand and tore himself away from me and out of the bedroom. His footsteps thudded across the apartment, and a moment later the door slammed shut.

He was gone.

His actions so much louder than his words.

CHAPTER TWENTY-SIX

DAMIAN

I'd asked for hourly updates from the security detail. That was the first thing I reviewed when I finally came to the next morning. All the reports were good. Jessa's apartment had remained safe.

Not like I'd slept much, despite knowing she had security. Even whiskey couldn't quiet my mind after that shit show of a Monday. The hurt on Jessa's face wouldn't leave me. Her entire spirit had crumpled when I'd told her that I couldn't do long-term.

I hated being the person to make her crumple. But I'd hate it even more if my being in her life meant even worse things came to her, or both of us.

Anxiety hummed beneath my skin as I forced myself to sit up, scrolling through the updates the security team had sent. I had ex-cops on patrol outside Jessa's apartment. Just in case. The Fairchild SUV would be waiting for her when she left the building.

She'd be safe. Even if she didn't want to come stay with me.

I tossed my phone onto the rumpled bedsheets and rubbed at my face. Everything hurt, from my muscles to my heart. I'd punished myself in the gym last night, and then I'd spent too long drinking and working in my bedroom.

I needed to get back to my regular MO, so I could at least feel like I had control. I exercised that control through gym time, working, and whiskey.

It was how I functioned.

It was the only thing that made sense.

But do you still want to keep doing this?

I quieted the voice, which had a distinct Kentucky-girl drawl to it, and hauled myself to the bathroom to get ready for the day. Splash cold water on the face. Pee. Stare at myself in the mirror until things made sense. Opt for a shower after all. Brush teeth. Deodorant. Cologne. More staring into the mirror, trying not to see Jessa in my mind's eye.

I dressed in the usual—business slacks and a button-down—and snatched up my phone from the bed before rummaging for a tie. I had three missed calls from Axel.

My gut knotted. It had to be bad news. There was no other option in my life anymore.

I called him back as I selected my tie.

"Okay, I'll just get right to it," he said in lieu of a greeting. "We've got a fucking mole at the office, and we need to figure out who the fuck it is."

My barely cobbled-together mood shattered at my feet. "What happened?"

"We're in the news again. All of us. Mom, Dad, all of us."

I squeezed my eyes shut. This was the last thing I wanted to hear. Our parents didn't need to be dragged into the tabloids. They could splash us there, but we wanted to at least spare them. "Ian?"

"Him and a lot more. I don't know what's going on here, but I don't fucking like it. Listen, you and I need to meet privately. And we need to do it outside the office. Where are you?"

"My bedroom. Just come up."

"Be there in five."

The phone went dead, and the air solidified in my lungs, making me fight for breath. I didn't fucking like it. This was a living, breathing, worst-case scenario. And at every turn, it managed to get worse.

How could I commit to someone long-term when my life was this constant hedge maze of bad news?

Jessa had to understand. That's what I kept telling myself. Maybe not now, but she would someday, when she saw how bad it got. This was for her own good—and mine. I didn't want to drag her into this muck. And deep down, I knew I didn't deserve to have such happiness.

You did the right thing drawing the line.

No matter how many times I told myself this, it didn't feel true.

Axel arrived in the private elevator just as I headed to the kitchen for coffee. The kettle had barely hit the stove when Axel brought out a sheet of paper and his phone.

"Here." He handed me the phone, where the article was pulled up. *Secret Family Splits the Fairchilds.* The headline alone made my head spin. Axel pulled out a pen and started scribbling on the paper as I read.

There were inaccuracies, of course. But the article laid out exactly what we were going through. Ian's appearance in our lives. The secret family. Our father stepping out on our mother.

It was all there in gut-wrenching clarity. Exposed for the entire world to see.

By the time I finished reading, I wanted to puke.

"We gotta call Mom," I whispered, bringing out my own phone to call her. Axel didn't protest. The phone rang a few moments later and our mom picked up, sniffling.

"Hi Damian."

"Hi mom," I said softly. "Axel's here with me too. You okay? We just saw the article."

"Oh, I'm gettin' by." She sounded so incredibly weary. "Nice way to find out I've been living a lie for the past twenty-some years."

Axel rubbed at his face, and I winced at her words. "We're just as surprised as you."

"More than Trace can say," Axel muttered.

"What was that, sweets?" Mom asked.

"Nothing, mom." I shot Axel a death glare. "Listen, what can we do? What's your plan?"

"I'm leaving," she said, her voice going watery. A moment later, a sob broke through. "I gotta get out of this house."

"Go stay at my place," I told her. "As long as you want. Forever. I don't care. It's yours, mom."

"Thank you, sweets," she whispered through tears. Part of me was glad I couldn't see the devastation on her face. It would just hurt so much more to see her reduced and humiliated like this.

"You want us to come out?" Axel asked, his voice cracking.

"You boys have enough to deal with," she said. "Besides, I don't want you to hear the words I've been using with this man."

"We'll be out there soon," I told her. "Once you're done saying all the nasty stuff he deserves. Then we get a turn."

We sat with her for a few more moments as she cried, sighed, and swore under her breath. When we hung up, Axel and I just watched each other heavily for a few moments.

"How did this leak?" I whispered as I pushed the phone aside.

"That's what we've gotta figure out." Axel pointed to what he'd drawn on the sheet. Columns were labeled according to salacious detail: *secret family. Ian Fairchild.* "We're going to write down who knows about each one of the details that came out. Because this shit..." He paused, shaking his head. "This shit was close to the chest. Whoever betrayed us..."

I sighed, resting my elbows on the countertop so I could cradle my face. "I fucking hate this."

"We gotta do it. And we've gotta take action. *Today.*"

He was right. Of course he was right. But deep down, I knew where this was headed.

We laid out the names of who knew about each detail. The overwhelming majority featured only two names: Francis and Jessa. Felicia and Madison, our receptionists, showed up in a few columns, but there were too many details on this sheet that they'd have no way of knowing, short of sonar hearing and mindreading. Ian had access to the nitty gritty details about his own existence, of course, but there were too many particular details about the SEC investigation in the article that Ian would have no access to. We discounted Trace, since we agreed that he wouldn't leak a secret brother to the press after keeping it a secret from *us* for almost fifteen years.

Besides, this hurt Trace, too.

"So," I said, my gaze raking over the two names that appeared the most frequently. "What's our takeaway."

"That this fucking sucks?" Axel rubbed at his eyes. "I don't know, man. You're the data guru. Tell me what we should do."

"Data says it has to be one of them." I tapped my thumb against the sheet, my own words sounding hollow, forced.

Axel shook his head, squinting over at me. "But it just doesn't seem possible."

I didn't truly believe it could be *either* of them.

"But it has to be," I said, more as a test than a fact. "Right?"

We stared at each other for an eternity, wracked with doubt.

"Right," Axel concluded, looking at me severely. "If we had to pick one, who would it be?"

My mouth went dry. "I don't know."

"Who needs money more?"

I pinched my eyes shut, the realization crashing over me. Of course the press would pay well for news like this. Money had to be the main motivating factor. It always was.

"Jessa's family is pretty much always hounding her for money," I said quietly, not even wanting to speak the words. "I thought we paid her enough. Maybe they were asking for too much."

Axel crossed his arms, staring at the list. "I don't think she'd do it, though."

"Me neither," I whispered.

More silence. More confusion.

"But neither would Francis," Axel whispered. He knocked his knuckles against the countertop. "Okay, we've gotta take our emotions out of this shit. Here's what I know. Francis has been around sensitive information for *years*. He has a proven track record. Jessa doesn't."

I stewed over this, remembering what Jessa had told me in the car returning from the Hudson Valley.

"Jessa has a new roommate, Kendra," I blurted. "Maybe it was her. She could have broken into Jessa's phone, or her email...I pulled up some information on her but didn't look it over yet." I swiped through my phone, accessing my secure documents. I'd run a background check, which had come back clean. Seeing that had satisfied me for the moment, so I hadn't combed through the specifics of this woman's life.

"You think a new roommate could have anything to do with this?" Axel asked, doubt in his voice.

"I don't know jack shit anymore," I replied, scanning the information as quickly as I could. Place of birth. Siblings. Degrees obtained. Place of employment. "Except that it couldn't have been Jessa."

Axel sighed, rubbing at his face as I scanned the information as quickly as I could.

"Hold up," I said, displeased to find some familiar words on the screen. "Kendra works for *Big Apple Mag*."

"Fuck." Axel slammed his fist against the countertop.

I dragged my hands down my face. Everything inside of me wanted to avoid this conclusion. But it was a brightly lit pathway. The only logical choice. When all the facts lined up...how could I avoid the data?

"Jesus Christ."

Axel heaved a sigh, shaking his head. "I know, man."

"I don't want to believe it. It can't be her."

"Tell me honestly then. What would you do if Jessa *wasn't* Jessa?" Axel asked. He put his hand on my shoulder, forcing me to meet his gaze. "Seriously. Be real with me. If this was some girl off the street that you'd hired, what would you do?"

The truth of matter crashed over me in unpleasant, sickly waves. My mouth went dry. "I'd fire her."

Axel nodded, eyes fastened to the list. "Right."

Silence stretched between us as we confronted this reality.

"It's a security breach," Axel said gravely, and when his gaze met mine, I saw the meaning written there. *If it was anybody else, it was grounds for termination.*

I spent a few moments mulling over this turn of events, trying to find different angles. Some way to absolve Jessa. Any opportunity for salvation here.

But I came up with nothing.

I had to fire her. Between her and her roommate, this was too great a risk to bear.

"I don't know if I can do it," I said, massaging my face. "This is gonna suck."

"I know, man." He sniffed.

"We gotta call Jeremy too," I said. "What the fuck are we gonna say to him?"

"I don't know, dude."

"And Trace," I added. "He's gotta know."

Axel's face darkened. "You can handle that one. Honestly, I'm leaving this up to you. I'll follow your lead."

We spent some more time sitting with our thoughts, wrestling with the hows and the whens of it all. Axel finally went back to the office, and I stayed in the kitchen, drowning in my thoughts.

No matter how many times I went over it all, something didn't feel quite right. But I couldn't identify what was off.

It had to be my personal feelings for Jessa, the way she'd infiltrated my life and my heart, despite my best attempts to prevent it. The softness and grace she brought, the sweet healing of her smile. My chest tightened, and another wave of despair crashed through me. That's all this was—an emotional response when there should have been none. Logically, I had to go through with it, because the data paved the way.

I had to fire her.

And firing her would solve another problem that clawed at me. It would rid me of the constant temptation to dive deeper, to get closer, to lose myself with Jessa.

The deepest parts of me wanted to avoid this outcome for so many tender, loving reasons.

But I was nothing if not data driven. And the safest path forward involved ridding myself of the largest threat to my stability.

Staying isolated had always been my plan. It was what made sense. It offered protection. It offered a shot at normalcy. Inviting in love opened the doorway to heartbreak. It was already too late— heartbreak was here knocking. Time to throw the bolt.

I needed to get back to basics.

Single. Unattached. Impervious.

Firing her would ensure I returned to my status quo by tomorrow. Maybe I'd be licking my wounds for awhile, but doing the right thing didn't always come easy.

These were the sacrifices required for my kind of life.

Despite the rationalizations, it took me hours to rally. I dreaded this task, more than almost anything I'd ever done. I knew it would hurt. It would sting. It would haunt me at night when my thoughts grew too loud. But it had to be done.

For the sake of my sanity. For my stability. For the future of my company.

I finally made it down to the office after lunch. My legs felt leaden, but I powered through. Jessa's crystal blues found mine as soon as I rounded the corner into the hallway and my stomach bottomed out. I couldn't fire her. Something wasn't right.

I cleared my throat as I breezed past her desk. "Jessa, can you come into my office?"

Here went nothing.

I rounded my desk, and Jessa was in front of me a moment later, looking every grade of nervous.

"What's up, Damian?" She sat facing me, nibbling at her bottom lip as she fanned her dress out around her. I struggled not to notice her. I stared at my computer screen, groping for the right words. Waiting for anything to come to me.

You can't do this. It's not right. Something is off.

That intuitive sentiment warred with the pulsing need to get back on track. To return to the hard-won stability I'd enjoyed before she'd shown up and rocked me off my foundation.

I'd wanted to help her, to help her family. I'd done that. Now, I needed to help myself. I needed to get back to safety. To solitude. To the depressing aloneness I'd convinced myself was the only path forward.

"I don't know how to say this," I started.

She drew a shaky breath. "Oh God."

I steepled my fingers, finally daring to meet her gaze. *Just do it. Get it over with.* "I think it's time for us to part ways professionally." Hurt slashed through her gaze, making my chest tighten. But I forced myself to not look away. To come across as firmly as possible. This would be final. "A few things have come to my attention recently. You haven't been performing up to expectations. And given the recent information breach, there isn't much doubt about where it came from."

Her eyes were so wide I thought they might pop out of her head. She didn't move for what felt like a full minute.

"What are you talking about, Damian? What information breach?"

"Private information is leaking out of this office. Family issues. I'm not pointing fingers, but we are restructuring as a result. I'm sorry this had to happen. We'll offer you a severance package to make the transition easier. You'll find it to be pretty generous."

She cupped her cheeks in her hands, staring at me like I'd just grown a third head. "Am I having a nightmare right now? What is going on?"

"We can have someone pack your desk up for you if you'd like to avoid the spectacle." I turned my gaze to my computer. Her reaction reflected my internal state, and I didn't need any more of it. "Otherwise you're free to go."

Her mouth turned into a frighteningly thin line. She stared at me so hard, it was like she could see through me. "Why are you saying all of this? Do you think I leaked something? Damian, I never shared anything with anyone. I swear to God above. What happened? What did I do to make you think—"

"Jessa, this is a company decision. I appreciate what you did while you were here, but there's an element of liability I have to consider." I paused, forcing myself to meet her gaze. "Your new roommate works for *Big Apple Mag*. They're the ones who published the last two exposés about our personal lives, within the last two weeks. Follow the trail, Jessa. It's obvious."

Her mouth opened and closed, but nothing came out. Finally, she forced out, "But...I never...there wasn't..."

"It's done, Jessa. I'm sorry. You can leave now."

Her bottom lip quivered and she tore out of my office. Once the door shut behind her, I rested my face in my hands. My heart still pounded, every inch of my body feeling gelatinous and foreign.

But I'd done it. The band-aid had been ripped off.

And now things could start getting back to normal.

CHAPTER
TWENTY-SEVEN

JESSA

Back at my apartment, I didn't know what to do first.

So I just cried. And cried. And then cried some more.

I'd stuffed the contents of my desk unceremoniously into a box, and every time I glimpsed it in the corner of my room, more tears gushed out.

I felt like a failure. A disappointment. A complete and utter fool.

Even Damian, the man who was supposedly so close to me, so enchanted by me, couldn't be convinced of my worthiness.

I didn't understand how Kendra's job at *Big Apple Mag* could have led to me being fired, especially when she barely knew I worked there *and* had only spent one night here so far. That wasn't enough time to dig up any dirt. The hardest hitting question she'd asked me was whether the brothers were as hot in real life as they were in photos.

Nothing made sense. Yet I couldn't stop myself from combing through everything in my mind, trying to find the turning point, the moment when I'd fucked it all up. I certainly hadn't leaked information to anybody. So how could Damian be so convinced I was the breach?

It was almost four o'clock by the time I felt like I could breathe again. The universe must have sensed my ability to function, because a phone call came in just as I tossed out my last tissue and took my first clear breath.

Tara.

I deflated, staring at the vibrating phone as I debated whether answering. Did I have the strength for this? I considered just letting it go to voicemail but changed my mind at the last second.

"Hello?"

"Hey." Her voice sounded flat. She was pissed about something. Anxiety snaked cold and foreboding through me. "Thought you'd like to hear the latest."

"I don't know," I said with a small laugh. "Do I?"

Tara cleared her throat, and I could practically see her adjusting her position in her chair the way she always did when she sat down to tell it like it was, a scowl on her face. "Probably not. Mom relapsed."

The words settled in me like deadweight. Though I'd been hoping for the best, I'd also been expecting this. But I'd never admit it.

"Shit bricks," I whispered.

"And I think we can safely say it's your fault this time," Tara went on, her tone snippy as hell. "We came up short on the halfway house payment, so she got kicked out. Her being back on the street, where do you think she ended up, Jessa? So thanks a lot for turning your back on your family. Is this what you wanted? Because you got it."

The line went dead, and I was left gaping at my bedroom wall.

The tears returned in full force a moment later.

Back to crying, moping misery.

The logical side of me knew that my mother's relapse couldn't possibly be my fault. But Tara's words cut deep all the same, regardless of my understanding of addiction. Because if she thought that, others thought that. Tara would be telling her kids the worst lies about me, leveraging my absence as proof that I was ruining the family. That my decision to follow a different path had left the rest of them on the road to disaster.

I didn't want to believe it. But maybe she was right. Maybe she'd been right all along. There was still the chance that I'd simply been the one too foolish to recognize the truth.

I was on my way to the bathroom for another box of tissues when Kendra came home. The big grin on her face dropped immediately when she spotted me.

"Yo, new roomie. Everything okay?"

I laughed in spite of myself. My eyes were swollen, my face red, hair mussed. I was the dictionary definition of a hot mess. "Not really. But I'll be okay eventually."

Kendra dropped her bags near the front door and came up to me. "Want to talk about it?"

"I don't know. I'm so tired of thinking about it and crying about it. My life just completely imploded, Kendra. And you just moved in. I don't want to scare you off." I dabbed at the corners of my eyes with a tissue, emotion still bubbling inside my chest.

Kendra squeezed my arm. "I hear that. If you want to talk, I'm here, okay?"

I nodded. "Off the record, right?"

She tipped her head. "What do you mean?"

"Like if I tell you something, you wouldn't use it at work or anything...right?"

She blinked, confusion still written on her face. She tucked some hair behind her ear. "Right. Our home is a confidential space. Maybe we should have talked about this before. But you don't have to worry about anything you tell me leaving these four walls."

I nodded, mildly relieved. That protected this space at least. But what about things I'd told her elsewhere? I raked through my memories for the hundredth time, trying to remember anything salacious or unsavory I might have told her during the interview process.

But there was nothing.

"I lost my job today," I said quietly. "The Fairchild brothers let me go because they suspect I'm connected to the latest article that *Big Apple Mag* published about them."

Kendra's brows knit together. I could see the gears turning behind her blue eyes. "I saw that article today. The one about the secret family?"

"Yeah."

"A senior editor worked on that. I heard he had an informant." Kendra narrowed her eyes, her gaze drifting off as she thought. "I can talk to him tomorrow and see what I can find out, if you want me to."

I nodded, looking down at the tissue in my hand. "I would appreciate that. Thanks, Kendra."

She jerked her chin toward the kitchen. "Wanna have some tea? I've got some crazy gingko stuff I've been dying to try out. Supposed to make your brain work better. I'm down for whatever might help, you know?"

I smiled briefly, drawing a cleansing breath. Maybe some better brain function would help me get out of this mess. Or at least help me discern the next steps. "Yeah. That would be nice."

I sat on the cracked leather couch that faced the kitchenette, tucking my legs underneath me as she moved around the kitchen—filling the kettle, turning on the stove, finding mugs. It was nice to have someone else here. Especially now that I'd be spending a lot more time here, struggling to figure out my next move.

"For what it's worth," Kendra said a few moments later, long after we'd both sunk into our own thoughts. "I saw someone from Fairchild at our office recently. I don't know his name..."

"Oh?" I swung my head to look at her. "What did he look like?"

"A bigger guy. I saw him in the office yesterday when I came to pick up the key. He wore a Gucci suit. And he set my gaydar pinging, for what it's worth."

My mouth went dry. *Francis*. It had to be. But I couldn't know for sure.

"Are you sure it was him?" A strange nervousness pinged through me.

"I thought it was. Who knows. Coulda been his doppelganger. In a city this size, it's possible. And he was staring at a tablet the first time I saw him."

Maybe it hadn't been him. But the mere idea of Francis heading to *Big Apple Mag* had my palms itching and curiosity swarming.

It felt like a lightbulb moment, but I had no idea what to do with the insight. I didn't even have proof, much less a messenger bag full of evidence. Damian would need proof. *Data*.

"So." Kendra brought out two steaming mugs, setting them on the rickety coffee table in front of the couch. "Let's hear about this day from hell."

"Well, I didn't just lose my job," I told her. "I also lost Damian."

"What do you mean?" She cradled her mug, bringing it to her lips for a sip. "Ouch. Too hot. Don't try it."

"I sure won't." I looked down at the steaming green liquid.

"Your accent is so nice," Kendra said.

"I have an accent?"

"Well, yeah. A Kentucky accent. Didn't you know?"

"I don't notice it, obviously." I laughed.

"Do the Fairchilds have one too?"

I shook my head. "Nah, they sorta lost theirs. They've been living here a long time. Damian's comes out when he gets drunk though." I paused, thinking back on all those late-night conversations we'd had when I still thought we'd be able to keep things mostly-chaste. Back when it was just phone sex and my fashion portfolio. Damian's lilt had always presented itself then, just like it did at the tail end of fundraisers and galas, after a healthy handful of drinks.

Sadness streaked through my heart. Had I missed something with Damian? Was he drinking a lot more than I'd ever realized?

Kendra grinned over the lip of her mug. "That's cute. So what happened?"

"We had been kinda...I don't know...seeing each other." I fiddled with my earlobe, trying not to remember how many times Damian had bitten me there. When I touched that spot, it didn't elicit any reaction. But when his mouth or teeth went there, watch out, panties. "I've been in love with this man since seventh grade. Secretly, of course. But working for him just reignited what I always felt, even though it sounds so...stupid."

"Not stupid. Sometimes you fall in love early and it never goes away." She shrugged.

"Well, I wish it would go away," I muttered. "Damian wasn't happy with my work, I guess. At least that's what he told me. He got angry when I forgot an important task, which I understand. But he made it sound like I dicked off on the job constantly. I always keep my sketch pad out for down time; it's doodling, it's second nature for me. I guess he took that to be too much of a distraction. I was really trying at that job, Kendra. It was intense, and I gave it my all. But it wasn't enough."

Kendra wrapped an arm around me. "That's all you can do. But answer me one thing. What are you more upset about? Losing the job or losing the guy?"

"The guy." The answer flew off my lips. "I don't care about the job even half as much as I care about Damian. And if I'm being honest, getting fired was a small relief. That job sucked up so much of my time, and it's not what I came here to do. I did my job as well as I could, but it wasn't what I wanted to be doing."

She nodded. "I believe you can be doing what you want to be doing. And this might be your doorway."

Kendra's optimism was sweet. But it couldn't penetrate my sadness, which steamed fresh and pungent inside me.

The truth was, the doorway to the future didn't matter right now, because I was too stuck in my failure.

I'd lost both the guy *and* the job and let down everyone who had ever relied on me.

I'd never felt so worthless. And that voice inside me urging me to just pack it in and crawl back to Kentucky was screaming louder than ever.

CHAPTER TWENTY-EIGHT

DAMIAN

Normal.

Things were back to normal.

I settled back into the routine I'd once preferred and accustomed myself to the empty desk outside my office. The mere sight of it made me think of Jessa, though, so I had it removed on Thursday.

Out of sight, out of mind.

If that were even remotely true, I would have had a fighting chance at returning to my regular modus operandi. But I didn't need to see things that reminded me of Jessa to think about her. She just existed in the back of my head all the time, every day. Practically anything I tried to focus on led to more thoughts of Jessa.

All I could do was hope they would diminish over time. Even if it took decades.

Maybe by the time I reached old age, dementia would finally banish Jessa from my mind.

What a future to look forward to.

But this was the only path to stability that I knew. Returning to the status quo. Overworking and whiskey until my focus returned and my mind shut off.

Yep. The future of your dreams.

It seemed so much more unsavory now that Jessa was gone. I was shriveling—colorless, a boring husk, depleted—without her warmth, her joy, or her appreciation for shrimp cocktail.

Trace came back to the penthouse on Friday morning, tanned beyond belief and looking too relaxed in a loose tee and linen pants. I caught him as he rolled his bags into the penthouse. He took his sunglasses off, jerking his chin into a nod.

"Welcome back," I told him.

"I'd say it's good to be back, but"—Trace folded his sunglasses and hung them on the collar of his shirt—"that would be a lie."

"Yeah. I take it you read the article?"

Trace nodded, his dark gaze stuck on the floor. "I don't know who the fuck could have leaked that. Unless it was Ian himself."

"There's no way," I said. "Ian knows about the secret family, but there was too much in that article that Ian had no way of knowing."

Trace's jaw flexed. "So what now?"

"Still trying to figure that out." I checked my watch. "In fact, I'm supposed to be doing that now." The three of us had always started our weeks with a Monday check-in, but Axel and I had added a Friday meeting, given the absolute shitshow of our reality these days.

"You have a meeting with Axel downstairs?"

"I'd say yes, but I'm not supposed to tell you, so..."

Trace arched an expertly judgmental brow my way. "Let him bitch. I'm coming."

I held up my palms in submission. "I'll deny any knowledge."

Trace strode away, suitcase wheels clicking over the tiled floor. I headed for the elevator, already a minute late to the meeting.

Axel tapped his pen impatiently on the conference table as I took my seat.

"Glad you could finally join us," he said.

"Oh, cut me a break. I was two minutes late."

"*Five,*" he corrected me.

"Fine. Five. Can we start?"

Francis looked between us as though giving us one last chance to air our grievances. And then he spoke. "Great. Let's get this meeting underway."

Trace strode down the hallway, visible through the glass walls. He nodded at a few employees as he passed. Axel groaned.

"Who the fuck invited him?"

"Wasn't me," I said, fighting to hide my smile as Trace pushed open the door, sunglasses still hanging on his shirt.

"Jesus fuck," Axel complained.

"Long time no see, Trace." Francis lifted two fingers in a salute, tipping his perfectly shellacked head in a greeting. "You look so much tanner than before."

"I'd hope so. I lived exclusively on the water for weeks."

"Can we fucking start already?" Axel said, the annoyance in his voice almost cringeworthy. "There's a lot of noise in here that I can't fully understand, and it's distracting me from the real work we need to do, unlike some people who abandon work and obligations and morals in favor of other choices."

"I can't help but feel like that was directed at me," Trace murmured, looking my way.

"It probably wasn't," I teased.

"Well, I can see this is going to be a fun meeting," Francis said, tapping his pen on the table as his gaze darted between the three of us.

"Extremely fun. Let's proceed," I said.

"Well, I suppose I should update Trace for the sake of continuity," Francis said, sweeping his arm in Trace's direction.

"What are you gesturing at?" Axel asked.

"At Trace," Francis said.

"What?" Axel asked.

Trace lowered his chin, sending Axel his best death glare. "Knock off the childish shit, Axel."

"God, it's windy in here. It's just like a lot of hot air blows through here sometimes," Axel said, looking at me. "Should we hire an HVAC person to check it out? We might have a critical leak."

"Guys," I snapped. "Can we knock it the fuck off? It's time to strategize, not act like idiots."

Silence stretched across the table. Axel let out a terse sigh.

"So, moving on…" Francis opened up something on his tablet and went down a list, updating Trace on the latest developments. The last item on the list was, of course, Jessa's dismissal. Trace looked over at me, surprise etched onto his face.

"She's gone?"

"She's gone," I confirmed.

"It's for the better," Francis added. "Any weakness in the company should be rooted out. If they aren't loyal, they need to be gone."

"That's a shame. I thought she could have become an asset," Trace mused.

"Not surprising to hear from someone who regularly hides information from others," Axel muttered.

"Excuse me? I thought you could only hear hot air," Trace shot back. "Unless you learned how to talk to the wind?"

"I'll fucking respond to who I want, when I want," Axel said, jabbing a finger in Trace's direction.

"You guys," I barked out. "Shut the fuck up so we can at least get *something* done today."

Silence descended over the table once more. On days like today, I felt like the father. And in a way, I had been the father figure of the Haynes family, until Axel and I were placed with the Fairchilds. Maybe that's why I'd naturally become the mediator between Axel and Trace—and sometimes, the discipliner.

"What's next on the agenda?" I snapped at Francis.

"The lawyer has news," Francis said, positioning the conference room speakerphone equidistant between the four of us. "He's calling any minute now."

My stomach wrenched and I buried my face in my hands. I didn't like anything that was going on. Not one bit of it.

And this is the normal you were trying to get back to. By ridding yourself of the one bright spot you'd found.

The phone rang—the thing looked like a UFO with a number pad attached to one side—and Axel answered it with a smooth push of a button, not betraying an ounce of our collective tension.

"Hey guys, hope you're all doing well." Robert Fields's brusque, formal voice filled the conference room. We all leaned closer to the phone in the center and muttered pleasantries before he delivered his news. "I spoke to my contact at the SEC yesterday. They're no closer to a decision yet, but they're considering embezzlement charges, which brings a hefty fine and serious prison time. He's confident they'd recommend a ten-year prison sentence to whoever is determined to be the engineer of this fraud, instead of the typical thirty years. After all, you're not bilking little old ladies here, so that should help you."

The weight of the world on my shoulders sank heavier. The air in my lungs disappeared, and I could barely understand the rest of the words coming from the phone.

"We're not bilking *anyone*," I said, but I couldn't tell whether the words even made it past my lips. It was pointless now. We couldn't turn this train around. All I could do was hang on and hope I didn't spend the next ten years of my life in prison.

"They couldn't give me a timeline on when they might come to a conclusion about filing charges. They've got all the documents they need now, and we'll be in touch as soon as we hear more. Okay, guys? Chins up."

My gaze slid over to Axel's. I found the same worry in his eyes.

At least one of us was heading to prison. It might be him, me, or maybe all three of us. We sat suspended in silent disbelief.

"Was that supposed to be good news?" Trace asked eventually.

"Jesus fuck," I muttered, dragging my hands down my face. "I can't take this shit anymore. It's gonna eat me alive. I probably won't even live to see the sentencing. The stress is gonna kill me before we get there."

"Don't say that," Axel snapped.

"It's fucking true," I said, beating back waves of nausea. I wanted to puke. I wanted to rage. I wanted to launch an emotional appeal to whoever the head investigator was to make sure they understood just how much good we were doing in the world.

"You need Jessa back," Axel said, and from the look on his face I knew he was speaking seriously. "She's the only one who could get your head out of your ass."

"Nothing worth seeing up here," I bit out.

"You should still try to enjoy life," Axel said. "We've got our freedom right now. Why wouldn't we take advantage of that?"

"You think I should shack up with the woman who leaked our info to the press?"

Axel sighed, betraying the fact that he was torn, just like me. Neither of us truly believed Jessa had leaked anything. But she was the only one who made sense. And if not her, *then who?*

"Damian, you're better off," Francis added consolingly. "Harper is a catch, and I'm sure she'd love to start coming back to the office."

I schooled my annoyance. "I don't need the love life input, thank you, Francis."

"You never liked Jessa, did you, Francis?" Axel asked, jerking his chin in Francis's direction.

"Not one bit," Francis said, which made my heart wrench. "Those dresses were *too much*. And she always needed everything repeated. It took her a million years to catch on."

I fought the rebuke that so desperately wanted to erupt from me. I didn't want Francis—or *anyone*—talking about Jessa like that. Furthermore, that didn't sound a bit like Jessa. She'd always been so snappy, so smart. Sure, she'd needed time to adjust to life in New York. But all transplants did, and she'd done it quickly.

"Can we just not talk about Jessa, please?" I snapped, my fingers clenching into a fist beneath the table. I couldn't hold it in. The next negative word directed at Jessa would result in a punch to somebody's face.

Axel looked over at me, mildly amused.

Trace lifted a brow. "You're a lot snippier now that Jessa is gone."

"Okay, are we done here? I have work to do." I pushed to standing, more than ready to get the fuck out of here. I needed space to process. And more than that, I needed Jessa.

She was all I could see, all I could think about. I knew she'd have something comforting to say, something to yank me back into perspective. But I'd fucking fired her.

Every cell of my body knew it had been wrong. The more time that passed, the more confident I became. Even *without* the data, which disturbed me. But I knew there was something waiting for me out there. Some clue, some piece of information.

I just needed to find it.

"I think we had some more to cover—" Francis began.

"You can finish without me," I told them. "I need to think." I lifted my fingers in lieu of goodbye and left the conference room.

Once the door to my office clicked shut behind me, I let out a deep, raggedy breath.

Everything continued to dissolve, despite my ejecting Jessa from my life.

What if you had kept her around?

I needed to clear my head, and the best route to even attempt such a feat was through work. I sat at my computer, pulling up the call logs Jessa had collected for me on Monday. I also started some computer scans—aka light hacking—in the background that searched for keywords like *Jessa Walton, Big Apple, Ian, Gary,* and more.

A phone call interrupted my search—Jeremy.

I sighed, unsure if I should answer it. It could have been the most awkward call of my life. But I had just fired his sister, and he was probably curious for my side of things. I owed him that much at least.

"Jeremy," I said, trying to sound jovial when I was anything but.

He let out a long sigh. "Damian. I heard what happened."

"Yeah...I wondered if you'd...you know. Talked to Jessa."

"I am so, so disappointed," Jeremy said. "She said that some leaked information was attributed to her or her new roommate but that she wasn't sure how it had gotten out. I don't know, it kind of confused me. But it sounds like she dropped the ball."

"It's a tough situation for everyone," I said, eager to move past this conversation.

"I knew she couldn't hack it out there," Jeremy said mournfully. "We all warned her."

Sadness tremored through me. None of Jessa's family had ever believed in her. *Fuck.* I rested my forehead in my hand as I spoke.

"Let me be clear, Jeremy. She did a good job for me. She really did. But these were extenuating circumstances...I was left with no other choice. It's nothing personal. I still think she's a good person with tons of smarts, and no hard feelings, buddy."

"I appreciate that, Damian. I really do. I suppose it's probably for the best that she's heading home, then."

I straightened, a strange pit forming in my gut. "What?"

"Yeah, she's coming back. Finally!"

"To live?" I forced out.

"Well, I can't say for sure, but it's likely. Really, this is where she belongs."

All I could see in my mind's eye were the flashes of Jessa in New York—those big, freckled grins, the elegant dresses, the absolute delight at being flanked by important people, shrimp platters, and glittering chandeliers.

But more than that—the bubbling enthusiasm for her dresses. The constant creation and focus on fashion. The stars in her eyes when she showed Cora her designs or made new connections at events.

She couldn't find that back home, not at this level. Oakville wasn't for her. Even I knew that.

Jessa belonged in New York City.

"I guess I'm kind of surprised," I finally muttered. "She seemed to like it here. I thought she'd find a new job and try to stay, but...I guess I was wrong."

"We're going to make sure she stays where she should," Jeremy said. "After all, her mom needs her right now. She relapsed again this week. So we're all dealing with that."

"Fuck. I'm sorry Jeremy." Disappointment crashed through me, but more for Jessa. I knew Tara would have said something cruel to her by now. And I wasn't there for it, to help her sift through the rubble after the dust settled from Tara's latest missile.

This all felt wrong. Pieces out of place.

But hell if I knew how to put them back together.

"Well, I'll let you get back to work," Jeremy said. "I know how busy you all are. Promise you'll come visit soon."

"I will. Hey, Jeremy—when's Jessa planning on heading down?"

"I think she's got a flight next week. She'll be staying with me, so don't worry. She'll be taken care of."

We said our goodbyes, and I hung up the phone and shook my head.

Moving back in with Jeremy was the last thing I imagined Jessa wanting.

But nobody in her family even cared what she wanted. They just wanted her to do what *they* thought she should want.

Frustration bubbled up inside me, the urge to correct Jeremy, Francis, and anyone else who spoke poorly about her so fierce I didn't know what to do with it. It was one of the reasons I'd needed to leave the conference room. Another bad word about Jessa and I would have socked Francis in the fucking throat.

And here I was, ready to go to bat against Jeremy, her own brother.

What the fuck is wrong with you?

I needed hyper-focus. That was all I had left in my toolbelt. I needed to get so lost in work that everything else ceased to exist.

I gathered my things from my office and headed for the penthouse. I was done with socializing, done with interruptions. I just need to retreat.

I holed up in my bedroom, remembering to grab a protein bar and a water bottle before I did, and sank into death metal and hacking.

Axel started pinging me around five. I ignored everything. Trace joined in around seven. I had no time for responses—only advancing in my hunt and refilling my tumbler with ice from the mini fridge.

By eleven, my bottle of whiskey was a quarter gone. There was pounding on my door. I turned the music down and twisted to look at the door.

"What?" I called out.

Axel stuck his head into the room. "Dude. You gotta take a break."

"Why?"

The door swung all the way open, and Axel crossed his arms, tipping his head as if to say *seriously*? "You've been at it since late morning. That's more than twelve straight hours in this chair."

"I've peed a few times," I told him, but the words withered in the space between us.

"I know how you get," Axel said succinctly. "You need to stop, and you need to go to bed."

I shook my head, turning back to my computer. "No, dude. There's too much to do."

"*Damian.*"

Axel's tone made me turn back to face him. He looked serious now. More serious than I'd expected.

"You've been acting crazy since you fired Jessa," Axel said in a low voice. "You're being an overboard workaholic now, even for you. It's kinda freaking me out." He pointed to the whiskey bottle. "Was that full when you started?"

Frustration tore me in two, and I sighed. "What else am I supposed to do? I can't let up. Not letting up is the only way I can make a fucking difference, Axel. What am I worth if I'm not making a difference?"

Axel's face softened and he came into the room, his footsteps falling softly on the carpet. "Do you really believe that?"

"Yes."

"Do you realize that no matter how hard you try, you can't save the world?"

I huffed and shook my head. "Axel—"

"All we can do is inject a little bit of good here and there." He dotted his finger in different places in the air. "That's it. That's the most we can hope to accomplish in our lifetimes."

"Yeah. And even with those few spots of good, there's so much bad that comes with it," I mumbled.

"That's life, brother. A healthy mix of shit storms and rainbows." Axel shrugged. "What are you gonna do but find the ones you love and hang on for dear life?"

I hefted with a laugh, but it faded quickly. "I've got you and Trace. That's all I need." I started to turn back to my computer, but Axel stilled my chair with his hand.

"What's the deal with Jessa?" There was no sarcasm in his voice, no game between us. This was a raw, honest question. And it nearly brought me to my knees.

"I think I made a mistake, Axel," I said, squinting up at my brother. "I know we had some evidence and data, but I think we were wrong. Everything in my body rejects what we decided. I almost fucking punched Francis in the conference room for what he said about Jessa's dresses."

Axel hung his head, shoving his hands into his pants pockets as he listened to me.

"But I can't take it back. I fired her because I needed her to be away from me. Because I fucking fell in love with her, Axel. And I just...I can't have that."

"Why not? Don't you want love?"

For a moment, I didn't even know what to say. It seemed so obvious. Loving Jessa meant risk. It meant more things that could be taken from me. More ways to destroy my hard-won semblance of stability. Having Jessa in my life meant accepting the fact that I was loveable—worthy of love—after the failure with my sisters.

"Of course I want love. But that doesn't mean I get to have it. Losing Jordan and Kaylee was my responsibility. My fault. No matter what I do, I can't convince myself I deserve her, because I lost our little sisters."

"Damian—" Axel reached out for me, but I barreled on.

"And if I lost them, I could lose her. You see what I mean? It's too dangerous to get involved with someone who means that much to me."

"But Trace and I mean that much to you," Axel said. "You don't worry about having us in your life."

"I do," I told him. "Because that's the other side of this stupid fucking coin. Whenever something good comes my way, something much worse comes right behind it. It's happened enough times to be a fucking data set."

Axel looked unconvinced.

"Don't believe me if you don't want to."

"It's not that I don't believe you. I'm just thinking—that's life. Bad things happen to good people. You can't control it. You can just roll with it. It's like ice cream and drownings."

"What the hell are you talking about?"

"Ice cream sales and deaths from drowning increase on exactly the same curve. Doesn't mean eating ice cream if gonna make you drown, though. It just means it's summer."

I looked away, but this time, it was Axel who had more to say.

"Remember the fundraiser? You and I were stressing the fuck out about the protestors. Then Jessa came and you just...lit up. You hopped on board the solution train. She came up with a great idea, and we made it happen. It was magical."

My heart wrenched in my chest remembering that night. That was the night I'd realized I couldn't resist claiming her as my own anymore. The night I stopped caring if coworkers and colleagues saw us. Because our passion was too great to be contained.

"*That's* what a good relationship is about," Axel went on. "Because whether or not you're with her, bad things are gonna happen. People are gonna drown regardless of how little ice cream they eat. What does matter is who's at your side and how you weather the storm. Together."

I sat on his words for a few moments, letting them sink into me. He had a point. But the reality his words encouraged was terrifying.

"I liked you two together," Axel finally said. "A lot. Way more than you and Harper."

"Yeah. Well, I fired Jessa, so that's been ruined."

"So what are you gonna do about it?"

"Nothing," I told him, turning back to my computer. "I'm going to sit here and rot and fester in the consequences of my actions with whiskey at my side."

Axel laughed—a real, deep belly laugh. "I don't believe that shit for one second."

"It's what I'm supposed to be doing, right? She was the leak. Her roommate works for *Big Apple*. What else can I say?"

Axel rolled his neck in a slow circle, his gaze fastened to the far wall. "Do you ever think it might have been Francis?"

"I don't know what to think anymore. Other than I'm positive it wasn't Jessa."

Axel clapped his hand on my shoulder. "All right. Get back to your festering and rotting, since that's clearly what you're going to do."

His sarcasm was back, along with his wink. He knew the truth as well as I did.

When it came to Jessa, I couldn't sit still for long.

CHAPTER TWENTY-NINE

My flight touched down in Louisville on Sunday afternoon. Not even a week away from Damian and the Fairchild brothers and I still felt disjointed and lost.

The disjointedness was made worse by the fact that I was headed home to Oakville, for the first time since August. I hadn't wanted to come really, but with the holidays right around the corner, Jeremy had started to unload an immense amount of pressure for me to come home and touch base with the family.

God bless my older brother, he tried so hard for us to be one of those Hallmark families. Even though we were better fit for one of those failed reality TV shows that followed a dysfunctional family around and then never got renewed for a second season. *What a Fucking Mess with the Waltons* – that's what they'd name our show.

Between the holidays and Jeremy's mounting pressure, I felt like I had no other choice. Besides, I'd skipped Thanksgiving, and Jeremy's Martha Stewart energy was ramping up to dangerous levels. My fashion course had already paused for winter break, so I had a few uncharted weeks ahead of me with no plans, no direction.

Why not create the next episode of *What a Fucking Mess with the Waltons?*

Though I didn't want to be completely aimless over the winter break. I planned to work ahead for my final portfolio project, so there would be no chance of missing important deadlines or not being prepared. That was the big silver lining in being fired. My final portfolio was coming together, and I was so proud of it.

Except I was the only one who was proud of it.

I just had to get myself used to that idea. Strange how after so many years, I still expected those closest to me to share my excitement.

But Damian had proved I couldn't trust anyone. His dig about my sketchbooks during our return trip from the Hudson Valley was etched into my heart. It was clear he'd never supported me. Not truly. He'd only tolerated my fashion inclinations as an inconvenient side gig with some pleasant results.

Amazing how a little time and space could clarify a perspective.

I'd gotten caught up in the New York rat race. And while returning home in the midst of my mother's relapse was not what I would call a *good time*, I needed to touch base with my homeland.

Not permanently. Just to reorient, regroup, and then return to my chosen path.

Kendra called me on my way from the airport. I'd hired a ride share instead of renting a car, because Damian hadn't been lying—the severance package was more than generous, and I could survive another year in New York on that alone if I scrimped and split rent with Kendra.

"Hey, you miss me already?" I teased after picking up.

"The apartment feels empty without you," she said. "When are you coming back?"

"In a week, most likely. Unless everyone convinces me to stay a little longer. Which, now that I'm unemployed...I could."

"Well, I wish I could tell you this in person. But this can't wait."

I watched the Kentucky landscape roll by as we made it past the city limits. Wooden fences, some ramshackle, some pristinely white or black, lined sprawling pastures, horses grazing lazily. "Tell me. I have to know."

"I got some more information about the informant for the article," she said, her voice lowering to a conspiratorial hush. "The editor wouldn't give up any names, but I did some digging of my own. I checked the security logs from the past four weeks, and Francis's name appears once in our records here."

I sucked in a sharp breath, dizziness overcoming me. "Oh my God. So it *was* him."

"We at least know he was in the building," Kendra assured me. "I can't say much more than that. But we can draw our own conclusions from there."

"Thank you," I gushed. "Oh, this is such a relief. I know it's not the cold hard evidence I need, but it's *something*, and that's better than nothing."

"You got it. I'll see you when you get back."

I hung up the phone, all smiles for the rest of the drive. Jeremy had been so upset about what had happened with the Fairchilds; he'd be happy to hear this turn of events. It still didn't prove without a doubt it was Francis, but it at least cast some suspicion onto him and off of me.

I needed to tell someone from the Fairchild camp about what I'd learned. But it couldn't be Damian—not after what went down. I was also hesitant to call Axel, since I knew he'd probably been involved in the decision to fire me. Trace was probably still in Bali, so who did that leave?

Cora.

I called her just as the ride share turned into my brother's winding, spaced out neighborhood. Plastic reindeer dotted the front yards of a couple houses, some of them toppled from the wind. Green garland wrapped around porch railings; big wreaths dotted with ornaments on front doors. The holiday sights tugged at me in a strange way as the phone rang.

"Hello?" Cora answered breathily, and I wondered what I'd interrupted.

"Hi, Cora. Please don't hang up." I winced, suddenly second-guessing myself. The entire Fairchild crew probably hated me, and here I was calling Cora like an idiot.

"Why would I hang up?"

"I just...I don't know how you...feel..." I swallowed hard, at a loss for words. "I just need you to give Damian a message for me. Well, Axel and Damian. I wasn't sure if it would be appropriate to call them after they fired me."

"Oh, right. I'm so sorry about what happened." She paused. "I actually wanted to reach out to *you* but was kind of hesitant for the same reasons." Her nervous laugh took some of the edge off.

"Really?"

"Yeah. I have a friend who's opening a boutique, and she really wants to feature some up-and-coming designers. I recommended you, and I was hoping to connect you two soon."

Tears came to my eyes, and I clamped a hand over my mouth as the car slowed to a stop outside Jeremy's house. "Are you serious?"

"Of course. I love your designs. I just want to make sure we proceed with tact, I suppose."

"Yes, yes. We'll be tactful. So tactful." The words were pouring out of me now, my heart beating like I'd run a mile. "Oh my gosh. I can barely remember why I called. You've made my day. Thank you, Cora. Please, count me in for anything."

Her throaty laughter was a strange comfort. I missed these people. If I didn't know better, I'd say they were *my* people.

"Now, what did you want to talk about?" she asked.

"Oh, right. Yeah. Um—" I slapped a hand to my forehead. The driver had parked and gotten out of the car to open the trunk, which meant I needed to get out of the dang car too. "I'll have to summarize quickly, because I just got to my brother's house. But my new roommate, who works for *Big Apple Mag*, told me today that she found Francis's name in the visitor log at the magazine. He was in their office sometime within the last four weeks. I know the brothers think I leaked their sensitive information via my new roommate, but I didn't. And now there's a sign that it might have been Francis after all. I just need you to tell them that. We parted on bad terms, but I don't want to see them continue with someone untrustworthy, no matter how things ended for me."

"Thank you, Jessa. That's very sweet of you. I'll pass it along."

"And Cora? One more thing." I nibbled on my lip, wondering if I should even go there. "Do you think Damian has a drinking problem?"

A soft sigh erupted from her. "I think he self-medicates with whiskey for the stress. And I've seen him doing that more since the SEC investigation came around."

"Thank you, Cora," I whispered. "I just want Damian to feel good. But sometimes I think that man is his own worst enemy."

I swiped the phone off and hurried out of the car, apologizing profusely to the driver, who already had my things out on the gravel driveway. The front door clanged open, and my nieces tumbled out of the house in their pink puffy winter coats, screaming "Aunt Jessa! Aunt Jessa!"

A moment later, four arms were wrapped around my torso and hips, giggles and shrieks filling the air.

Jeremy stepped out onto the cement block porch in his deer hunting coat, smiling wearily, his dark brown hair grown out so far he could almost tuck it behind his ears.

"Hey there, big brother." I waddled his way, my nieces still attached to my midsection, arms outstretched. "Join the pile."

"I missed you, Jessa." He wrapped his arms around me, forming a Walton group hug. We all laughed. "God, you look different."

"Do I?" I stepped back to size him up, finding the familiar signs of exhaustion and worry on his face. "Is that a good thing or a bad thing?"

"You look like a big city girl," he admitted with a small laugh. "Look at this purse. How much did this cost?"

"I got it at a thrift store," I said, swatting his arm before he grabbed my luggage and headed for the house. "That's the key to New York City. Find the right thrift stores, and you can score big. That or renting the runway."

"You can rent a runway?" Izzy scrunched up her nose, looking at me like I'd just told her the moon was made of cheese. "What does that even mean?"

We walked toward the small brick ranch while I explained the concept of renting fashionable clothes that were too expensive to buy, especially if you only needed them for a single event. Inside the house, everything was dark and cramped. Jeremy's threadbare couch faced an oversized TV—the main form of relaxation for my brother—and dolls littered the floor.

"Where's Chelsea?" Jeremy and his wife Chelsea had been together for a lifetime—they'd started dating in the seventh grade and never broken up.

"Ah, she's uh..." Jeremy sighed, then clamped his mouth shut as the girls raced around us. "Girls, go get Aunt Jessa some cookies from the kitchen. Go on, now."

The girls scampered off, and I turned to my brother, sensing something amiss.

"Where's Chels?" I repeated.

He frowned when he looked over at me. "She's been staying with a friend."

Understanding shivered through me. "For how long?"

"A few weeks."

"Why didn't you say anything?"

He laughed emptily. "I didn't want to believe it."

"What sort of...friend?"

The girls rushed back into the room, sharing the duty of presenting me with a plate of cookies. "Aunt Jessa, your cookies are here!"

"The kind of friend you'd imagine," Jeremy said dryly.

Shit bricks. I needed more details, but I got the gist well enough. I popped on a smile as my nieces doled out cookies between all of us. We munched happily, though Jeremy's smile was strained.

We spent that first evening together enjoying time as a family. My dad came over for dinner, and we shared chicken wings while we watched football on TV. Just like always.

But we couldn't go on forever like that, avoiding talk about my mom or Tara. Monday morning, after the kids had gotten on the school bus and Jeremy was racing around to get ready for work, Tara showed up.

"Oh. Hey there." Her face registered only distant surprise as her gaze washed over me. She wore the standard red polo shirt required at the local fried chicken restaurant, under a tan fur-lined coat. She'd been manager there for the past four years. "Didn't think you'd be coming around these parts again."

"Good to see you, Tara," I forced out.

"Jeremy, I'm dropping Mom's bags off, okay?" she called out. Jeremy's muffled agreement sounded from the back of the house.

"What did he say?" Tara asked, more to herself than to me.

"Is mom coming here?" I asked.

"That's the plan. She'll stay in the spare room." Tara stuffed her hands into the pockets of her coat.

The spare room. Where I'd slept last night and had thought to continue staying. "Good to know."

Footsteps sounded down the hallway, and Jeremy showed up a moment later, still tucking his work shirt into his jeans. "Hey, Tara. We all doing dinner tonight then?"

"Yeah. Gotta run. See you at six." Tara pushed open the front door and hurried back to her car, which sat idling in the driveway.

I looked over at Jeremy with wide eyes. "Mom's coming to stay here then?"

He grimaced. "I meant to tell you…"

"It's fine. I can go somewhere else."

"Well, we wanted to talk to you about that." Jeremy checked his phone, then he swore under his breath. "I'm running late, Jessa. Listen, we're all gonna have dinner tonight. You, me, Tara, mom, the kids." Our father was usually not included when mom was around. Kinda like how I wished I wasn't included either. "We'll have a nice family meal. Talk everything out."

I watched him go, caught between dumbfounded and irritated. There was nothing to talk out. Unless they had plans for my life again. Plans that I never agreed to.

I spent most the day sketching and working on my portfolio while I watched reruns of *Friends.* The show had always been a favorite, but the slice of 90s New York was more comforting to me than usual.

Because that big, crazy city felt like home to me now. Less than six months living there and I'd fallen for its chaos, its insanity, its never-ending surprises and fascinations.

Not only that—I'd fallen for one of its premier inhabitants. Damian Fairchild.

I'd spent too much of my tenure at Fairchild Enterprises imagining our perfect Manhattan life together. We'd even lived it, briefly. Walking hand-in-hand along the High Line. Attending galas.

Make-out sessions in elegant hallways. Trying new foods together, then rushing off to a hotel room around the corner.

My heart ached. The city was inextricably linked with Damian, and I wasn't sure I'd ever be able to inhabit Manhattan without lamenting the love I'd almost grasped with the one man who had forever carried a piece of my heart.

I'd loved him from afar for almost fifteen years. What was another fifteen?

As I sank deeper into my thoughts and feels, sadness bubbled to the surface.

We'd been so good together. That was the part that hurt the worst. All my fantasies and expectations had been wildly surpassed.

Until it came to the long-term. Until it came to trust.

Tears welled up in my eyes as I sketched a long ball gown. I reached for my colored pencils, alternating between filling in the shades of gray I'd chosen and fanning my eyes to dry the tears. I had to believe that I was doing the right thing in the right way. This was the only path that seemed natural. The only path that seemed right.

But what if I was doing things all wrong?

Maybe I'd been expecting too much out of life. Trying for too lucky a hand. Trying to squeeze mimosas out of sour oranges.

Mom and Jeremy showed up just after the girls had gotten home from school. My insides tightened as they always did when I spotted her, a response I couldn't control after a lifetime at her side. Her dark hair had been bleached blonde a while ago; dark roots had grown out by several inches. Her limp ponytail hung over one shoulder as she came toward the house, smoking a cigarette and frowning down at the ground.

Jeremy came into the house, Mom right behind him. She blew out a big puff of smoke as she stepped in.

"There's my baby girl," she said in her smoker's rasp. She came my way for a hug, which I accepted stiffly. She gripped my shoulder hard enough to hurt. "You been good?"

"Mm-hmm." I waved my hand to disperse the cloud of cigarette smoke. "Mom, the girls are in here. Smoke outside."

"Oh, come on." She dismissed my words and headed to the couch, where she sat and peered at Izzy and Hannah. "Y'all don't mind if Nana smokes, right?"

The girls shook their heads dutifully, glancing back at me.

"See? They're fine." Mom collapsed onto the couch with a sigh. "It'd do you good to loosen up a little, Jessa. Like I been telling you."

Everything inside me felt disjointed and unpleasant. I felt ill in a way that I couldn't expel from my body via the usual methods. This was a deep illness. A sickness I couldn't touch.

"So you doing good?" I asked, packing up my things as quickly as I could from the coffee table. A couple of my colored pencils rolled off, and Izzy hurried to pick them up.

"Ooh, this one sparkles," she cooed.

"Yeah, I'm good. Same old bullshit, but good. Hey, whatcha coloring?" Mom jerked her chin toward Izzy. "You gonna draw Nana a pretty picture?"

"These are Jessa's," Izzy said softly, looking between mom and me.

Mom cackled. "Ain't you a little old to be coloring?"

I took the pencils from Izzy's outstretched hand. "It's for a project I'm working on. And there's no age limit to coloring, anyway. It can be therapeutic."

Mom crossed her legs, her foot bouncing as she tapped the cigarette into the ashtray. "Yeah, yeah. I know. They tell me that plenty. Hey, what are we having for dinner? I can go get a case of beer if we want."

"Makin' ribs," Jeremy called out from the kitchen. "Been marinating these suckers since yesterday. Y'all are gonna flip."

"Ooh, that sounds good. You need anything, Jer? I'll head to the store now."

"Naw, I'm good, Mom. Take my car, okay?"

"Sure thing." Mom hopped up, extinguishing the cigarette in an ashtray on the end table before heading out the front door. Once the car had revved and she was gone, I wandered into the kitchen to find Jeremy. The girls scampered down the hall to their room.

"You let her just take your car?" I asked softly. "Don't you think she's gonna just try to score?"

He sighed, wrist deep in a mixing bowl of marinade and ribs. "Jessa, she's gonna score if she wants to, no matter what. Whether or not she's got my car."

I leaned against the countertop, crossing my arms. "She doesn't look good."

"She's looking better than she did before."

"Do you really want her here with the girls?"

He set his jaw but didn't answer.

"I wouldn't," I said.

"It's what family does," he said softly.

And that was the whole problem. What the Waltons expected family to do was depressing. It involved bending over backwards to accommodate people who may or may not have been using heroin. Family meant accepting cigarette smoke in children's lungs. Family meant thinly veiled distaste and outright disrespect when someone didn't behave how you thought they should.

Family meant forsaking anything you wanted for yourself in order to bow to the needs of someone in relapse.

If they could stand by Mom like this, and enable her decisions, why couldn't they do the same for me? Frustration scorched through me, curling my fingers, making me itchy. I heaved a sigh and pushed away from the countertop.

"Where you goin', Jessa?"

"To check on the girls."

"They're playing in their bedroom."

"Then I think I'll start packing." I turned for the spare room.

"Why you gonna pack?" Jeremy called out.

"I'm not staying with Mom here," I called over my shoulder. "I'll get a hotel room."

"Jessa, that's gonna be too expensive."

I entered the bedroom and put the few things I'd taken out of my suitcase back in. "I don't care," I shouted.

"What's all this racket?" Tara's voice suddenly entered the mix. The front door slammed shut a moment later, and I heard her issue stern instructions to her kids to sit on the couch and stay quiet. I wasn't as close to Tara's kids, but they were all teens who preferred to be engrossed in their video games anyway.

"Jessa thinks she's getting a hotel room." Jeremy called out from the kitchen.

"Miss Moneybags would," Tara said, loud enough for me to hear. "Spends all that money on herself and can't even toss a dime to her mom."

I huffed and ignored them, but the frustration inside me had kicked up to a boil. I packed blindly, just trying to get it done as quickly as I could.

Seeing family was always like this. We knew how to push each other's buttons. If anyone thought they were healed or mature, a quick visit to home would rid them of that idea. That's what I'd learned in this short time, at least.

I thought I'd come to get a gulp of air in the wake of what had happened on Wall Street. To throw my siblings a bone and show the support to my mom they demanded.

But I saw now that coming back had merely shoved me into the past. Made me feel small, worthless, and useless. I couldn't do anything right here. Couldn't say the right things. Even being propositioned by a grown man twice my age couldn't win me an ounce of support. Sometimes it felt like my sin was simply that I had the audacity to *breathe*.

I rolled my suitcase into the living room, setting it near the door.

I'd come for a breath of fresh air, but I'd wandered into a sulfurous cave.

"Leaving so soon?" Tara asked.

"Hi, Klay. Hi, Penny. Long time no see." I greeted my niece and nephew first, offering a bright smile. They barely looked up at me from their handheld video games, mumbling a greeting.

"They'd see a lot more of you if you were around," Tara said, slipping her coat off and hanging it on the rack near the door. "Where's Mom?"

"She went out to get some beer," I said.

"And you let her?"

I let out an exasperated breath. "Jeremy let her. He said she'd score when she wanted, with or without us."

Tara had changed her shirt, but the smell of fried chicken clung to her ever so slightly as she breezed past me, headed for the kitchen. "You need help in there or what, Jer?"

"I got it," Jeremy said.

I crossed my arms, surveying the living room. Tears already threatened to spill, and we'd barely started this get-together. I wasn't gonna last. I could feel it to my bones. I couldn't remember why I'd come, and all I wanted to do was find some space.

"Klay, Penny, you wanna go play with Izzy and Hannah in their room?"

Tara's kids shook their heads silently.

"How's school been going?"

Two shrugs. Typical teens. I wandered into the kitchen, intent on turning this reunion around. Jeremy had laid all the ribs out on a sheet pan, and Tara was mixing coleslaw in a bowl.

"Can I help?" I asked.

Tara looked over at me, distaste written across her features. "Do you even remember how to cook?"

"I don't know why you think I'd forget," I said, leaning against the countertop, bracing for her vitriol. Tara's favorite pastime was shitting on me, talking down to me, making me the reason everything was wrong.

But the frustration inside of me was too hot, too roiling.

I'd always been good at schooling myself around her, at making myself small. But after what happened with Damian and after so many years of being painted as the villain, I'd fucking had it.

"Tara, I'm not even sure why you're here tonight if all you're gonna do is talk down to me," I said, my cheeks heating up as soon as the words had left my mouth.

Her brows shot up and she looked over at me slowly. "Excuse me? What sass was that coming from your mouth?"

"It's no secret you hate me," I said, sniffing. "So why spend an evening with me? That's all. Honest question."

"It sounds like you're telling me to leave," she said, a hard edge to her voice. The tone sent ice spreading through my limbs.

"I'm not. Just asking an honest question."

"I'm here for Jer and Mom," Tara clarified. "You're just an extra that nobody asked for."

"Tara," Jeremy scolded softly. "Why you gotta be like that?"

"I'm not being like nothin'," she claimed, jamming her spoon into the slaw.

"You act like that, she ain't gonna help us," Jeremy warned in a low voice.

"Was she helping us before? Musta missed that part," Tara muttered, tugging the fridge open and storing the bowl inside.

"Quit being a bitch," I spat out. I regretted the words instantly, but they'd flown from my lips without even thinking. I never talked to Tara like that, because I knew what the consequences would be. But I'd reached my bullshit limit sometime back in New York.

"I'm being the bitch? Miss Hoity Toity Money Bags waltzes in here in these expensive dresses trying to tell *me* I'm being the bitch." Tara tugged a gallon of milk from the fridge and slammed it on the counter. The lid popped off, spraying milk all over the cabinets.

"Jesus, Tara," Jeremy said, grabbing for a towel.

"I suppose you'll blame that on me too," I said snidely.

"Why wouldn't I? Your attitude made me do it," she shouted. "Wouldn't have sprayed shit if you'd kept your mouth shut."

The front door open and closed, and footsteps approached the kitchen.

"I got a twelve pack," Mom said, wedging herself between Tara and Jeremy to reach the fridge. She opened up the case and cracked a beer before putting it inside. "Feel free, if you want one. What do you drink now, Jessa? Cocktails only?"

"Mostly wine," I said, my whole body vibrating and hot. I wanted to punch Tara so much. I wanted to scream until my vocal cords disintegrated. But more than that, I wanted her to shut the hell up forever.

"I think I should leave," I said abruptly, smoothing the front of my dress. "Tara and I mix as well as bleach and ammonia, and I don't want to poison the air for the rest of you. This is supposed to be a fun evening, not miserable."

"Hey, we're having fun," Mom said, sipping her beer. "Ain't we?"

"You've been waiting to leave since you got here," Tara muttered.

"Tara, knock it off." Jeremy's fatherly voice came out gruff and annoyed. He turned to me, his hands covered in burgundy marinade. "Jessa, don't leave. Or at least stay long enough to hear me out about something."

"What is it?" I crossed my arms, trying my best to ignore the seething, miserable vortex of Tara behind him.

"I've been thinking. Since you lost your job and you're kinda floating right now, I was thinking maybe you and Mom could get a place here in town for a bit. Or closer to Louisville, if you wanted that big-city feel."

"She won't do it. You're wasting your breath," Tara muttered.

"It would be good for everyone," Jeremy went on, raising the volume of his voice as though this would counteract Tara's presence behind him. "You'd be back here where you belong. You and Mom could catch up, share groceries, all that good stuff."

"I'd be into it, sissy, what do you think?" Mom lifted her beer can in my direction. "Just like old times."

Old times. Like when I'd have to do my homework from the waiting area of the Emergency Room, because whatever prescription pill she was abusing didn't mix well with alcohol. Or like when her ex forced himself on me when I was a junior in high school. Dread washed over me. "Well, the idea sounds nice," I started, but my words stalled. A blockade had formed. I couldn't continue lying.

"See?" Jeremy said, looking back at Tara.

"Truth is, I'm not really drifting right now, Jer."

His face fell, and he turned back to the ribs. "What do you mean?"

"I'm in school," I told him. "I'm finishing my certificate in mere months. I'm going back to New York. That's where I live now."

Jeremy's mouth turned into a thin line. Now *he* was pissed.

"*See?*" Tara retorted, sneering at Jeremy. "I told you she wouldn't do it."

"You can shut your fat mouth, Tara," I snapped, my heart racing. There was so much inside me that wanted to explode. And I didn't have the energy to keep it inside anymore.

"I can't believe you'd call anyone else fat with how you look in that dress," Tara said, laughing bitterly.

This was when the tears used to come. But now, it just increased the pressure inside me.

"I don't care what you have to say about me or my life anymore," I hissed at her. "No matter what I do, no matter what I say, it's wrong. You're the one who's constantly nagging for me to come home, and now that I'm here, you can't wait until I'm gone. You ask for help and mock me in the same breath. You've been nothing but a bitch to me since the day I was born. And honestly, I don't really care why anymore. There's no hope of getting along with you in this lifetime *or* the next. So how about you shut the fuck up and we never speak again? That would really help family relations, Tara. Shut up and butt out."

"Gladly," she spat, glaring at me so hard I thought my dress might catch on fire.

"I just wish you two would get along," Mom lamented, but she looked unbothered. Maybe even secretly entertained. She had probably shot up while she was out.

This was the textbook definition of a toxic family dynamic, and I was ready to say goodbye forever.

"That chance ended the day you two turned your backs on me," I said, pointing at her and Tara. "It's why you and me, Mom, we're never living together. Sorry to burst your creepy family bubble here, but I'm not taking care of you, because you never took care of me. I don't owe you shit after you defended that scumbag, and I'm done tiptoeing around it. And besides, that's not my job. It's not any of our job. You're a grown-ass woman, Mom. Figure it out. I know you're struggling, but I've helped you as much as I can stand. And now? I need *all of you* to lay the fuck off."

My chest heaved when I was done. They all watched me with varying degrees of disdain.

"What, nothing to say about Jeremy?" Tara goaded. "I knew he was always your favorite."

"Save it, Tara." I huffed and spun on my heels, finding four pairs of wide eyes. That spectacle had been fully absorbed by all the nieces and nephews in the house.

"Sorry you kids had to hear that," I said softly, stepping past Izzy and Hannah. Tara's kids on the couch quickly buried their heads in their handhelds again.

"Are we ever gonna see you again, Aunt Jessa?" Izzy's voice trembled with emotion.

"Of course you will, sweetheart," I said, bending down to eye level with her. "I'll come back just to see you kids, okay? I promise. Be good girls for me." Hannah came up, and I was wrapped in their arms. I hugged them tightly, wishing I could carry them with me. I needed to leave. Immediately.

I gave them one last squeeze and let go. I could feel all eyes on me as I scooped up my messenger bag, stuffed with my pencils and sketchbooks, and rolled my luggage behind me. Nobody chased me down.

I paused at the door, looking back at the kitchen. Jeremy was the only one who met my gaze. He looked sadder than I'd ever seen him, but I couldn't give away my life just to help a woman who barely wanted to be helped, a family that constantly tore me down.

That's not what I was here for. And I was done pretending they had the right to demand that I change my course just to suit their agendas.

I tore open the door, finding dusk spreading across the calm neighborhood. Damn these early sunsets. The crisp evening air stole my breath as my eyes adjusted to the outside world, spotting the bare trees in the distance first.

And then I noticed the sleek black sports car in the driveway.

I blinked. I had no plan, no ride arranged, no nothing. This wasn't my car. So who was it?

I decided it didn't matter. The shininess of the car distracted me as I barreled past it. It seemed *too* nice. *Too* shiny. Was that a Mercedes Benz?

My feet hit the asphalt of my brother's street. I hadn't made it three steps down the road when I heard a familiar voice shout gruffly, "*Jessa!*"

I swallowed, an annoying kernel of hope fluttering inside of me. That voice couldn't belong to who it sounded like it belonged to. Unless I was hallucinating now, on top of everything else going wrong around me. Surely the imaginary audience of this doomed reality TV show was *loving* this turn of events.

"Jessa, please."

The emotion cracking the baritone voice was unmistakable. My entire body lit up like a firecracker, hope trembling against awe. I turned slowly.

There stood the last man I'd ever expected to follow me here.

Tall, broad-shouldered, excessively handsome Damian Fairchild.

Brooding, moody, excessively intelligent Damian.

My Damian. At least, I'd thought.

He walked toward me, hands stuffed into jeans pockets, wearing a thin black parka. Seeing him here, in the context of our hometown, sent me tumbling into the past. Yet he was all adult, all modern Damian, his strength evident even through the thin parka, the longish but well-maintained chestnut hair falling into his eyes, his gaze so intense I thought I might unravel on the spot.

"Damian?" I breathed. "What on God's green earth are you doing here?"

CHAPTER THIRTY

DAMIAN

My heart hammered in my chest so hard I thought Jessa could hear it. Like the Looney Tunes characters in love, hearts leaping away from chests, barely contained by skin.

This was the shit I'd tried to stay away from. This was the shit that could kill me.

But so could flying in my helicopter. So could the whiskey I consumed. So could any chance encounter on the street.

Going after Jessa was a risk, but the benefits were immeasurable. Chest-leaping arrythmia be damned.

"I wanted to see you," I finally said, the words withering in the air between us. What I wanted was so much more than that. Seeing her here, after a week that had felt more like a year, was a greater relief than I could even begin to understand. Looking at her made sense. It made my life make sense. It let me breathe easier. "And a few other things."

"But why did you—" She seemed to quietly scold herself. "Actually, never mind. I've gotta go. Maybe we can schedule a conference call or something." She hoisted her messenger bag and marched away, her luggage *click-click-click*ing on the asphalt behind her.

"I know you're probably still mad at me," I called out, jogging to catch up with her. I barely noticed the brisk air as I kept pace at her side. I tugged at the strap of her messenger bag. "Let me carry that."

"I've got it," she snapped.

I let her carry it, nervousness making my palms damp. I'd ditched my jacket specifically because of this. I was so anxious I was over-heating. And throwing my heart on the line like this was going to only make it worse. "I heard about your plans to move home. I have to say, I'm...surprised. But if that's the case, then I want to help however I can."

"The severance package was enough, Damian." It sounded like she was fighting tears. My chest tightened, and I knew I had to make this right, and fast.

"You can use my house." The words rushed out of me. "I brought you a key. It's out on Tyler Road, the last one in the cul-de-sac. You'll probably want a place to call your own. A place to work on your designs in peace. I want to give you that until you...find your feet. And maybe I could see you there too."

She stopped, looking up at me with eyes shimmering with tears. "You came all this way to say I could housesit for you? You could have just called Jeremy."

"No, I couldn't have," I told her, already lost in the crystal swirl of her eyes. I could never go this long again without looking into their depths. All the confusion and pain of the last week melted away as we stood on the edge of Humm Road in the encroaching dusk, amber and scarlet hues wending their way around us and through the naked trees.

"I needed to see you," I said. "And it's not house sitting. It's...more than that." A shaky sigh escaped me as I struggled to find the right words. I had to strike that delicate balance between *grand gesture* and *totally fucking insane,* without steering too far to the wrong side. "I planted autumn cherry trees."

"What?"

"I mean, I haven't yet. It's too cold. But in the spring, I..." I raked a hand through my hair. "Maybe it sounds like I'm luring you there or something," I said with a small laugh. "In a way, I guess I am. But I, I want you to feel at home. There's ten going in at the start of spring to line the driveway at my house here. For you."

She sighed, pinching her eyes shut, then finally turned away from me. *Click-click-click.* "I've got to go."

"Jessa, please. Can we talk?"

She looked over her shoulder at me, then at my car idling in Jeremy's driveway a block behind us. "Go get your car and meet me at the park. Then my family won't be spying on us and shoving popcorn in their faces as they watch."

Humm Park sat two more blocks north, just over a little hill. I raced back to my car, catching the quick flashes of a few faces behind Jeremy's curtains. I'd touch base with him later; now, I needed to make Jessa understand that I'd made a mistake.

I wasn't just sorry. I was ready to fucking grovel.

Jessa and I made it to the park at the same time. Gravel crunched under the tires of my Benz. Jessa parked her rolling luggage in its own space, draping her messenger bag over top, and zipped her coat up a little closer to her chin. She looked toward the five chain-link swings, two of them tossed over the top bar so that they couldn't be used. A basic jungle gym sat off to the left, in the middle of a bed of rubber tire fragments.

My fingers twitched from wanting to touch her. To take her face in my hands and kiss her until our lips went numb. I planned to do everything in my power to make sure that was the outcome.

But I wasn't sure. I didn't know.

You might have fucked it all up.

"Where are you heading?"

"I don't know, Damian. I just told off my entire family, and I'll probably never speak to Tara again. I'm kinda just seeing where the wind takes me."

Let it take you to me. I stepped closer to her, and she stepped away. I pointed at the swings. "Can we swing?"

She followed hesitantly. The two on the far end hadn't been vandalized, so I sat on the farthest one, the chains groaning under my weight.

"Did you tell Tara where to shove it?"

"I told her to shut up and butt out. And probably severed my relationship with everyone in the house." Jessa frowned down at the ground. "It needed to be done. But it doesn't feel good."

"You can't change them, Jessa. It doesn't matter how hard you try. Tara's committed to misunderstanding you. Your mom is committed to...well, you know. And Jeremy is committed to keeping all of you miserable but together."

"It's an impossible job," she lamented, looking out at the neighborhood in the distance. "I could only take so much from Tara and Mom. I had to draw the line. But drawing the line makes me the bad guy again. That was the catch. There is no way for me to win in that family." She squinted over at me. "I can only be hated or gone. And now I'm both."

I drew in a deep breath. I could feel the heaviness in her heart. I craved the chance to hug her until the pain went away, even just an ounce. But it was too soon for that. Instead, I decided to distract her.

"Come on. I bet I can swing higher."

"I'm wearing a dress, Damian," she said with a little smirk.

"Maybe that's part of my plan," I said with a sideways grin. She sent me an amused look and started swinging gently. I did the same, resting my forehead against the chain as I watched her. Her gaze drifted between me and the ground. The air between us was both comfortable and bloated. Nothing needed to be said, yet we had so much to say.

"I came to apologize," I finally said, my words shattering the silence that had only been filled by dead leaves skittering across the gravel parking lot. "I'm sorry, Jessa. I'm *so* fucking sorry. I'll be sorry for the rest of my life."

She peeked up at me from under her eyelashes but didn't say anything.

"I'm sorry for firing you. I'm sorry for not believing you. I'm sorry for pushing you away. I'm sorry for being the biggest fucking idiot in the world."

She started nibbling on her lip. A single tear rolled down her cheek.

"I'm not trying to convince you to come back to work. That's not what this is about. Firing you was a mistake, but I know you didn't really belong there."

Hurt slashed across her face. "Was I that bad?"

"No. Not at all." I stopped swinging and stood, unable to prevent myself from being closer to her. I went to her swing and grabbed the chains, stilling her so our gazes could meet. "You were great. But you have your own career to pursue, and it isn't at Fairchild Enterprises. That's all I meant."

Her bottom lip trembled slightly, and then she looked away suddenly, dabbing at the corner of her eye. "I take it Cora told you what we talked about yesterday?"

"I haven't talked to Cora."

Her brows drew together, searching my face. "Are you serious? I told her to tell you, and—"

"Tell me what?"

Jessa's throat bobbed, and she brushed away a lock of hair that had blown across her face. "Kendra did some digging at work. She found Francis's name in a visitor log within the past four weeks. I know it's not hard evidence, but I thought it would give you a place to start. I don't want you to have a mole in your midst, no matter how shitty things ended."

My throat tightened, and I grabbed her chin between my thumb and forefinger, directing her gaze toward me. "I didn't need Cora to tell me that. I knew in my bones you didn't do it. I only went through with firing you because I thought I needed to. To protect the way I thought life was supposed to be. But ending things between us caused the worst outcome I could have imagined. I don't want them to end. I want them to begin. Properly, this time. Like you deserve."

Her eyes shimmered with tears, and her nostrils flared as she looked up at me. I had more to say, and she seemed to know it, waiting for me to go on.

"I was terrified to admit to myself that I love you. My whole life, I've been convinced that I don't deserve love because of what happened with my sisters. I've taken the blame for their disappearance and death, and I told myself that any good that comes my way will be followed by bad. Because I don't deserve the good." I paused, looking out at the bare treetops, laughing a little. "I still believe that, actually."

"You deserve love, Damian," Jessa said in a low, trembling voice. "You deserve all the good things. You might not believe it, but I do. Your brothers do. We all believe it so much that someday, I know you're gonna believe it too."

"Well, since the investigation was announced, the anxiety has increased tenfold. I've been drinking more than ever. Working more than ever. My brothers have been worried."

"*I'm* worried," she added softly.

"I don't want to keep going like that," I whispered. "Not while I've got a chance to turn things around. I've seen what happens when people get chances and just let them pass by. You know probably better than anyone, after everything your mom's put you through."

Her bottom lip trembled, and she nodded.

"I want to be better because you deserve better," I said.

"And *you* deserve better," she rushed to add. "You have to do this for yourself, Damian."

I grinned. "You knew I wasn't gonna say that part, huh? Fine. I want to be better because Jessa Walton says I deserve better, and I believe everything that woman says, so if she says it's true, then it must be true."

Her eyes watered as she bit back a smile. "Now you believe me, huh?"

My gaze fell to her lap, coasting over the geometrical pattern of her dress, up over her coat, up to her hands clutching the chain links of the swing.

"Can I?" I reached for her, and she unclenched her hand, allowing me to cradle it in mine. I brought her knuckles up to my lips, making sure her eyes were on me.

"Jessa Walton…"

She swallowed, eyes widening. "Oh lord, Damian."

I laughed, then pressed another kiss to her knuckles. "This isn't a playground proposal. *Yet.* But I have to kiss you somewhere or I'm going to fucking unravel."

Pink stained her cheeks, and she batted her eyelashes at me. "Go on."

"Jessa Walton…you are gorgeous. Your smile is medicine, and it's the only thing I need to function in the insanity of life. Your entire being calms my raging anxiety, and just one glimpse of you has the power to calm, excite, and make me harder than fucking iron. I want to be your man, for as long as you'll have me. Even though I don't think I deserve you, I can only hope that someday I'll be worthy of you. Will you please, for the love of God, be my girlfriend?"

She covered her mouth with her free hand, giggles erupting. "Now that was the most romantic thing I've ever heard."

I brushed my lips over her knuckles again. "I need an answer here, Jessa. I'm dying."

"Of course I will!" She nearly shouted it, laughter edging her words. "You big doofus, I've been your secret girlfriend for almost fifteen years. How could I say no to you? Especially after you're aiming to plant ten of my favorite trees on your property? Sign me up, baby."

I wanted to celebrate, but I needed to ask the big question first. "Would you be willing to wait for me if I go to prison for ten years?"

Her eyes softened and she touched my cheek with her fingertips. "Is that what they're thinking you'll get?"

"Nobody knows yet. But it's definitely on the table."

"Damian, I've waited fifteen years for you. Ten more is nothing. Even if it happens, which I know it won't, we'll find a way to make it bearable."

For once, in the face of such abysmal anxiety and uncertainty about the future, I felt hope. I believed Jessa. Together, we would find a way to make it bearable. Axel's words returned to me: *You should still try to enjoy life. We've got our freedom right now.*

Maybe that was part of what I had to come to terms with. Being okay with not knowing what the future held and making the most of what I had right in front of me.

And what I had in front of me here was everything I fucking needed.

I scraped my teeth over her knuckles, making sure she knew what I was getting at. "May I kiss you?"

"Please," she whispered, and I took her face in my hands, stroking my thumbs over her cheeks as I dove in for the kiss I'd been waiting for.

Our lips met hungrily, sloppy, desperate kisses unfolding, far more explicit than what this playground normally saw. Thankfully there were no children here on this chilly December dusk. Jessa whimpered, her head turned up to receive my kisses as she white-knuckled the swing.

We broke for air when darkness had fully settled on the park. My headlights were the only thing illuminating our encounter. My cock was throbbing, and I hadn't even gotten to the best part.

"We should go back to my house," I whispered.

"I've heard you have lovely marble countertops," she whispered back. "Your mom told me all about it one day at the Sav-A-Lot."

"Well, she'll be able to tell you about the other features of the house once we get there," I added, still whispering. "Because she's been staying there."

"Oh! We get to spend the night with your mom!"

I laughed, brushing my thumb over her lips. "I promise we'll have plenty of room. And she won't even hear an echo of your sexy cries, because we'll stay in the guest house out back." I brushed my lips over the line of her jaw, desperate for so much more. "What do you think about having your own design studio?"

She blinked a few times. "I think it sounds like a dream."

"Once you get your certificate." I placed feathery kisses across her cheeks, down the center of her nose. "The building my brothers and I bought over the summer, from Margulis Realty—I'm thinking you could have an entire floor if you need it. I started working on some plans, but really, I want you to make the decisions. Since it'll be yours."

Jessa clamped her hands over her mouth, tears coming to her eyes. "Are you serious?"

"So serious."

"Oh my god, Damian." She pressed her palms to my chest. "You really are a dreamboat. Even more now than the time you put together shrimp cocktail for our romantic dinner."

"I was hoping this might win over shrimp cocktail," I said, pushing my palms over the swell of her hips, "but to be honest, I wasn't sure. Sometimes, shrimp cocktail wins."

She threw her head back, a peal of laughter erupting from her.

And all I could do was smile. Watching her, taking her in, loving every second of her in my arms.

Jessa was the only one for me. I'd known it some way, somehow, since high school. And now we were here making it official in the town where it'd all begun.

The old me would have called this too big of a risk, too dangerous to go after.

But now? I knew it for what it was.

Passion. The only risk worth taking.

CHAPTER THIRTY-ONE

JESSA

White linen–covered tables filled the room, over sixty place settings awaiting their designated guests.

It was graduation day for my fashion class, but I hadn't planned this party.

I hadn't even conceived of it. I'd simply sat back and shown up.

"This place is fabulous," Veronica said in a low voice, leaning over the table so I could hear her, the array of flickering candles in the middle of the table casting strange shadows on her face. "This is, like, the ritziest place I've ever been."

I smiled at her, my gaze drifting to Damian as he headed our way across the event room. We had rented an entire famous fusion restaurant in the Garment District, just for one evening. Damian had wanted to celebrate my certificate, and in doing so, opted to celebrate *all* of us. He'd collaborated with Mr. Mitchell to bring this event to life. Graduates were allowed to bring guests, and all the students wore their best pieces—in my case, the black lace gown that I knew drove Damian crazy.

Which was why his bedroom eyes were out as he grew nearer.

A shiver of excitement raced up my spine. We'd been boyfriend and girlfriend for two months, and it still felt like we'd kissed on the playground swing a day ago.

"When Damian gets an idea, there's no talking him out of it," I told Veronica. "And when it comes to dinner ideas, he's always got the best ones."

Kendra stepped into the dining room a moment later, her eyes wide with wonder as she beheld the scene. I waved at her, which also caught the attention of Cora, who'd come in just in front of her.

My smile stretched so wide my cheeks hurt. I headed to greet the new arrivals, gliding effortlessly across the floor since I'd made the necessary alterations to the bottom of the dress. Trace stepped into the room just as I started a round of hugs.

"I'm so glad you could all make it," I gushed, my gaze washing over everyone. These were, definitively, *my people* now.

"This is so exciting," Cora said, squeezing my hand. Her green eyes were like exotic gemstones as she met my gaze, her dark hair pulled back into a low, glossy bun. "I heard about the plans for the Tenth Avenue building too. We're going to be neighbors!"

"It feels like a dream to me still," I said with a laugh. "I won't believe it until the first day there!"

"Well, the good thing is, it'll be so much closer to your new place," Damian said, sliding a protective hand over the small of my back.

"*Our* new place," Kendra said, sliding into the convo.

"You're moving?" Cora asked.

"Yes," I told her. "Kendra and I opted for a new place in Chelsea. Damian was insistent after I got robbed last month. And we love it! We signed the papers yesterday."

Insistent didn't even cover it. Damian had been hellbent on getting me out of our place in Brooklyn while still respecting my desire to maintain my own apartment and at least the appearance of separate existences. I ended up spending most nights with Damian anyway, but the separate spaces were perfect for us, even though I knew we'd likely give up the illusion altogether.

"That's thrilling," Cora said, giving Kendra and me a warm look. "Housewarming party sometime?"

"Uhhh, I'd be honored," Kendra said, touching her chest. "If Cora Margulis ever set foot in my home, I could die happy."

Cora batted away the comment. "Kendra, you've always been too kind."

I blinked, looking between them. "Wait. How long have you two known each other?"

"Kendra is the reporter who collaborated with me to publish my expose letter in *Big Apple Mag*," Cora said off-handedly.

I blinked a few more times, looking between them. "Seriously?"

"We only ever spoke on the phone," Kendra said. "And my senior editor got the byline."

"What a small little Wall Street," I mused. Practically every day showed me just how tight the elite circles were. It had turned out that Cora's friend who was opening the boutique and needed my designs was none other than the daughter of the woman I'd met at the Programmer's Ball—Mrs. Bancroft, who had the link to Anna Wintour. I was fresh out of fashion school and already rubbing elbows with Anna Wintour—with two degrees of separation, of course.

Axel joined our group, slinging his arm over Cora's shoulders. "Anything I should be informed of over here?"

Cora laughed, eyes twinkling as she looked up at her boyfriend. "No, CEO. You can stand down."

"Good. Just checking in." He saluted with two fingers and wandered off, giving Trace a wide berth as he headed to the bar. The rift was still deep between all three brothers, but worst between Axel and Trace.

Trace stepped up, sliding his arm around me for a side hug. "Man, my brother knows how to throw a party, doesn't he?"

"We haven't even started, and it's one of the best I've been to," I told him.

"You weren't at Jessa's party, the Programmer's Ball," Damian interjected. "That one was the best."

"You're just saying that 'cause you like me," I teased him.

"And you'll let me," he whispered into my ear, snagging a quick bite at my ear lobe.

"I'm shocked you didn't invite Francis," Trace deadpanned.

A laugh rocketed out of me. "You know, I thought about it. All those attempts to make it seem like I was the one fucking you guys over—they were so sweet and thoughtful of him. But you know..." I shook my head. "Not gonna happen in a million years."

Francis had been formally dismissed from Fairchild Enterprises immediately after Damian and I converged on the Kentucky playground. Axel and Damian were able to find other tiny clues in the call logs at the office and a few scrubbed emails that Francis had thought he could get past the tech wizard.

Axel and Damian confronted him in the conference room before he'd left for good. When they slapped him with a lawsuit related to violating the non-disclosure agreement required at Fairchild Enterprises, he'd squealed like a pig in exchange for a speedy settlement. Apparently, the ultra-loyal and unflappable Francis had seen a sinking ship with the Fairchilds, thanks to the SEC investigation, and had thought he could have his cake *and* stuff his face by raking in extra cash from leaking information to the magazine. He'd used me—the vulnerable newbie—to divert attention from him. His professional reputation was ruined—at least with anyone who valued transparency and honesty—and now he was officially broke. Great job, Francis.

I knew the betrayal stung for the brothers. They'd worked with him for years and had considered him one of the last trustworthy, reliable outsiders they'd met on Wall Street.

But now their circle was a little smaller.

"Hey there!"

A gruff, Brooklyn accent broke through. I swiveled and found Legs, wearing a black button-down shirt and black pants, stepping into the room.

"Legs! You made it!" I held out my arms for a quick hug, and he received it with a nervous smile.

"Glad you came, buddy," Damian said, clapping his shoulder. Trace reached out to shake his hand.

"Thanks for inviting me," he said, looking between us. "Ain't too often we get to hang outside of the car."

"You were such an instrumental part of supporting our lives as I finished my coursework," I told him, leading him deeper into the room. "It was only right to invite you."

"You want a drink?" Damian asked him.

"Yeah, I'll take a Manhattan." Legs looked pleased with himself. "Seems right for a place like this."

Damian stopped a passing server to give him Legs' order while I pointed out who was who in the room to Legs: Mr. Mitchell, Kendra, classmates, the various details of our featured outfits.

"And you made this dress?" Legs asked me after I mentioned my own project.

"Of course."

"One of the best designs she's ever made," Damian said, smoothing his hand over my hip as heat pooled in his gaze. "Tied for number one with a certain green and white dress I'm fond of, as well."

"Maybe you could help me make something sometime," Legs said, his gaze skating around the room. "I've always wanted to make a special shirt. It's been in my head for years, I swear."

"I'd love to," I told him. "A Legs-Jessa collaboration. Hey, speaking of which—" I grabbed Legs' wrist. "How many rides have I taken with you? Have I earned the backstory of your name yet?"

He started a low chuckle, and Damian and Trace joined in.

"Why are you guys laughing like that?" I asked.

"Think it's time?" Legs asked Damian.

"It's up to you, buddy," he said, lifting his palms.

"This is making me a little nervous," I admitted. Legs jerked his head toward the side of the room.

"Come 'ere. I'll show ya."

"Oh. I need to be *shown*?"

Damian simply followed with a mysterious smile on his lips.

"I gotta see this again," Trace said, joining along.

Once we were tucked away in the mauve drapes of the corner, Legs bent down and lifted his pants leg up to his knee.

"You won't believe the size of his legs," Damian said, crossing his arms as he watched. Legs's meaty calf was exposed, sprinkled with dark leg hair. But meaty was an understatement. His leg was simply *dense*.

"Wow," I said.

"Like salami tubes," Legs said, turning his leg. "It only gets worse the farther you go."

I giggled into my hand, bending down to look closer. "Those are some pretty thick legs, Legs."

"You should see him in a bathing suit," Damian said. "Nobody dares wrestle this man, because his leg lock will kill you."

I laughed, looking over at Damian. "How often are you guys wrestling in your bathing suits?"

Damian and Legs shared a guilty look. "It was only that one party..." Legs started.

"Sure, sure. Honestly, it doesn't matter. You know why? Because now I've been initiated." I tossed the men a pleased smile.

"Oh yeah, you're in," Damian said, slinging an arm around my shoulders. "My girlfriend deserves to be in the circle."

"One would hope," I teased.

"What's going on over here?" Kendra poked her head into our gathering, but Legs's pant leg had already dropped. She'd missed the show.

"Just chatting," I told her, "and reveling in the fact that I've finally been initiated into the Fairchild circle."

"Someday soon it'll be my *fiancée* who's in the circle," Damian murmured into my ear. Happiness snaked through me, slow and prickly.

"Don't go whispering sweet nothings in front of everyone," I chided Damian jokingly.

"Yeah, that's not fair to the rest of us sad, single people," Trace teased.

"Oh, you don't have anyone?" Kendra piped up, stepping closer to him.

"Trace hasn't had a single date since I got to New York," I said.

"He doesn't date," Damian corrected.

"Have you ever? Isn't there at least one who got away?" I asked.

Trace smiled, but it looked more like a grimace. He contemplated a spot in the distance, unknowable to everyone but him. "Yes, I've dated. And yes, there is one who got away."

"Oooh, tell us more," Kendra said, batting her eyes at him.

"Do you know who it is?" I asked Legs, who shook his head.

"That's all you'll get from me," Trace said, looking around. "Now where's the bar?"

"At least tell us where she lives," I said. "Is it someone in the city?"

Trace seemed to be weighing his words. And then he said, "She's in Louisville. And now that *is* the last you're getting from me. Who needs a drink?"

Kendra and I shared an intrigued look before rattling off our drink orders. Damian had started tugging me away from the conversation and crowd, inviting me to step back and take it all in.

"You know how amazing you are, right?" he asked me, pushing his fingertips along my jawline.

"I don't know about *amazing*," I answered shyly.

"Just your daily reminder." He pressed a soft kiss to my lips, the kind that confirmed every fantasy and sealed every hope. The type of kiss I'd never tire of, from the one man I'd always loved. "You know how much I love you, right?"

I giggled, tipping my head. "Why don't you tell me..."

"Crazily. Abundantly. Excessively."

"I love you crazily, abundantly, excessively too, Damian Fairchild." I wrapped my arms around his waist, pressing my forehead against his chest.

The feel of his arms around me was all I needed in this life. The solid foundation that grounded me. The security that pushed me take risks.

Damian acted as the roots of my autumn cherry tree. He made it safe for me to lay dormant and then bloom, to let out my fire and wild dreams. To allow this crazy, abundant, excessive love to fill my heart.

Neither of us could say what the future had in store for us. But with Damian at my side, the details didn't matter.

I had the most important part of my future already.

EPILOGUE

ONE MONTH LATER

DAMIAN

Another Monday signaled another week of groping blindly without a trusted assistant at our side. This shit was hard to do, week after week. But after what happened with Francis, my brothers and I trusted no one.

Not a soul.

Which meant we'd stumble forward blindly on our own. We'd started on our own, and we could continue on our own. As long as the three of us could stay somewhat connected, we could stay strong under the oppressing weight of waiting for the SEC to finish their investigation.

But now, even our connectedness was at risk. As Trace, Axel, and I converged for yet another Monday focus session in the conference room, Axel's frown seemed to have become a permanent fixture on his face. Even five months after learning of Ian's existence, things weren't right between Axel and Trace. Because all of Axel's initial hurt and anger had made him lash out, which meant Trace had been lashing out in return. Now there was a river of bad blood between these brothers, and all I could do was hang on to the life raft and hope they pulled themselves out.

Axel had a heart of gold, but it was lined with unsightly barbed wire protecting his morals and expectations. Trace had a heart of gold, too—but he could only be pushed so far.

"Shall we begin?" I asked, thumbing through screens on my iPad.

"Please," Axel said with a sigh. "Though I could use some coffee."

"I already asked Felicia to bring some," Trace intoned, staring at his phone.

"That's at least one good deed you've done recently," Axel muttered.

"Make sure you write it down," Trace said, looking up at him with a hard gaze. "Next to all the other fucking things I've done for you since you became family. You ungrateful jerk."

"Guys," I said softly. I was tired. The fighting, the sniping, the division—it was so fucking exhausting on top of everything else we were dealing with.

Thank God I had Jessa to balance me, to pull me out of my funks, to heal me with her smile at the end of every day. I'd taken to spending most nights at her new place, though we occasionally came back to the penthouse. It had become lonely to me though—Axel and Cora mostly stayed in the Hamptons, and Trace had started hiding out at his apartment in Tribeca. Our brotherly penthouse, the home we'd shared for years as we built Fairchild Enterprises, felt like the empty shell of a ghostly former life.

The life we'd led as brothers. As family. As *friends*.

It was a life I wanted back, but I didn't know how to get there.

"That's a pretty strong f-word you used there," Axel said, sniffing. "You sure you're prepared to defend it?"

"What, fucking?"

"*Family*." Axel stared at Trace, his face a neutral mask.

Trace scoffed, shaking his head. "You're a real piece of work, Axel. Unbelievable."

"Says the man who lied to me for over a decade."

Trace let out a sarcastic laugh, tapping the bottom of his pen maniacally against the table. I knew he was about to say something harsh, so I hurried to say, "Enough! Can we continue? I want to hear something *good* that's happened recently. Let's start there."

That was a consequence of loving Jessa. She made me count my blessings, made me focus on what I was grateful for. It had started bleeding out into other areas of my life, and I couldn't say I minded.

"Sure," Trace said, the acid tone still thick in his voice. "I've got one. I've been connecting more with that very strong F-word Axel likes to beat me with. And it's been very rewarding."

I blinked, turning to squint at Trace. Axel looked similarly confused.

"What now?" I asked him.

Felicia glided down the hallway with our tray of coffees, pushing open the conference room with her back. She sent us big grins as she set the tray down and set out our drinks.

"Time to caffeinate, boys," she said.

After a relieved sigh and a muttered "I fucking love coffee", Axel turned his attention back to Trace.

"Please elaborate on your cryptic sentiment."

"I'm connecting with family." Trace held out his hands as if this sentence summarized everything perfectly. "That's my bright spot as of late."

"What family?" I asked.

"Ian."

I could see the wall of distaste come slamming down around Axel. His lips turned downward again, and he leaned back in his chair slowly. Lethally.

"Come again?" Axel said.

"I've been connecting with Ian," Trace said. "I wanted to be honest about it, because that's the type of person I am."

Axel let out a sarcastic laugh.

"How long have you been meeting up with him?" I asked.

"Just a couple weeks," Trace said. "He was back in New York for a business trip. I let him stay at the Tribeca apartment while he was here."

"So he's gone now?" I asked.

"Yeah. He went back to Louisville a couple days ago." Trace sniffed, something hard sliding over his features as he looked over at Axel.

Axel swore under his breath, crossing his arms over his chest. "Are you fucking serious?"

"Why would I lie about this?" Trace demanded.

"I just can't believe you'd engage with such a wildcard at a time like this," Axel spat, anger rending his voice. "We need to keep everything under wraps, and you invite the fucking dude right into your house?"

"This is my half-brother," Trace said succinctly, leaning forward to jab the table for emphasis. "My fucking blood relative. Of course I want to get to know him."

"This is some grade-A bullshit right here," Axel seethed.

"What if it was Jordan, huh?" Trace said, his voice bordering on shouting. "What if she showed up after being gone your entire life and wanted to reconnect? What would you fucking say?"

"That is fucking *different*," Axel hissed, standing up and pressing his palms to the table. "And you fucking know it."

"Sit down!" I barked at Axel.

"Jordan and I already connected," Axel barreled on, completely ignoring me. "We knew about each other from day one. She lived with me. My daddy didn't lie to my mom about her existence. And I never hid her existence from *anyone*, let alone my own family. And that's more than you can fucking say."

Trace stood now as well, mimicking Axel's posture. "Why do you fucking act like it was me who cheated on mom?"

"Because you knew about it the whole time and never did *shit* to save our family," Axel shouted, spit flying from his mouth. And I, like always, just stayed in the middle. Absorbing both sides. Understanding everyone's reactions.

"Staying quiet *was* saving our family," Trace said, leaning closer. "It was the only way I could think of protecting you and our family at the time. Because saying something would have meant the whole family fell apart. And we couldn't have handled it then."

The tension in the room skyrocketed. Someone was about to get punched, and it might very well be me if I tried to stop the two of them in the wrong way.

I stood, heading for Axel, who I suspected would be the first to throw a fist.

"Sit the fuck down," I hissed into his ear.

"What would our mom think?" Axel went on, oblivious to my warning. "You think she wants you to be out there acting like Ian's bestie?"

"That's not what's going on," Trace said through gritted teeth. "And yes, I think our mom understands perfectly well that Ian has no fault in this. It's our daddy's fault. And you'd know that too if you could stop for one second and pull your head out of your ass."

Axel surged forward and I intercepted him, wrapping my arm around his chest. I knew he'd be the first to pounce. I shoved him into his chair, positioning myself in front of him.

"You ready to calm the fuck down?" I asked him.

Axel glared at me, settling back into his chair. He only grunted.

"I'm sick and tired of this," I said, looking back at Trace. I noticed employees in the hallway, staring through the glass-walled conference room with wide eyes, but they scattered as soon as my gaze met theirs. "You've gotta stop this shit, or else everything is going to tank. And I mean that."

Neither of them responded. An uncomfortable silence filled the room.

"This only works if we stick together," I reminded them, looking from Axel to Trace to Axel again. Once Axel's chest had stopped heaving, I was confident he wouldn't pounce again, so I returned to my chair. "And to be honest, this shit is starting to scare me."

"It's all him," Trace muttered. And honestly, I agreed. Mostly.

"Well, I know a solution," Axel said, his voice edged with something I'd never heard before. He swiveled to face me, a strange light glinting in his eye. "Maybe you'd like to hear?"

"I'm all ears," I told him.

Axel looked back at Trace, a sneer twisting his lips. "I want you out of Fairchild Enterprises. That way, we don't have to worry about our differences. I'll buy you out. We can draw up the paperwork today."

Trace blinked about a hundred times before he finally croaked, "You've gotta be fucking kidding me."

"I'm not."

"And this is how you treat family?" Trace boomed. I let my head drop into my hands. I felt lower than ever, and for the first time, I didn't know how to talk my way out of this argument.

No amount of cajoling would get this meeting back on track.

"Family doesn't do this," Trace said, his voice louder and more commanding than ever. "Family doesn't stonewall. Family doesn't act like a petulant fucking child. And that's all you've done recently. Should I remind you of all the ways I've stepped up as your brother throughout the years? What about all the times I covered for you when you'd go on your fact-finding missions even though you were grounded? How many fucking times did I finish all your chores so you could go out early with whatever flavor of the week? Not to mention all the thousands—and then millions—of dollars I made for you, to pay for your schooling, to help us start this business?

What about the clients I hunted down for us, all the big names I brought your way?"

"I was the one who schmoozed them anyway," Axel muttered.

But Trace wasn't done. "What about all the times I stopped you from drinking yourself to death over Cora, huh? Or all the times I joined your campaigns to stamp out the bad guys, all the questionable shit I did for us just to bring Yagel down and stop him from trafficking more girls through his company? You act like I've done nothing but lie to you since we met, but Axel, all I've done is honored your cause, because you're my brother. And you want to sit here and fault me for getting to know a blood relative."

Axel didn't say anything; he simply examined his nails while the echo of Trace's words festered and steamed in the air around us.

"Un-fucking-believable." Trace pushed away from the table, pacing the far wall. I massaged my face, unsure where to go from here.

Axel wanted Trace gone. Trace wanted Axel to understand. And I just wanted us back to the unshakeable trio we'd always been.

But this had shaken us down to our core, and I didn't know if we'd recover.

Something buzzed, and Trace paused in his pacing, snatching his phone from his pocket. He stared at the screen a moment then swiped it to answer. "Hello?"

I listened to Trace's side of the conversation—"Mm-hmm...this is him...okay"—as I watched his brows knit closer and closer together.

"I'm sorry, what did you say?" Trace exhaled a moment later.

Both Axel and I stared at Trace, curiosity so thick in the air it almost choked me.

"To Kentucky," Trace said.

Axel and I shared a look.

"Okay. Thank you. I'll be there as soon as I can." Trace swiped his phone off and pocketed it again, staring into space for a moment before he turned to us. Something raw and foreign had wrenched at his features, and for a moment, it seemed like he might cry.

"That was Child Protective Services," he whispered. "I was listed as the legal guardian for a baby girl who's recently been turned over to the state. I need to get to Louisville immediately."

THE END

Ready for more? The Fairchild saga is far from over! Continue on in THE PRICE OF INFAMY, Trace's second chance romance with the one who got away...

The Fairchilds aren't the only brothers I've written about. Have you met the Daly brothers? They're alpha, they're stubborn, and they're learning how to mend their broken family in my rom-com Bayshore series, which is now available on all retailers! Book #1 is MAKE ME LOSE.

Did you read the free PREQUEL to the Bad Boys of Wall Street series? We see what happened in the early years of Axel and Cora's relationship (before the brothers were billionaires) in THE PRICE OF A PROMISE.

ACKNOWLEDGEMENTS

This book would not have been possible without the stellar assistance and feedback from my plotting and beta squad: Elisabeth Nelson, Angela Howard-Seely, Whitley Cox, Kat McIntyre.

Big thanks to Jamie Bishop for dating the ex that allowed the story of Legs to come out.

Endless thanks to my husband (HORGLES!) for continuing to support this dream, even when I schedule releases in the middle of the busiest part of the year for the business that he and I built together.

And my largest, most humble, most incredulous thanks goes out to every single reader who has followed me along this writing journey. I still cannot believe this is real, that you found my book and you (hopefully) enjoyed it. This is what my 10th grade self was too afraid to even hope for. THANK YOU!

LET'S STAY CONNECTED!

Stay connected with me via my newsletter (http://bit.ly/EL-newsl etter), where I share teasers, sales, and other exciting news.

Or join my reader group, EMBER'S BLOSSOMS, to hang out up-close and personal! Early looks at new covers, exclusive access to ARC sign-ups, and more.

FACEBOOK
INSTAGRAM
GOODREADS
BOOKBUB
http://www.emberleighromance.com/

And before you go...

Please consider leaving an honest review about this book! Even just a few words or a line mean so much to us authors.

ALSO BY EMBER LEIGH

WINTER HARBOR
(co-written with Whitley Cox)
The Bastard Heir
The Asshole Heir
The Rebel Heir
The Matchmaking Heirs

THE BAYSHORE SERIES
Make Me Lose
Make Me Fall
Make Me Yours
Make Me Choose
Make Me Hot
Make Me Smile

THE BREAKING SERIES
Breaking the Rules
Changing the Game
Breaking the Sinner
Breaking the Habit
Breaking the Fall

* 9 7 8 1 9 6 5 1 8 2 0 8 6 *